STACY M. JONES

The Magician

For Lily
Hope you enjoy your character & thank you for sharing your tarot knowledge

Acknowledgments

Thank you to the detectives, special agents, and forensics teams I've had the pleasure of working with through the years and the knowledge and expertise shared with me. Your support when writing this story and all of those in my FBI Agent Walsh Thriller Series has been why these stories are so beloved by my readers. Anything I get wrong is my fault. Thank you!

Special thanks to 17 Studio Book Design for bringing my stories to life with amazing covers. Thank you to Dj Hendrickson for your insightful editing and Liza Wood for proofreading and revisions. Thank you to my early readers for their feedback and my loyal and new readers who have truly made this series a success.

I'm so happy we are continuing Kate's journey together.

CHAPTER 1

Forearm deep in pumpkin guts, the last thing FBI Agent Kate Walsh expected was to have a photo taken. This had once been a rare occurrence for her, this kind of domestic revelry, so it made sense that her partner turned boyfriend, Agent Declan James, wanted to capture the moment. The kitchen table in her brownstone in Boston's Back Bay was littered with the remnants of pumpkins.

Kate winced her eyes shut as she used her other forearm, not the one elbow deep in pumpkin, to wipe the strands of hair from her face. "I'm a disgusting mess."

"I like it," Declan assured her and sat down across the table. He had already finished gutting his pumpkin and was waiting for her before they started carving. "I can't believe I'm getting you to carve a pumpkin. This is something I never thought I'd see."

"I haven't done it since I was a kid. I'd sit right here with my parents and we'd make a whole afternoon of it." Kate had a smile on her face even though she missed her parents terribly. She was only recently feeling like the cloak of grief she'd worn since their deaths when she was twenty-two, and just about to graduate from Harvard, had started to fall away. Declan had found many ways to bring joy back to her house.

It had started last Christmas with decorating the house then carried over into the new year. They had marked each holiday in the way she had done with her parents, also honoring some of Declan's family traditions.

Over the year, Kate had felt herself changing, softening, and letting down her guard.

They had woken early that fall morning, strolled hand in hand to their favorite restaurant for brunch, and talked over breakfast about how each of them was glad for the changing leaves and turn of the season. They were equally as glad for the reprieve from work over the late spring and into the summer.

With the break in their schedule, Kate had given a few guest lectures at colleges and universities in New England about investigating serial crime while Declan worked at the FBI Boston Field Office. Declan had given her more than one worried glance when she came home from a day of teaching more exhilarated than she'd been in a long time about casework.

Kate had no intention of giving up her work in the specialized unit of the FBI where they both worked. She was just happy to know that if she ever did want to leave, she could comfortably make a living on the lecture circuit.

When brunch was finished, Declan had a mischievous glint in his seafoam green eyes. Kate had tentatively asked him what he had planned. They ended up at a pumpkin patch where they got pumpkins for carving and hot apple cider donuts. For a few hours, they got to forget all the ills of the world and the responsibilities that lay on their shoulders. It had been the perfect day that carried over to early evening as they sat in the kitchen and carved their pumpkins.

Kate pulled her hand out of the sticky guts and dropped a handful of seeds into the bowl. She dug in for more before using the spoon to scrape the insides clean. When she was done, she rinsed her hands at the sink and dried them with the towel.

As she returned to the table, Kate said, "I want to make sure we get more candy for the kids this year. My house is always dark on Halloween and I want to make up for it."

"Full-sized candy bars?"

Kate nodded with a smile. "As long as you don't eat all the Reese's."

Declan laughed. "I make no promises, so buy extra."

"You're worse than the kids."

"You like that about me." Declan pulled her chair closer and smacked his lips against her cheek. "You know what I think we should do now?" The question was barely out of his mouth when the doorbell rang. Declan groaned in annoyance.

Kate started to get up but he stopped her and told her he'd get it. They weren't expecting company. At nearly five on a Sunday evening, she had no idea who it could be. She heard Declan yell that he was coming when the doorbell chimed again. The front door let out a familiar creak and Declan let out a surprised hello. A familiar voice echoed through the hall – one Kate had not heard in a few months.

She stood then and made her way out of the kitchen and down the hall. Leo Lamiere stood at her front door. The Phantom, as he was once known, was the most infamous international art thief the world had ever known. After helping the FBI with two murder investigations, Declan convinced Spade, their boss, to let Leo on their team. He had spent the last six months in training.

Leo raised his dark eyes to hers as she got to the door. She offered him a nervous smile and ducked under Declan's arm as he held the door open. "Leo, you're back from training. Come on in." She had to nudge Declan out of the way as his large frame blocked the doorway.

"I don't mean to bother the two of you at home," he said, looking at Declan. Kate was sure it was Declan's presence that had stopped him from coming over before now.

She felt a familiar rumble in her stomach that she had hoped would have dissipated after not seeing him for a few months. Leo stood a few inches taller than her five-foot-eight. He had dark hair and a permanent five o'clock shadow. He spoke with a French accent. Kate knew he was fluent in several languages and had strength and agility beyond most men.

Their relationship, as it was, had started when she was his hostage on a rooftop in Paris. It was an odd start and an even odder development. They had grown...*close* was the only word that came to mind for Kate. Probably too close for an international criminal and an FBI agent.

It had been Declan who had provided him a way out of his life of crime. As Kate had grown to know him, she'd been surprised by his life story and the real mission for his thievery – stealing back Nazi-looted art. He was still a wanted man. But he had skills the FBI could use.

They faked his death, the Phantom went back to his real identity as Leo Lamiere and he'd spent several months at the FBI training center in Quantico. Now, here he was standing at Kate's door and the familiar rush of feeling for him that she had forgotten, because she was with Declan after all, came rushing back.

Kate did what she was best at and ignored the feelings that bubbled up inside of her.

Declan stepped back, letting him enter. "You're on our team now and our neighbor. It's good to see you," he said through gritted teeth. "I assume construction is done on your brownstone."

In addition to joining the team, Leo had surprised them by telling them he had bought a brownstone down the road from Kate's. Neither she nor Declan had been quite happy with the news but for very different reasons.

Leo stepped inside the foyer. "Construction was finished a month ago and furniture was delivered. You should stop over and see the place when you get the chance. They did an incredible job restoring it to how it looked when it was built in the 1860s. Of course, there are modern amenities now, but the hardwood floors, wainscoting, and unique features of the time have been salvaged and brought back to life." He leaned forward to look inside Kate's home. "I see we have about the same layout. Yours, Kate, is still as glorious as I'm sure it was when it was constructed."

Kate thanked him. "I've made similar upgrades to the kitchen and bathroom." She tugged Declan's arm as she pulled him back away from the door, allowing Leo to fully enter. As she shut the door and gestured toward the kitchen, she noticed the manila eight-by-ten envelope in a sealed evidence bag in Leo's hand. "What do you have there?"

Leo handed it to her. "I was in Washington D.C. this morning and Spade wanted me to bring this to you. He didn't discuss the contents with me but suggested that what's inside is alarming if it's real. Spade said it could be your next case."

Kate didn't need to ask Declan to run upstairs and grab the gloves. He had already departed for the stairs by the time she registered the information. Alone with Leo, she asked, "How's it really going? This must all be quite a change for you." She guided Leo back to the kitchen and asked if he wanted anything to drink.

He declined but thanked her. "It's good to see you, Kate. How have you been?" The question was weighted. Kate knew he wanted to know how the relationship with Declan was going. While their attraction was mutual, Leo had made it clear that he'd never do anything to disrespect Declan, and neither would she.

"It's going well," Kate said and gestured toward the table. She knew he'd understand what she was about to say in a way most people couldn't. "It's been nice the past few months to be able to enjoy simpler things in life that I've missed out on over the years because of work."

Leo nodded. "We aren't normal though, Kate. Enjoy it while it lasts."

She looked down at the bagged evidence. "I have a feeling this might be the end of it." She raised her chin to look at him. "You didn't answer me. How was the training?" Kate paused for a moment and lowered her voice. "I'm asking as much personally as I am professionally."

"It's going," Leo said with a hint of a smile on his lips. "I'll forever be grateful to Declan for finding me a way out and protecting me from going to prison. Your training is tougher than I considered. It never even occurred to me when we were on that rooftop in Paris that you could have gotten the best of me. I might have been caught right then."

Her inability to save herself that day had been a haunting memory. "It can be grueling," she admitted. "How is everything else?"

"Spade has been treating me well. Testing my loyalty at every turn."

That sounded like Martin Spade, their boss and head of the specialized FBI unit that Kate had called home during her entire career. He was something of an enigma at the FBI and not one to ever be crossed. "It's all part of the process. Once he feels like he can trust you, he'll give you his full respect and trust until he can't. At that point, nothing will save you."

Leo laughed. "He said as much." He leaned in and was about to say something when Declan entered back into the kitchen. Leo immediately pulled back.

Kate took the gloves from Declan and snapped them on. She went to the kitchen's center island and unsealed the evidence bag, carefully pulling out the manilla envelope. She unclasped it and shook out the contents – a white business envelope addressed to Kate at the FBI headquarters in Washinton D.C. Her name and the address were typed and the envelope had been slit open at the top.

Kate pulled out the white printer paper. As she unfolded it, two tarot cards dropped to the table. The Magician and The High Priestess. Kate knew next to nothing about tarot cards. The names were written across the top.

While the envelope had been typed, the letter inside was handwritten in scrawling black ink.

Dearest Agent Walsh,

No opponent has ever been a better match for me than you. You are The High Priestess. Make no mistake, even with all the intelligence and instinct you possess, this will not be easy for you. I harness all the elements – cups, wands, swords, and pentacles – and I use them masterfully.

Are you ready? I have already started. The Fool is dead.

Yours truly,

The Magician

Declan's breath was hot against her neck. "What is all of that supposed to mean?"

"I have no idea. I don't understand." Early in her career, Kate had arrested a scammer who was selling psychic services out of a shop. She had swindled millions of dollars from unsuspecting clients with threats of blackmail in the form of curses if clients didn't continue to pay for spellcasting and readings. It was a rare case that went through the judicial system because of money laundering and blackmail.

Among the items that had been collected at the shop were numerous tarot decks. Kate had no idea how the woman used them or how one could predict the future with them. She'd never had a psychic reading in her life nor did she believe anyone had the power to see anyone's fate.

"Are those tarot cards?" Leo asked from behind her.

Kate felt him hovering at her other shoulder, opposite Declan. She picked up the two cards and turned to show him, bumping right into him. He stepped back apologetically. Declan hadn't brought gloves for Leo, so she held them up and he studied them. "Do you have any idea about their meaning?"

"I do," Leo said, studying the cards. "This is from a Rider-Waite Tarot Deck."

"How do you know that?" Declan asked, looking between the cards and Leo.

"Its artistry. Tarot is much older than people think. From the 1400s in Italy." Leo paused and studied the cards some more. "It seems this killer has taken on the attributes of The Magician and has identified you as The High Priestess – the second and third cards in what they call the major arcana. They are mates, matched in skill. The Fool is the first card in the deck."

Kate glanced over at Declan and he shrugged. She turned back to Leo. "We need to know everything you know about tarot."

Leo locked his gaze on her. "Take a seat then. This is going to take some time."

Declan pulled off his gloves and went to clear the table of the pumpkin mess.

Kate shuddered as she looked at the cards again. They felt like an ominous presence in her hands.

CHAPTER 2

Once they were all seated around the table, Leo began. "We know from historical records that the first recorded tarot decks came about in the 1440s in Italy, specifically in Milan, Ferrara, Florence, and Bologna. Additional trump cards with allegorical illustrations were added to the common four-suit pack – the playing cards you know today. The tarot cards were not used then for divination but were used for a game known as tarocchi, which was similar to bridge. These early tarot decks were hand-painted and commissioned by wealthy families as a symbol of their status."

Declan pointed to the cards. "Are you saying these are similar to normal numbered playing cards?"

"Sort of."

Declan furrowed his brow, not understanding. "You said major arcana. What does that mean?"

Leo sat back in the chair. "There are cards in tarot similar to playing cards as you know them. They are called the minor arcana. These cards go from one through ten and then each suit has a page, knight, queen, and king. The pentacles are representative of the diamonds, cups are hearts, swords are spades, and wands are clubs."

"That makes sense," Kate said aloud, not meaning to interrupt him.

He pointed to the cards on the table. "What you're seeing here is what I called the major arcana. That is a set of twenty-two cards that represent significant life lessons, themes, and energies. Each card has its own unique symbolism and meaning. The Fool, for instance, is the journey of a new beginning. The major arcana closes with the World card, representing completion and fulfillment."

Kate said she understood even though she'd have to go buy a deck to explore the other cards. "You said these were from the Rider-Waite. Does that have a particular meaning?"

"There are many different types of tarot cards, all with the same meaning. The artistry of them is different." Leo pulled out his cellphone and typed a few words then turned his screen so Kate and Declan could see. "There are hundreds, maybe thousands of differently designed tarot decks. I've seen Art Nouveau decks, African decks, angel decks, and even popular television show decks. You name it, they have been created. The Rider-Waite deck is among the most popular. It was created by A. E. Waite, who was a spiritual seeker and mystic. In 1889, under the pseudonym Grand Orient, he published *A Handbook of Cartomancy, Fortune-Telling and Occult Divination*, one of the first books in English on how to read tarot. He created this deck in 1909."

"Is there any special symbolism to this deck?" Declan asked.

"I don't believe so. I don't think it's more spiritually powerful if that's what you're asking."

Declan pulled back in surprise. "Don't tell me you believe in all of this."

Leo slowly shrugged. "I learned a long time ago that I don't know what I don't know. With the rise of Spiritualism in the late 18th century, there was a lot of fraud."

"There is a lot of fraud today," Kate said, this time meaning to interrupt. "I don't know that I've ever come across a psychic or medium who wasn't a fraud."

Leo didn't argue. "There are more frauds than not. I can't discount all people. There was a woman I knew in France when I was young. She was a friend of my mother's. I saw the power of the tarot and what she could do with it. I watched with my own eyes as she told my mother true things. If only my mother had listened to her. I saw the woman later in life, she was well into her seventies by then. People lined up outside her shop to hear her read their fortunes. She only took enough money from them to survive and nothing more. If someone couldn't pay, she still read for them. I believe she had a real gift."

It wasn't a surprise to Kate that Leo believed in something beyond what he could see with his eyes and hear with his ears. He was far more open and worldly than most people she had met. His experiences in life far surpassed hers. All that aside, they were potentially dealing with a real killer – someone with flesh and blood who was threatening to harm others.

"I can't focus on the psychic aspect of the tarot right now," Kate said, hoping she never had to. "I will need to go out and buy a deck to understand the rest of the cards. What does he mean when he calls me The High Priestess?"

"I'm not an expert at this by any means," Leo admitted, suddenly a bit shy to share.

Declan encouraged him to continue. "This isn't a test. Tell us what you know. The more you can catch us up to speed, the faster it will go."

Leo said he understood. "From what I remember, The High Priestess is the guardian of divine intuition and wisdom. There are things hidden and yet to be revealed. The biggest takeaway from the card is that she indicates you're going to have to retreat, reflect on the situation, and use your intuition to guide you. She's an intelligent woman who gets things done. She has divine support in her endeavors."

It was too weighty a description for Kate. "What about The Magician?"

"Power and mastery over the elements." Leo gestured for Kate to slide the card to him while promising not to touch it. His finger hovered over the card as he pointed out the different elements. "It's like he said in his note. See here, each of the four suits – pentacles, cups, wands, and swords – are represented. The Magician has all at his disposal. Depending on how the card is laid in a tarot spread, it can indicate a person has all they need to manifest their desires, or if the card is laid in reverse, it can indicate someone who is a trickster and skilled at manipulation."

Declan rolled his eyes. "That sums up every killer we have ever faced."

Leo didn't seem surprised by that. "Do they often give you warnings like this?"

Kate shook her head. "Not all of them. Those who want to play a game with us will." She wanted to ask Leo what he thought about a person who'd use the tarot in this way. She hesitated for too long and both Leo and Declan were looking at her with curiosity. She smiled and laughed. "I wish you both would stop reading me like that."

Declan didn't let the moment pass. "There's something on your mind."

"I was going to ask Leo what he thought of the person who could send something like this. Then I realized he wouldn't know any more than we do."

"I have no idea, Kate," Leo assured her that she was correct.

"We don't know if this person is serious," Kate said, staring at the cards. "There hasn't been any news about a body. If he sent this to Washington D.C. he could be anywhere. If there is a body they might not even connect it to this." She knew as soon as she said it she was wrong.

Declan knew it too. "He's going to make it known, Kate. If he knows enough to address this to you, he might also know you're in the Boston area. You've been on the news before and Boston was mentioned during your testimony in front of Congress."

Kate was trying hard to forget that had been televised for the whole world to see. "Did Spade mention when this arrived?"

"This morning, Kate," Leo said and explained how when he was meeting with Spade his administrative assistant brought him the letter. He didn't open it in front of Leo but had called him back to the office later to give it to him. "Spade wanted you to have this right away. I wasn't even scheduled to come back to Boston for a few more days. He sent me back early to make sure this was hand-delivered to you."

If Spade was taking it that seriously, then Kate had to take it seriously, too. She raised her head to Declan. "He said the first target is represented by The Fool. Leo, you said that's the first card in the deck. What kind of person does that represent?"

Leo's features stiffened. "It's far too broad to know."

Declan gestured to him and asked him to pull up The Fool card on his phone. He studied it. "This person looks like they are stepping off a cliff. Could that be an indication of how he killed them?"

It was Kate's turn to echo the same response he had given her. They simply didn't know anything. She raised her head to Leo. "Did Spade give you any other information?"

"No. He said to give this to you and you'd know what to do with it. He asked that you call him once you had a chance to digest it." Leo pushed back from the table, seeming uncertain about what to do now.

"Please, head home and relax," Kate said, letting him off the hook. She could see how uncomfortable he was either with the information or maybe being there with the two of them. "Once this case officially starts, there probably won't be much of a chance to do anything. We keep a suitcase packed with clothes ready all the time because we often don't get much notice. You might want to do the same."

Leo thanked her for the tip, shook Declan's hand, and headed toward the front door. Declan followed him out while Kate studied the cards. She was glad Leo had left because she wanted to be alone with Declan while they called Spade. She didn't know if he had kept information back from Leo and she wanted him to be able to speak freely.

"What do you think, Kate?" Declan asked as he returned to the kitchen. He had taken off his gloves and tossed them on the table. "Do you think this is real or some sick joke?"

"I don't think Spade would have sent this to us if he wasn't taking it seriously." She read the note over again. "The Fool is already dead. We have to assume he's already killed someone and he will make that known to us."

Declan pulled his cellphone from his pocket and punched in the numbers. He set the phone down between them on the table and hit the speakerphone button so they could both hear. Spade was quick to answer. "Leo dropped off the information, Spade."

"Is he there with you?"

"No," Kate said, leaning toward the phone. "I figured it would be better for the three of us to talk."

"Either way is fine for me. He's part of the team now. I know it's going to take some time to trust him. He excelled at training and is more than ready."

"Leo has already been helpful." Declan relayed the information he provided about the tarot cards. "He's more knowledgeable on the subject than us. What are we looking at here, Spade? Has there been a body?"

Spade cleared his throat. "I'm surprised you hadn't heard it on the local news. A man jumped from a brand new condo development in downtown Boston. I don't believe he jumped. We think he was pushed or thrown off his balcony." Spade gave her the address.

Kate knew the building. It was now the tallest residential building in Boston and one that had been hotly anticipated. It was the new *it* place and cost a small fortune. Kate explained that they had been out for most of the day and hadn't watched any of the news. "What time did this occur?"

"At three this afternoon."

"Are you sure it's connected to this case?"

"The Fool card was tucked into the man's pocket." Spade explained that he'd already been in touch with the medical examiner's office. "Dr. Melissa Nagel from the Suffolk County Medical Examiner's office is anticipating your call. She said she'd be happy to meet with you and you can see the body. I've already spoken with Det. Harris Briggs from the Boston Police Department homicide unit. You've worked with him on a previous case."

Kate was glad that he'd been assigned. He was an excellent detective and they had all worked well together. "I don't understand how he knew to call you, especially if the case was labeled a suicide."

"Only initially labeled a suicide," Spade corrected. "I called the D.C. Metro Police and the Boston Police Department earlier today. I figured the killer would strike soon or already had and he'd leave a message for us. They were anticipating it. When the medical examiner's office found the tarot card in the man's pocket, they knew to call me immediately. I wanted to give you time to digest the information before telling you the details of the first murder."

Kate didn't like the way he had said *first*. Spade knew there'd be more. "We will head over to the medical examiner's office now."

"I'll let you know if any more mail comes in relating to the case. Clearly, he likes to communicate." Spade started to say goodbye and then added, "Let's let Leo sit this out until morning. Go get a handle on the case and then read him in."

"Good idea," Declan said then glanced up at Kate.

Her mind was already spinning up a profile of the killer. She knew he was already in the process of targeting his next victim. As Spade had said and Kate agreed, the killer wasn't going to stop with just one.

CHAPTER 3

Kate and Declan arrived at the medical examiner's office an hour later. After a quick call to Det. Harris Briggs before leaving the house, they had timed their arrival with his.

"Sick people out there," Det. Briggs said as he held the door open for Kate. He stood just about her height and had dark eyes and skin tone. His black hair was closely cropped to his head. It had been about a year since Kate had seen him but he looked about the same. "If Spade hadn't alerted us, this would have remained a suicide, which is what the first cop on the scene suspected. It wasn't until Dr. Nagel called to tell us about the tarot card that we knew it was a homicide."

"Has the Boston PD already gone through the man's condo?" Declan asked as they signed into the office and showed their badges.

Det. Briggs guided them through the double doors while he talked over his shoulder. "The initial cops on the scene were in his condo but nothing had been disturbed. There were no signs of a struggle and there was no note found. I went over there shortly after Dr. Nagel called me about the note. I wanted to see the place for myself. The railing to the balcony is high. I'm still having trouble imagining anyone having the strength to lift the guy and throw him over the side. The killer must have exceptional strength. The victim, Kirk Eagen, was a little over six feet and close to two hundred pounds. It wasn't an easy feat to throw a man of that size over the balcony. He might have forced him over."

Kate thought that sounded more likely. "What else do we know about him?"

Before he could respond, a short woman with dark hair stepped out into the hall. She introduced herself as Dr. Melissa Nagel. "I'm fairly new here at this office. I moved up from Florida."

Declan extended a hand to her and introduced them both. "Usually people go the other way."

"I was ready for a change," was all she said, then ushered them into the autopsy bay. They walked over to the stretcher, which was holding the man's body under a white sheet. "He was pushed from the fifteenth floor. He landed on his back and has catastrophic injuries." She described the man's injuries in detail and then unceremoniously pulled back the sheet.

Kate winced as she looked up at Dr. Nagel, not staring at the body any longer than necessary. Impact wounds of that kind often obliterate other wounds that could have been made to the body previously. She was surprised that he had remained intact. "Are we sure that he was pushed from his condo and not somewhere else in the building?"

"That's an excellent question and one I've not explored yet," Briggs admitted. "It was an assumption on our part. We haven't received reports of anyone seeing him anywhere else in the building. The security is pulling video for us. They should have it ready by morning."

"No witnesses on the ground?" Declan asked, gesturing for Dr. Nagel to cover the body.

"Only after impact. I haven't found anyone who saw him on the way down."

That was frustrating to Kate but not surprising. The area around the new condo building was under construction. She assumed that it also happened too fast for anyone to have been paying attention. She directed her question to Dr. Nagel. "Are there any other injuries to the body that were not caused by the impact?"

Dr. Nagel shook her head. "As you know, the impact shattered bones and caused organ damage as well as split open the man's skull. Everything I'm seeing so far is consistent with the impact on the ground. I might know more when I open him up."

That's what Kate had assumed. She also knew that it would be some time before toxicology came back. "What about the tarot card? Do you have that?"

Dr. Nagel went to the counter at the side of the room and returned with the bagged card. "I almost didn't find it. As you can see it was folded in half and tucked into his pants pocket. We were notified earlier in the day by a Martin Spade with the FBI to keep an eye out for any unusual cases or ones related to the tarot. This certainly qualified."

Kate gave her the overview of what they knew so far. She turned to Declan to see if there was anything he wanted to add but he shook his head. Kate turned her attention back to the doctor. "I can only assume this will be the first case of more to come."

Dr. Nagel raised her thick dark eyebrows. "You think there will be more?"

Kate hated the only answer she could give. "I can assure you there will be. He's put too much thought into this little game to only kill once. I don't know enough to tell you where, when, or who. If I knew all of that, we could get in front of this."

"What do you need from me?" Dr. Nagel asked, her tone reflecting the stress that Kate was feeling.

Kate gestured toward the deceased. "Anything you can find on the body that might indicate what happened to him before his death. Declan and I have not had a chance to see the scene yet. What has me stumped is if the railing is as high as Briggs described how anyone would get him over it."

Dr. Nagel agreed that it would be a feat for even someone bigger and stronger than the man. "As I'm sure you know with the body in the condition it's in, it's going to be difficult to tell if there was any kind of prior struggle. So far, there's nothing to indicate that from what I can find. As soon as I know anything, I'll let you know."

Kate turned to Briggs. "Did the deceased live with anyone? Any notifications done?"

Briggs shook his head. "I didn't see anything to indicate he lived with anyone. I spoke briefly to a neighbor who said that Eagen had recently moved in, roughly two months ago. He started a new job at a prestigious criminal defense firm downtown. The neighbor didn't believe he was married or had children. The neighbor hadn't seen Eagen with anyone and he never spoke of anyone. That doesn't mean much. He could have been getting settled and planned to move his family later. I'll need to cover some ground to get enough information to make the death notification."

"Who initially identified the body?" Declan asked.

Briggs explained, "It was the neighbor who identified him at the scene. He was able to assist us in identifying Eagen and then directing us to his condo. The officers on the scene got a key from maintenance and entered the unit."

"That makes sense then," Declan said. He asked Briggs a few more questions about what took place when the police arrived on the scene. Briggs did his best to answer but he didn't have much information. With nothing else to do at the medical examiner's office, Declan suggested going to the scene.

Twenty minutes later, Kate stood in the middle of the condo recently purchased by Kirk Eagen while Declan and Briggs interviewed the neighbor. Declan wanted a chance to speak to him and hear the information firsthand. Kate had been anxious to get into the condo and have a look around.

The space was sterile. If she didn't know better, Kate might have assumed it was a staged condo used by the real estate agent. The living room had what looked like new furniture, but as Briggs had told them, it was devoid of anything personal. The kitchen had pots, pans, dishes, glasses, and silverware all in place, neatly lined up in cabinets and drawers. Fresh fruits and vegetables were on the refrigerator shelves along with some basic condiments and bottles of iced coffee concentrate. There were bananas on the counter next to a tub of protein powder. Eagen didn't have any dishes in the sink or the dishwasher.

The condo had two bedrooms. In the main bedroom, the bed had been made with crisp military corners and precision. The clothes and shoes were lined up in the closet the same way. There were rows of suits and then more casual clothes. The dressers had the same level of neatness. The connecting bathroom had nothing on the countertop. Kate opened the cabinets and found neatly stacked products. There was a bar of soap and some men's shampoo and conditioner in the walk-in shower. Nothing looked out of order.

It wasn't until Kate reached the spare bedroom that she realized Eagen hadn't been done unpacking. There were ten moving boxes stacked up against the side wall and the spare bed had not been made. The comforter was folded with a stack of folded sheets on top as if he planned to make the bed soon. The spare bedroom closet had a few dumbbells stacked in a row on the floor. Other than that there was nothing in the closet, no clothes or shoes or boxes.

"Kate," Declan called from the living room. She left her search of the spare bedroom and walked down the short hallway to the living room. "Security will be sending us the video but they have a clip of Eagen with a man. They enter the condo at around two and the man leaves shortly after. We are going to need to look at the timing of his death. It might be around the same time."

Kate had yet to walk out onto the balcony. She had been waiting for Declan. She gestured toward the sliding glass door of the living room. "Let's see if he could have forced him over the side. Do you know the name of the man who had been with him?"

"We asked the neighbor down the hall and he didn't know him."

Declan and Briggs put on gloves as Kate opened the sliding door to the balcony.

The wind whipped her face as she stepped outside. If this had been her condo, Kate wasn't sure she'd spend that much time on the balcony. She didn't have a fear of heights but the enclosed space was small and the railing, which was made of a wall of thick blueish glass, was much higher than she had anticipated. It gave the whole space a closed-off feeling even though they were outside. Eagen didn't have any furniture or plants or anything outside in the space. It looked unused.

The top of the wall came up past her chest almost to her clavicle. It would be lower on Declan. She supposed he could pull himself up and over if he so desired. She had no idea how strong Eagen was. It would be possible but awkward. She saw what Briggs meant when he said it would be hard for someone to throw a person off the balcony. The victim would need to not only be totally compliant but also helpful in the endeavor.

Kate couldn't imagine anyone allowing themselves to be tossed over the side.

She turned back to Declan and Briggs. "You didn't see Eagen leave the condo again after the man left?"

"No. Security said that no one leaves or enters the condo until the police."

"Do we know if anyone entered while he was out?"

"Security doesn't believe so, but they are still going through the footage."

Kate was trying to make sense of the situation. She stared back at the thick glass and looked for scuff marks or anything to indicate a struggle against it. She saw none. "There's no chair or anything out here. If Eagen was going over, don't you think he would have pulled a chair out here to make it easier? He'd need considerable upper body strength to pull himself up and over. Even then, you'd think you'd see some scuff marks on the glass. There isn't anything. By the same token, it would be difficult for anyone to heave him over the side. Again, if there was some kind of struggle out there, we'd see that reflected in the glass." To prove her point, Kate went to the glass and scuffed the front of her shoe against it, leaving a streak.

"It seems," Declan started, "that is as much a mystery as who did it."

Kate took a breath, feeling the weight of the unknowns. "I guess he is The Magician."

CHAPTER 4

Later that night, Kate sat against the headboard in her bed with the covers pooled on her lap. Declan had turned on the news then went to his office to look through some witness statements Briggs had provided. Kate had skimmed them but was more interested in reading through the book that went with the tarot cards she had bought at a bookstore on their way home.

Kate had felt foolish buying the cards but the cashier didn't seem to think it was strange. She had complimented Kate on the choice of cards and wished her luck with them. The shop had been out of the Rider-Waite Tarot deck and she had opted for something called The Golden Tarot.

As soon as she got back to her brownstone, Kate unwrapped the plastic around the box and pulled out the deck of cards. She flipped through each of them, pulling out what Leo had called the major arcana. She set those aside and then separated each of the suits into piles from the first card in the suit to the king at the end.

Kate carefully studied each of the suited cards before setting them aside for the major arcana. She had no idea how literally to take the imagery or if it held only symbolic meaning for the killer.

After going through each of the cards, Kate went back to the beginning to study The Fool. It had a 0 at the top and depicted a young man dressed as a court jester with a stick thrown over his shoulder with a sack attached to it. He stood next to a small dog on the edge of a cliff. Its meaning highlighted new beginnings and opportunities. There was a downside or negative aspect to each card, too.

Kate was most interested in the imagery and the part about the new beginning because it resonated so clearly with Eagen's life. He had moved to Boston to start a new job and it was a huge opportunity for him. The condo building was also brand new, not even opened for three months.

Kate wondered if the killer had been watching the building and waiting for someone who fit the ideal. *Could Eagen have also been a fool for trusting the killer?*

Kate flipped the page in the book, bypassing The Magician and going right to The High Priestess. She wore a blue dress and cloak and had a gold crown on her head. She stood between two pillars and in front of a veil that symbolized the break between this world and the spirit realm. The open book in her hands symbolized higher learning and wisdom. Leo had been right about what The High Priestess represented. It was a tall order for Kate to match up to the energy in the card.

"I bet you were hot in college, all nerdy and focused," Declan said as he leaned against the doorjamb, watching her.

Kate turned her head. "I was hot in college," she teased him back. "I didn't go for jocks so you would have missed out."

Declan clutched his heart. "I was so much more than a jock."

Kate tried to hide her smile and gave a noncommittal shrug. "I might have been a little attracted to you. You were too flirty back then for me to have really considered it."

"It's true," Declan said with a sigh. He crossed the room to the bed and slid in next to her, planting a kiss on her lips. He gestured toward the small book in her hands. "Are you learning anything?"

Kate explained the similarities between The Fool card and Kirk Eagen. "It matches up closely. I was learning about The High Priestess when you came in. It's big shoes to fill."

"No one expects you to live up to a description in a book, Kate. This killer is playing a game with us. What comes after The High Priestess?"

Kate flipped the pages to show him. "The Empress, who matched with The Emperor. The female and male energy of basically the same cards. She represents fertility, motherhood, and a happy home. He represents protection, order, rules, and fatherhood."

"Do you think he will target a couple next?"

Kate couldn't be sure. "There is also The Lovers card, which is depicted with a couple. I assumed he'd target a couple for that. I was hoping by studying these cards, I might be able to anticipate what he's going to do."

Declan laid his hand on top of hers. "Don't go down that road. You'll drive yourself crazy trying to guess his next moves."

Kate knew he was right. She closed the book and tossed it on her nightstand. She'd have time tomorrow to study it more intensely. "Cases are harder when they communicate. It's like dangling a carrot we can chase but never catch. I don't know if he'll stay here in Boston or go someplace else."

"Not that I want the people here in Boston to be at risk, but I'm hoping he stays here. We know the city better and we have Briggs on our side. We also have the FBI forensics lab here. Sharon is heading to the condo in the morning and will go over it with her team."

Sharon Esposito was out of the FBI field office in Boston. She had recently been invited by Declan to join their team. She had accepted a few months back. She was tough and smart and Kate was looking forward to working with her.

Before leaving the condo, Declan had found information on Eagen's previous address in Chicago. After a quick search, Declan found the man's family and called the FBI field office in Chicago to send out an FBI agent to make the death notification to Eagen's parents who were in their seventies. Declan would follow up with a phone call.

Kate was glad that it had initially been reported as a suicide to the media. It would buy them some time. She couldn't even be sure that Eagen hadn't thrown himself off the balcony, surely under duress and probably forced. The one clear thing was there hadn't been a struggle.

As if reading her thoughts, Declan asked, "When do you think we need to make a media statement? If there are more deaths and the media knew we were holding back information, it's a liability for us."

Kate knew that to be true. "After we speak to the law firm and learn more about Eagen, then we can call a press conference. I want to get in front of this more before we make any statement to the press."

Declan took her hand in his and snuggled in next to her. "Do you have any ideas about a profile for the killer?"

Kate had been mulling that over for the last couple of hours. It's what she was most skilled at and the reason she had been asked to join Spade's specialized FBI unit. Where Declan was the best she'd ever witnessed at assessing a scene, catching what others missed, Kate was a skilled interrogator, had a specialty in forensic linguistics, and was one of the FBI's most skilled profilers. If anyone were to ask Spade, he told them she wasn't one of the best – she was the best.

It often left Kate feeling as if she were carrying the weight of the case on her shoulders. A profile only went so far. It didn't direct them to the suspect. It was merely a way to better understand them and to hone in on their peculiarities to help catch them. It was even more important during interrogation. If Kate knew what psychological buttons to push, it gave her an advantage. Like playing a verbal chess match.

After taking far too long to respond, Kate glanced over at Declan.

"He wants total power and control over the case. He didn't have to tell us he had already killed someone. He wanted us to know he's one step ahead of us. Narcissism is overplayed in our society today. It's a throwaway word at this point for every form of maladaptive behavior. I don't like using it, but I suspect we are dealing with someone who truly has narcissistic personality disorder. I can tell that in his writing. He's calling himself The Magician and while he's calling me his counterpoint, he believes that we will never catch him. He's intelligent and knows tarot. I suspect he also knows how to kill and get away with it. Meaning this isn't his first. He didn't wake up one day and decide he wanted to kill people and came up with this big elaborate plan. His violent tendencies go back far, possibly to childhood. He gets off on the game of it."

"It's theatrical," Declan said, agreeing with her.

That was the word that most described it. The description had been gnawing at the recesses of her mind. Declan had put it simply enough. "That's right. This is his production. He's the director and the main character and we are pawns in his story. Not even side characters with a purpose. He's going to direct us and we will play as small or as large a part in it as he determines." Kate looked down at him. "That's what he believes anyway. He chose me as his adversary without thinking through exactly what we do. He probably saw an image of me on the news from the Congressional hearing and decided I wasn't a threat. He saw me being dressed down by Congress and wanted a piece of the action."

"Do you think he's local to Boston?"

"I don't know. We are going to have to wait to see how the case unfolds. If he remains killing in Boston, then I'd say, yes, it's highly likely he's living here and knows the area well."

"Do you think he works a day job?"

Kate had been going back and forth on that. "I believe he's college-educated. I suspect he might have trouble holding a job unless he's the boss. He's got time on his hands whatever it is."

"Age range?" Declan asked, knowing that he was pressing his luck with questions at this late hour. He did this sometimes to get Kate thinking, knowing she didn't have the answers yet. It was as much his process in the case as it was hers.

But she had no idea of the killer's age. "I assume he's in his forties, give or take a few years."

Declan was done with his questions for now. "I keep thinking about how he got Eagen over that balcony. It came up to my chest and you were right about the scuff marks. No matter how he pulled himself over the side, he would have left a mark on that glass. If he had used a chair, then someone was there to take the chair away. Any sane person would have fought someone trying to get them over the railing. There would have been signs of a struggle."

Kate agreed with all of it. She didn't want to talk about the case anymore. She yawned and rolled over to shut off the bedside table lamp. She snuggled down into the bed and rolled over to face him. "We had such a perfect day before Leo showed up."

Declan wrapped his arms around her and pulled her close. "We had the perfect summer too. My mother keeps telling me how happy she is we finally got together. She said she saw it all along and was waiting for us to wake up."

Kate loved Declan's mom. With her parents long deceased, it had left a hole in Kate's life. Declan's mom was doing a good job of filling it. "I appreciate how kind your parents have been to me." Kate's eyes slowly closed and she forced them open again. She leaned into Declan and kissed him before drifting off.

Declan pulled her closer then released her as she rolled to her side away from him. "Sleep well, Katie." She had fallen into a dreamless sleep only to wake sometime later as the bed shifted under Declan's weight.

Kate reached her hand behind her to find the bed empty. She rolled onto her back hearing his voice off in the distance. She was still in that middle ground of asleep and awake, not sure if she was truly hearing him.

Kate inched herself up to a sitting position, opening her eyes to the darkened room.

"Declan," she called out and waited. Kate reached for her phone on the nightstand and checked for any messages she might have missed. There were none. The time read 4:34 a.m. It was too early in the morning for anyone to be calling unless it was an emergency.

Declan returned moments later, his face pale even for sleep. "There's been another murder, Kate. Two actually." Before Kate had a chance to react, he explained. "That was Briggs who called me. He was just called to the scene."

There was something he wasn't saying. "Who is it, Declan?"

"Bernard and Audrey Davenport," he said releasing a breath.

Kate gasped as she clutched her chest. "That's right near us." The Davenports were one of the wealthiest families in Boston. They were old money and Bernard's family's roots in the city were as deep as Kate's, going back to the country's founding. His family were leading merchants and Bernard had followed in the same footsteps. He had his hands in finance, shipping, and commerce. He also ran a successful hedge fund and his wife was a charity darling, sitting on every prestigious board in the city. Kate started to ask a question but Declan shook his head.

"Let's get to the scene as quickly as we can. Briggs said he already received a call from a reporter."

Kate scrambled out of bed and rushed to get dressed, panic already setting in as sirens wailed in the distance.

CHAPTER 5

Given how close the Davenport mansion was to Kate's brownstone, they walked the short distance down Marlborough Street, took a left on Dartmouth Street, and then a right onto Commonwealth Avenue. It was then they saw the line of Boston Police Department cruisers and the barricade that had been erected.

Kate and Declan passed the media that had started to gather outside the barricade. Neither had on their FBI windbreakers, so they looked no different than any other couple on the street. Their badges were tucked inside their clothes. The last thing they wanted was to get swarmed by the media before they even reached the scene.

It wasn't until they approached the uniformed cop and flashed their badges that the media knew the FBI was on the scene, raising the stakes for the case to something beyond a local crime. Reporters shouted questions. Kate and Declan passed through the barricade without looking back.

The Davenport mansion stood five stories high and within its walls were fifteen thousand square feet of residential space on a lot that touched both Commonwealth Avenue and Marlborough Street. The front of the home had a Commonwealth Avenue address while the back of the home was on Marlborough. It spanned two plots that covered the entire city block between the two streets. The mansion had a sleek, pale façade with bright mosaic detail. Construction had started in 1899 and finished in 1902.

Kate and Declan had walked by the mansion countless times. As a child she had stood outside the wrought-iron gates, staring up at the double doors that boasted ornate columns on each side. The doors were massive in size and had gold looping hand pulls attached to the round gold doorknobs. Eight small square windows in two rows, four across, sat atop each door.

"Twenty-three bedrooms and twelve baths," Declan said as he whistled softly to himself as he read the details off his phone. "What does anyone need with that many bedrooms? How many children did they have?"

"Two," Kate said absently as she stared at the house, pulled by the horrors that went on inside. "I went to Harvard with the son, Chase Davenport. His sister, Rebecca, went to Yale. She was two years older than me. I didn't know Chase well. We only had a history class together. We didn't run in the same social circles."

Even though Kate's parents had been wealthy, her father a distinguished professor at Harvard and later an ambassador, they didn't encourage her to run in a wealthy crowd. Instead, they had lived simply and valued experiences, education, and travel over wealthy possessions. It was much the way Kate lived now. Without knowing her address, most wouldn't assume her net worth based on her government salary.

As Kate and Declan paused at the bottom of the front steps, one of the front doors opened and Briggs stepped outside. He gave a stiff wave as he descended the stairs. "It's a real mess inside," he said stiffly. "I've never seen anything like it."

Kate wanted the details but they could wait. "Who found the bodies?"

"One of our officers," Briggs explained. "A silent alarm was tripped from the back door. When the security company called and no one answered, they alerted the police. Around the same time, a call came into the station from a man who said the Davenports were dead. He left no details and hung up before the person who answered the phone could ask any questions. They called me out. I called Declan immediately. It's too high-profile of a murder to not be connected to the case. I figured it was the next one."

Kate wasn't surprised. "Have you been studying the tarot?"

Briggs offered a slight nod. "If tarot is going to play an important role in this case, I wanted to get ahead of the curve." He zeroed in on Kate. "Do you think the Davenports represent The Empress and The Emperor?"

"A wealthy older couple. I would assume so. Did you find any tarot cards with the bodies?"

Briggs explained he hadn't touched the bodies. "I wanted you to see the scene exactly as I saw it. I called the medical examiner's office but told them to hold off until we had a chance to assess the scene. I assumed you'd want your forensic team out here before the bodies were removed."

"That's a good call," Declan said. He pulled out his phone and called Sharon, asking her to come to the house. He gave her the address before hanging up. "You met Sharon on a previous case."

"I remember her." Briggs pointed out the box of gloves and booties outside the front door and waited for Kate and Declan to put them on before entering the mansion.

Briggs went in first and paused to wait for them. "The space is amazing. I've never seen anything like this."

Even with his praise of the mansion, Kate and Declan paused to take in the magnificence. In the great hall, as it was known, Kate's eyes were drawn to the tall fireplace and vaulted ceiling. The front stairs were under a proscenium arch of Tiffany mosaic tiles. At the top of the first landing and seen from the foot of the stairs, a trompe l'oeil Greek temple reflected the light.

"Is this a home, or a museum?" Declan asked as he tipped his head back to look at the ceiling. He lowered his gaze to Briggs. "What was the point of entry?"

"I believe the back door. It was the only alarm that tripped. Oddly, I believe it had to have tripped as he was leaving rather than arriving." Briggs constricted his facial features as if he were in pain. Quietly and with emotion, he said, "It appears he took some time with them. You'll see once we go up to the second floor."

Kate turned to him too. "Have you done a thorough search of the home?"

"I had officers each take a floor and search. The place is massive. From what we can see nothing other than the couple's bedroom is disturbed. I can't account for how he entered the home."

"Take us to them." Kate followed behind Briggs as he ascended the stairs to the second floor. He walked down a long hallway going toward the back of the property. They passed two doors in the front and stopped in front of an open doorway at the end of the hall.

Before he crossed the threshold, Briggs explained, "This is one massive suite. There is the sitting room first, which flows into the master bedroom and separate his and her bathrooms with closets. This space alone is bigger than my first apartment." He guided them through the sitting room with its cream-colored couch and plush carpeting.

Kate noticed the blood droplets on the carpet first. As she raised her eyes toward the back of the sitting room and beyond, she noticed the blood droplets become more frequent and larger.

"They are in the bedroom part of the suite?" Kate asked, stepping toward the blood.

From behind her Briggs said, "It looks like the killer pulled in chairs from the sitting room next to the bed." He pointed out two areas of the carpet that had indents from the legs of the chairs. "I believe he surprised them when they were asleep and then subdued them."

Kate heard what he said but her gaze was focused on what was to come. The only sound she heard was the thump of her heart in her ears. Other than a small table lamp in the sitting room, the rest of the suite was dark. Kate asked Briggs if he had found it like this. He confirmed he had.

Kate took a few more steps and then wobbled ever so slightly at the sight in front of her. At the right-hand side of the bed, the couple was propped up in high-back chairs, facing each other. Their arms and legs were bound to the chairs. Angry red lines slashed their necks and dark red blood stains covered their pajamas. It was only a small area of the sleeve of Audrey's nightgown that hinted the garment had once been yellow.

Kate took a tentative step toward them, her feet sinking into the plush carpeting. "We need light in here," she said as she got close to the couple. There was barely an area on them or under them not covered in blood. Kate's mind flashed to being tied to a chair and watching as Declan was murdered in this way. She quickly shoved the thought aside. The horror the couple must have experienced in the time leading up to their deaths. It was almost too much to bear.

Declan let out an audible groan from behind her as he stepped into the room.

"I need light in here to find the cards. They have to be here someplace." Kate stared down at the couple, trying not to stand in the blood that had soaked the carpet. It was hard because it had pooled under the chair and seeped in every direction. Kate ran her gloved hand over Bernard, tugging the front of his pajama shirt forward so she could look in the small breast pocket. Nothing.

She crouched down at the side of him and ran her hand over the side pants pocket but she didn't feel anything but the gathered materials. She did the same to the other side and came away with the same result. As Kate stood to her full height the room was bathed in soft white light.

"The cards are here, Kate," Declan said, standing next to the bed. He pulled back a stack of pillows that had been arranged on one side. "The Emperor is taped to the headboard." He moved around to the other side of the bed and pulled back the other stack of pillows to reveal The Empress.

Kate left the couple and went to where Declan stood. She resisted pulling the cards from the headboard and inspecting them. They'd need to wait until Sharon arrived and photographed the scene as it was. They looked like standard cards from the Rider-Waite Tarot deck.

"I don't see signs of a struggle," Declan said as he took in the scene. "It looks like the killer walked into the room, got them out of bed, tied them to the chairs, and slit their throats. I wonder who he killed first."

Kate had no idea. "We won't know if there are any signs of sexual assault. I assume not in this case. A sexual motive hardly seems to be at play here." Kate had seen other similar cases where the man was subdued and the woman assaulted. Sometimes the killer would kill the man first to take the biggest threat out but other times, he'd make the husband watch as he tortured the wife.

The one thing Kate knew for sure was the blood was fresh. The couple couldn't have been dead for more than an hour or two. She turned to look out into the sitting room. "Briggs, what time did you say the alarm was tripped?"

Briggs stepped into the room, focused on Kate and averted his eyes from the couple. "Three twenty-eight. The security company called when the alarm wasn't disengaged and then sent a security officer to the residence. He found the back door open and called the Boston

Police Department. He didn't want to go inside alone. Rightly so. We had officers out here quickly."

"Your officers came in here?"

Briggs nodded. "There was concern about the safety of the couple, so the two officers came into the home. They had the security officer wait outside. They started a search of the house but didn't get far before they found the couple. They called it in right away and then continued with a search of the home. When I arrived, they brought me right here to the bedroom. I was concerned the killer might still be inside, so we did a more thorough search of the home. Honestly, Kate, the place is so massive that it's hard to know if the killer was inside the whole time. He could have slipped out while we were searching. I was trying to balance safety with preserving the crime scene."

Kate could tell that Briggs was concerned they had done something wrong. "You did exactly what we would have done. Did you notify the family?"

"I haven't gotten that far."

Kate said she'd take care of it. "I knew the couple's children. Not well. I haven't seen either of them since college. Still, though, I'll make the death notification."

"What about the media outside?"

They would need to address that. She turned to Declan. "What's the ETA on Sharon?"

"I'm already here, boss," Sharon said as she entered the room carrying her bags. She was already suited up in her head-to-toe crime scene gear. "Officers downstairs told me it's a messy case." She leaned to the left to look around Kate. "I'd say it is. The rest of my team is downstairs. You'll need to clear the room so we can get to work. Is there anything else you need in here?"

Declan moved out of the bedroom to Sharon. "You made it here quickly."

Sharon gestured toward Kate. "I wanted to impress the boss. You already like me. Spade said I had to win her over."

Kate didn't know if Spade had truly said that. "You've already won me over," she said truthfully. Sharon was a spitfire. She packed a lot of punch in a tiny body. She didn't stand more than five-foot-four and had a twist of dark hair on top of her head. "We're glad you're a part of the team. You remember Briggs?"

Sharon looked in his direction. "We worked a case a couple of years ago."

"We did. I held off calling the medical examiner as I figured you'd want to start with the scene as it was found. The only difference is the light was off."

Declan gestured toward the bedroom. "I also turned on one of the bedside lights. The tarot cards are taped to the headboard."

Sharon shivered. "Creepy. Especially right around Halloween too."

Even though they had been carving pumpkins when the case started, Kate hadn't considered it as being connected to the holiday. She turned to Declan to see his reaction. He seemed as surprised as she felt. "It's the creepiest case we've ever had," she said to Sharon before thanking her for arriving so quickly. "We'll be searching the rest of the house if you need us."

The three of them filed out of the room.

There was a lot to be done and only a little time before they'd have to face the media.

CHAPTER 6

Later that morning, Kate sat with Leo at her kitchen table updating him about the case. "I'm sorry we didn't bring you with us."

Leo held his hand up to stop her. "You don't owe me any explanation. I'm not even sure how I'd be able to assist in this case. It's far out of my depth. Something related to art theft, sure. A serial homicide case like this – I know nothing. I'm not the least bit upset that I missed going to the morgue or the awful scene you described to me. How are you doing?"

There was weight behind his words. "This is what we do. I've become somewhat desensitized to it. I have to do my job." Kate appreciated his checking on her. She explained she bought tarot cards last night too. "I still need to study more, particularly as the killer seems to be sticking to this pattern. The cards were taped to the back of the headboard not far from where they were killed."

"This killer is sick. The way he killed that couple." Leo had a look of disgust on his face and he cursed in frustration. "I don't understand the mindset of someone like that. To hurt an innocent couple for no reason. I can't wrap my mind around that."

Kate wished she could say the same. "It's a pathology. Killers like this don't think the way we do. They don't process emotions in the same way. Some don't have emotions like we have them. They are not easily understood, which is why most people don't do this work."

"You understand them." It was more a statement than a question.

"As much as anyone can understand," Kate admitted, not sure of his point. "Luckily, there aren't many like them. It's kind of a rare breed who kills strangers for the thrill of it or sexual gratification. It's easier to understand people who kill over money, revenge, or even lust. These killers don't have motives like regular killers."

Leo reached for her but retracted his hand before he touched her. He stared at her with a thoughtful expression on his face. "I never asked you why you chose to do work like this. Surely, you could have been in law enforcement, even the FBI, without having to subject yourself to cases like this."

Not many people had ever asked Kate that question. In all the time she had known him, Declan had never asked her that. She wasn't sure she knew the *why* herself. Kate gave him the only answer she had. "I don't know that I chose this. I showed an aptitude in graduate school for understanding the pathology of killers like this. I showed a skill set for profiling and interrogating them. That's why I was recruited for the FBI. In the academy, my skills only increased. It was easy for me in the way it wasn't for others. The job chose me more than I chose the job if that makes sense."

The corner of Leo's mouth turned up in a smile. "Kind of the way my profession chose me. Maybe we would have been better off stepping back and going after what we really wanted. I know my life would have turned out much differently had I been able to go after what I wanted instead of doing what I felt called to do."

Kate knew he had some regret about the way his life had turned out. He had admitted to her that his life of crime and living in the shadows had robbed him of relationships. He hadn't been able to marry, have children, or even maintain a normal relationship with a woman. "What would you have done? It never sounded to me like you had an interest in much else. Once you found out that your stepfather Lucien had Nazi-looted art, your path was set in stone."

"Ahh," he said with a sigh. "That is probably true. I would have liked the opportunity to see what else was out there for me. Did you have any other interests?"

Kate had only talked a little about her parents with Leo. "As you know my father was an American history professor at Harvard. I often thought I might have followed in his footsteps. I spent a good deal of time this past summer giving lectures at colleges and universities about the work I do now. I enjoyed it quite a bit and could see myself retiring early and teaching. But I have a great love of American history like my father. If I wasn't doing this, I'd probably be teaching and researching."

Leo seemed to like her answer. "I can see that for you, Kate. Retirement may surprise you." He held his arms wide. "This is not where I thought I'd be. I owe that to you."

"Declan," Kate reminded him. They were waiting for him to get back from finishing up with Sharon at the crime scene. They had gone their separate ways so Kate could update Spade and read Leo into the case.

"You're right," Leo said with a nod. "It was Declan who suggested it and pushed for me to be here. It still surprises me."

Kate felt a warm rush over her as she thought about Declan. "He has a way of surprising all of us. He knew I'd never be able to arrest you and I wouldn't be able to stand knowing you were in prison. The more I got to know you, the harder it was to separate what you did from why you did it. The motive was pure even if the action was criminal."

Leo's mouth set in a firm line. He looked as if he wanted to say something profound. He held back whatever it was and looked away. "You have a strong sense of justice that I admire." Leo smiled in the kind way to which she'd grown accustomed. "Now, back to the case. What else do you think I should know? I'm happy to help where I can even if I'm out of my element."

Leo was right, they needed to refocus their attention. Kate leaned her arms on the table. "After looking at the tarot book last night, it appears the killer is going in order. First, he killed a man who represented The Fool. Not only from the victim's new beginning here in Boston but to how the man died. It was represented in the card quite poetically. Then he assigned himself The Magician and me The High Priestess. I think that will take some time to determine if it's a true representation. Next, he killed The Empress and Emperor. I think we'd be safe in assuming that he's going after The Hierophant. Do you believe that's a safe assumption?"

Leo agreed with her. "Do you understand The Hierophant card?"

"I read about it in the book. The descriptions are short. Do you know something that might not have been in the book?" Kate knew this was the area where Leo could be most helpful.

Leo sat back and propped his ankle up on his opposite knee. He gestured with his hands as he spoke. "Some might say that The Hierophant and The High Priestess are a match. Many historians I know on tarot don't see it that way. She is more of a match for The Magician, using the tools she has been provided like he is using his. The Hierophant is…" Leo trailed off as if trying to find the right words.

"He looked like the Pope," Kate said, helping him along. "He's an imposing figure sitting on a throne between two pillars, wearing three robes of different colors with a triple-pointed crown on his head. He has one hand held up as if speaking and two fingers pointed toward the sky as if he's mid-lecture. In his other hand, he holds a scepter while two people sit below him listening. He seems inaccessible to me."

Leo pulled back in surprise. "For someone who didn't know anything about tarot yesterday, you're a quick study. You were able to see all the symbolism of the card and interpret it well. The

Hierophant is inaccessible as some might say. He's the conduit between the heavens and man. Some might say God and man or whatever higher being you believe. He represents traditional values and institutions. He has a focus on conformity, marriage, and commitment. It depends on what kind of reading you are doing how the card will be interpreted."

Kate followed along well. "Is there anything we can take from the card or its meaning to help us to know who he is targeting next?" Kate had her own ideas but wanted to hear Leo's.

Leo pointed toward the front of her brownstone. "You have the seat of the Catholic church right here. The Archdiocese of Boston is the fourth largest in the United States. Catholics are the predominant religion here. I wouldn't be surprised if he went after the cardinal or a priest."

Kate swallowed hard. It had been exactly what she had been thinking. "As soon as I saw the card, I thought about Cardinal Michael O'Connor. He's not as well protected as one might think. Given this killer went after the Davenports, I assume he might be going after well-known targets."

"Did Kirk Eagen have great power or prestige?"

Kate was a little surprised Leo had remembered the man's name. "I have a meeting with his law firm today. He's from Chicago and had worked as a criminal defense attorney there. I don't know much about his background. I was hoping to find that out today. The Davenports were quite well-known. I grew up with their children and it was a hard call to make to their son Chase. Both of them are living out of state now and I wanted to deliver the news myself. We sent FBI agents in Chicago to inform Eagen's family. We sent agents to see Chase Davenport, too. They handed him a phone and I delivered the news. Given I knew him, I wanted to deliver the message myself and I'm glad I did."

"Did you find out anything that's helpful?"

Kate wasn't sure how helpful it would be. "The Davenports were in the process of retiring. Bernard was ready to turn his business empire over to his son and his wife was going to be giving up her board positions. They wanted to travel. Chase said several people knew this. They were scheduled to leave for a six-month trip next month. Chase also said he believed his father would have tried to fight the intruder. There were no signs of a struggle. The live-in housekeeper has also been on vacation."

"People think they will fight when confronted like that. Fear can do many things when it comes right down to it. I suppose that's why you train so much. It has to be second nature." He locked his gaze on Kate and they held steady eye contact, neither of them looking away. "I'm sure you feel the fear, much like I did. You've learned to fight through it."

Kate let him hold her gaze for a few beats longer. He was interested in getting to know her more. She felt the wall go up around her the way it did sometimes when people were getting too close. She needed to keep Leo at bay for more reasons than one. "I think all humans feel fear. It's a good response. It's what keeps us safe and gets us out of danger. You're right, though, the FBI trains us to feel it and go forward regardless. We have a job to do."

Leo shifted his eyes away from her, sensing rightly he was getting too close. "Were the Davenports robbed? I'm sure there was money and other valuables in the home."

"There were many valuables," Kate confirmed. Chase had asked her the same question. "As far as we know, nothing outside of that bedroom was disturbed. Chase will be in Boston tonight and I'll walk through the home with him. There was no forced entry. We are still trying to figure out how the killer got in. We know he left through the back door but no alarm was tripped on the way in. I have a feeling this killer might be getting close to his victims before killing them. That also might be why Bernard didn't fight. He might not have felt a need to until it was too late."

"Perceptive." Leo grew quiet for a moment. He looked around Kate's kitchen and admired her recent renovation. He turned to her when he was done. "You know, Kate, most people set their alarm codes to something familiar to them. When I went into private collectors' homes, there was always an alarm. More often than not it was set to the birthday of someone in the home, usually the wife. Sometimes the children but rarely the man of the house."

Kate had no idea it was that common. She thought back to the discussion with Declan when she had a new home alarm system installed. She was going to set it as the month and day of her birthday but Declan said that was too obvious. "Declan has the Davenports' alarm code and we can look into it."

Leo's tone grew serious. "The other possibility is that the killer was already inside the home. If he knew the Davenports maybe he spent the night, which is why the alarm code was tripped only when he was leaving. He didn't need to worry about going in because he was already there."

Kate felt the sweat start to pool on her back. She couldn't remember now if it was Declan or Briggs who had raised the same question about the Eagen murder. They still didn't know the identity of the man who had walked in with Eagen the day he died. But the killer might have been already inside waiting. It was all too murky still.

Kate wanted to focus on the future, getting a step ahead of the killer, even though Declan had warned her against it. "I think it's fair to say the killer is going after The Hierophant next. What's the likelihood it's going to be Cardinal Michael O'Connor?"

Leo's eyes flicked up back to hers. "I'd say high enough we should go warn him."

That's exactly what Kate had been thinking.

CHAPTER 7

Getting a meeting with the head of the Archdiocese of Boston wasn't as easy a feat as Kate had assumed, even with her FBI credentials and the expressed concern for Cardinal Michael O'Connor. The staff there had initially stonewalled her and told her that getting a meeting that day would be impossible. When Kate insisted, the woman on the phone said that Kate could meet with staff but that Cardinal O'Connor wasn't available. Kate would see about that once she arrived.

Before leaving, Kate had called Declan to ask if he was available to come with her. He was meeting with Sharon and Briggs to compare the two crime scenes. She was fine with him focusing on the physical evidence. It was more his skill set anyway. Declan agreed with her that she should warn the cardinal and promised to meet up with her as soon as he was done. When she asked if they had found anything of interest, he paused in the way that indicated he had. He wouldn't tell her then. Declan said he wanted to explore more and assured her as soon as they knew anything conclusive, he'd tell her.

Instead of Declan, Kate sat in the front lobby of the Archdiocese with Leo. It was only once they had arrived that they were informed Cardinal O'Connor would be willing to speak to them. Kate wasn't sure why there was so much confusion over a simple meeting. They were told to wait in the lobby and someone would come for them when it was time.

"Were you raised with any religion?" Kate asked, keeping her voice low. With the building's hardwood flooring and high ceilings, everything echoed. The space was so quiet and serene that the only sounds were the squeak of shoes on the floor.

Leo's shoulder had been resting on hers as they sat side-by-side. He shifted himself to look at her. "My mother raised me Catholic. Lucien was nothing but pure evil. I don't think he believed in anything but himself and his power. I went to church with her as a child. I grew away from all of it once I was in my teens." Leo had a far-off look on his face. "I've often thought about coming back to it."

"Declan and I had similar upbringings. His family is far more religious than mine," she offered. Kate wanted to ask him more. Before she had the chance, a stern-looking woman with pressed blue pants and a white blouse approached them. She had a wooden cross around her neck. "Cardinal Michael O'Connor will see you now. I'm Sister Elizabeth."

Kate stood and extended her hand. The nun's hand was thin and cold. "I'm sorry for disturbing your office today. We came across something in one of our ongoing cases and we must speak to the Cardinal."

Sister Elizabeth's back stiffened. "As you said on the phone. Cardinal O'Connor has opted not to have the Archdiocese lawyer present. I think that's a mistake but it's not my call to make."

Kate pulled back in confusion. "I'm sorry. I don't think I understand." As she said the words, the full weight of the nun's meaning finally sank in. Kate felt a rush of concern that the Archdiocese had mistaken the meaning for the visit. "This isn't about any sexual abuse investigation, Sister Elizabeth. Cardinal O'Connor is not the subject of my investigation. We have some information about a case that doesn't relate in any way to the Catholic Church or the Archdiocese.

We felt given what we know and the way the case has been going, the Cardinal might be in danger."

"Oh," Sister Elizabeth said as she put her hand over the wooden cross around her neck. "You should have said that on the phone. You had the office all in a tizzy today."

Kate apologized for the miscommunication. She had been so focused on the case that the Catholic Church's sexual abuse scandal that had broken wide open in Boston had been the last thing on her mind. "I said on the phone that I'm not from the FBI Boston Field Office. I work from a specialized unit based out of the FBI headquarters."

The nun looked over at Kate as if she were clueless about her power. "Is this case happening here in Boston?"

"Yes. The Davenports were murdered last night."

"Oh, my." The nun whispered words of prayer. But that was all Sister Elizabeth needed to hear to rush Kate and Leo out of the lobby. The Davenports had been large donors of the Catholic Church and Audrey had sat on the board of Catholic Charities. She'd also been on the board of a Catholic all-girls prep school. "I don't think Cardinal O'Connor knows of the news yet."

"We haven't released many details. It happened in the early hours this morning." Kate was a little surprised they didn't know. The media had been camped in front of the mansion. Declan and Briggs had given a joint statement. They had not released any other details about the case. So far, the media had not connected the Eagen murder with this one. Why would they? It was a different victim type and method of killing. Most still believed Eagen's death was a suicide. Kate knew the details would need to come out sooner rather than later. They had all agreed they wanted a better handle on the investigation before they publicly connected the two.

Sister Elizabeth walked Kate and Leo to Cardinal O'Connor's office.

She rapped once on the door and a woman told them to enter. An assistant sat behind a large mahogany desk. Kate wasn't sure if the woman was also a Catholic nun or a layperson. She didn't introduce herself just pointed to the door on the left side of her desk. "Cardinal O'Connor is waiting for you," was all she said.

Kate turned to thank Sister Elizabeth but she was already gone. "Okay," she said mostly to herself. She took the lead and Leo followed right behind her. Kate wasn't sure what to expect from Cardinal O'Connor. She had not met the man or his predecessor.

Kate walked through the open door of his office, which had a wall of windows in the back letting in the natural sunlight. His desk was a match to his assistant's. O'Connor had a head full of white hair, a round affable face, and a pleasant smile. He was dressed simply in black pants and a shirt with a white collar. In some ways, Kate had been expecting more opulence, as if maybe she was having an audience with the Pope.

"Agent Walsh," he said and got up from his desk chair. He crossed the office and greeted her with a handshake. "I knew your parents. It was a tragedy what happened to them."

Kate accepted the handshake. She had no memory of ever meeting him.

Before she could respond, Cardinal O'Connor noted the confusion. "I was a chaplain at Harvard a million years ago," he said with a wider smile. He turned to Leo. "I'm sorry, I don't know your name."

"Leo Lamiere, I'm a consultant with the FBI."

Kate apologized for not introducing him. "I apologize for causing a ruckus at your office today."

"No bother at all. My staff gets themselves all worked up over nothing usually. They were running around like chickens." He gestured toward the couch and chair. "Please, let's sit down and have a chat. You were quite insistent about seeing me, so it must be important."

Kate stood for a moment to deliver the news while Cardinal O'Connor sat in the brown leather chair. Leo sat on a matching couch facing it. She waited until they got settled to start. "This morning Bernard and Audrey Davenport were found murdered in their home." She gave him time to respond with his shock and then sadness. "It's a blow to the community. The case is not isolated."

O'Connor didn't understand. "What do you mean? Was someone else killed in their home?"

"No," Kate said then sat on the edge of the couch, folding her hands in her lap. She went on to describe the Eagen murder then went back to the initial letter and tarot cards she had received. "I don't know much about tarot. I'm learning as I go. I had to go out and buy a tarot deck to understand it."

"Curious motive," O'Connor said, less horrified than Kate would have assumed. "He doesn't know your address in Boston, does he?"

"No," Kate said with a firm shake of her head. "The initial letter was sent to the FBI Headquarters in Washington D.C. I suspect he's from here. Given how he's choosing the victims and what he knows about them in advance. He might even be befriending them."

O'Connor took in all the information as Kate continued to explain. He was only left with one question at the end. "How does this relate to me? The Davenports were well-known by a lot of people in this community and I considered them dear friends. I don't know Kirk Eagen."

Kate had taken a photo of The Hierophant card before she left the house. She pulled out her phone and showed O'Connor the photo. "This is the next card. We believe the killer will go after someone who represents this to him." Kate went on to describe the meaning of the card and how they had ended up in his office. "Of course, I don't have any facts or specific threats against you or anyone related to the

Catholic Church. That said, given what happened to the Davenports, we thought it best to warn you."

O'Connor studied the card and handed Kate back her phone. "I can understand why you think that would represent me or someone related to the church. I have the means to pass the warning to our parish priests and others. Do we have any idea when he might strike?"

Kate was afraid the victim had already been chosen. "I suspect his plan has been in motion for a long time. He may already be interacting with his victim. Is there anyone new in your life?"

O'Connor didn't even need to consider. "No. I'm out very little other than saying mass and visiting the parishes. I meet new people all the time but no one has taken any particular interest or visited me here or where I live. Do you have any idea who is doing this?"

"No. I have worked up a basic profile but we can't be sure that it's accurate." Kate described the killer based on her profile. "All of that said, he's a chameleon. If he's meeting people ahead of time and worse befriending them, then he's blending into their environments and gaining their trust. I'm afraid this is someone who walks among us and is blending in. Is there a way to keep a low profile for now?"

"I will take extra precautions and I will pass the warning on. But, no, I will not hide. I have events scheduled and things I need to do. The people around me have been with me for years and are trustworthy." He smiled over at her. "Sister Elizabeth is a stickler for protocol and, as much as I think she'd like to knock me about the head some days, I do not think she's a real threat." There was a twinkle in his eyes even though Kate knew he was taking the threat seriously.

"How would you feel about us sending an FBI agent over as protection?"

He didn't even take a moment to consider. "If there was a specific threat against me that would be one thing. There is none other than this speculation about the card. Many other religious denominations could be a match here in the city. I will not take up valuable resources from the FBI to protect me while so many others are at risk. If it's God's will he comes for me, I will handle that then."

"Are you certain of that decision?" Leo asked.

"I'm certain." Cardinal O'Connor stood, signaling the end of the meeting. Kate and Leo stood with him. He extended his hand to each of them. "I will be praying for you both to stop this madman before he does more damage to the city. I assume the Davenport children know about the murder?"

"I notified Chase earlier today. He is on his way to Boston. His sister is out of the country and will return as soon as she can. Did you know them?"

"Not as well as the parents," Cardinal O'Connor admitted. "I will reach out to them later."

As Kate was wrapping up the meeting, there was a knock on the door.

"It's Evan Crandall. He is my right-hand man here at the Archdiocese. He keeps me on task," Cardinal O'Connor said with a smile. He called the man in and introduced them.

Evan Crandall stood about five-eleven and had sandy brown hair and blue eyes. He was thin but the muscles showing through his shirt were well-defined. He extended his hand to Kate.

Kate turned back to O'Connor. "If you change your mind about the security, please let me know." She saw the concerned look on Evan's face as they exited the room. She had said it purposefully. If Evan was his right-hand man, then maybe he could convince O'Connor to protect himself.

Kate and Leo made it to the parking lot when Evan called from the doorway of the building. "Agent Walsh!" he shouted again until she turned around. He jogged over to her. "I wanted to speak to you out of earshot of Cardinal O'Connor. You said he was in danger?"

Kate gave him a fast update, leaving out most of the details she had shared with the cardinal. She stressed the last part. "I don't have a specific threat against him. It's more of a general warning based on the tarot card. It could be anyone this killer deems representative of The Hierophant. I thought Cardinal O'Connor was the most likely. I'm glad he's passing the warning down to local parish priests. Everyone should be on alert."

Evan's features pinched in concern. "Do you have any idea who we should be watching out for related to this threat?"

"No," Kate admitted. "We are too early in the investigations and don't have any suspects. The case is barely a couple of days old."

"What can I do?"

Kate wasn't sure there was anything he could do. "Cardinal O'Connor refused the FBI security I offered. I think all you can do is ensure his normal protection. Watch out for anyone trying to get too close to him."

Evan pursed his lips. "If that's the best we can do, we'll do it. I know Cardinal O'Connor can be cavalier sometimes about his security. I'll make sure the rest of the staff is aware of the threat."

Kate thanked him and then they were on their way. She checked the phone as she was getting in her car. Declan had texted her – there hadn't been a development. He wanted to meet back at her brownstone rather than the Boston Police Department. It was a curious request but she texted him that she'd be there soon.

CHAPTER 8

Kate pulled into the small parking lot behind her brownstone. Declan's SUV was already there as was a car she didn't recognize.

"Is it normal to meet the team at your house?" Leo asked as he climbed out of her SUV and shut the door.

"Never." Kate glanced up at the back window and saw Briggs standing there. "There must be a reason why Declan wanted to meet here rather than the Boston Police Department or even the FBI Boston Field Office."

Kate entered the back door into her kitchen with Leo right behind her. Declan and Sharon sat at her kitchen table while Briggs stood near it. She glanced at Declan who was deep in conversation. "You said you found something?" she said not wasting any time.

Leo moved away from the group and stood near the kitchen island. He leaned back and observed. Kate appreciated that he was hanging back and taking time to learn from them.

"Sorry to be meeting at your house, Kate. It's lovely," Sharon offered.

Kate took the chair across from them. "Thank you. What's going on?" She looked up at Briggs and hitched her chin toward the other chair. He took a seat but Kate could tell he seemed uncomfortable. "It's okay that we are meeting here. I know it's unusual. I'm fine with it."

"I didn't want to show up at your house like this. Declan insisted."

"It's fine," she assured him. "What's going on?"

Sharon flipped her laptop around and showed Kate an image of what looked like a small piece of plastic with traces of red. "It's silicone. I believe the killer has used silicone over his fingertips to avoid leaving prints. The red you're seeing is blood. I assume he wore gloves during the murder or there'd be a lot more blood on it. Of course, I don't know exactly when this fell to the floor."

Declan added, "We think it's how he's getting in and out of these scenes without leaving prints. It's also how he's interacting with people ahead of time but not arousing suspicion. If you had someone over here casually and they were wearing gloves, you'd question it. If he's got silicone over his fingerprints to mask them, you probably aren't going to notice."

Kate had heard of people doing that before. She didn't know how well it worked long term. "Is this something you found at the Davenports?"

Sharon spun her laptop back to face her. "It was found slightly under the bed near the pillows. I imagine it fell off while he was trying to tape the cards to the headboard. I can't be sure if he did that before or after he killed the couple."

"No other prints in the room?"

Sharon shook her head. "No. That house is far too big and there are many staff in and out of there so we were strategic about where we dusted for prints."

Declan leaned forward on the table. "Do you remember the spare bedroom that had all the sheets off the bed and just the bare mattress? We thought maybe they just didn't use that room. Sharon's team dusted it for prints and found none – the whole room had been wiped down."

Kate wasn't sure she was following. "What made you pick that room?"

"Because it was bare and it didn't match up with the rest of the house," Sharon explained over the rim of her laptop. She could see that Kate was still confused about the process. "We went through the whole place and every room was well decorated. Even rooms that were probably never used. Those rooms didn't have a speck of dust. That told me the housekeeper regularly cleaned those rooms even if no one was staying in them. Why would that one room not be made up like the rest? I got curious. Then when Declan mentioned the housekeeper had been off the last few days, I was even more curious about why that room would be unmade. I found the sheets in the dryer. I'm fairly certain Audrey Davenport wasn't doing her laundry and a good housekeeper wasn't going to let laundry sit in the dryer to wrinkle while she's on vacation."

"You're right," Kate said slowly, understanding the implications of it. Someone had been staying in that room and had cleaned up after themselves. "There were no fingerprints in that whole room?"

Sharon shook her head. "It had been wiped down thoroughly. Someone was trying to hide that they were there. They didn't do a good enough job though or they would have waited for the sheets and duvet to dry and would have remade the bed. There were no fingerprints in the attached bathroom or oddly in the couple's kitchen. I didn't even find their fingerprints in the kitchen. He wiped down every area where he probably touched. He didn't trust the silicone."

Kate was going through all the places someone could touch regularly in the home. She hit on something Sharon hadn't mentioned. "What about the pillows on the bed?"

"Gone," Sharon said, giving even more confirmation to her theory. "He must have taken them with him and dumped them. Each bed in that house has four pillows for sleeping and two decorative pillows. The decorative pillows were there but the other four were not."

Leo cursed under his breath, drawing everyone's attention to him. He apologized. "I was thinking about the level of detail and planning that had to go into all of that. Along with the time spent there. It's meticulous – all to kill two people."

Leo had a point that didn't escape Kate. It was not only meticulous planning but excessive. This whole thing was so much more than the kill for him. It was the ritual – the whole thing, the cozying up to the couple, getting to know them all the while plotting and planning their deaths. Kate didn't think there had been a sexual component to this crime but she was starting to wonder what kind of gratification the killer was getting from this whole thing.

"Kate," Declan said slowly, drawing out her name. "You look utterly lost in your own world."

Kate raised her eyes to him. "He's getting significant gratification from going through this ritual and duping his victims. It's completely psychopathic behavior."

Briggs had trouble relating. "This is beyond diabolical. By that logic then we can assume he's already in contact with his next victim."

Kate thought it might be more than that. "He might have the next six or seven victims picked out and already be interacting with one or two of them. This must have taken more than a year in planning. While I believe he must have a way of making money, this must be like a full-time job for him."

"Independently wealthy?" Declan asked.

Kate wasn't sure. "Either that or he's making money by some other means. Something where he's not working a regular nine-to-five kind of job. He also got in with the Davenports, so he's carrying himself in a way that indicates he has power and wealth. I can't imagine the Davenports would let a random stranger in their home."

"Did you ask Chase if anyone was staying there?"

"I didn't know at the time, Declan," Kate said, feeling like they were playing catch-up. "We didn't even know then that the housekeeper was away." Kate felt the implications of all of that settle into her gut. This killer had significant time with them. He didn't have to rush with his kill.

Declan read her mind. "This killer had all the time in the world to enact his plan."

"That's right."

They all fell into silence thinking about the dangerous predator already stalking the streets for his next victim. It was Briggs who spoke first. "What do we do with this information? The Hierophant is next."

Kate realized then she hadn't told them all where she had been earlier. "This might seem crazy, but I went to the Archdiocese and warned Cardinal O'Connor. He's the closest person in Boston that resembles the card. He refused extra protection but said he'd send the warning to the local parish priests. I don't know how other religious denominations work. If anyone has an in, please let them know." She saw the look on Declan's face and knew exactly what he was thinking before he said it.

"We have to go public with the whole thing, Kate." Declan was insistent. He said it again when Kate balked at the idea. He looked to Briggs and Sharon for support. They agreed with him that the time was now to bring it all out into the open.

When Kate still didn't seem convinced, Leo moved from the island over to the table. "Does anyone want my two cents?"

No one jumped at it other than Kate. "Please feel free to tell us what you think."

He gave her a look that asked if she was sure. When Kate nodded, he continued. "You have to make this public. I don't see any way around it. If the killer strikes and it's someone prominent again, then the FBI is in real trouble. I know when I was…" Leo faltered at the words.

Kate was ready to jump in and rescue him, but he didn't need it.

Leo recovered well. He ran a hand down his stubbled face. "I was going to say that the media can be used as pressure for a criminal. It can get them to be more cocky thinking they will never get caught and then they make mistakes or they can go underground and cool off for some time."

Spade had trained him well. Kate was impressed and she conceded the point. "Will Declan and Briggs continue to be the faces for the media during the case?"

They both agreed.

"We can craft a statement that highlights the two murders, the use of the tarot cards, and the warning about the upcoming cards." Declan gestured toward Kate. "Is there anything you want us to say directly to the killer? You know he'll be listening."

Kate took a moment to consider. "You can say we believe the killer is befriending the victims ahead of time and working to conceal his identity. I'd also add that we know he's meticulous in his planning and we know he's taking his time with the victims. I'd leave out anything about the evidence found." She thought for a moment longer then added, "You can tell him The High Priestess has accepted the challenge and she looks forward to sitting down to speak with him. Until then, she is going to do everything she can to stop him."

Declan raised his eyebrows. "You want to say that? Are you sure?"

"I'm sure," Kate said but not with the conviction she would have wanted. For the first time in her career, she was afraid of her adversary. He seemed smarter and more conniving and manipulative than most of the killers she went after. She believed him when he told her he was The Magician.

A knock on the front door interrupted them. Declan hopped up not giving Kate the chance. He told Sharon to share more of the crime scene analysis – not that there was much more to share. She had covered the important parts.

As Sharon started to give them the overview, Declan went to the front door. Moments later, he called for Kate, his voice tinged with urgency. He called again and again, his voice growing distant.

Kate and Briggs sprang up from their chairs and dashed into the hallway only to find the front door wide open, with Declan nowhere in sight.

"What's going on?" Briggs demanded, his hand instinctively reaching for his gun.

Kate swiftly unholstered her weapon, her senses on high alert. "Declan!" she shouted, her voice echoing through the house. She bolted towards the open doorway, her gun leading the way. "Declan!" she called out again and again, scanning the surroundings as she stepped onto the concrete landing. But Declan was gone.

She turned back to Briggs, whose gaze was focused on the floor. "I don't know where he could have gone that quickly. I don't understand what's happening." Kate lowered her eyes to the floor to see what had garnered his attention.

Briggs toed a slip of folded-over white paper that sat atop what looked to Kate to be a tarot card. "There's something here you need to see."

Kate stepped back into the house and bent down to look at it, not even thinking about putting on gloves to pick it up. She picked up the card, studied its antique-looking design, then unfolded the paper and gasped.

I know where you live, Kate. You are my High Priestess but you might also be Justice.

CHAPTER 9

Kate held the slip of paper in her shaking hand. It was written in the same style as the last letter. The fear permeated her body and caused her to lose her breath.

The killer knew where she lived.

"Kate," Leo said with concern as he laid his hand on her arm.

Everyone else had sprung to action. Briggs took off out the front door after Declan and Sharon snapped on gloves and tried to take the letter from her.

Kate resisted, not able to take her eyes away from it.

The stark white printer paper only had one line across the middle of the page. Dead center.

She had started as his opponent and now he was suggesting that she might be better matched as one of the other tarot cards – Justice. That felt like a better fit for her, except that it meant she was no longer his equal – she was a target.

Kate read the line again. She knew it was a taunt to rile her up and throw her off her game. The Davenport scene flashed in her mind and she shoved it to the side.

No. Kate wasn't going to be afraid in her home. She wasn't going to let this killer get to her.

Kate shook herself out of the trance and thrust the letter toward Sharon. "Bag this and take it for prints. Mine are already on file. I don't think there will be any others. We have to do whatever we can." As she started to head out the door to go after Declan and Briggs, Sharon called her back.

"Kate, it's okay if you're not okay," Sharon said as she slipped the letter and the tarot card into an evidence bag. "This creepy killer knows where you live. I'd already be packing my things."

"I'm not going to give him the satisfaction." It was the last thing Kate said as she jogged down her front steps not bothering to look back at Sharon or Leo. She could hear them talking about her, expressing their concern.

Kate knew she had every reason to be concerned and, if the letter had been sent to either one of them, the first thing she'd tell them to do was leave. Kate wasn't going to do that.

Kate paused on the sidewalk not sure which way Declan and Briggs went. She made a snap decision to go toward Boston Public Garden. There were enough winding paths and tourists to blend in quickly and get away. He could be sitting on a park bench right now watching Declan and Briggs scramble to find him.

That's the mindset of this killer.

Games. Manipulation. Fear.

Kate jogged down the block, watching the faces of every stranger who passed her. She hoped that her intuition might alert her if she saw him. It was probably wishful thinking. She waited for the light to change and hurried across the street into the park.

The path she chose was random chance. She'd walked about a quarter of a mile into Boston Public Garden when she came across Briggs. She called to him, "Did you find Declan?"

Briggs shook his head. "This area is too big to search alone. I've gone down a few of these paths and around to the other side of the water and back again. They could be down in Boston Common for all we know." He rubbed a hand across his bald head in frustration and let out a guttural growl. "They could be anywhere in the city by now. We don't even know that they went in this direction."

Kate took it as a good sign that Briggs had chosen this way too. "Declan came this way. I'm sure of it. He must have only been seconds behind whoever dropped that off."

Briggs looked at her with skepticism on his face. "Do you think the killer came to your door?"

Kate shook her head. "I don't think he'd do anything that risky this early on. He wanted to send me a message, not get caught. He sent someone and that person has seen his face."

Briggs was staring at her. "How are you not freaking out right now?"

"Who said I'm not freaking out?" she said with a nervous laugh. "My hand was shaking as I was holding the letter. I'm angry and that trumps everything." She pinned her gaze on him. "I'm not going to give this guy the satisfaction of seeing me afraid or flee my home."

"You have to leave, Kate," Briggs said, his tone serious but filled with emotion for her. "You can't put yourself at risk to prove a point. We all know you're brave. You're braver than all of us."

Kate was on the verge of disputing the matter when Declan's voice sliced through the air, summoning her attention. Her gaze darted around, searching for him. Suddenly, he materialized from between two trees, navigating through the foliage of a grassy knoll. His grip firmly clasped the arm of a man, blood trickling from his nose.

Kate rushed to him, fighting the urge to wrap her arms around him and kiss him right there in front of everyone. She had tempered her worry about him and focused on the letter. Seeing him now, safe, the rush of emotions she had been feeling bubbled to the surface. Kate knew she couldn't express it now. She focused on the man instead.

He was young, too young to be the killer. He had a ripped Grateful Dead tee shirt, jeans with holes in the knees, and blue ratty Converse that almost looked older than him. "You can't hold me like this!" the kid shouted as they approached. Declan dragged the kid toward them. He had his hands cuffed behind his back and a defiant scowl on his face.

Kate stepped toward the kid. She jabbed a finger into his chest. "Are you the one who dropped that note off at my door?"

The kid turned his head to avoid her eyes.

"He's the one, Kate," Declan said with confidence. "I saw him running away from the house."

"You don't know why I was running." He must have noticed the badge on Briggs. "Are you a cop? This guy tackled me and punched me in the face. I want to press charges. He can't do something like that. I know my rights!"

He reeked of pot and his eyes reflected that he was higher than a kite. Briggs ignored him.

Kate tugged the chain that held her badge from under her shirt and showed him the shield. "FBI Agent Kate Walsh. This is my partner, Declan James, who I assume identified himself."

The kid narrowed his eyes. "After he punched me."

"I tried earlier but you didn't hear me," Declan said with a hint of a satisfied smile on his lips. "I told you to stop running. All you had to do was stop."

"I didn't think you'd catch me."

Declan was fast and this kid was stoned out of his mind. "Why did you run?"

"Big goon like you coming after me. You'd run too."

Kate didn't care about the chase or his bloody nose. "Who gave you the note to leave at my house?"

He looked down at her. "I don't know anything about any note." He raised his eyes to Briggs. "Arrest him. I told you I want to press charges."

Briggs finally spoke up. "Not going to happen. You're coming in for questioning." He walked away from them to call a squad car to take them to the station.

"I didn't do anything!" he yelled and tried to wriggle out of Declan's grasp.

"Stop it!" Declan shouted at him and looked over at Kate. "We need to get him to an interrogation room. We can't do this here in the park."

"No, no, no. I'm not going anywhere with you," the kid said again. He must have figured out quickly that they were serious because he settled down. "I don't want you to call my dad. I'll tell you what you want to know. But I'm not going to the police station. You can't detain me for dropping off a note. I didn't hurt anyone. I didn't even read the stupid thing."

"You're admitting it then," Kate said, thinking this was good progress. He hadn't technically done anything more than drop off a note and that wasn't illegal. She had no reason to believe this stoned kid was the killer or even knew him. He probably did it for money. She went with her hunch. "How much did he pay you to leave the note?"

"Twenty bucks. It was supposed to be easy money," the kid responded with a shrug. "It was until this goon chased me down and punched me in the face. I'm going to sue you for this, even if that dumb cop over there won't arrest you."

Kate didn't care about his grumbling. She gestured away from the path toward two side-by-side park benches. Until they could get a squad car there to take him to the police station, she wanted as much information as possible.

Declan deposited the kid on the bench. "What's your name?"

"I don't have to tell you that," he snarled, holding firm until he got one look at Declan's face looming over him. "Fine, man. It's River."

"That's your given name?" Declan asked with skepticism in his voice. "What's on your birth certificate?"

"River Thomas."

"River," Kate said calmly as she sat next to him. "I need you to tell me about the man who gave you the note. Where did you meet him?"

"Here." He pointed down near the water. "I was laying in the grass enjoying the vibe and this guy approaches me and says he's got twenty bucks if I can drop off a note. I told him to go away and that I didn't care about the money. I was happy on the grass, you know?" He paused but Kate wanted him to go on. "He wouldn't leave me alone. He kept at me over and over again. He was ruining my vibe, so I got up and asked him where to drop the note. He gave me the address and it was super close, so I said yes. I figured it was the only way to get him to leave me alone. He handed over the twenty and I went. I don't see how I did anything illegal."

Declan folded his arms over his chest as he stared down at the kid. "You didn't think it was weird that some random guy was asking you to deliver a note he could have done himself?"

"I don't know, man. He seemed like a rich guy. I figured he didn't want to cross that busy street."

"What makes you think he was rich?" Kate asked, focusing on him. River was telling the truth. He was open in his body language and no deception in his tone. He was still angry about being detained.

River shrugged and said he didn't know. Kate pressed him and he grunted. "He was dressed nicely in pressed tan pants and a blue shirt. He had fancy brown loafers on too. Like the high-end stuff. His watch looked expensive too. I didn't see the brand."

It fit Kate's profile. She knew the killer had money. "What else can you tell me about him? How tall was he? What did he look like?"

"I wasn't paying much attention to him," River said with another shrug.

"Think!" Declan shouted, growing frustrated.

The harder River was pushed the more he'd shut down. Kate shook her head at Declan. "Can you go back to the house and update them, please?" She had wanted to tell him to knock it off, but she wasn't going to dress him down in front of the kid.

Declan left begrudgingly, looking back twice to make sure she was okay.

When he was out of sight, River looked over at Kate. "What is his problem? Is he always this angry?"

"We believe the man who gave you the note is a serial killer, targeting people here in Boston," Kate said and watched his reaction. River went from disbelief to fear in seconds flat. "That's why Agent James chased you. The note was delivered to my home address and it was a threat against me."

River shook his head furiously. "I didn't know. I wouldn't threaten the FBI. You have to believe me. I had no idea. I just delivered the note." He was practically on the verge of crying. His shoulders shook and his voice trembled as he spoke. "I'll tell you whatever you want to know."

"Had you ever seen the man before today?"

"No. If I did, then I don't remember him."

"What did he look like?"

River considered the question for a moment, actually taking his time to answer. Kate assumed that was a good sign. "He was taller than me, probably as tall as your partner. He had dark hair, kind of parted on the side. He had a full dark beard but trimmed like he just came from the barbershop. His appearance was neat and professional like he was about to go to a board meeting or on a yacht or something fancy."

"Color of his eyes? Anything distinctive about his face?"

"I don't remember his eyes. He looked like an average rich guy." River paused for a moment. "There was one thing that was weird." He pointed to just below his right ear. "His beard up here kind of looked weird. I noticed it when he was handing me the money. Almost darker or patchy. Something about it was off."

Kate thought back to what Sharon said about the silicone over his fingertips. "Could he have been wearing a fake beard?"

River scrunched up his features in uncertainty. "I don't know. It looked real to me except for that one area. I didn't get a good look at him."

Kate asked a few more questions but didn't get much else from him. She had one last one that she wanted to revisit. "If you were just dropping a note, why did you run?"

"When he came out and yelled at me, I thought maybe he was having an affair with some lady in the house and that guy was the husband. I thought he was going to hurt me, which he did."

Briggs approached them on the bench, pointing to the car that had arrived. "We can take him down to the station for a formal interview and statement."

Before River put up a fight, Kate said, "This is as much to keep you safe as it is to get the information we need. You're going one way or the other, so you're better off not fighting it. I'll take the cuffs off you if you go willingly."

"Fine, whatever." River leaned forward so Kate could undo the cuffs.

Briggs said he'd go with him and get the formal statement. He'd call her when he was done.

Kate didn't see any reason to go. She had the information she needed. As Briggs was walking River toward the car, she shouted a thank you that wasn't acknowledged.

Kate wrapped her arms around herself as she stared at the trees with their rich orange and red autumn leaves, many of which had already fallen to the ground.

This killer was coming for her. No one could protect her.

CHAPTER 10

Kate made it back to her brownstone just as Sharon and Leo were leaving. She had to get back to the lab to run some tests on the new note as well as follow up on some other pending evidence. Before leaving, Sharon offered her support in any way she could.

"I promise, I'm fine," Kate said even though she wasn't sure that she was. Sharon was too new to the team to see Kate falter. After Sharon left, Kate turned to Leo who was standing on the last step of her stoop, lingering there. "I'm fine, Leo. I know you don't believe me."

"I don't, Kate. Not for a second." Leo looked up at her brownstone. "I know I'm only down the street, which doesn't put you that far out of harm's way, but if the two of you want to stay with me, there's more than enough room. I have the entire third floor that I never use. There are three bedrooms up there and two baths. You can have your pick."

"I'm not leaving, Leo," Kate said, resolved, but thanked him for the kind offer. "I have an alarm system and Declan is here with me. We have faced threats before. This killer isn't the first criminal to send something to my home and he probably won't be the last." She realized what she said a moment too late. "I wasn't talking about you. I appreciated the painting."

"But you were freaked out that I had your home address." Leo realized then that he had caused her fear. The remorse was written

70

all over his face.

"It was a kind gesture, Leo. Don't overthink it. Declan was more concerned than I was," Kate admitted, shifting her gaze away from him. She hated to even admit that he had caused her concern. "I did wonder how you knew where I lived."

Leo didn't offer up the information. "I didn't know where else to send it. I should have thought better of the decision. I didn't mean to scare you. I hoped you knew I cared for you."

"I did," she said, wanting to talk to him more, but she didn't know how much longer she could hold it together. "I'll call you later."

Kate closed and locked the front door and she slid down to the floor, taking a moment for herself. She hadn't been trying to appease Leo when she told him other criminals had found out her address. This time felt different – this killer was more dangerous than the others. More theatrics and willingness to play the game. It meant he was a risk taker and would do just about anything to up the tension and the thrill of the case.

That made him the most dangerous adversary Kate had come up against.

Kate didn't know how long she sat on the floor. Part of her waited for the tears to come. The emotion swelled and then subsided just as quickly. She had a job to do. Kate got to her feet and called Declan's name. She made her way back to the kitchen and found Declan sitting at the table with his head low reading a document. He had earbuds in but Kate could hear the music through them.

"You're going to make yourself deaf if you keep listening at that volume," she said with a rap of her knuckles against the table. Kate didn't know if he heard her but he raised his head and clicked his phone to shut off the music.

Declan pulled out the earbuds never breaking eye contact with her. "Katie, I'm so sorry that this guy is targeting you." She pulled up the chair next to him and he leaned over and kissed her. "Did River say anything else after I left? I wanted to punch that kid so badly. It was good you sent me away."

Kate leaned into him as much as two people could in separate chairs. She rested her head on his shoulder, feeling a brief moment of relief. "Leo suggested we stay at his place. I turned him down. I won't be driven out of here."

Declan moved to accommodate her better. "If you want to go, I'll understand."

"No," she said again and he didn't fight her. Kate took a deep breath and righted herself. "River gave me a basic description."

"Is it enough to have him work with a sketch artist?"

"It is. Briggs will take care of it and call me if he needs me to head to the station." Kate checked her phone for the time. "I have to head to the law firm where Kirk Eagen was employed. Then I have to meet Chase Davenport. Are you coming with me or staying here?"

"I'm going with you to the law firm. I thought you might want to speak to Chase on your own since you know him." Declan arched an eyebrow in a question.

She appreciated that he was giving her space. "I didn't know the Davenports well. Chase and I were never really friends. I do think some one-on-one time with him might be good. You can be a bit intimidating."

"Me? Intimidating? Never," he said with a chuckle. "Sharon wanted me to take her back over to the Eagen scene later today. She went through there yesterday but noted she has a few more questions."

"How is she working out?"

"Perfectly. I don't know how I'd feel if we had to rely on Boston Police Department's crime scene techs. I don't know them and wouldn't have the immediate access Sharon provides us."

"Good. I'm glad the decision is working out for us. Why were you meeting here?"

"It was close and I wanted the privacy rather than heading to the police station. The media is camped out there."

"Understood."

"Did you mind?"

Kate shook her head. "It was probably better that we were here when the note was delivered." She pushed herself up from the table and checked the address on her phone. "Eagen's office is within walking distance. It's a few blocks up on Boylston Avenue."

Declan grunted a response Kate didn't understand. He repeated himself. "This killer is hunting in our neighborhood. Eagen lived farther away but his office is right here. There's not even a mile between the law firm, the Davenports, and your brownstone."

"He walks among us," Kate said, knowing it to be true. "He's close, Declan." She ran her hands over her arms as she shivered. Not from the cold but the fear that coursed through her veins. "How do you think he figured out where I live?"

As Declan gathered his things, he raised his head. "You're assuming he didn't already know it when he sent the first letter to Washington D.C. He might have known all along, Kate, especially if he's someone who has been in the neighborhood for a while."

Kate hadn't wanted to think about that. "It's true," she conceded, giving it some thought. They hadn't exactly kept a low profile. Then again, the house had been in her father's family for generations. Few people in the neighborhood didn't know the Walshes.

They walked the few blocks, entered the Prudential Center, and took the elevator to the thirty-third floor. They stepped out of the elevator onto plush carpets and high-end design features. There was a glass chandelier and a mirrored backsplash behind the two-person desk in the reception area. It wasn't so much a desk as a fortress they sat behind. Kate introduced herself to one of the women and showed their credentials. The woman who had short blond hair and pink lipstick asked their appointment time and who they were there to see.

"Bryce Truxell is expecting us," Kate said evenly. Her gaze darted around the office, wondering just how much the law firm pulled in each year. She knew from their website that they were licensed in several of the surrounding states and had defended some heavy hitters including major league sports figures, politicians, and a handful of Hollywood types who had found themselves in trouble on the east coast. She knew there were seven partners and twenty attorneys who worked for the firm. They weren't the biggest in Boston, but the cases they took netted them huge wins and financial rewards.

"Mr. Truxell will see you now," the young woman said as she gestured to the double doors at the side of the desk. "His administrative assistant will meet you on the other side of the doors." The young woman smiled up at Declan, batting her eyelashes at him. "You must be very brave to work for the FBI."

Declan barely paid her any attention. "It pays the bills," he said dismissively as he followed Kate to the door. He pushed open the door and held it for Kate as she entered first. "That was weird."

"She was trying to flirt with you," Kate said and looked up at him, wondering if he didn't know or if he was trying to make sure she wasn't jealous. If Kate were the jealous type, Declan wouldn't be the man for her. His rugged good looks caused women to swoon no matter where they went. She had grown accustomed to it over the years and even come to appreciate it. It could open doors for them when needed.

"I'm Kayla Reed," a young woman said as she approached. She had her hand extended to Kate. "Thank you for being on time. Anytime I've had to meet with law enforcement, they are late."

Declan eyed her. "Field work is unpredictable."

That was all that was said as Kayla walked them down the long hallway to a glass-enclosed conference room. "Bryce will be with you in a moment." That moment turned into roughly twenty-five. Kate had grown antsy in that time even with the large floor-to-ceiling windows that gave them a great view of the city. When Kate had reached the limit of her patience, Bryce finally showed up.

"I'm sorry," he said as he pushed open the doors. "I had a client keep me much longer than planned." Bryce stood about Declan's height and had a head full of auburn-colored hair. Not as dark as Declan's but coifed perfectly as if he had walked out of a salon that morning. Everything about him was crisp from the way he spoke to the pressed pleat in his tan pants.

Kate sat back down at the table as Bryce sat across from them. "As I said when I called, we are here to discuss Kirk Eagen."

Bryce shook his head. "Terrible. Terrible thing that happened. We had no idea he was having any trouble or experiencing any mental health issues."

Declan cocked his head to look at Kate then back at Bryce. "It wasn't a suicide as initially reported. Eagen was murdered in his condo."

Bryce sat back. "I don't understand. He jumped from his balcony."

"He went over his balcony. We are still working out how," Declan said, providing Bryce the details as they knew them, which still wasn't much. "There was evidence found to indicate that it was murder. We are still working through the particulars of how exactly that happened. We need to know if anyone was bothering Eagen. Did he have anyone new in his life?"

"I wouldn't know that," Bryce said, looking between Kate and Declan. "He was recruited to work here based on his outstanding work on several cases in Chicago. He had his choice of our New York office or here in Boston. He chose Boston. While he reported directly to me, he hasn't been here for long. He was working on one case and we were getting him up to speed on another. I didn't know much about his personal life."

"He never said anything to you about friends he had in Boston or people he was getting to know?" Kate asked, hoping to illicit something to go on.

Bryce smirked and tapped his fingers on the table. "This isn't that kind of law firm. We aren't a family or even friends. Kirk Eagen showed up at the office when he was supposed to be here. He kept his head down and was a good criminal defense attorney. He was sharp and could jump into an ongoing case and be up to speed faster than most. In his interview, he said he had connections in the city that could bring in more cases and we believed him. His references were outstanding. Outside of what happens at this office, his life isn't any of my business. We weren't friends, Agent Walsh. I knew very little personal information about him."

That was certainly one way to run an office. Not that Kate wanted a lot of her personal life mixed up with the professional, but to know almost nothing seemed strange. "Was there anyone here who knew Eagen better?"

Bryce shook his head. "It's not how the office works. We encourage our staff to focus on work. We don't incentivize anything else. We don't do staff happy hours. We aren't socializing outside of here. Not that our attorneys have much of a life outside work."

Declan shifted in his seat, resting his arms on the tabletop. "Let me ask this another way. Did you ever see or overhear Eagen with anyone?"

Bryce pondered for a moment, his hand gesturing as he spoke. "About two weeks after Eagen moved here, my wife and I were walking to a restaurant in the North End. I spotted Eagen on the sidewalk outside another restaurant. He was there with a man. They appeared to be on good terms, dressed casually and were waiting for a table. As we passed by, we exchanged greetings, but there wasn't much conversation. He didn't introduce me to his friend."

Declan leaned forward. "More than friends, perhaps?"

Bryce shook his head. "I doubt it. Eagen mentioned his divorce in one of our interviews. His ex, Lynn, is an attorney at his former firm in Chicago. That's part of why he wanted a fresh start. When I heard about his suicide, I began to wonder if his split with Lynn was less amicable than he led us to believe." He glanced at Kate. "Are you certain it was murder?"

"We're certain," Kate affirmed, though they hadn't yet determined how Eagen had plunged over the railing without leaving any discernible marks. "Kirk Eagen's murder is linked to the Davenports. They were all killed by the same person."

Bryce slouched back in his chair, his expression deflated. "They were my clients. Bernard Davenport utilized my services a few times. I suppose I'm connected to both cases."

"I suppose you are," Declan replied stiffly, implying it couldn't be a mere coincidence.

Kate didn't entirely buy into that notion. Wealthy individuals often travelled in similar circles.

Still, the connection was undeniably intriguing.

CHAPTER 11

There were still a few reporters lingering in front of the Davenport mansion when Kate arrived late that evening to meet with Chase. She brushed past them without making a statement. Briggs and Declan had already given them enough. The more she could keep herself shielded from the media spotlight the better.

She flashed her badge to the young officer stationed outside the mansion and ducked under the yellow crime scene tape. Kate ascended the steps and unlocked the front door with the key that had been found near Bernard's wallet in the bedroom. They had no other way to lock the door. Sharon had taken it into evidence, processed it, and given it back to them.

What else were they going to do until Chase arrived?

Kate stepped inside the grand foyer, trying to process the sequence of events during the murder. If the killer was someone the Davenports knew and they had already been inside the home, confusion must have been the first thing they felt. Here was a person they trusted enough to sleep in their home, attacking them in the middle of the night. It would be a jarring juxtaposition. It made sense to Kate why Bernard might not have tried to fight him off. He might have assumed he could have reasoned with him. Bernard probably offered him money or other possessions in the home in exchange for their lives. It wasn't what the killer was after.

The doorknob to the front door turned and Kate came face to face with a man she hadn't seen in a long time. The last time she saw Chase he was barely a man. He was twenty-two and graduating Harvard on his way to conquer the world of finance. She hadn't seen him since that day.

His blond hair had grown darker and the scruff on his face had lines of gray. There were lines now around his navy eyes. He extended his hand to Kate and then surprised her by pulling her into an awkward hug. Chase thought better of it once they embraced. He stepped back. "I'm so sorry. I'm not sure why I did that."

"It's okay, Chase," Kate said and meant it. "It's a terrible thing that's happened to your parents. It's been a long time since we've seen each other." People reacted differently to this kind of horror. She had seen all sorts of reactions and Chase wasn't acting out of the norm. "I'm glad you could be here. Is your sister on her way?"

"Yes. She caught a flight out but won't be here until tomorrow. She's so freaked out though. I don't think she'll be able to come to the house when she arrives." He paused and collected himself. "Not that I'm not freaked out. Kate, I..."

Kate knew exactly what he was feeling. She didn't know if he remembered that her parents were killed in an embassy bombing right before her Harvard graduation. She reminded him of that. "I understand everything you're feeling right now. It's like there are no words. You keep reliving what they might have gone through and then you have to stop yourself because it's so overwhelming. It's too painful to try to relive their last moments. Then you feel guilty for not being there and start questioning yourself about what you could have done to have prevented it from happening. It's weird circular thinking that leads nowhere."

"That's exactly it," Chase said and expelled a breath. He looked up the grand staircase. "Can you take me to the scene? I want to get that out of the way. I've been dreading it."

Kate reached out and touched his arm. "You don't have to see it if you don't want to. We can talk and I can call a crime scene cleaning company to come and clean the room. You don't ever have to see it in the state it's in."

Chase didn't even stop to consider it. "It would be doing my parents a disservice if I didn't see it." He looked over at her with emotion and determination in his eyes. "I need to see it."

Kate understood at a core level. She had gone to the bombing site in Kenya years after her parents' murder and stood at the site. She didn't get much from it after the fact, but had she not been twenty-two at the time of their deaths, Kate might have gone sooner. She regretted not going sooner. She wasn't going to force Chase to live with the same regret.

Kate walked with Chase up the stairs as she explained what he would see. She held back a few of the details that were more sensationalized that he didn't need to know. She might tell him later but not right before he would see the place where his parents took their last breaths.

"There's still blood on the floor," Kate cautioned him as she nudged open the bedroom door. "They were found tied to chairs at the side of the bed. We can only speculate how it occurred. I don't know for sure the sequence of events. But they were tied up when they died."

Chase grew quiet and drew into himself as he walked through the sitting room into the inner bedroom. His eyes lowered to the blood on the floor. "There's so much blood. I can't imagine what they went through."

"Don't try to imagine it." Kate wanted to tell him that they died quickly or didn't know what was happening – all of it would be a lie. Their last moments were brutal and terrifying. "We don't know if your mother or father was killed first. We believe they were in bed together and then the killer struck, getting them out of bed. There were two tarot cards taped to the headboard."

Chase pinched the bridge of his nose. "You mentioned the tarot cards when you called. I also heard it on the news. You think their murder is connected to another?"

Kate gave him the overview of the case to date, deciding at the moment what details to share or not. In the end, she added, "The killer also dropped off communication to my house. The case started with him taunting me to catch him. It escalated quickly to him threatening me. I'm not sure why there was such a quick escalation."

Chase expressed his worry for her. "Do you think it's because you got close to him already?"

Kate hadn't considered that. "I doubt it. We haven't met many people yet connected to the case. The other victim's family is in Chicago and hasn't arrived yet. We've only spoken to a handful of people."

"No suspects then?"

"No," Kate admitted as she watched his face fall. "That said, our crime scene team noticed some oddities. There was a bedroom unmade. The bedding was in the washer as if it had been recently washed. The room was wiped down as well as many of the other rooms – the kitchen, areas of the living room, the laundry room and the machines, and one of the bathrooms."

Chase didn't understand. "What do you mean wiped down?"

First, she wanted to move them out of the bedroom. She gestured toward the door and Chase followed. He took one last look at the room as it was then closed his eyes. Kate didn't know if he was saying a silent prayer or just taking a moment to himself. She allowed him the time as she stepped back into the sitting room area. She had no desire to rush him in the process. Kate waited in the sitting room, giving him a moment. When time went on, she left the bedroom completely and stood in the hall.

A few minutes later, Chase joined her. His eyes were red and watery and pink burned his cheeks. "Thanks for giving me a moment."

Kate put her hand on his back to offer some comfort. "Take all the time you need."

"Show me the room," Chase said as he composed himself. "It's unusual that a room would be left unmade and laundry left in the washer. My parents' housekeeper, Debbie Burns, would never leave a room like that or the laundry."

Chase was getting to the heart of what Kate wanted to know. "She's been on vacation. She always takes two weeks around this time of year. She heads down to Florida to see her sister. Their birthdays are a couple of days apart and Debbie takes an extended vacation. It's been that way for years."

"Nothing out of the normal then?" Kate asked checking what she heard.

"Completely normal. I suppose my parents could have had company and my mother could have thrown a load of wash in." Chase cracked a sad smile. "I haven't known my mother to do her laundry in close to thirty years, not since I was a child. Even then we had a housekeeper. If my sister and I made a mess, my mother would clean it up. She didn't want us making extra messes for the help. It seems odd. I assume she would have just left the room as it was for Debbie when she returned."

"You don't know of anyone staying with them?"

"No. My father would have mentioned it. As I said, he was turning his business over to me. We talked every day, several times a day."

Kate guided him to the room in question. "As you can see the comforter and the pillows on the bed are missing. There were no prints found in this room, not even in the bathroom. Someone was staying in here. The sheets were found in the dryer. Would it be unusual for a room to be left like this?"

Chase surveyed the room. "Even though hardly anyone ever spent the night here outside of family, my mother kept every room made up for guests. The beds were stripped every two weeks and everything was washed to keep it fresh, even if no one had stayed in the room in months. I can't imagine she'd leave a room like this unless the person came and went after Debbie was already on vacation." He walked toward the bed and stood at the end of it. "Still, it doesn't make sense that the pillows and the comforter could be gone. Why even bother washing the sheets if he was going to take everything else with him?"

That was the question Kate had. "Would your sister maybe know if someone was staying?"

"No. I talked to them more," Chase said and breathed heavily. He turned back to look at Kate. "As I said, I was about to take over my father's business. We mostly talked about that and the transition. The only people who ever stayed here were family and the occasional business client coming in from out of town. My father would have them stay here if they were doing a lot of work and it was easier for them to be here rather than a hotel. That was rare. I can only think about a handful of times that happened."

Kate watched Chase's face as he surveyed the room. It was as if he were searching for something. "Is something wrong?"

Chase furrowed his brow. "I find it odd that my parents would invite someone here while Debbie was on vacation. I called her the housekeeper but she was so much more than that. She did clean, but she was also their cook and my mother's assistant. She helped with catering events and scheduling. I can't imagine my parents would be entertaining anyone with Debbie gone."

That was a valid point. "Have you notified Debbie about your parents?"

"I left her a message to call me back. I didn't tell her anything in the message other than she needed to call me back." Chase pulled his phone from his pocket and checked the phone. "She hasn't called me back yet. I only called a couple of hours ago."

Kate got Debbie's number from him. She could call and have a conversation with the woman too. On her way over, Sharon had called letting her know that a partial print had been found in the kitchen. It came back to a petty thief. Kate didn't know what it meant. "Does the name Toby Neuman mean anything to you?"

"Why?" He glanced up from his phone to look at Kate. "What does he have to do with the case?"

Kate noted that he didn't answer her question. He had a look of concern rather than confusion on his face. "It's the name of the man whose partial print was found in the kitchen. Do you know him, Chase?"

"That's my cousin," he admitted slowly, drawing out his words. Chase seemed hesitant to go on. Kate encouraged him to speak freely. It was critical information she needed. Chase walked out of the bedroom and went downstairs to the family room. Kate followed behind him not sure what he was doing.

Once Chase got comfortable on the chair, he continued. "Toby is my mother's brother's son. He's been trouble since we were kids. I haven't had any contact with him in at least a decade, maybe longer. I didn't think my mother had any contact with him either. I'm not sure I'm following what you're telling me. What do you mean you found his fingerprint here in the house? Do you think he had something to do with the murder?"

"I honestly don't know if he had anything to do with the murder," Kate explained, sitting down in a chair across from him. "All we know is that Toby's partial fingerprint was found in the kitchen. I'll be honest that I wondered if he had done this to your parents."

Chase wasn't buying it. "Toby has done a lot of crazy things. He's never been violent. He'd rip off your last dollar and try to con you for more. He's never physically harmed anyone that I'm aware of. He had a good relationship with my mother even if they didn't see each other often. He knew she had to protect her reputation. Even for as much money as my family had, Toby never once asked us for any. He respected my father." He shook his head back and forth as if trying to make sense of it. "It can't be Toby."

"Why was he here then?" Kate asked as confused as Chase. She wasn't surprised by what Chase was saying. Kate's initial reaction was that the killer wasn't Toby Neuman.

Chase held the phone in his hand. "Let's call him and find out."

CHAPTER 12

Kate sat at the conference table in the FBI Boston Field Office. She had called a meeting to get them all on the same page and update them after her meeting with Chase. She chose the field office because Sharon had been hard at work and Kate didn't think, with the threat, anyone should be back at her house.

Sharon, Briggs, Leo, and Declan were watching her, eagerly awaiting her update.

"From the information I gathered, Toby Neuman is most likely not responsible for the murders," Kate said evenly. "Both Chase and his Uncle Lawrence, Toby's father, could not conceive of the idea that Toby had anything to do with the murders. Lawrence indicated that Toby had stayed with the Davenports a couple of weeks back. He left the same day that Debbie, the housekeeper, did. She confirmed that. He was in Boston and had an interview for a legitimate job. He stayed with the Davenports so Bernard could coach him before the interview. Debbie said that Toby was kind and helpful and even tried to do his laundry but couldn't figure out how to use the washing machine. There are legitimate reasons his prints were found in the kitchen."

Sharon asked, "Do we think the print was left on purpose or was it just a coincidence? Maybe the killer didn't wipe down everything as well as he thought he had."

It was Declan who answered. "I'm not ready to rule out anything until we speak to Toby. We have confirmation that he was there a month ago. No one has any idea if he came back."

"He was in New Hampshire two nights ago, Declan. Lawrence said that Toby was staying at the house and that he left for Maine the next morning. His father confirmed that he had made it to Portland and was crashing at a local motel," Kate explained, wishing that he wasn't giving her pushback on this. He had argued his point that they couldn't rule Toby out when she broke the news to him after the meeting. He was excited that a print had been found and wasn't going to give up that easily. It was why she called the meeting for all to be there. The last thing Kate wanted to do was waste precious resources going after the wrong man.

Declan crossed his arms over his chest. Kate could tell he wanted to dig in. "We need to get in touch with him and confirm he didn't go back to the Davenports. Unfortunately, the family hasn't been able to reach him since getting to Maine. We left a message at the motel desk for him to call us."

Kate drove home her earlier point. "He has no motive and he was most definitely not here in Boston to kill Kirk Eagen. His father provided him with an alibi for that night. If he didn't kill Eagen, then Toby didn't kill the Davenports."

"Are we sure the cases are connected?" Briggs asked, trying to be diplomatic. He had accurately sensed the tension between Kate and Declan when he got to the meeting and had raised an eyebrow at Kate in a question. She knew he was trying to appease them both.

While the question had been directed at all of them, Sharon explained, "There's no crime scene evidence to tie the cases together other than the tarot cards. The issue with the cases is there is no crime scene evidence at all. The homes have been wiped down. There are no witness statements that I'm aware of and there's no one who saw the killer with the victims. The best I can surmise is that the killer forced Eagen up on a chair and either pushed him over the railing or made him jump. Then returned the chair to the table. There was one chair that wasn't pushed in all the way and there was dust on the bottom that was found out on the balcony."

Kate was glad they now had a working theory on how that murder had taken place. The medical examiner had provided them the time of death and it was shortly before the person Eagen had brought into his apartment had left.

Kate didn't think the cases were separate, even with the lack of evidence. "The tarot cards are what tie the cases together. We didn't say anything to the media about the tarot cards after the Eagen case. Therefore, there is no way the Davenports could be a copycat." She didn't want to rub salt into Declan's perceived wound but it had to be said, "If a person of interest didn't kill Eagen, then they didn't kill the Davenports. It's highly unlikely that we are dealing with two killers."

"All right," Declan conceded. "Toby isn't our guy. It still begs the question why that was the only print left. Back to Sharon's question, did he leave it intentionally or was it by accident after he's been so meticulous with everything else?"

Briggs leaned his arms on the table. "He would have had to have known Toby was in the home and that seems highly unlikely. Then again, if we believe the killer is stalking the victims ahead of time, he might have met Toby in the house."

It was all too big of a leap for Kate. "I think we should move off Toby for now." Everyone agreed. They could come back to it if the evidence led there. Kate looked over at Leo who had remained quiet since entering the room with all of them. She raised her eyebrows in a question, wondering if he had any thoughts to add. He smiled over at her and waved her off. It seemed he was content listening.

Sharon, who saw the exchange, focused on Declan. "What about the guy on surveillance video at Eagen's condo?"

Kate had been waiting for this information too. Declan had told her he'd share at the meeting. He had a small removable drive and had brought his laptop with him. He fired it up now and slipped the drive in. He clicked a few buttons on the keyboard and explained, "This same man has been seen a few times on surveillance video with Eagen. They had some prior established relationship. But as you can see, he knows where the cameras are so he avoids them. Keeps his hat on and head low. He almost uses Eagen as a shield. After he leaves, surveillance downstairs catches him leaving the building and exiting out the door heading east. He doesn't speak to anyone and his face is blocked from view. He's wearing a black baseball cap with no lettering or image on it that he's pulled low on his face. He has a black jacket and dark jeans. He's also wearing black boots." When he was finished explaining the video, Declan clicked play as they crowded around the laptop to watch it.

Once the video played all the way through, Briggs asked him to play it again. Each one of them took a turn closely studying it and then Declan would hit play for the next person. Kate watched the man, who was a little over six-foot in height and had a muscular build, walk confidently down the hall. He had a swagger as if he had no cares in the world, even though he had just killed a man.

Declan, having shaken off his earlier mood, gestured toward the screen. "I think we need to put the full video out to the media and ask for help from the community in identifying him. We can also put the sketch that Briggs has of the man who approached River in Boston Common."

Kate angled her head to speak to Briggs directly. "Was River able to give a good description?"

"For a stoner kid, he was good." Briggs pulled up a photo of the sketch and slid his phone to her across the table. While she was looking at it, he explained, "Turns out River is not the drop-out we first thought. He's a third-year Harvard student who was ditching classes for the day and in the park. His father is a Massachusetts Supreme Court Judge. The whole reason he was freaking out about being arrested was he didn't want to get in trouble with his father or cause a media issue."

Declan wrinkled his nose. "He was dressed like a homeless person. I thought he had wandered in from the bus from out of state."

Briggs put his hands out wide. "I guess the saying is true that you can't judge a book by its cover. Given how smart he must be, it did surprise me that he was willing to drop off the note for a twenty. As he said though, the guy was bugging him and ruining his high. He figured he'd walk the note down a block, grab a cup of coffee, and come back to his grassy spot. Declan chasing him put a hitch in that plan."

"He should know better than to run from a cop," Declan countered gruffly.

Kate hadn't told him what River had said. "He thought you were a jilted husband who was finding out his wife was having an affair. He assumed rightly that you were going to hurt him, and he didn't hear you say that you were FBI. I can see why he'd run if he's trying to keep his reputation intact for his father's sake. All the way around, River didn't make good decisions. We can chalk it up to him being high."

Declan shrugged it off. "I've made worse decisions stoned."

No one seemed shocked by his admission.

Kate focused her attention on the photo of the sketch. While she couldn't see the face of the man in the video surveillance, the shoulders and upper body of the man River encountered were a match to the man in the video. River had been able to describe good detail for the man's face, even the weird marking near his ear that looked like it was part of a beard pulling off his face. Kate couldn't be sure if the beard was fake from the sketch. Although, she wouldn't be surprised if this killer was wearing a disguise and changing them up as he went about his crimes.

Declan tapped on the table to get her attention. "What do you think, Kate? Should we release it all to the media?"

"I think so," Kate said but she wanted to check in with Spade first. She explained she was going to call him and stepped out of the conference room to do so. She hadn't been able to update him much since he had sent her the initial letter from the killer. When Spade answered, Kate provided him with a quick rundown of everything that had been happening. She hesitated telling him that the killer had sent a message directly to her home.

"Declan already called me, Kate. He's concerned and wanted my advice about staying in the house or leaving," Spade explained. "I told him you could make that call."

Kate met that information with silence.

Spade wasn't going to deal with it. "Don't be angry with him. He did what he should have done by calling me. We both know you can dig your heels in and get stubborn."

Kate pursed her lips together in a slight grimace. "I'm staying, Spade."

"That's what I told him." He paused for a moment, letting Kate settle into her feelings about it. He was good at giving her a minute even when she didn't acknowledge to herself that she needed one. "About the media," Spade said, speaking again. "What do you want to do?"

"I think we go public with it. The reality is that everyone is a target with this killer." Kate leaned against the wall for support as she spoke. "I've never seen anything like this, Spade. He's seemingly choosing people he either knows or he's spending time to get to know them to make sure they fit his target for each card. He's gaining their trust and then killing them. He hasn't used the same method of murder either.

Eagen was forced off that balcony and the Davenports' throats were slashed."

"It's performative."

"That's what I said at the start with the first letter. We've never had a performative killer like this. Can you think of one on record?"

"Zodiac," Spade responded quicker than Kate would have thought. "He had the ciphers and letters to the media. Plus he wore a costume of sorts at the Lake Berryessa murders. He switched from a gun to a knife. The Zodiac is represented in the tarot as well."

Kate knew they were trying to use new Ancestry DNA to try to identify the Zodiac killer. He'd never been caught all these years later. Not too long ago, she and Declan had watched the movie *Zodiac* with Jake Gyllenhaal and Robert Downey Jr. It was a good movie. She wouldn't have wanted to work that case.

"I can see some similarities but this one is different," Kate responded after thinking it through.

"It is. Since Zodiac was never caught we also don't know that his motive and crimes were performative on his part. It's the closest one we have on record that I'm aware of that could be similar."

Kate didn't know how a case in the sixties would help them today, especially since the killer had never been caught. She thanked Spade for his help with the media. "We will try to get this on the news as soon as possible with a warning to the public."

Kate ended the call thinking about the Zodiac killer's crimes, knowing she wasn't going to walk back into the conference room and bring up that infamous killer – she wasn't going to bring that vibe to this case.

CHAPTER 13

Kate, Declan, and Briggs spent the rest of the late afternoon and early part of the evening running down the few leads they had, following up with neighbors of Kirk Eagen and the Davenports to see if they heard or saw anything suspicious in the days leading up to the murder.

There was nothing. The killer was a ghost.

They could have had the story lead the evening news. It would have been preferable to the newscasters. They had decided that it wouldn't make a big enough splash and many people might still be heading home in the after-work traffic and miss it. They wanted a special broadcast right as people were sitting down to watch their evening television programs.

"I want to interrupt everything," Declan had said and the rest agreed. That's just what they did.

They called a live press conference right in the middle of Boston Common for eight that evening. The FBI public affairs office had made sure the podium was set and the lighting perfect. There was something about the overall dark Common in the middle of fall that gave the whole thing an ominous feeling. The mood hopefully helped drive home the warning.

Kate and Leo stood in the back watching from a distance. Declan was about halfway through the press conference when Leo said, "He's good at this, Kate. Has he always been the spokesperson?"

"Neither of us likes interacting with the media. If we can get someone else to talk to the press or avoid it altogether then we will. Declan has been handling the media on the last few cases." She looked up at the podium with a certain sense of pride. Kate never paid too much attention to the press conferences. She was usually watching the crowd as she had been before Leo redirected her attention. "He does have a certain commanding presence for it and the reporters respond well to him."

The reporters practically fell all over themselves as they asked him questions. There had always been something about Declan, a natural charm, that allowed him to be a guy's guy but a charmer to women too.

"Did the two of you get over your fight quickly?" Leo asked, rocking back and forth on his feet. He had a mischievous smile on his face, which Kate knew meant he was teasing her. "Everyone knew. You two don't hide it well."

Kate didn't like that they were speculating about the relationship. It was only natural though and she didn't take it to heart. "We get over things fairly quickly. Declan and I have a good balance on cases and I like that he fights for what he thinks is right. Usually, as quickly as we have a dust-up, we are over it. If anything, I hold onto things longer than he does."

Before Leo could respond, they heard Kate's name being called from behind them.

Leo stepped in front of her to shield her.

Kate stepped back surprised at how quickly he moved to protect her. He shielded her whole body with his. Kate had to step around him to see who was approaching. As soon as she spotted who was calling to her, she put her hand on Leo's arm as if calling back her guard. "It's Evan from the Archdiocese."

"I see that now. I didn't see who it was at first, Kate," Leo said by way of explanation.

"Evan, what brings you out here tonight?" she asked, glancing back at Leo who's posture remained rigid and ready to strike.

"Cardinal O'Connor received a message from the killer. He called the FBI office but the person who answered said you were all at the press conference." Evan raised his hand and it was then Kate saw he had a large manilla envelope. "He and his private secretary were the only two who touched it with their bare hands. I pulled on gloves and slipped it in this envelope for you. I figured it was better not to let anyone else touch it and to get it to you right away."

Kate didn't have gloves with her. She knew Declan had some on him. He always carried them. She'd have to wait until she had them to look inside. Kate took the envelope from him. "I appreciate you getting this right over to us. Can you tell me about the message?" She explained why she wasn't opening it right there.

"It came in our regular mail today. His private secretary didn't get to the mail as early as she usually does. She was working late and only had the chance to review it about an hour ago. As you'll see the white envelope was handwritten and addressed to Cardinal O'Connor. Mail comes all the time for him so it didn't raise any suspicions right away. It was only after his secretary opened it and shook out the contents that she became alarmed." Evan's eyes were wide. "That's a bit of an understatement. She screamed so loudly that the few of us still working rushed to her. Cardinal O'Connor was still in his office working after dinner. He was the first to reach her, which is why he touched it before I had a chance to stop him."

Kate said she understood. "What did the letter say?"

With his voice stiff and growing with concern, Evan explained, "It said Agent Walsh was cleverer than he thought. Cardinal O'Connor had a choice. He could sacrifice himself or one of the parish priests would be a target – he had to choose."

Kate stepped toward Evan, closing the distance between them. She lowered her voice to not draw attention from the reporters nearby. Her tone was rushed and insistent. "Where is the cardinal now? Please tell me he's not going to offer himself up to this killer."

"No," Evan responded but didn't sound sure. "He said he was going to retreat to his chambers. That it was all too stressful for him."

"Did the letter say how Cardinal O'Connor could sacrifice himself?" Leo asked, moving to Kate's side. He asked what she was about to ask next, which Kate took as a good sign that he was learning.

"It was unclear. The letter said the cardinal would know what to do. That he had twenty-four hours to decide and that if his death wasn't announced someone else would die."

Kate cursed loudly, drawing the attention of reporters near them. She grabbed Evan by the arm and moved them back into the darkness of the Common. "Is there anyone with Cardinal O'Connor now?"

"No. He retired for the night." Evan saw the fear in Kate's eyes. "He assured us that he wasn't going to sacrifice himself, Agent Walsh. He'd never do something like that. We all know what suicide means in the Catholic Church. He'd never." Evan was so insistent Kate felt bad for him. His naivete had put the Cardinal at risk.

"We need to go there now," she said, commanding them. Kate turned back to the podium as Declan finished up. She looked at Leo. "Wait here and let me go get Declan."

"Let me go ahead, Kate. I'll go with Evan and you can meet us there."

Kate had already started to move. She didn't have time to consider. Leo was right, the faster someone got there the better. "If you're comfortable doing that, then go." She didn't look back but heard Evan say where he was parked as she raced toward Briggs and Declan at the podium, parting the sea of reporters who were beginning to realize an emergency was happening around them.

Kate got to the makeshift stage and whispered the details to Briggs. She was impressed that his face remained neutral giving nothing away. He simply nodded in understanding then went to Declan, touched his arm, and took his place in front of the crowd.

Kate waited for Declan to rush off the stage. He started to ask her what was going on. She couldn't run and explain at the same time. "We have to get back to the house to get my car. I'll tell you once we are on the road." She didn't wait for him as she sprinted off through the Common with Declan close on her heels.

Once they were in the car, navigating through the streets of Boston toward the Archdiocese, Kate caught Declan up to speed. "I'm worried he's going to sacrifice himself, Declan. I bet this is exactly how this killer got Kirk Eagen over the side of that railing. Maybe he threatened his family and said if he didn't kill himself, he'd target someone Eagen loved. He sacrificed himself."

Declan gripped the bar overhead as Kate hit the gas, turning left and right, zooming through the city streets. He absorbed the information quickly and she didn't have to repeat anything. "Do you honestly think O'Connor is going to kill himself, Kate? That's the most insane thing I've ever heard."

Kate felt like it was the most insane thing she had ever thought. "Cardinal O'Connor knows this killer means business. He's already killed three people. I warned him of the threat, which he didn't take all that seriously. Evan took it more seriously than he did. I don't know what he's going to do, but he's alone after reading that letter from the killer. If he believes the killer is going after some parish priest if he doesn't sacrifice himself, then I believe Cardinal O'Connor might do it. I don't know, he's the ultimate power of the Catholic Church here in Boston. If he doesn't sacrifice himself, then a parish priest will die. I don't know the man well enough to know what he'd do."

"Isn't there anyone there with him? He must have staff around him?"

"Evan said he retreated to his chambers alone. I assumed that was his bedroom," Kate said, frustration tinging her voice.

They weren't getting there fast enough. She hit the gas and bounced off a curb as she careened the car right at the light. She felt herself rambling. "Evan came to find us after they received the letter, Declan. He had to have been worried O'Connor was going to do something. It might have been better if he stayed there with him. If O'Connor sent him to find us, then, yes, maybe he sent Evan away so he could kill himself."

Kate pulled to a stop in front of the Archdiocese building next to a blue Honda SUV. She assumed it was Evan's car. It looked like he pulled in so fast that he didn't care if the car was straight. She noticed as she put her SUV in park that the driver's side door was left slightly ajar.

They exited her SUV at the same time as they unholstered their weapons. Declan reached the front door of the building first and opened it. "I assume Evan left this open for us."

This was the administrative building, not O'Connor's home. Kate knew that much. "I don't know why Evan would come back into this building. He said Cardinal O'Connor was at home. You go this way and I'll go around back."

"Wait, Kate," Declan called to her and traced his steps back out of the building and followed her. "The last thing we should do is split up."

Kate heard his voice, but she pushed it aside, focusing solely on the path ahead as she sprinted down the side of the administrative building towards the rest of the property. Earlier that day, she had noticed a small chain-link fence at the back of the building, with a brick walkway leading to a gate. She suspected that it was where O'Connor resided.

Dim lights dotted the walkway, casting eerie shadows. Kate hurried down the path, passed through the gate, and turned left. It was then, amidst the trees, that she spotted the small brick house. The front door stood wide open, and from a distance, there appeared to be a figure sprawled on the grass.

Declan caught sight of it. "Are we too late?" He briefly paused, then dashed past Kate toward the person on the ground. The body lay face down as if it had collapsed while running towards the house.

From where she stood, Kate could only see the soles of the person's shoes.

"It's Leo!" Declan exclaimed as he knelt beside him. "He's breathing, but he's unconscious."

"What?" Kate's mind reeled, struggling to understand the scene as the wind picked up, rustling leaves in the grass. She hurried to Declan's side, bending over to see him. Leo had a wound to the back of his head, blood seeping through his dark hair. But he was alive. Kate's gaze darted around the yard. "Where's Evan?"

Declan didn't respond immediately. Instead, he rose to his feet, calling for an ambulance and backup. Kate rose from the damp grass, leaving wet stains on her knees, and hurried up the steps to the house, her gun at the ready.

"Evan! Cardinal O'Connor!" Her voice echoed through the silent house as she moved from the living room to the dining room and kitchen. There was no sign of disturbance downstairs.

Calling out their names once more, Kate finally heard faint sounds of distress emanating from upstairs. A low, guttural moan. She ascended the creaking stairs, reaching the landing and turning first right, then left. The moan led her to a closed door at the end of the hall, dim light seeping through the crack beneath.

Approaching cautiously, Kate steadied her gun and called them again. She nudged the door open with her foot.

Evan lay sprawled at the foot of the bed, blood pooling beneath him.

His lips parted in a feeble moan as he uttered her name.

Kate took a few more steps into the room aiming the gun at the bed. As her gaze landed on the scene, she turned her head in horror. A scream caught in her throat.

Cardinal O'Connor had been beaten. His face was barely recognizable.

CHAPTER 14

Kate pushed through the revulsion, her focus fixed on the bed. She needed to confirm whether O'Connor still clung to life amidst the chaos. Determined, she reached the bedside and extended her hand to check his pulse.

Her mission stopped cold by the crumpled item in the man's hand.

She pressed her fingers on his wrist. No sign of life, no hint of a heartbeat. She hesitated briefly before prying open his stiffened fingers, revealing The Hierophant card. Stepping back, another sound drew her attention, a moan that snapped her back to the present.

"Evan!" Kate rushed to his side, panic rising as she took in the blood seeping through his shirt. With urgency, she rolled him onto his back, revealing the source of the bleeding – two puncture wounds in his abdomen.

Declan rushed down the hall toward her, stopping at the door's threshold to take in the scene.

"See if there's towels in the bathroom. I need to apply pressure," she barked orders at him, not sure what else to do. Kate leaned over Evan. "Who did this to you?"

Evan's eyes flickered in and out of consciousness. "He was already dead."

"You're going to be okay," she said in response.

A moment later, with the towels Declan had found, she applied pressure to Evan's wounds. Sirens wailed in the distance outside the home. She pressed the towels against the pooling blood as she looked back up at Declan. She opened her mouth to speak but there were no words to be said.

"I know, Kate. I know." Declan's eyebrows furrowed. "He's trying to say something."

Lowering her head to Evan's level, Kate reassured him, urging him to speak. "You're safe. Tell me, we're here with you."

"Mace," Evan whispered, his voice weak but insistent. He said it twice more.

Confusion clouded Kate's features. "You were maced?" she questioned, but the lack of its distinct odor perplexed her.

"No," Evan groaned, his strength waning. He closed his eyes and his breathing became shallow.

"Evan!" Kate's desperation peaked, her voice pleading. "Stay with me, please." But he'd lost too much blood. He slipped away from her, unconscious but alive.

Hours later, Kate and Declan stood in the upstairs hallway of O'Connor's home as Sharon and her team processed the bedroom. The body had been removed by the medical examiner and Evan was at the hospital listed as stable but still in and out of consciousness. He'd lost a considerable amount of blood and had needed a transfusion.

Leo had a significant concussion and was being kept for observation. Kate and Declan would need to go to the hospital and get their statements. They were still operating in the dark, not sure what had happened. The only clue was Evan telling Kate that Cardinal O'Connor had been dead by the time they arrived. They wouldn't know the official time of death until the medical examiner finished the autopsy.

"I found something," Sharon called from the bedroom, beckoning them. As Kate and Declan entered the room, Sharon held up a prescription pill bottle. "As you said, Kate, there are no signs of a struggle. You said early on Cardinal O'Connor had either been asleep or hadn't fought back at all, accepting his fate. I think he tried to kill himself first and the killer wanted to make sure he had finished the job. This is a bottle of OxyContin, prescribed by a local doctor. The prescription is fairly new, only a few days old. I remember reading in the newspaper that he had fallen a couple of weeks ago and had hurt his back. The bottle is empty. A glass of water on the nightstand too. I think Cardinal O'Connor probably took these and was out cold by the time the beating started."

That was some relief to Kate but not much. She remembered what Evan had told her. "Do you see any signs of mace?"

Sharon shook her head, slightly confused by the question. "Why would there have been mace? Did Evan try to mace the killer? I didn't see any bottles or signs of it here."

"Evan said the word a few times before he finally passed out," Kate said, still trying to make sense of it. "I don't know what he was talking about."

Sharon said the word a few times to herself before she exclaimed, "I know what he meant!" She yelled it so loudly and with such force Kate and Declan were startled by the exclamation. "Sorry for startling you both. He didn't mean mace like the spray. He meant mace like the weapon. It's like a type of club that has a heavy head that can deliver powerful strikes. It can be designed on the end or pointed like a spike, which is what could have caused Evan's puncture wounds. It could also account for the pattern of wound injuries to Cardinal O'Connor."

Kate was sure she had heard the term before. She couldn't recall where. But as soon as Sharon explained it, the image of a mace burned in her mind.

"It makes sense," Declan said, agreeing with Sharon and drawing Kate's attention. "During medieval times, maces were carried during the processional for popes and cardinals. They have now been replaced with processional crosses. There's some speculation that knights and priests carried maces in warfare too as to not draw blood with a sword."

"What is the figure holding on The Hierophant card?" Kate asked, stepping around the pool of blood left by Evan. She inched toward Sharon who had bagged the card.

Sharon held it up in the bag. "A golden staff with three crosses at the top?"

Kate thought back to the letter and the card that had been delivered to her house. It hadn't been from the Rider-Waite tarot deck. She did a quick search on her phone for other, older tarot decks. She found exactly what she was seeking. "These cards here are much older than the decks the killer has been using, The Hierophant is holding a mace in his hand. It's ornately designed at the top and has the spike that Sharon mentioned."

Sharon hadn't seen the card but she agreed. "It must be what Evan meant."

"It had to be," Kate agreed. "You didn't find anything in this room?"

"No. There's no murder weapon in here."

Kate rushed to the doorway and stared down the hall. She hadn't seen any blood on the way up. She moved out into the hallway watching her footsteps as she walked. There was no blood there or on the stairs. It didn't make any sense.

Kate bolted back to the room. "Why is there no blood out here? If the killer was carrying an object like you described that he'd use to beat someone to death with and then stab Evan, it had to have been covered in blood. Yet, there's no blood anywhere other than in this room." She turned to Declan. "Was there blood in the bathroom?" There was an ensuite bathroom off the bedroom that Kate hadn't noticed when she had first come into the bedroom.

"I wasn't looking for blood, Kate. I was looking for towels."

No one had gone back in the bathroom since Declan. Sharon had been so focused on the bedroom scene and the team processing the rest of the home that she hadn't made it to the bathroom yet.

Sharon finished what she was doing and hurried past them. She flicked on the bathroom light and called out to them, "There are droplets on the floor. Two of them." She came back to her crime scene bag and pulled out the luminol. It was used to test for blood that had been cleaned up.

Kate and Declan stood on the edge of the doorway as they watched her work. She sprayed the solution then flipped off the light. The entire tub glowed a pale blue.

"He washed up," Kate said almost to herself.

Declan heard her and agreed. "Spray more of the bathroom."

Sharon turned the light back on and sprayed down other areas including the floor and bathroom counter, sink, and cabinets. She turned off the light again and the whole room glowed. "There was blood everywhere," she said in a rush of breath.

It wasn't an understatement. There was indeed blood on everything in the bathroom. As Kate scanned the small room, Declan zeroed in on one area across from the sink. There was a row of cabinets with brass handles.

"That bottom one there. Is that a handprint?" Declan stepped into the bathroom to get closer. "There's a bloody handprint on this handle. Sharon, come look at this." He hadn't needed to ask her, she was hunched over at his side looking at the same area. He stepped back to give her more room.

With her gloved hand, avoiding the bloody handprint, she eased it open. Then Sharon stopped and stepped back. "This isn't a drawer. It's an old fashioned laundry shoot. Look, there's nothing inside." She didn't wait for them to look. She grabbed the bottle of luminol and sprayed it inside the chute. It glowed the same pale blue. "He threw something down there."

Kate didn't wait for Declan. She was closest to the door and took off down the hall, descending the stairs so fast she nearly fell. Once at the bottom, she headed for the kitchen where she remembered seeing a door.

Kate tugged it open and felt for a light switch on the wall inside. When she found the switch, she flipped it into the upright position, illuminating the stairs and basement floor. By then Declan was right behind her.

They got to the basement floor and turned in all directions looking for where the chute would exit. "There," Declan said, pointing to what looked like an old gray laundry cart. It was wide, bigger than something needed for one person's laundry. It looked to Kate like it was something once used in a hotel.

Declan beat her to the cart as he bent over and peered inside. He gasped. "My God, Kate. He threw his bloody clothes in here. They are right on the pile." He reached a gloved hand in and pulled out a pair of blue coveralls. "Not clothes exactly. He had on coveralls like a workman would wear."

Kate drew up to his side and peered in. "What else is in here? The murder weapon?" Kate wondered how the killer could casually stroll out of the home with a mace that had once been covered in blood. It might have been rinsed off, but it wasn't the kind of thing that wouldn't draw attention.

Declan sifted through the items in the cart, coming up empty. "I don't see anything other than what I assume is Cardinal O'Connor's dirty clothing and these coveralls. No murder weapon."

Kate stepped back and cursed. "We are going to have to update Briggs and make another statement to the media before the Archdiocese beats us to it." Kate wanted to be out in front of the story which would surely bring shame to the FBI. Not only had they not stopped the killer, a well-known and popular Catholic cardinal was dead in one of the biggest archdioceses in the United States. There was a chance the FBI, specifically Kate and Declan, would never live it down.

Briggs had gone to the hospital with Leo and Evan. He also assured them he'd make the call to leadership in the Catholic Church to inform them what had happened at the archdiocese. Kate had no idea the process that would take but Briggs seemed to know what to do. They had let him run with that to save time.

Declan's phone buzzed against his hip. He ripped off his gloves to answer it. It wasn't a phone call though. It was a text. He read it and cursed loudly. "It's already made the news, Kate. My mom just texted me asking if it was true that Cardinal O'Connor had been murdered in his bed."

Frustrated and angry, she practically growled, "Does she say anything else?"

"She said it was an unconfirmed report and the media appears to be camped out near the archdiocese building." Declan raised his head from the phone with a question. "They must be out front. Do we go out there and give them an official statement now? We can't leave them to speculate."

That was exactly what they would be forced to do – give the media a statement while they worked with few facts and were no closer to the identity of the killer than when they had started the case a couple of days ago.

"We don't have a choice." Kate had been hoping to speak to Leo and Evan before informing the media. "Let's go get that done and then get over to the hospital."

Declan saw the worry in her eyes. "You go upstairs and tell Sharon what we found down here. I'll go make the statement to the media.

I'll meet you outside and we can go to the hospital together."

Kate shook her head. She couldn't let Declan alone be the public face of this failure. "We'll face them together." She pulled off her gloves, straightened her clothes, and left the way they had come in to face the awaiting press.

There were television vans from all the local and national networks parked in front of the archdiocese. Cameramen and photographers started as soon as Kate and Declan approached. Microphones shoved toward them as they steadied each other.

Declan gave a brief factual statement, asking them to hold for questions. "There isn't a lot we can tell you right now. We are still assessing the scene. We know that this case is connected to two others, Kirk Eagen and the Davenports." He went on to explain the little they could share. Then he took questions. As the press conference wound down and Declan had answered all he could, a reporter in the back had one last question.

"Can we assume The Lovers are next?"

All they could say was yes.

Kate's fists clenched and released. She knew the killer was already stalking his prey.

CHAPTER 15

The next morning was a flurry of activity. Declan went to the FBI Boston Field Office to meet with Sharon and then he was headed to meet with the medical examiner. Kate had an important meeting with Suffolk County's District Attorney Carmen Langston.

She and Declan had planned to go to the hospital first thing that morning to interview Leo and Evan. Their respective doctors had asked them to hold off until later in the day. They were still monitoring them and didn't think either would be up for an interview early. Kate pushed the doctor on the phone but he didn't relent.

Declan had rolled with the punches and said he'd rather see what forensics were coming back and what, if any, information came in regarding the autopsy. Given the high status of the deceased, Cardinal O'Connor's autopsy came first before anyone else in Boston.

Briggs was busy interviewing other archdiocese staff and running down potential witnesses in the neighborhood, including searching for any street surveillance cameras.

Someone, somewhere, had to have seen something.

Kate was tasked with meeting Carmen Langston – the district attorney who was known for not pulling any punches and for being a spitfire. She had all but taken over their one previous case in Boston, making demands that could not be met.

If Kate didn't regularly go up against Spade, she might have been afraid of Carmen. At the mere mention of the woman's name, Declan had simply declined any possibility of attending the meeting. Dealing with her on the last case was enough for him.

Kate appreciated Carmen's direct approach and her candor. But being called out for not protecting O'Connor, which Kate assumed was the focus of the meeting, was not something she was looking forward to.

"Ms. Langston will see you now," the young woman behind the desk called out, shaking Kate from her wandering thoughts.

Kate rose from the chair, thanked the young woman, and headed down the short hallway to Carmen's office. She rapped once on the slightly ajar door and was told to enter. Kate took a few steps into the office and found Carmen perched on the edge of her desk. Her black pumps had been tossed below her on the deep cream carpet, one upright and the other on its side. Her skirt hitched above her knees and her blouse wrinkled untucked. Her legs swung back and forth.

Kate couldn't remember the color of her hair the last time she'd seen her. Carmen was known to change it often and it all looked amazing. This time her dark blonde hair had been cut in a blunt bob at her chin line and her eyes hinted that she'd had little sleep.

Kate wasn't sure what she was witnessing.

The woman looked undone in every sense of the word.

"Ms. Langston," Kate said tentatively, taking a few steps toward her. "Are you okay?"

"It's Carmen and you're Kate. We've already gone through the formalities. We have no time for that." Carmen gestured toward the chair. "I'm most definitely not okay."

Kate sat and crossed her legs, looking up at Carmen. Her angle on the desk forced Kate to tip her head back to look at the woman who was otherwise several inches shorter. "I know that you're probably focused on the murder of Cardinal O'Connor."

"Stop right there." Carmen waved her off. "We can be frank with each other, can't we?"

"Certainly." Kate had no idea where this was going. She might have wondered if Carmen was drunk by her demeanor, but it wasn't alcohol that was causing this. It had a distinct smell – fear.

"I know we should be focused on Cardinal O'Connor." She blew out a frustrated breath and gestured wildly with her hands. "Lord knows the Catholic Church around here gets all the focus from the sexual abuse scandal they caused years ago to now this very public murder and everything in between. That's not why I called you in. I'm sure you are doing everything you can on this case. I heard a rumor that he threatened you with tarot cards or some such nonsense. Is that true?"

"That is true," Kate said evenly, trying to slow the pace before Carmen became frantic. "He is using tarot cards as his signature and so far he's been killing in order of the cards. This all started when he sent a letter to FBI headquarters."

Carmen jabbed her index finger toward Kate. "That's why I called you in. Three more and it's Justice, baby! I'm Justice. I'm the epitome of Justice! Have you seen the card? He's targeting prominent people. The Davenports. Cardinal O'Connor. What better trifecta than taking out the District Attorney? I'm a walking dead woman." Carmen pinned her gaze on Kate, the rims of her eyes red with lack of sleep. "What do I do? I don't want to die. I have a lot of life left in me. There's so much still to be done to clean up this city."

Kate nervously licked her lips. She wasn't nervous about the case anymore. She was nervous about how she was going to contain this five-foot-four powder keg. Kate chose her words carefully. "I completely understand how you're feeling, Carmen. The killer delivered a note to my home yesterday that indicated I might be Justice."

Carmen's eyes grew wide. "Are you kidding me? He knows where you live?"

That was a bit of information that they had not made public. No one had shared it with the media. Outside of the team, now Carmen was the only other one who knew. "He gave the letter to a guy in Boston Public Garden to deliver to me." Kate paused and considered something for the first time. She wasn't sure why it hadn't occurred to her sooner. "The guy who delivered the note was River Thomas. We later learned that he's Judge Keaton Thomas's son."

"Our Supreme Court Justice Keaton Thomas?" Carmen said her voice going up several octaves. "I might not be the target after all. Have you warned him?"

"No," Kate said, not believing she hadn't connected the dots before now. She watched Carmen who hadn't taken her gaze off Kate. She decided to do something she rarely did with anyone but Declan, she wanted to process the case. "Given the letter about the Justice card was focused on me and how quickly things have been coming at us, I didn't stop to consider that River Thomas might have been targeted intentionally and it was a clue to us that the killer was focused on his father. I didn't connect all of those pieces until right now."

Carmen hopped off the desk, landing on her bare feet. She tucked her blouse back in her skirt and slipped her heels back on. She smoothed down the strands of her bob. "We have a lot of work to do on this. Do you have any suspects at all?"

"Not one. As I'm sure you saw on the news last night, we have a composite sketch of the man who approached River and some video surveillance of a man seen with Kirk Eagen."

Carmen didn't seem to understand. "He had a fake beard though."

That's what Kate had thought. "River thought he might have shaved weirdly."

Carmen let out a light chuckle. "How stoned was River when you picked him up?"

"Fairly stoned but he got a good look at the guy."

"It's obvious in the sketch that it's a fake beard," Carmen said as she went back behind her desk. It seemed she had a renewed sense of herself since realizing she wasn't the most prominent justice figure in Boston. "If you're willing to share some details with me about the case, I'm willing to listen."

Kate gave her a brief overview of the three cases so far. "It wasn't on the news last night but we believe Cardinal O'Connor overdosed on some prescription oxy before his death. The killer had given him a warning that he either take his own life or some local parish priest was going to die. I don't know if the killer changed his mind or if he was only toying with O'Connor. The threat helped us to solve one of the questions we had about Kirk Eagen's death. We didn't know how he went over the railing. There were no signs of a struggle and there should have been. Eagen was a big guy. There's no way he wouldn't have put up some fight. But if the killer threatened someone he loved, then maybe Eagen sacrificed himself."

"That's utterly diabolical," Carmen said with a grimace.

Kate shifted in the chair, uncrossed and crossed the other leg. She was growing to like talking to Carmen. It was nice to process with another strong woman. "That's the best word we have to describe this killer. Evan, the Cardinal's assistant, was stabbed and one of our men was struck on the head. The killer could have easily murdered either of them. He chose not to. Evan lost a lot of blood, but the wounds wouldn't have killed him. I believe the killer knew we'd get there in time. He rendered Evan unable to chase him. But he didn't kill him." Kate waited for those details to sink in. Then she added, "We will interview both of them at the hospital later today. Their doctors didn't want us to this morning to give them more time."

Carmen asked a few more pointed questions that Kate didn't mind answering. "What can we do here at the DA's office to help you?"

Kate wasn't sure how much they could help. Resources were always good. "The Lovers is the next card. My partner, Declan, and I were talking last night that he might target a couple having an affair or a couple in a lover's lane situation. The Chariot is after that. We talked about the potential for him to target a public transit worker – cabbie, bus driver, or train operator. Then there is Justice. I believe once we have more information, we need to go public in a big way with this information. Then we need more patrols on the streets and possibly get security for the Supreme Court Justices and yourself. The FBI has some resources, but if the county can pitch in that would be helpful."

Carmen agreed without hesitation. "You have the full support of this office." She sat behind her desk and leaned on it, leveling a look at Kate. "When you catch this guy and I know you will, I want him brought in alive. Prosecuting him will be the biggest case this office has ever handled and I will do it personally. I want others out there who think they get away with this in Boston to know – not our town, not now, and not ever."

Kate appreciated Carmen's conviction. "I don't know that this killer will allow himself to be taken in. He has a God complex and those types aren't usually taken alive. I will do everything in my power to try to bring him to justice that way."

Kate doubted that they'd have the chance to bring him in alive. She wanted Carmen on their side and most importantly, focused and calm. The way she was when Kate first entered the office wouldn't help anyone. Kate had never seen her that way and now that Kate knew she had the propensity for that, it concerned her. She needed Carmen level-headed and calm.

As if reading Kate's mind, Carmen smiled. "I know I seemed out of it when you first arrived. I was spiraling for sure. The murder of the Davenports, who were dear friends, and now Cardinal O'Connor is terrifying. I thought for sure he was coming for me next."

Kate weighed what she said next carefully. "There has been no specific threat against you. Just as I could be a match for the Justice card so could you. I don't think you should assume anything either way. I'm taking more precautions at home. It would be wise if you did the same at home and in the office. If you receive any threats or notice anyone that seems out of the ordinary in any way, let us know."

"I get it," Carmen said a little too dismissively. She seemed to have two speeds – terrified for her safety or too cavalier. Kate had been hoping for something in the middle. She might be embarrassed by her earlier state and covering for it. They talked for a few more minutes about the case and anything Kate might need.

As she got up to go, Carmen came around her desk. "This is probably completely inappropriate to ask, especially with everything going on. I'm not known for my appropriateness."

"Sure, ask anything," Kate said assuming either it was personal to her or another question about the case.

Carmen pressed her tongue to her top lip and held it there for a moment before smacking her lips dramatically. "Tell me, that partner of yours, Declan James. Does he have a girlfriend? I heard he got divorced some time ago and I know he's living with you. That made national news during your hearing. You said then there was nothing between you. I thought I'd take my shot."

Declan had told Kate during the last case that Carmen had flirted with him. She hadn't cared then and thought it was all in his head – the way he sometimes assumed all women flirted with him. Kate wasn't sure which annoyed her more. The fact that a little jealousy was bubbling to the surface or that he was right. Kate didn't know what to say.

She hoped her cheeks weren't burning red. "He's been seeing someone. Declan doesn't share much about his personal life, but he's very much involved."

"Too bad," Carmen said with a click of her tongue. "He doesn't seem like the kind of guy to settle down. Maybe I'll have my shot later."

"Maybe," was all Kate could say and she headed for the door. She had three missed calls from Declan and two texts asking her to meet him at the hospital. It seemed Leo was ready to talk and be released. He was giving the doctor a hard time.

Leo wanted to be sprung and wasn't taking no for an answer.

CHAPTER 16

K ate met Declan in the hospital hallway outside Leo's room. "Did Sharon find anything of interest?"

Declan leaned against the wall, frustrated. "She's still going through everything. She said there might be some trace DNA on the overalls. It might be from Cardinal O'Connor. She won't know until later. The medical examiner said Cardinal O'Connor was still alive but probably unconscious during the beating. It's what killed him before the oxy could. The bloody print wasn't anything useful."

"The silicone?" Kate asked and was not surprised when Declan confirmed. "I met with Carmen Langston."

Declan pulled a face. "She's terrifying."

"I thought you liked strong women."

"There's strong and then there is absolutely terrifying, Kate." He chuckled lightly. "Did she scold you and tell you that we need to get it together?"

Kate explained the reason for the visit. "Did it occur to you that the killer might have sought out River intentionally, trying to tell us Keaton Thomas was the target?"

"It didn't," Declan admitted. "I guess in retrospect it should have. I was more focused on your safety and that he had your address."

Kate wasn't sure if she was going to tell him what else Carmen had to say. She hesitated a beat too long and he looked over at her with a question on his face. "I hate admitting this, but you were right. She probably was flirting with you during the last case. She asked me if you were single."

Declan broke into a wide grin. "I knew she was flirting with me."

Kate knew telling him was a bad idea. "I can set you up if you'd like," she said, dripping with sarcasm.

Declan pulled her into him and dropped a kiss on the top of her head. "I've got more than I can handle right here. Besides, Carmen is hot but she's terrifying. Did you tell her we were involved?"

Kate allowed herself to be hugged right there in the hospital hallway. "I told her you were involved. I didn't say it was with me. We can't have everyone knowing. I'm still afraid that Spade will separate us if he knows." That was a real possibility. Spade would consider it too much of a liability to have them together. If Declan wasn't broke from his divorce, Spade might have a problem with them living together. Declan had shown great growth as an FBI agent since living with Kate. She assumed it was why they were getting a pass.

"Are you two done making out in the hallway? We have work to do," Leo called from inside the hospital room.

Kate leaned her head against Declan's chest and laughed. "I think he's feeling fine."

"Is that what we have to look forward to on cases?" Declan said with a wry chuckle. "If so, I say we kick him off the team."

"I heard that!" Leo shouted louder. He was teasing them and quite effective at it.

Kate left Declan and went inside the hospital room. She found Leo in a hospital gown sitting up in bed eating lime Jello.

He held the plastic container up. "This is disgusting. Can I get some real food, please?"

Kate had no idea what kind of diet Leo had been put on by the doctor. She went to his bedside and sat in the chair. "We will get you some food as soon as we can. I need to speak to your doctor first. Did they say when you'll be released?"

Leo turned his head to look at her. "I wanted to be released this morning but they told me I need to go for a scan. My brain is perfectly fine. It was a little bump on the head and they are acting like I sliced off a body part. I've been through worse and never saw a doctor."

The gown slipped from Leo's shoulder, revealing a long faded scar across his shoulder and down toward his chest. Kate couldn't see how far the scar went. It looked like an ugly injury. "Like what's on your shoulder?"

Leo craned his neck to the side, seeing his shoulder was exposed, and yanked the gown back up. "I don't want to talk about that." He turned his head from Kate to Declan. "Are you ready for my statement from last night? We need to get on with this. I saw on the news what happened to Evan and Cardinal O'Connor and I feel terrible I couldn't have been more help."

Declan's mouth was set in a firm line. "Leo, don't think like that. There was nothing you could have done. O'Connor was dead by the time you arrived. Tell us what happened." Declan moved from the doorway to the end of his bed.

Leo relaxed back and folded his hands in his lap. "Evan was upset on the drive over realizing that with him gone, there was no one to protect O'Connor. When we got there, he took off out of the car without me. It took me a minute to figure out that he wasn't going into the main building but to the house in the back, which I'm sure you saw. It was dark and I didn't have my bearings. I thought I saw someone lurking behind one of the trees. With the lighting, it could have been a shadow. I stopped for a moment to assess the house before entering like I learned at the academy. I didn't even hear someone behind me. I felt the hit on the back of the head and before I could react I was out cold. That's all I remember until I came to in the ambulance. Even then, I was in and out and couldn't make sense of what was happening."

"You don't remember anything else?" Kate asked, drawing his attention.

Leo frowned and tugged on the covers in his lap. "Unfortunately, not. I assumed Evan was already in the house at that point. I didn't see him go in. He took off out of that car so fast. As I said, he was freaked out and feeling guilty for leaving Cardinal O'Connor alone. He left me alone out there to figure out where I was going. I didn't see him go into the administration building. He ran around to the side of it. I thought at first there was a side door but everything was dark. It wasn't until I went down the path a little that I saw the fence and then the house in the distance."

Kate had the same experience when she arrived on the scene. "You said you thought you saw someone in the shadows. Do you believe now that it was someone standing there?"

"I don't know," Leo said regretfully. "I don't know, Kate. With the wind and the leaves, it's anyone's guess. I thought I caught someone out of the corner of my eye. When I turned to look, no one was there. I assumed then it was just a shadow or maybe an animal. I didn't have much time to process before I was knocked out."

Declan pointed toward his head. "Can I take a look at your injury?"

"Sure. The doctor had to shave some of my hair. I haven't even seen it. It hurts more than anything I've ever experienced. It felt like he hit me with a baseball bat with spikes on it."

Kate winced at the description. "We think the killer was using a mace." She started to describe it to Leo, but he stopped her.

"I'm familiar with those. I've stolen a few."

"Don't say that too loudly," Declan cautioned him as he came around to the side of the bed opposite Kate. He had Leo lean forward so he could assess the wound – what he could see of it around the bandage.

"I can't tell what hit you but they got you good."

Kate got up to see it for herself. She went to Leo's bedside and leaned over to see it. The thick white bandage covered most of the crushing blow to Leo's skull. "Did the doctor say anything about your injury?"

"Not much. Just that it required close to thirty stitches to close it. I lost some blood, not enough to need a transfusion, and I had a solid concussion." Leo grew quiet for a moment. "The only confusing part was him asking me questions about myself. I don't know exactly what I told him. Keeping my real identity and this new one separate while concussed might have been too much for me. I'm a bit worried I blew my cover."

"It's okay," Declan told him, trying to offer support. "We can sort that out for you. Do you mind if I snap a few photos? I know you said the doctor has some. I want some to compare to what the medical examiner has."

"Go right ahead."

Declan opened the camera on his phone and snapped a few photos from different angles. Kate watched him work and said she was going to find the doctor. As she got to the door, Leo called out to her.

"I listed you as my medical proxy and my emergency contact."

Kate didn't hide the surprise on her face well enough. "That's okay," she said, trying to recover.

"I don't have anyone else." He glanced back at Declan and then at Kate with a look that was a mix of embarrassment and apology. "You two are the only people I have."

Declan spoke first, patting Leo on the back. "It's okay, Leo. We get it and Kate's happy to do it."

Kate smiled back at the both of them, happy these were her people. "It also makes it easier to speak to the doctor, so we can follow his advice."

Leo pulled a face. "No more lime Jello no matter what he says."

Kate found the doctor down the hall coming out of another patient's room. She asked him a few quick questions about Leo's condition. The doctor explained he was cleared to leave with a few restrictions. He could go back to eating anything he liked. That would make Leo happy, but the fact that he needed to stay still for a while would probably grate on his last nerve.

"Leo told us you took some photos of the injury while you were stitching him up. I need to see those." Kate wasn't asking the doctor. She didn't want to leave any room for debate about the issue.

"Of course," he said easily. He led Kate down the hall to his office. He pulled up a file on his laptop and turned it to her. "It was a strange pattern mark that I've never seen before. The injury didn't come from a fall. He was struck with something heavy and I assume metal. You can see the imprint of a crown there. That didn't make a lot of sense to me. Maybe some kind of walking stick with a handle in the shape of a crown."

"It was a mace," Kate explained to the doctor. "Cardinal O'Connor was beaten to death with the same or a similar weapon."

The doctor expelled a breath. "That's terrible. Do you have any suspects?"

"No," Kate admitted echoing the stress in his eyes. "Is there anything else I need to know about Leo before we take him home?"

The doctor hesitated for a moment. Then replied, "He said some strange things when he first came in. His accent was thicker and he said he lived in France. I chalked it up to the concussion."

Kate steadied herself, hoping her expression wasn't giving anything away. "It was partially the concussion. Leo was undercover in our last case. He probably had memories of that or got confused and reverted to playing the part."

"Oh," the doctor said with a smile. "I didn't even consider that. It makes perfect sense then. If you see anything of concern or if he has memory issues, please bring him back in. He suffered a real blow to the head. He's stable and fine now. But keep a good watch on him."

Kate assured the doctor she would. She had one last question. "I'm also looking for Evan Crandall. He was brought in at the same time as Leo. Do you know where I can find him?"

The doctor cocked his head to the side. "You didn't hear?"

Kate sucked in a breath, thinking he might have succumbed to his injuries. "I haven't heard anything other than you said we couldn't speak to him or Leo this morning."

"That was my mistake," he said and apologized. "Evan left. He walked right out of the hospital and refused treatment after he woke up this morning."

Kate stepped back, confusion falling over her face. "I don't understand. He needed a transfusion last night. I saw those stab wounds. How could he just walk out of here?" Kate wasn't sure how the man could walk at all.

"I'm not authorized to discuss treatment with you. All I can tell you is he left against the doctor's orders. He wasn't being held by law enforcement, so we couldn't do anything other than let him go." The doctor watched Kate for a reaction. She knew because of HIPAA she couldn't ask much that he would answer.

"Did he have any visitors? Anyone who might have threatened him?"

"I don't believe so. He was under observation by our staff for most of the night." The doctor reached for a file on his desk and opened it. "As I said, I can't tell you much about his condition. You are aware he needed a transfusion. He was stable when he left. Alert and awake. Leaving like he did opens him up to future infection and other medical difficulties. As I said, we strongly advised against it."

Kate knew the doctor was giving her far more than he probably should. She didn't want to push his boundaries further, but she wanted to know about the nature of the wounds. "We believe the mace had a metal spike at the end. We assumed that's what the killer used to stab Evan. Would you say it was consistent with that?"

The doctor studied the file, raising his eyes to Kate when he was done. "The strange thing about his wounds was that while they bled a lot, they weren't very deep. Definitely not deep enough to cause internal injury. If he'd been stabbed any deeper, he might not have lived. This was an injury to wound not to kill."

That didn't necessarily surprise Kate. "Is that the only thing strange?"

"It's just so precise – almost as if he'd been lying still when it happened and he let it happen. I'm not saying that's what occurred. He was clearly under duress when he was brought in here. The wounds were clean in and out, spaced rather close together. He didn't have any other injuries on him – not defense wounds, for instance." He saw the confusion on Kate's face. "I don't know what it means, but that's why I'm sharing this with you."

"I understand," Kate said as they shared a silent message between them. The doctor was giving Kate access to what she might not otherwise have without a court order. The doctor believed that whatever happened to Evan didn't add up – didn't make sense.

With him taking off, there was more to the story than they knew.

CHAPTER 17

L ater, when they were home after getting Leo settled at his house, Kate unscrewed the cap on a bottle of water and chugged it back. She had told them both about Evan taking off, something none of them could understand. Kate hadn't shared the information about the wounds with Leo. She waited until she and Declan were alone.

"The doctor seemed to think it was strange that the wounds weren't deep. They appeared deliberately shallow and he had no defense wounds. Evan didn't fight the killer at all. Why not fight?"

Declan watched her carefully. "What do you think is going on?"

Kate finished off the rest of her water and tossed the bottle in the recycling bin near the back kitchen door. She sat down at the table. "How was the killer inside the house killing Cardinal O'Connor, cleaning up, stabbing Evan, but also outside to strike Leo on the back of the head? Evan couldn't have gotten inside that much before Leo that the killer had time to stab him and then clean up and make it outside. Leo would have made it inside the home by then. So was there someone outside who hit Leo and then ran back inside?"

Declan didn't dismiss the possibility. "Maybe the killer was already outside. He saw Evan run into the house and then saw Leo hesitate. He struck him in the back of the head and went upstairs to Evan. He stabbed him twice, cleaned off the mace, and left again."

"Why?" Kate asked, looking over at him, confusion in her voice. That didn't make any sense to her. The killer would have been home free. There would have been no point risking a confrontation if he was already outside the home. "I don't think that's what happened. It doesn't fit the pattern of this killer. He's only going after particular people who fit his victim profile. Leo was hit to stop him from going inside of that home."

"Then the killer was already outside," Declan said, striking a logical point.

Kate was going through different scenarios to try to make it all add up. None of it did. "I can't make sense of it. The killer went back inside the house for some reason even though he was free."

"Why do you think he might have done that?"

"I don't know." That was the honest answer. There were now four dead and two wounded and Kate couldn't get a handle on this killer. She often felt like this at the start of a case but after a while, the killer's motives started to make sense to her. That was a pattern. Like taking a new lover – all of it was new at the beginning, but over time she knew what turned them on and got them off. This killer was a stranger to her in every way – random victim selection other than what he determined to fit the tarot cards, changing murder weapons, and even how he went about the crime. Worse still, he had attacked her team and was threatening her life.

"Maybe I've lost my touch," Kate said after a few moments. She knew she was being defeatist but she couldn't help it. She saw the concern on Declan's face. She shook off the mood. "This killer isn't like any we've seen before. We are going to have to think outside the box to catch him. Our usual methods aren't going to work. What does the scene tell you?"

Declan was the best she'd ever worked with at assessing the scene of a crime. "He's taking his time. He's methodical in what he's doing.

The wounds on Cardinal O'Connor might have looked frenzied but they weren't. The victims aren't fighting him. That tells me what you already said –threats go along with murders." Declan paused for a moment and Kate didn't push him. He was thinking through the murder scenes. Kate knew he was taking each one separately and then mentally thinking about them as a whole.

When Declan was ready he spoke again, his voice even and strong. "What you said is correct – he's getting to know them enough that he knows what the psychological pressure points are. Of course, he knows enough to identify them as a victim who'd match what he needs. It's more than that. He's getting to know them enough to know what will cause them to kill themselves. We didn't necessarily see that outright with the Davenports, so it might not be every time. You said Chase was surprised his father didn't fight back."

"That's correct," Kate said, reiterating what Chase had told her. "Even when he visited the scene, Chase couldn't make sense of it. He didn't say it outright. But it was obvious to me."

"We have no idea what the killer said to them. He could have told them if they sacrificed themselves, the killer wouldn't go after Chase and his sister. I think any parent would do what they could to protect their children."

Kate couldn't argue with that. In her way, she might have been the one who reinforced that with Cardinal O'Connor. She went to warn him, but in the warning suggested that if it wasn't him it might be one of the parish priests. The one thing she knew about him from the news was that after the sexual abuse scandal, he was someone who was brought on to clean things up in Boston. He had removed several priests from duty. He had a moral sense of right and wrong and could make difficult decisions his predecessors couldn't or didn't. Cardinal O'Connor had an ingrained sense of responsibility that informed his choice to overdose on the oxy.

Kate knew no matter what – once the killer had targeted him, he was as good as dead. Even at the end of his life, O'Connor was going to do everything he could to protect others. It was a basic human instinct that could be exploited.

The victims were carefully chosen – that was the only thing they knew for sure.

"What are you thinking, Kate?" Declan asked as he watched her process.

Kate wasn't sure how to articulate what she was thinking. She tried the best she could. "He is methodical and yet he wants to play a game with us. He's going in order because he wants us to be scrambling to figure out who he's going to kill next." Something was nagging at her. "A part of this for him is the psychological manipulation in their deaths."

Declan squinted unsure of what she meant. "Explain that to me."

Kate gestured with her hand as she spelled it out. "Take Kirk Eagen. This killer befriends him and gets to know him. Then one day turns on him, threatens him, and gets Eagen to jump. He's getting off on the psychological manipulation of having these people participate in their deaths. I think we need to go back to Eagen's family and see who he was close to. I want to know the threat. We know the threat for Cardinal O'Connor and we can assume it for the Davenports. I want to know what got Eagen over that railing."

"I can call his father," Declan said and put his phone on the table. He pulled up the contact and hit the call button. Ringing echoed through the phone followed by a strong male voice answering.

"John, this is Agent James. I'm here with Agent Kate Walsh," Declan said when the man answered. "We have a few questions for you."

"Just one question, really," Kate corrected. "We hate to bother you with this during this difficult time."

John told her it was no problem. "I'm willing to do anything you need to help find who killed my son."

Kate wished she could say she was. "I'm sure you might have seen on the news Cardinal O'Connor was murdered last night."

"That was connected to my son's murder?"

"Yes." Kate explained a few of the details that were on the news about the murder. "One of the things we know this killer is doing is convincing these victims to participate in their murders. The Davenports didn't fight back, even though by all accounts Bernard was a fighter. He would have protected his wife. We found no defense wounds on him. He never fought back. Cardinal O'Connor overdosed on oxy before his death. He would have died either way. We know that your son had to have thrown himself over because there were no marks on the railing to indicate a struggle. Given the railing height, he couldn't have been simply pushed over. We need to know who your son would have been protecting above everyone else. Is there someone he would have chosen to die to protect?"

John audibly released a rush of breath, nearly a groan. "Kirk would have done anything for his family. I don't know that he'd allow himself to be murdered for us. I think if I were being threatened, he would have told me. He knows we'd help him. I'm a cop and so are his two brothers. I don't think he'd be intimidated like that."

"Is there anyone in your family who might be vulnerable?"

It took John a moment but it came to him. "His niece, Christa. She's twenty-one and took off three years ago. She got into a bad relationship when she was a freshman in college. She dropped out and ended up getting addicted to drugs. We have not had much contact with her. Even with all of our collective resources, she's been missing for some time. Part of the reason he was excited about the job in Boston was because it put him potentially in closer contact with her. He was going to look for her since he was there."

Kate leaned toward the phone. "What do you mean, Christa is here?

In Boston?"

"We weren't sure. She had been attending Emerson College. She is a phenomenal artist but then got caught up in a toxic relationship with some guy she met. She got addicted to drugs and dropped out. She's been off the grid for a while." John's voice shifted from concerned grandfather to the detached tone of a hardened police officer. "You know once a kid gets addicted like that, you can't reason with them. There's only so much you can do. Her father and I went to Boston to look for her. She was living in Salem. She had broken up with her boyfriend and was living in some commune. She said she was tapping into her metaphysical side, dropping acid, and doing some crazy things. If it was the sixties, you'd say she had turned from a straight-A student to a dirty hippie. Christa has always been impressionable. I don't know if she's up there in a cult or what she's doing."

"Are you saying that if someone found out about Christa and threatened her, your son might have been willing to trade his life for hers?" Declan asked, getting straight to the point.

"I think he would. He was close to Christa when she was a child and had been so proud of her going off to Emerson. He was her godfather. I think he would have done anything to make sure she was safe. If someone was threatening her, Kirk knew no one could protect her."

Kate swallowed hard at the implication and mention of Salem. The tarot cards certainly fit Salem's infamous reputation. Even though she knew the real tragic history of the community, the connection between witches and tarot didn't escape her. The handful of times she'd been to Salem, she'd seen more than a few psychic shops. "How long ago was Christa in Salem?"

"We were up there about six months ago. We've had no word that she's moved on anywhere else."

Declan asked the next logical question. "Do you know if Kirk went up looking for her?"

"The first weekend he was there," John explained. "He found her and was keeping in contact. He was hoping that she'd live with him in Boston. She wasn't ready to leave."

Kate knew then they'd have to go to Salem. "Do you have the names of anyone he spoke to or the address where you had found her?"

"Not on me," he said. "I can call you later with the information."

Declan had one last question. "Is there anyone in Kirk's life who knew the situation with Christa?"

"A couple of close friends here, but it wasn't something the family discussed openly." John yelled to someone on the other end of the line, leaving them to wait. When he came back, he said, "I have to get going. Please let me know if there's anything else you need."

Kate promised they'd be in touch as soon as she knew anything.

CHAPTER 18

The last place Kate wanted to visit in the middle of October was Salem. Mostly, because she knew the crowds filling the city streets would make searching for Christa nearly impossible. Kate had felt strongly that they needed to try to find the young woman no matter the challenges it presented. She also felt drawn to the city for reasons she couldn't explain.

They had no other leads to run down in Boston. It was a longshot but one worth pursuing in Kate's opinion. She sat in the passenger side of Declan's SUV thinking about Evan Crandall as Declan drove them the short fifty-minute drive north.

After speaking with John on the phone, Kate and Declan had gone in search of Evan. They went to the Archdiocese first to get his home address. No one had heard from him since Cardinal O'Connor's death. If there was hesitation about turning over personal information, when Kate told the staff Evan had been badly injured, had checked himself out of the hospital against doctor's orders, and wouldn't respond to calls and texts, they had quickly provided whatever information about Evan they had desired.

No one had reason to suspect the long-time employee. He had worked side-by-side with Cardinal O'Connor for the past five years and had been his private secretary when O'Connor had worked as a priest in Maryland. No one knew quite how far back the relationship between the two went. All they knew was that if there were hard decisions to be made, Evan was in on the conversation. It didn't surprise anyone that Evan might have rushed to the aid of O'Connor.

What the staff didn't know at the time, something Kate and Declan only knew after going to his home, was that Evan Crandall was missing. They had gone to his house in the North End of Boston and spoken to a neighbor, who saw Evan come home, limp up the front steps of the porch, and then leave with a bag an hour later. When asked if he was okay, Evan said he had fallen at work and was taking some time to heal. He'd explained that he'd be gone for a while and asked his neighbor to take in his mail.

Declan had pulled up a few old addresses for Evan in Baltimore. They had called phone numbers listed and scoured the internet. While Declan was suspicious of him, Kate had tried to see the situation from Evan's viewpoint. If he hadn't done anything wrong, then he had likely seen the killer. He'd been face-to-face with him. While the injuries might not have been life-threatening this time, Evan might have been threatened like the rest of them.

Kate wanted desperately to interview him, but for all she knew the killer told him to leave town or he was next. Evan might have simply been doing whatever he could to keep himself alive. If there was evidence to suggest Evan was involved in the murders, it hadn't presented itself yet. They could only work within the confines of the case. Even if they found Evan, they couldn't compel him to talk to the FBI or hold him for anything.

Declan cleared his throat, drawing Kate out of the maze in her mind. "We are about fifteen minutes out and traffic is getting heavy. What's your plan?"

Kate reached over and caressed the back of his neck, tickling the sensitive skin with her fingertips and making him shiver. "Was I supposed to have a plan?"

He squirmed under her touch. "You always have a plan. You've made me come to Salem in the middle of their Halloween festivities. You have a plan, Katie. I know you do." He swatted her away "Stop that."

Kate withdrew her hand back to her lap, curious about his sudden shift in mood. She had a plan – although she wasn't sure it was the best idea. His mood seemed to grow darker as they got closer to Salem. She knew he didn't want to go, but he didn't need to be that grumpy.

Kate refocused on work. "I have a meeting scheduled with someone who knows tarot and who might have insight into this killer. If this killer knows tarot as well as I think he does and Christa is in Salem, then the community might be small enough that a local has encountered one or both of them."

"Okay," Declan said, applying the brake as traffic slowed to a crawl at the Salem exit. "That's a plan I support. Even if nothing else comes of this trip, it might be beneficial to speak to someone who knows the tarot well. Did you have a psychic in mind?"

"Lily Patterson."

"Never heard of her."

Kate had spent the evening researching Salem and reading reviews on psychics in the area – ones who were local and well-connected to the community. She had never been to a psychic before but had encountered frauds during a criminal case. The good ones, who scammed people for serious money, could read people, asking questions that elicited information that they could use later, and convince people of wild things that Kate could never be persuaded to believe. That said, most of the people who were scammed were in high emotional states and struggling in an area of their lives that they were desperate to resolve or improve. It made them highly vulnerable to this kind of scam.

When they were told they were cursed, which is how most of the scams started, they believed it because in many ways they felt cursed.

The psychics then asked for large sums of money to help remove the curse. Inevitably, the psychic would come back time after time, claiming the evil was just too much and more work was needed. Some psychics asked for gift cards and expensive clothing and jewelry for the spell work with the promise that it would all be returned to the client in the end.

It was all just one big financial scam on a vulnerable person who'd do anything to fix their situation. Kate understood how people could fall into it. It was often the same way people fell into cults. Someone else had the answer, the fix for their problem. The power imbalance was used against them.

That's not the kind of psychic Kate was after today. There were other psychics, she found, who didn't scam their clients. They provided a service in exchange for payment. For people like Kate, she didn't believe in psychic abilities. But the service was a fair trade for payment.

As they crawled through the narrow city streets of Salem and Declan navigated between the throngs of people walking on the sidewalks and in the road, Kate turned her body to look at him. She was curious about something. "Have you ever spoken to a psychic?"

Declan shifted his eyes to the side. "Once but not intentionally."

She didn't hide her surprise. "How does one not intentionally see a psychic?"

Declan stared straight ahead. "My mother, if you can believe it, knew a woman who claimed she was psychic. When I was about fifteen, she asked me to deliver some fresh bread she had baked. The woman insisted I come inside to chat. Then she took my hand and read my fortune."

For as much as Kate didn't believe, she had to know. "What did she say?" she asked, a little too excitedly.

"I thought you didn't believe."

"It's still kind of fun to think it might be real." She poked him in the stomach. "Come on, tell me."

"She told me I would not turn out like my brothers. I would go the opposite way into law enforcement and I'd get married, not have children, and get divorced later. She said that I'd have a long and happy life and I'd eventually find true love."

Kate cocked an eyebrow. "Are you making that up? It sounds like, for the most part, that's what's happened. I mean you haven't found true love yet. You know, it might be Carmen."

"Stop with that," Declan said but finally the corners of his lips turned up in a smile. "Tell me about Lily."

Kate was satisfied with Declan's response. "She's been a psychic for close to forty years and has lived in Salem her whole life, according to her website. She offers a range of different readings and some candle spell work, whatever that means." There was still a lot Kate didn't know.

After finding a parking spot, they walked through the waves of excited people, some of whom were dressed for Halloween. Kate wanted to keep focused on the mission at hand, but she couldn't help people watching as they went, especially the excited little girls talking about witches.

Declan asked Kate for the address and she rattled off the house number. Lily lived on a short side street between Essex and Debry Streets. They walked down the tree-lined street to the two-story colonial home that had been painted blue with white shutters on what looked like newly installed windows. The home was in pristine condition and the walkway appeared to have new paver stones and rebuilt white railing posts. Lily had the home landscaped perfectly with fall flowers in window boxes and brightly colored mums on the porch steps.

"Looks like she does well for herself," Declan said as he stood on the porch beside Kate and rang the bell. A dog barked inside the house causing Declan to chuckle. "I expected a black cat."

Kate rolled her eyes. "Maybe don't stereotype before we start the interview." No sooner were the words out of Kate's mouth when a small black cat curled itself around her left leg and then snaked through to her right and curled against Declan's ankle. She glanced down at the small creature. "I spoke too soon."

A moment later an older woman with white hair and an easy smile pulled open the front door. Kate introduced them. Before Lily let them enter, her gaze fell to the ground and she scolded the cat for always being underfoot. She raised her eyes to Declan. "Luna is my people barometer. She doesn't like many, so this is a good sign. The dog you hear is Pepper and he likes everyone."

Lily stepped out of the way, the silver bracelets on her wrists jingling against her flowing purple skirt as she moved. Where the outside of the home had been remodeled, the inside had an old-world charm with wide plank wooden floors and lower ceilings. It was brightly decorated with knickknacks and bright pops of color.

"Your energy is tense," Lily said as the two sat at her small round table. Pepper, a black labrador, had followed them back to the kitchen and lay on a rug in the corner of the room.

The cat was nowhere to be seen.

Kate had called Lily and set up a time to speak. She hadn't provided many details at the time. "We are here related to a case we are working on in Boston and a missing girl known to be here in Salem. Her name is Christa." Kate watched as Lily's face fell for the first time since they arrived. "Do you know her?"

Lily's tongue darted between her lips and remained there for a moment. "Possibly. First though, the case in Boston. Is it the one I think it is? The tarot case?"

"It is," Kate said evenly. "We need your help to understand this killer."

Lily approached the table and reached for Kate's hand. When Kate made no motion to provide it, Lily insisted. "Please humor me."

Kate glanced over at Declan who gestured to give it a go. They had to play the game if they were going to get what they needed. Kate turned back and slipped her hand into Lily's, which was cold to the touch and aged, the palms calloused.

Lily closed her eyes and took a deep breath that raised her chest. She held it for a few beats and then violently threw Kate's hand back at her. She stumbled back, holding onto the counter behind her. "You're in grave danger," she said in a rush of breath as if she had startled herself. "Grave danger. Your life is at risk."

CHAPTER 19

"This killer knows where Kate lives," Declan said, not waiting to see if Kate was willing to share. "This case started because he sent a letter with two tarot cards to Kate through our office in Washington D.C. The second came to Kate's house in Boston. This time he indicated that instead of his match The High Priestess, she might be Justice instead. It was a direct threat."

Lily absorbed the information then gestured with her finger toward each of them. "You're romantically together, no?"

While Declan said yes, Kate had hesitated. "Why does that matter?"

"The Lovers. You both could be at risk." Lily poured herself a glass of water and gulped it down in a few sips. She offered them water but they declined. She left the glass in the sink and sat back down at the table. "I'm getting ahead of myself here. It's just that the energy is so strong. I know you don't believe, Agent Walsh." She turned slightly to face Declan. "You're a curious one – a non-believing believer. You don't want to believe but it calls to you. You're drawn in, even when you try to rationalize. The energy here will affect you. Be careful with that."

Declan shifted uncomfortably in his chair. Kate knew he didn't like being under a microscope any more than she did. While his expression remained neutral, the twitch in his eyes gave him away.

"I'm open to believing that I don't know everything there is to know."

That was all he'd admit and Lily didn't press him further.

She turned her attention to Kate. "You need to allow your mind to open a little more to solve the case."

"What does that mean? Are you suggesting that the killer is a psychic turned psycho?" There was an edge of annoyance in Kate's tone she wished she didn't have. It was hard to hold back given the situation.

"No," Lily said, keeping her composure. "I'm suggesting that this killer has studied the tarot. He knows the ins and the outs. It's a case that has many layers. He might also be a student of energy and spell work."

"That's not real," Kate said, interrupting her. She wasn't going to go down this path. She needed real information that could help the case. Not a bunch of hocus pocus nonsense. "Witches aren't real." But that wasn't true. Kate knew the Wiccan religion was very real. She also knew that people of different faiths cast spells.

Lily raised her hand to stop her. "I'm not going to debate my spiritual beliefs with you. You came here to better understand the killer. Is that correct?"

Kate settled down, realizing she was getting worked up and defensive for no reason. "That's correct."

Lily picked up Kate's hand from the table and held it between her hands, one on the bottom, the other laid over it. "All I ask is that you listen to what I have to say and make a judgment call about your belief about it later."

Kate had one request of her own – a ground rule of sorts. "In turn, I need to know if the information you're providing is based on your knowledge and experience or if it's psychic insight. I promise not to judge one more truthful than the other, but I need to be able to keep it separate."

Declan agreed with that request as well, admitting, "This is an area where we are both out of our depth of knowledge. Having a foundation for how you know the information will help us."

Lily's expression appeared as if she wanted to protest. In the end, she let it go. "I'll tell you the psychic information first and we can get that out of the way. Yes, I believe this man is into some dark magic. I don't believe that it does what he thinks it does for him. He thinks it means he can control people, get them to do his bidding."

"How do we stop him?" Kate found herself blurting out.

Lily looked Kate dead in the eyes. "You will stop him. I can't see how or when. All I know is that you will stop him, but not before risking your life. If you're not careful then you could lose your life. Either way, it will be done and he will be stopped."

Declan reached for Kate's hand under the table and squeezed it. "Can you tell us anything about him?"

"He's been close by." Lily didn't say anything for a moment, as if she were trying to sort out the information coming to her. "It might be that you saw him on the street and had no idea of his identity. I'm not able to see him. He shows himself to me in a dark cloak with his face covered."

"Anything else?" Declan asked with impatience in his voice. Kate was sure he wanted to get past this as much as she did. While she appreciated the psychic insight, Kate couldn't take it too seriously.

Lily paused for a moment and stared off past them at something neither of them could see. "He has help or he did have help. Then he crossed a line with this person helping and he's not helping any longer. He might be in hiding."

"The killer?" Kate asked.

Lily shook her head. "The person helping him. Remember I said this case has layers."

Despite herself, Evan Crandall came to mind. Kate neither confirmed nor denied it directly. She skated around the issue, probably coming across as more transparent than she intended. "We might have a situation like that. A person was injured during the last murder. He's since checked himself out of the hospital against doctor's orders and cannot be located."

Lily nodded along with Kate as if that was exactly what she had seen. "He's in hiding, afraid for his life. The situation got out of hand. He was blackmailed into helping."

Declan squeezed Kate's hand under the table as she swallowed hard. Kate had no idea how Lily was coming by this information but she was correct. "We have had some questions about how this killer makes his victims take certain actions," she admitted, finding herself sharing more than she intended. "We believe the killer threatened one victim to jump from a balcony. The threat was strong enough that he complied."

"That's what led you here," Lily said without missing a beat.

"Possibly."

"I'm telling you – that's why you're here." Lily didn't leave room for Kate to argue with her. "Now enough of the psychic insight. I don't have more to share. This killer knows the tarot. I knew that from what was shared on the news. Agent James, you're good at giving a press conference. You project strength and are insightful even when you don't have much you can share. Tell me about the case."

Declan turned his head to Kate. He was looking for permission he didn't need to share the information with Lily. He still had a hold of her hand and Kate squeezed his in confirmation. He focused back on Lily. "He started with sharing tarot cards – The Magician and The High Priestess, which he said were symbols of him and Kate, respectively. He said he already killed The Fool – we found the card with the first victim. He went on to kill The Emperor and The Empress. Then The Hierophant. Before he killed Cardinal O'Connor, he met a young man in Boston Common and asked him to deliver a note to Kate's house with the Justice card and a direct threat. He's not only using the cards as a threat, but he's also choosing his victims based on them and his method of murder."

Lily seemed nonplussed by the information. "Tell me more about the murders."

Kate gave her the overview of how each of the murders took place, not sharing all the details but enough for her to understand. "The one thing that's most clear to me is that he's studied the symbols in the cards. One victim, he got to jump off his balcony. The Davenports he stabbed to death and Cardinal O'Connor he bludgeoned to death with a mace. Although, on that card, The Hierophant was carrying a wooden cross."

Lily thought the mace was curious. "What tarot deck is he using?"

"The Ryder-Waite Tarot," Kate said as she reached for her phone. "The Justice card he sent me though was from another deck, one that I couldn't find anywhere." She brought up the photo of the card and turned her phone to show Lily.

She asked if she could take the phone. When Kate let go of it, Lily brought the photo closer to her face, studying it. "This one is old, ancient. I can't be certain but this looks like a card from the tarot deck from The Order of the Magicians."

"What's that?" Declan asked.

Lily handed Kate back her phone. "An old order of male mystics. It grew after the Salem Witch Trials. Once all that quieted down, a handful of men were interested in the topic of witchcraft and why it was so abhorrent to people, outside of the religious connotations at the time. They began to study and legend says that they found a book that explained how to gain great power over people. They formed an order to keep the knowledge they learned a secret and only passed it down from one generation to another – a secret society so to speak. There are even stories about some of the founding fathers participating in the Order of the Magicians."

Declan let go of Kate's hand and leaned on the table. "I assume The Magician refers to the tarot card rather than what most people associate with magician?"

"That would be correct. My understanding is that they even created a special tarot deck." Lily pointed to Kate's phone. "I can't be certain as I've only seen the deck once, a long time ago. But that looks like one of the cards."

Kate wasn't sure she understood the implications. "Can those tarot decks be easily found today?"

Lily shook her head. "You won't find them anywhere outside the order. That's why I'm not even one hundred percent sure that it's from that tarot deck. I've only seen a couple of the cards and they were created in the same color and style. I do recall that in that tarot deck, The Hierophant had a mace."

Kate expelled a breath, wondering what it all meant. "Can we assume this killer is a part of the Order of the Magicians or connected to someone who is?"

Lily hesitated to answer and Kate wondered if she was sorting out fact from psychic insight. Kate pressed her to say whatever was on her mind. "I don't know that the order still exists today. Now that spirituality has evolved to be more out in the open. You hear about people even selling courses on how to be more psychic, how to manifest, and so forth."

"I assume this isn't information we can look up online?" Declan asked, pulling out his phone. When Lily told him no, he placed it on the table. "Then where do we find out more? Where did this start? How many supposed members does it have?" Lily told them she didn't know the answer to any of those questions. Declan finally settled on one important question. "How do you know about it?"

"There's been talk over the years among the people here in Salem. If it were me, I would have been too afraid to start something like that here so soon after that devastation, but we are talking about rich, powerful white men. They could fly under the radar in a way most couldn't back then. My mother and grandmother told me most of the stories."

"Is there anyone here in Salem who might know more?" Kate pressed her. She didn't know if this would lead to anything, but this was the kind of information she had hoped to gather here. Besides, the name of the order was literally what this killer was calling himself. When Lily didn't respond, Kate leaned toward her. "We wouldn't be here if we weren't desperate for information. We aren't any closer to finding this killer than when we started. If you believe the tarot card he sent me is from a secret order and not accessible to most people, then that narrows things down for us. If you don't know, you don't know. But if you do…" Kate didn't need to finish that. Lily had risen from her chair and went to the hook near the back door, grabbing a brown cardigan.

"I'll take you to someone who can help. While you talk to him, I'll go find the girl."

Kate had nearly forgotten that they were there to find Christa too. "This information can save lives, Lily. It might save my own."

Lily raised her eyes and met Kate's. "That's why I'm doing it. I cannot have your death on my conscience all to protect an order that no longer needs to remain secret."

Declan leaned into Kate. "Does that mean she knows more than she's telling us?"

Kate thought so, but as long as Lily was willing to bring them to someone who knew more, she wasn't going to call her out on it. "Do you think this person will be willing?"

"No," Lily said definitively as she grabbed her house keys and ushered them toward the front door. "But he owes me a favor."

That was good enough for Kate.

CHAPTER 20

Baird Howe's home was not unlike Lily's. It was a two-story colonial painted a barn red with dark black shutters flanking each of the windows. The wide front porch looked out over the front yard landscaped immaculately with rows of planted flowers lining the driveway, overflowing in window boxes, and baskets on the porch.

When Kate remarked about the flowers, Lily explained that it had been Baird's wife who was the gardener but that she had passed a few years ago. He had a landscaper now. Baird had many skills. A green thumb wasn't one of them.

Lily pointed to a porch swing and told them to sit while she went inside to talk to Baird alone. He'd need some convincing, Lily said, and she needed the space to do that properly. She wasn't asking Kate and Declan to wait, she was telling them and they abided by whatever she needed.

"This is actually kind of nice," Declan said as he used his foot to glide them back and forth. "I'd like to find a small town like this in retirement."

While the relationship was new and going well, this was the first time Declan had mentioned anything with her that long-term. Sure, there had been jokes about the relationship and their old age. Kate had never taken it seriously before now. She had thought he was teasing her. Declan wasn't teasing this time.

His tone was serious. "What do you think?" he said again, forcing Kate to turn her head and look at him. Declan's expression was as serious as his tone.

"I haven't thought about real retirement. I think about quitting the FBI about every other month. It's lovely here though." Kate avoided reacting to Declan's long-term plan. She wasn't sure if he was baiting her into a conversation or not. This wasn't the time nor the place for it.

"Don't get me wrong. I love Boston and your brownstone is great. I just thought it might be nice to have a place outside the city. Somewhere near the water," Declan said, rambling about investing his money and how he needed to get his affairs in order.

Kate had never heard him talk like that. "What's going on?" she asked suddenly suspicious.

"Nothing," he replied, staring straight ahead. "I've been thinking about the future a lot. I also feel badly living in your brownstone while I get my financial sea legs again." He turned to look at her. "Planning isn't bad, is it?"

"Not at all." Kate sometimes wondered what had happened to the Declan she knew, the one who drank too much and chased women for sport. Before she could respond to him, an older man who appeared to be in his late seventies followed Lily outside.

He stood about five-foot-ten and had a slender build with a bit of a belly that rounded out his frame. He had pale blue eyes, a bald head, and a kind smile. "Agent Walsh. Agent James. It's nice to meet you both. Although, as Lily described, it should have been under better circumstances." He hitched his thumb over his shoulder toward the front door. "We can go inside to talk or speak right here. It's a lovely day to be outside."

He didn't wait for them to respond. He tugged over a wicker chair with a barn red couch cushion that matched the paint color of the house. He gestured to the chair opposite him for Lily. Once they were seated and comfortable and Declan used the toe of his shoe to stop them from rocking, Baird said, "I heard Lily told you about the Order of the Magicians."

"She told us what she knew, which wasn't much. It's not something we have heard of before now," Kate said honestly. "I don't know if this killer is connected to this group, but if the tarot card is connected, then he might be."

"Can I see it?"

Kate pulled up the photo and handed it to him while she explained how it had been delivered to her home. She assumed Lily had caught him up to speed about the case. "He's using the Rider-Waite tarot deck during the murders. This card was different in design. He used it to threaten me."

Baird said he understood while he studied the card. "Do you have the card with you?"

"No, it's in evidence," Declan said. "Is that card connected to the Order of the Magicians? It's what he called himself from the start – The Magician. It's why we were so interested when Lily mentioned it."

Baird did not take his gaze off the phone while he spoke. "This card is from the original tarot made for the order." He tipped his chin up to look at them. "Only twelve decks were made using this design."

"How can you be sure?" Kate asked.

"I know the deck."

It wasn't much of an answer but Kate accepted it. "Did the members use those cards for divination?"

"Yes," Baird said slowly his tone suspicious. "Is there a reason you're asking?"

Kate explained about how the card had felt. "It wasn't like a card that had been preserved well. Do you know how playing cards get a bit beat up and softer with a lot of use? That's how this card felt. I assumed the killer pulled the card out of a tarot deck he'd used frequently. It had a distinct feeling different from the cards found with the victims – which were stiff and new."

Baird had a look of understanding. "The cards are very old. Divination was the purpose for creating them. Each member had a deck to infuse their energy into."

"Is the Order of the Magicians still around today?" Declan asked.

Baird sat stone-faced, not uttering a word of response.

It was clear to Kate that Baird did not want to give up his secrets.

Kate wasn't going to let him stop now. "This is about murder, Baird. It's going to continue if we don't catch him. If he works his way through the major arcana, there is still the minor. We have to stop him. If you know something, you need to tell us."

Baird sat back in the chair and crossed his legs. "My last name is Howe. My ancestor, great-grandmother back several times, was Elizabeth Howe. I'm the eldest son of James Howe's line. Elizabeth was accused of witchcraft for bewitching a neighbor's child. She was tried, convicted, and hung on July 19, 1692. It was James, her son, who was one of the original Order of the Magicians. He and some of the other children of the accused came together to better understand what had happened to their mothers and also to learn if that kind of power truly existed. The original tarot deck has been passed from generation to the next until it came to me."

They were sitting in front of a descendant of one of the originals. Kate had so many questions but had to focus on the murders. "Do you believe this killer could be someone connected to the Order of the Magicians?"

"If not someone like me, then someone close," Baird said, pinching the bridge of his thin nose. "You see, Agent Walsh, the Order of the

Magicians is not like most secret societies where the secrets eventually get out. No one even knows about them. Nothing has ever been written. They had to keep the secrets to survive back then. If found out, they'd be hung just like the others. What they were doing was risky, too risky. It's not something I would have done. Even in families the order is a secret, passed down to the oldest male heir when he comes of age. Most wives of the members didn't even know it existed. The other children didn't know either. Maybe someone in a family line spilled the secret. I can't rule that out all of these hundreds of years later. But the Order of Magicians is not something read about in books – there are no written documents about the order. It's all oral tradition and stories handed down. There's no one meeting house. There's not even a hint about this order outside of Salem. So, yes, if someone is using that card, it's someone connected to the order."

That certainly narrowed things down for Kate. "How many of you are out there?"

Baird drew his mouth in a firm line and exhaled through his nose, flaring his nostrils. "There are only five of us left. The rest of the lines have died off through the generations."

Kate grew excited at the small number. The look on Baird's face told her to slow down.

"It's not that simple, Agent Walsh. I know all four of the other men and they are old like me, two even older. I can assure you none of them are your killer. The lines die out. My line will die with me. I never had children for me to pass on the information."

"What about the tarot cards?" Kate asked. "If every one of your families had a set, can we see yours?"

"No." The way Baird said it left no room for debate.

Frustrated, Declan said, "If it's not any of you, then information must not be as secret as you claim. You just said yourself this must be someone connected. If the other lines died out, then someone must have the cards. They went somewhere. If you refuse to show us yours, how do we know you're telling the truth."

"I have no reason to lie." Baird stared at them for a few seconds, not giving in about the cards. "Let me speak to the other members and get back to you."

"I want their names," Declan said, moving to the edge of the swing. Kate put her hand out to stop him from doing something rash. She understood how he was feeling. They were on the precipice of getting information and they kept running into roadblocks. It was time they didn't have.

"I can't give you that information, Agent James. I will speak to the remaining members and see if we can come up with anything for you. That's the best that I can do."

Kate focused her attention on Lily who had spent the entire conversation on her phone. She had said she'd track down Kirk Eagen's niece, Christa. Kate hadn't thought she meant by phone. She shifted her attention back to Baird. "It sounds like this might be from a small pool of people. I trust that you will be able to get information more quickly than I can. I assume most won't even speak to me. We appreciate that you are willing. That said, this is our only lead right now. We have two ties back to Salem. We are in search of a young woman. After we find her, we are heading back to Boston. Please call me if you find out anything we should know."

Kate stood and pulled a business card from her pocket. "My cellphone number is on there. Call me day or night. I'm trying to prevent another murder and bring justice to the families of the deceased. He's going after well-known targets and we need to understand his motive."

"That I can tell you," Baird said, surprising her. He saw the look on her face. "You didn't ask me motive before, but it's clear in what he's doing."

Kate wasn't going to sit back down. She stood there towering over him waiting for the information. "Well," Kate said expectantly, "are you going to tell me?"

Baird flicked his eyes up to her and stared for a moment before he spoke. "This killer believes that with each person he kills, he gains their power. Their energetic essence so to speak. The Magician in the tarot represents someone who has all the powers and tools of the tarot. The founders of the order believed that through death a person can steal another's energetic power for their own. It was the ultimate act and one that was forbidden. To steal another's energy is to invite evil into yourself. Not only karmic energy from the universe that must be paid back, but while you take on another's energy it morphs and changes once it's inside you. The founders forbade any one person from having that much power. It corrupted the soul. They witnessed the destruction of that kind of power here in Salem. They were adamantly against it. Still, the legend of gaining that kind of power was discussed. That very well could be this killer's motive and why he's sticking so closely to the tarot – using a representative from each card to enhance the power. It's ultimate power and it's intoxicating for some."

Kate found herself wanting to ask if that could possibly be real when Declan asked for her.

"You're kidding, right? That's absolute nonsense." He stood up from the swing right next to Kate.

Baird didn't seem to be dissuaded by his skepticism. "I'm telling you what he might have learned from the Order of the Magicians. Take it or leave it." Baird stood then and shoved his hands in his pockets, clearly offended by their not believing.

Kate tried to apologize but Baird brushed them off.

It was Declan who extended his hand. "It's not that I don't believe you. I'm having difficulty believing that anyone can so cruelly and violently kill people in the pursuit of power. I see murder every day and it still baffles my mind." It was no apology but it was a peace offering. "Thank you for sharing the information that you did. I'm sure it felt like you were breaking generations of trust."

"I'll be in touch," was all Baird said before saying goodbye to Lily and heading back inside.

All hope was not lost.

"I found the girl," Lily said, telling them they must quickly go.

CHAPTER 21

Lily brought them to a communal house down near the water's edge. It was a home that had once been stately. Its glory had faded through years of neglect and sea spray. The front porch needed repair, the landscaping was non-existent, and the front screen door was off one hinge.

"This house is a stain on the community," Lily said as she carefully climbed the porch steps. "We get throwaway kids here – the ones who come to find the witches and then stay to learn the craft, never realizing that it's not what they see in the movies. It's a religious practice and not casting black magic against their enemies. Most who are practicing Wiccan in these parts practice white magic – the do no harm kind of magic that bores these kids."

Kate followed right behind her. "How did you find her?"

"My friend, Eleanor, brings food to the house now and then. We don't want the kids to starve and we don't want them begging on the streets. Not only will it scare off tourists, but they could get arrested." She sighed as if she wasn't sure what else they could be doing. "They are all of age, most of them dropped out of college, looking for something in their lives, and don't seem to have anywhere else they want to go."

"Any of them working?" Declan asked.

"Some do odd jobs here and there. A couple of the girls were working as waitresses. It's that age you know. They like the community and the community takes care of them."

Kate wondered if she knew Christa had been here all along. Surely, Lily would have seen her here if she was at the house as much as she said. "Have you interacted with Christa before?"

Lily offered Kate a sad smile. "That's the thing, Agent Walsh. Not all of them use their real names. I'm not here as much as my friend Eleanor. I don't know Christa well. I knew her by the name Daisy and she's changed her hair since that photo. She's nearly white-blond now and her hair is longer. I wasn't sure when I looked at the photo you provided. Eleanor confirmed for me that Daisy is Christa."

It was a reasonable explanation and Kate had no reason not to trust her. "Did Eleanor say anything about what Christa has been doing?"

"She works at a local diner in the evenings. Nothing during the day, so she should be home."

They had been standing on the porch talking for so long, Kate was surprised no one had spotted them and come to the door.

"I'm going to take a walk around back." Declan jogged down the steps and disappeared around the side of the building. Kate knew he was feeling anxious to get things done. If he was forced to sit and talk to people for too long he got antsy.

Lily pointed in the direction he went. "He was good with Baird." Lily gave her a knowing smile. "You two make a good team both at work and at home."

Kate didn't confirm what the woman already knew. "We've been working together for a long time."

"You have a lot longer to go, dear." Lily turned back to the door and knocked once. A young woman with short purple hair and a row of earrings up each side of her ears answered the door. Kate didn't think she looked much older than eighteen. She had the rail-thin body of a heroin addict. It didn't look natural or healthy and Kate was immediately concerned for her wellbeing.

"We are looking for Daisy," Lily said, holding the broken screen door open. "I know she's inside. Eleanor sent me over. You remember me, right? I brought chicken and dumplings over last week."

The young woman didn't say anything as she stepped back and let them inside. She waited until they were fully in then turned and made her way up a staircase that groaned under her slight frame. Kate hoped she wasn't going to need to climb that. The third stair up was missing and what was left was a gaping hole. "How has the city not been in here and shut this place down?"

Lily agreed with her. "I think the city officials want to contain the problem. Eleanor was able to get some volunteers to come in each week and start repairs. If you can believe it, the house is better than it was. There's still work."

Kate hitched her chin in the direction of the young woman. "Is she okay? She looks like a heroin addict."

"No drugs if you can believe it. She's been dealing with an eating disorder and has been seeing a local counselor." Lily sighed heavily. "There are a lot of things here more broken than the house. The kids take care of each other and we try to take care of them. Some weeks are better than others."

Kate was about to praise Lily for her efforts when Declan's voice interrupted the conversation. She heard heavy footfalls behind her. When Kate turned, she came face to face with him and a young woman he was holding onto.

"Meet Christa. She decided it was a good time to slip out the back door when we arrived."

The tall girl with a nose ring jerked free of his grasp. "It's Daisy and I wasn't sneaking out. I was going for a walk, which I'm free to do. Are you arresting me?" When Declan didn't answer, she smirked. "I didn't think so, which means I am free to do whatever I want to do including not talking to you."

Declan looked ready to slap the cuffs on her. Finally, he realized he wasn't going to win and threw his hands up. "I'm going outside."

Kate had to hold back a smile. She liked Christa on the spot and turned to the young woman while Declan left. She introduced herself. "You're not under arrest. When was the last time you spoke to your father?"

Christa eyed her suspiciously. "I don't think he can send the FBI to come get me."

Kate assured her that wasn't why she was there. "You're an adult and you're free to do whatever you want. When I leave today, I'm leaving you here because I need to go back to Boston. If you want me to get your father and grandfather to come get you, that I can do. I'm not here for you per se."

Christa narrowed her eyes. "Why are you here?"

Kate hated to deliver a death notification. It seemed the young woman had no idea her uncle was dead. "Have you watched the news lately about what's been happening in Boston?"

"The tarot murders." Christa chewed on her bottom lip. "I heard that my uncle was one of the victims."

"That's right," Kate said softly, feeling a wave of relief that the girl already knew. "My partner and I are investigating those cases. As you might know, it was reported that your Uncle Kirk killed himself."

"He would never," Christa said, cutting off Kate. She gestured toward the living room. "I'll talk to you if it's about my uncle."

Kate was glad about that. She followed the young woman into the living room. She didn't tell Lily not to follow along, but the older woman decided to head out of the house. She told Kate she was heading back home if she needed anything else. Kate was glad for the privacy.

As Christa folded her legs under herself and eased down on the well-worn brown sofa, she asked, "What do you want to know? I saw my uncle not that long ago. Maybe a week before it happened."

"That's why I'm here. I spoke with your grandfather and he said Kirk was happy to be in Boston because it would be closer to you. How was your visit with him?"

Christa shrugged and lowered her eyes to her hands. "I wasn't exactly nice to him. He wanted me to get my life together and go back to college or at least go home and see my parents. I didn't want to do either of those things. We argued a bit." She raised her head to look at Kate. "By the end of the visit, he gave up trying to convince me and we had a nice lunch together. He said that as long as we were going to be so close I should try to come to Boston to visit him. He said he'd pay for the train. He gave me money before he left too. All in all, it wasn't a bad visit. I was glad I got to see him one last time." Tears formed at the corner of her eyes and she aggressively wiped them away. She was trying to show that she was tough, but Kate didn't buy it.

"Did anyone ask about your uncle after the visit?"

"What do you mean?"

Kate had to watch her words. She didn't want to imply in any way that Christa was responsible for her uncle's murder or that she had made him vulnerable. "You work at the diner. Did anyone meet your uncle at work or any of your friends here? I'm just wondering if anyone you know from Salem talked to you about your uncle after the visit."

"A few people, I guess," Christa said and paused as if she was thinking about it. "There were a few of the girls here who knew and then a couple of customers. Not really too many people."

"What about any men who might have asked questions about your uncle? Did anyone ask where he worked or when he moved to Boston? When you were out with your uncle, did you introduce him to anyone?"

Christa looked out in the hallway. "A few of the girls who live here. A couple of the customers when Kirk came into the diner when I was working. He showed up there first. I don't think he knew where I lived but knew where I worked."

"Tell me about any overly friendly customers. Asking questions and wanting to learn more about your uncle."

Christa shifted uncomfortably on the sofa. Her back grew rigid in a way that Kate knew she had hit on something. "There was only one person like that. He said he saw me with a man down near the common and asked who I was with. That's when I told him about my Uncle Kirk. He asked a lot of questions – where he was from, what he was doing in Boston, and where he was living."

"You didn't think that was strange?" Kate asked, keeping her tone even to not sound judgmental.

"He always asks a lot of questions about everyone. I didn't think much of it."

"Do you know his name?"

Christa nodded. "He goes by Ronny. I only know his first name, not his last name. He pays in cash, so I've never seen a credit card. What does this have to do with my uncle and the murders?"

Kate didn't want to tell this young woman, who she could see was emotionally fragile in ways Christa wasn't admitting, that the killer had used her as leverage to get her uncle to kill himself. It was only a working theory and not something she'd lay at the feet of a young person. The emotional scars that could leave might be too hard to come back from. Christa was already on the fringes.

"I don't know that it has anything to do with the murders," Kate lied with ease. "We know that the killer might have a connection to Salem and might have met your uncle before and knew a good deal about him."

Christa was more perceptive than Kate thought. "You think

something I said to him made Kirk a target?" Kate didn't respond right away and Christa persisted. Her eyes filled with genuine fear.

Kate had no answer for that. "When was the last time you saw Ronny?"

Christa seemed to let it go. "A couple of weeks ago. He usually comes in a couple times a week but he said he was going on a trip. He didn't say where and I didn't ask."

It certainly sounded like Ronny could be connected. Kate pulled her phone from her pocket and walked over to Christa. "Does this man look familiar to you?" She showed her a photo of Evan Crandall. When Christa shook her head, Kate wasn't sure if she was happy or disappointed. "You never saw him here in Salem or with Ronny?"

"Not that I can remember."

"Does Ronny know where you live?"

"Everyone knows where I live. It's not a secret." Christa got up from the sofa and stood in the middle of the room, her breathing shallow. "What can I do to help?"

"I'm going to need everything you know about Ronny."

CHAPTER 22

Ronald Pallazzo was a forty-five-year-old man from New Hampshire, at least according to what people in Salem knew about him. Kate and Declan had spent the afternoon interviewing as many people as they could find who had interacted with Ronny, as he was known. Christa had no idea where Ronny lived and didn't know much about him.

They had no choice but to spend time in the community speaking to people to help both identify Ronny and locate him. Kate was hoping the man was still on the vacation he told Christa he was taking and wouldn't hear that the FBI was looking for him. She assumed if Ronny was back he would have been seen at the diner, which is the one place he was known to frequent.

Kate and Declan flew under the radar as much as they could roaming around the community trying to find locals who might know Ronny. The few they found all had the same thing to say – they knew him but not that much about him. Some people said he was an odd duck and stayed clear of him while others chalked him up to an eccentric living in a witchy town where weird things were the norm. People said he was from Maine, others said out west in California or Washington State. More than a handful had said New Hampshire but no one knew the town.

What Kate had gleaned from these interviews was that Ronny was a liar and had crafted stories about his life and his past to fit whatever conversation he was in with no regard for how neighbors might talk to one another. No one had a photo of him and the diner didn't have cameras.

They were going off a basic description – five-foot-ten, medium build with dark hair, no facial hair. After they were able to get in touch with Lily again, she had a whole lot to say about the man. She hadn't liked him at first meeting and had only grown more uncomfortable with time. He stood too close when he talked. Asked endless intrusive questions and stared with the eyes of a "dead fish" as she had put it. No one seemed to know when Ronny had arrived in Salem, just that one day he was there among them. He had no close relationships with anyone from what Kate and Declan gathered but he didn't stay hidden in his home either. He went to community events, ate at the local diner, and chatted with his neighbors. At the end of the day though, no one truly knew the man.

The most interesting fact about Ronny, which they learned from Baird, was that he lived in the home of Edwin Langmore, who was not involved directly with the witch trials as a victim or accuser but who had a son who was an originating member of the Order of the Magicians. The Langmore line had died off back in the 1990s. It was the only line that had never turned the original tarot cards back over to the order when the line ended. Baird had failed to disclose that to Kate and Declan initially.

Upon hearing that Kate and Declan were curious about Ronny that information seemed pertinent enough to share. The Langmore house had remained in the family for several generations, fell into disrepair, and was used as a rental house by the city who took over the house when no heirs came forward after the last Langmore death. It was bought by Ronny several years ago when city officials were trying to determine if it should be torn down or if it could be saved.

Ronny had hired a construction crew and rebuilt the house based on the original plans. The community had been grateful, even if Ronny wasn't everyone's cup of tea.

There was no telling what he found hidden in the home. Kate assumed the tarot cards and possibly other information about the Order of the Magicians, even if Baird said nothing had ever been written down. No one knew what the Langmores did over the years inside the family home or what secrets were passed down with it.

When Kate asked Baird if Ronny had ever talked about the order, he confirmed that no one outside of the order knew the identity of the members. Declan had asked one important question that Baird could not answer – *what if someone in the Langmore line had written down the names of the original members and Ronny found that list with the tarot cards inside of the home?*

Baird assured Kate and Declan that simply didn't happen and wouldn't even entertain the idea that it *might* have happened. But his expression told them something entirely different – it was more than possible.

The reality was Lily knew that Baird was a member. There could be others in the community.

Kate didn't believe it was as secret as he believed, at least not locally.

After exhausting a search of Salem for anyone who might know something about Ronny, they retreated to Lily's house, who offered up her dining room as a workspace. There wasn't much left to be done. Kate and Declan had gone to Ronny's home and found no one there. They had no information that would substantiate a warrant. All they had was a story about the Order of the Magicians, which might have nothing to do with the case.

Lily made them some tea and slid a tin of cookies onto the table. "I can make you something more substantial if you're hungry."

Declan raised his head from focusing on his laptop. "This is more than enough. Thank you. We should be out of your way soon enough."

"It's no bother," Lily said, waving him off as she sat down next to him. "Do you honestly believe it could be Ronny who is killing people? He's an odd duck for sure. Just, murder…" She couldn't finish her thought. She shook her head in disbelief.

Kate didn't know what to tell her. They had no way to know for sure. "It's hard to think of someone you know as a killer. Most go about normal things like the rest of us and have this secret life on the side. It's not easy to understand the mind of a killer."

Lily said she understood. Her features constricted in a question.

"Is there something wrong?"

Lily took a moment before she said, "I'm concerned about Christa, or Daisy – whatever she goes by now. If Ronny is the guy, she might not be able to act calm enough if he shows back up at the diner. If she does something to give it away, he could come after her."

Kate had been considering that. "I tried to get her to call her father and grandfather. I told her that it probably wasn't safe for her here. She had enough interaction with Ronny and shared enough about her life that she might be a target no matter what she says or does. There might come a point where he wants to clean up after himself and take out anyone he considers a threat. That is if we can't get to him first."

"If Ronny is the killer," Declan reminded her. "That's a big if. We don't even have enough information to get a warrant." He focused more on Lily than Kate. "This is a lot of wild speculation right now based on some circumstantial evidence. We have no proof the Langmores left anything behind in the home about the Order of the Magicians. We have no proof that just because Ronny knew Christa and had heard about her uncle, he killed him. We have no proof of anything."

Lily nodded her head in understanding. "I'm only concerned for Christa, that's all. I've had my suspicions about Ronny for quite a while now. Nothing to this level of evilness, of course. It's hard to believe he's the killer."

Declan's jaw tensed. "We would appreciate it if you kept your suspicions to yourself. We came to you and Baird for help in the investigation. Disclosing anything we told you could harm the investigation. You don't know who in the community might have ties to Ronny. If the rumor starts going around the community that the FBI thinks he's a serial killer, he could vanish for good and never come back here."

Earlier Kate and Declan had debated if Ronny would ever come back to Salem. They had decided that if he never got wind that the FBI had shown up in the village there was no reason for him not to return to his home. They had spoken with the local police who'd be keeping an eye on his house and watching out for him. Any rumors that reached him would ensure he'd never return unless he had few other options.

Lily heeded Declan's warning. "I won't say anything to anyone about it. Not only do I not want to ruin your investigation, but I also wouldn't want to ruin an innocent man's reputation if it turns out not to be true. Still, is there anything I can do to protect Christa?"

Kate reached for the tea Lily had provided. She took a sip and savored it. It was warm, infused with honey and soothed her instantly. She thanked her for the tea. "If you think you can befriend Christa, do that. Maybe over time you can convince her to go home or back to college. Salem is a wonderful place to live, but not for her right now. Those girls she's living with seem troubled. I don't get the sense that Christa is as troubled as the rest of them. She's here for a reason. I just don't know what that might be."

"You're perceptive," Lily said with a smile. "I don't believe Christa is running away from anything like the rest of the girls in the house. I believe Christa is on pause, not sure of the direction she wants to go, and is here for the time being. A respite from the pressures of life. She'll get it together, eventually. I can speak to my friends and maybe between us we can try to convince her to go home."

Kate could only hope that happened before it was too late. She had seen young women pulled down by others in their immediate environment. But there wasn't much Kate could do about that if Christa wasn't willing to leave.

They chatted for a few more minutes while Kate finished her tea and Declan finished the work he was doing – reading over reports Sharon had sent him about the evidence. Not that the killer left anything behind.

Before they left, Kate had one more question about Ronny. "Do you know what he did for work? A few people said he worked from home. No one seemed to know what he did. Maybe he had a favorite topic of conversation."

Lily considered the question. "I didn't speak to him much. When we did talk, it was more about the community, who was doing what, and what events were upcoming. Did you speak to Ned Fillmore over at the library?"

Kate shook her head. "We stopped in the library and a young woman was working. She said she didn't know Ronny. We didn't see anyone else working there."

"Stop back over," Lily advised. "Ned was probably busy. He's been the town librarian for more than fifty years. The few times I saw Ronny, he was usually on his way to see Ned or just coming back."

Kate turned to Declan. "We should stop there before we leave."

Lily pointed to the clock on the wall. "You better get going then. Ned closes up around five and you've got about fifteen minutes to get over there."

They quickly gathered up their things to go, thanking Lily again for all of her help. Kate wondered if she was going to have any parting words for them, some last bit of psychic insight she'd give them. Not that Kate believed it.

Lily offered words of encouragement and reminded them of her earlier warning that Kate was in danger. The last thing she said was, "Take care of each other."

No psychic insight was offered and Kate found herself weirdly disappointed by it. She didn't have time to process why as they raced the few blocks toward the library – easier to run than take the car in all the traffic.

They reached the double wooden doors of the library and navigated through a swarm of people who were gathering for another tour. Declan gently moved through the crowd until he got to the door. Kate ducked under his arm and pulled the door open, holding it for Declan as the two of them jetted inside, up a few steps and directly to the desk.

"We are here to see Ned Fillmore," Kate said, slightly out of breath, to the man behind the counter looking at them wide-eyed. She flashed her badge and introduced her and Declan. "Is he here?"

The man who had thick gray hair, piercing blue eyes and a wide smile said, "I'm Ned. I wondered how long it was going to take you two to get over here. Word around town is that you're investigating Ronny Pallazzo." He didn't wait for Kate or Declan to respond. He pointed to a high wooden table that sat to the right of the desk. "See that stack of books? Those are every book Ronny has borrowed from here. He has some interesting reading taste. I think it might help your case."

Kate and Declan shared a look – the trip to Salem was worth it.

CHAPTER 23

Kate expelled a relieved breath. "I'm so glad we found you before we left for Boston. We only heard about you a few minutes ago. We were told you were friends with Ronny."

"I should have called you myself when I heard you were looking into him," Ned admitted. "I was so busy with the tours and people here today. I'm short-staffed. I would have called you, probably too late. I wouldn't say we were friends. Ronny is…" His voice trailed off as if he couldn't find the right word to describe the man.

Kate helped him along. "We've heard odd duck and a bit off. Was that your impression of him?"

Ned cocked his head to the side and squinted his eyes. "That's certainly one way to describe him but not quite accurate in my perception of him. He's highly intelligent, and inquisitive, asks a lot of questions, and wants to know a lot of information. He can absorb it quickly and make logical inferences from it. He's manipulative and a bit of a chameleon."

Kate's heart started to race. It was all the things she had assumed about the killer. "What do you mean about chameleon?"

"Ronny shared with me that he grew up poor in the Midwest."

Kate stopped him. "We heard he was from New Hampshire."

"I don't believe so," Ned said quietly. "That's one of the things I mean. Ronny would say whatever he thought would make him attractive to

168

people. He could switch it up no matter who he had in front of him. I thought he was doing that with me for a while. I started asking him specific questions and letting my guard down in the hopes he'd do the same. I thought at first he was a troubled person running from a difficult past and maybe he just needed a friend."

"That changed at some point?" Declan asked.

"Yeah," Ned said through a breath. He gestured to one of the long wooden tables in front of his desk. "Let me lock up the doors and we can talk. If there's anyone in this community who might know the real Ronny Pallazzo, and I don't think that's his real name, it's me. I'm happy to help however I can."

As Ned went to lock the front door, Kate and Declan sat at the table. She leaned into him. "You doing okay?" He had seemed stiff and agitated for most of the day. The way he had when he brushed off her touch in the car when they first arrived.

Declan looked over at her. "I'm okay. This town has a weird… energy…I guess that is the word. I don't know. I can't explain it any better than that."

"The town does have a weird energy," Ned said as he approached the table. "It can impact people differently. I've lived here my whole life. Some people love it here. They get into the spook factor. Others don't feel that at all and just see a lovely New England town with a storied history. For some, they can feel a dense negative vibe – like standing at the site of a horrific incident and that heavy feeling stays with them the whole time they are here. Those people visit once and rarely come back."

Declan blinked rapidly at first trying to deny that he was feeling that heaviness, trying to explain it another way. Finally, when he ran out of words, he gave in to the description. "It's odd how it's impacting my mood. I've been walking around feeling angry all day mixed with being sad for no reason. Your description of heavy is apt. I didn't know I would feel this way."

Kate knew he had been acting out of character. He had snapped at Christa and then at Lily. Even rightfully so, he would have normally taken a different approach. Kate had no idea that he was feeling this way. All she could do was reach her hand into his lap and take his hand, the way he had taken hers before. He shook it off and she retreated. Feeling stung, Kate tried not to take it personally. They'd be home soon enough and could shake off the whole vibe of the place.

"I believe Ronny felt a lot of that heaviness too," Ned said, acknowledging Declan's feelings. "When he first arrived in Salem, he was a more likable guy. A little more easygoing, friendlier to people. He still had a way about him, wanting to impress people and show off. I've heard countless lies about his background and don't know that any of us know the truth."

Kate asked, "What did he say he did for work? No one mentioned how the man made a living or was able to afford that house. I couldn't find one person who said he was employed here in Salem."

"He wasn't," Ned confirmed. "Ronny was involved in investing and was a day trader. According to him, he had family money that was left to him when his parents died. He invested it and then basically started day trading. That's where he said he made his money. Ronny said he owned a good deal of real estate around the country. I don't know if that's true or not. He had money that was for sure. Where he got it is anyone's guess. He had that air about him and that part wasn't an act. He was also well-educated. He had the diverse vocabulary of a reader and the entitlement of an Ivy League graduate. College is why I think he came here to New England and stayed. Something made him angry though – there was a deep anger inside of him that he tried to fight. Being here in Salem only seemed to fuel that rage."

Declan didn't take his gaze off Ned. "Did you see that temper firsthand?"

"It wasn't explosive. It was a quiet simmering anger." Ned paused and had a thoughtful expression on his face. He zeroed in on Kate. "I believe it was that simmering anger that put most people off. They could sense that about him and it made him dangerous. No one knew what to expect."

Kate understood that perfectly. She had seen that with other killers they had caught – it was an unpredictability that made people uncomfortable. Couple that with an ability to lie with ease and manipulate and it was the perfect storm to create the kind of person who'd kill for sport.

Anger was one thing. Kate needed to know the most important thing about Ronny. "Do you believe that he could kill?"

Ned didn't even need a moment to think about it. "I do. When I heard about those cases in Boston and remembered back to some of the conversations I had with Ronny, I suspected right away that it might be him. I went to his house to see him only to find that he wasn't there. I spoke to his neighbor who said Ronny had been out of town for the last two weeks. I didn't have enough information though to call the FBI. I didn't think making a wild unfounded accusation would help you."

Kate could appreciate that. "How often did he come into the library?"

"It was sporadic. Sometimes he'd be here several times a week. Then there'd be times I saw him once a month. He did a lot of research."

"Research?" Declan asked, clarifying. "About what?"

"That's what I pulled for you." Ned got up from the table and grabbed the stack of books he had pulled for them. He set them down in the middle of Kate and Declan. "As you can see by the titles, Ronny was obsessed with the metaphysical. It ran the gamut from astrology to witchcraft to tarot and everything in between. He was obsessed with the afterlife and reincarnation."

Kate's gaze was drawn to the books. She counted nine in all. She turned her attention back to Ned. She didn't hesitate to ask the question. "Did he ever talk to you about the Order of the Magicians?"

Ned sat back in the chair, a knowing look on his face. "That's a bit of a town legend. I know from history the order was active throughout the years, centuries I should say. They were real and centered here in Salem. I don't know the names of the families or if anyone is active today. To answer your question, yes, Ronny spoke about them several times. He was fascinated with the history and who might have been a part of it. He was also curious about their rituals and the power they might have possessed. He wanted to know if I had any books on the subject. Of course, we don't. That's history that's never been recorded."

"What if it was?" Declan asked, venturing into a subject Kate hadn't planned to disclose.

"Then I don't know anything about it. It's not books we have here at the library or town government. I'm on the board of the Salem Historical Society and they have no written history of the order. Few, if any, people I've spoken to can even confirm its existence. If the order did exist, then the members were ultra-secretive and never shared the information outside of the original member families."

"Do you believe it existed?" Kate asked, trying to gauge Ned's belief.

"I do," he said after a moment. "I think there's enough chatter out there about it. Given the time in which it was created, there was a real interest in mysticism and in understanding witchcraft. People lost their lives over this thing that couldn't be proven. It was so universally feared. Not only here but in Europe. What happened here in Salem pales in comparison to what happened in Europe, particularly Scotland. In the 16th and 17th centuries, it's estimated some twenty-five thousand people accused of being witches were executed. It's about five times the average across Europe. There was a deep-rooted fear in the unknown but also an interest."

Kate had no idea that had happened in Scotland. The sheer numbers were astounding. "What's your sense of what the order did here in Salem?"

Ned gave the question consideration. "I can't say for certain. I believe they were trying to understand both what had happened here to make sure it never happened again and to understand this thing people were being accused of doing. They wanted to study it and understand it. I don't believe they wanted to practice it, but I can't be sure. I can't say that it didn't morph or change down the line. I believe the original intention was good."

If Ned knew more from a personal standpoint, Kate was sure he wasn't going to admit that.

Declan asked, "What did you tell Ronny about the order?"

"Nothing," Ned said with a shake of his head. "I don't know much. What I told you, which is only my opinion, is about all I know. I was curious how he came to learn about them and had such an interest. I don't know many people who have heard of the order outside this town. Given Ronny was an outsider in Salem, I found it curious he knew. He never told me how he knew." Ned checked his watch. "If there's nothing else, I need to get home."

Kate looked down at the stack of books. They had no time to go through them.

Ned saw the look on her face. "Take them with you. You can return them when you're done." Ned shifted his gaze between them. "Is there anything else you need to know?"

Kate turned to Declan, who was looking tired and worn out from the day. "Anything?"

Declan shook his head. "If there is, we can call you. We appreciate everything you have shared."

Kate had one last question before they left. She pulled her phone from her pocket and scrolled to a photo of Evan Crandall. "Do you know this man?"

Ned leaned on the table, looking at the photo. "He was in here today. I've never seen him before today though."

"Are you sure?" Kate leaned forward with the phone. "Please look closely."

Ned leaned in. "Yeah, I'm sure. He was holding his side as he walked. I wondered if he was injured and I was going to ask him if he was okay right after I helped the two women I was talking to when he came in. When I was done, he was gone."

Kate was sure then Ned had seen Evan Crandall. "Do you have any idea what he was doing in here?"

"I don't. He didn't check out any books. He would have had to come to the desk. I never saw him leave. He was here and then he was gone. For all I know he came in to use the bathroom. Tourists do that sometimes," Ned said his voice unsteady. He had sensed Kate's concern. "Who is he?"

Kate explained Evan's connection to the case. "He disappeared from the hospital in Boston."

"If I see him again, I can call you."

Before they left, Kate leveled a warning. "If Ronny is the killer we are tracking, he's killed four people so far. We know that he's threatened the victims to make them do what he wants. You can identify him and you know things about him no one else seems to. You need to be careful."

Ned assured them he'd be careful and call them if he found out anything else.

When they were back out on the street, Declan turned to Kate. "As much as I want to get on the road and get back to Boston, let's swing by Ronny's house one more time. We can drop the books in the car on the way over."

"What do you want to do about Evan?"

Declan stared off past Kate. "Call it a feeling but I think it's going to sort itself out."

175

CHAPTER 24

Declan's intuition proved eerily accurate. A glaring light emanated from the front room of Ronny Pallazzo's house. An SUV parked askew at the curb. Not just any SUV, but the very one Kate had seen outside the Archdiocese in Boston.

"Is that Evan Crandall's ride?" Declan's question echoed Kate's observation.

"It sure looks like it."

Declan chuckled. "I had a hunch he'd be here, but I didn't want to sound like I'd lost it."

"Nothing fazes me anymore," Kate replied knowingly. It was akin to the inexplicable sense she'd felt since setting foot in Salem – a deep intuition, beyond mere gut instinct. Kate unholstered her gun, and Declan followed. They weren't taking any chances.

Declan led them down the sidewalk to the corner of Ronny's driveway. Leaves rustled against the distant chatter of tourists. This part of the neighborhood was quiet, except for two approaching figures. Spotting their weapons, the pedestrians froze in their tracks.

Kate waved them off, flashing her badge. With a single nod from the shorter of the two women, they retreated out of sight.

"If we're doing this, it has to be now, before a crowd gathers," Kate asserted.

"We're overstepping our jurisdiction," Declan reminded her, though it didn't deter him from advancing toward the house. Technically, Evan Crandall was a free man, and Ronald Pallazzo remained a suspect without solid evidence. Still, they pressed on.

Creeping up the driveway, Declan halted, motioning toward the window. Through the sheer curtains, they spied Evan Crandall rummaging through the living room while also clutching his side in discomfort. "What's the plan, Kate?"

Suspecting Ronny wasn't home, Kate decided to approach the front while Declan covered the rear. "Are we certain there are only two entrances?" Declan asked.

Kate admitted uncertainty. "We don't have much choice."

As Declan disappeared toward the back, Kate ascended the porch steps. A creak echoed through the stillness as she reached the top, prompting her to pause. She had intended to knock, but peering through the front windows, she reconsidered.

She tapped lightly on the glass, calling out Evan's name.

His head snapped up, peering into the darkness. He didn't speak a word in response.

Kate persisted. "Come out, Evan. We just want to talk."

Evan hesitated, glancing around, perhaps wondering if he could flee.

Kate urged him to cooperate. "We are here to talk, Evan." Before she could speak again, Declan's arrival behind Evan caught her attention. She kept her focus on Evan, imploring him to understand their intentions.

Evan remained still, his demeanor shifting only when Declan got close enough to put a hand on his shoulder. Kate couldn't hear their exchange, but she saw Evan's posture relax, revealing a troubling patch of blood on his shirt – far worse than Kate had anticipated.

Kate stepped back from the window as Declan and Evan disappeared to the back of the home. She rushed down the porch steps and around to the driveway. She met them halfway to the back of the house.

Declan had a hold of Evan, urging him down the driveway. It wasn't that Evan wasn't coming willingly, he was shuffling his feet as if it was difficult to walk. "He broke in, Kate. Smashed the back window to get to the door lock."

"I'm not worried about that right now," she said, brushing it off. She didn't care that he had broken in. She wanted to know why he was there at all.

Declan didn't argue with her. Simply raised an eyebrow in a question.

The last thing Kate wanted to do was call the local police department and alert them that their only witness had just broken into the home of their prime suspect. It might upend the entire case. Who knows what evidence was in that house? If Ronny was labeled the victim of a home burglary, he'd be notified immediately and know the cops were onto him. He'd be on the run long before they'd ever have a chance to find him. The risk was high that he'd go elsewhere and continue the murders.

Kate didn't think that once he had started he could stop.

With Kate not willing to call the local police department, Declan gestured toward the man's midsection. "He's hurt, Kate. We need to get him to the hospital."

Before Kate could respond, Evan said, "We need to leave here now before he comes back." He had real fear in his eyes. "I know I shouldn't be here. I had to find him and avenge Cardinal O'Connor. He promised me he wouldn't kill him."

All at once the words he was saying sank in.

Declan's eyes grew wide and he shifted his head to look at Evan.

Kate took a step toward him. "Are you saying Ronny Pallazzo killed Cardinal O'Connor? Do you know that for sure?"

"Yes," Evan said barely above a whisper. He sucked in a sharp breath.

"He promised me he wouldn't kill him. I did everything Ronny asked me to do. That's who was in O'Connor's room when I got up there. He stabbed me but not enough to kill me. He said he was going to let me live, so I could suffer for what I had done."

"What did you do, Evan?" Kate asked, inching closer to him. "What did you do for Ronny?" At that moment, she didn't care that he was bleeding through his clothing or needed medical attention. She was so close to the truth she could taste the justice hot on her tongue.

Evan's mouth twisted up in anger. "He said he was going to kill my mother. She's seventy-five years old and lives alone in Cambridge. He said if I didn't help him he was going to kill her. I couldn't let her die." He hung his head as his voice cracked. "All he wanted was the Archdiocese directory with all the priest names, addresses, and so forth. I didn't think he was going after Cardinal O'Connor. It didn't even cross my mind at the beginning."

Declan released his grip and turned on him. "When did it cross your mind?" he asked, his tone brimming with rage. "Why didn't you call the police when he approached you?"

"I didn't know what he was going to do. I swear it!" Evan said, a sob getting caught in the back of his throat as his hand went to his stomach. "This was months ago before the murders started. He told me he was a private investigator and investigating a potential sexual abuse scandal."

Declan wasn't buying it. "No private investigator is going to threaten to kill your mother."

"No, you don't understand," Evan said, shaking his head as if trying to make sense of what he was saying. "He didn't threaten that at first. I went to Cardinal O'Connor when he showed up at the Archdiocese and made the request. O'Connor told me to tell him no. I thought that would be the end of it. I figured there had to be another way to get the information if he wanted it that badly. He left and I went back to work. About a week later, he returned and told me he wanted that directory, and if he didn't get it something bad was going to happen to my mother. He didn't say what. I didn't believe him but he insisted. Then he showed up at my house." He raised his eyes to Kate. "How did he know where I live?"

"What happened when he showed up?" Kate asked, wondering how it was that Evan was still alive. "Did he tell you his name?"

"Ronny Pallazzo and he said he lived in Salem. He was so straight-forward with me and wasn't trying to hide anything. When he was in my house, I knew he'd be able to get to my mother. I gave him the directory. I didn't think anything of it until a week ago." Evan grew quiet again, his breathing a bit labored now.

Declan wasn't going to let him off the hook. "What happened a few days ago?"

Evan's breathing grew even more uneven. He was struggling to talk and the blood stain started to spread. "He showed up and told me I had to choose the priest who was going to die." Evan furiously shook his head. "I wasn't going to pick someone to die. That's when he said he'd kill my mother and Cardinal O'Connor if I didn't pick someone. He told me I had to pick someone whose house was easy to get into. I didn't know. I haven't been to every house in the diocese. How was I supposed to know that? I didn't know why he was doing this to me. I believed him that he'd kill my mother and Cardinal O'Connor if I didn't tell him what he wanted to know."

"You gave him a name," Kate said, her pulse rising. It was all a game to the killer – the ultimate manipulation. "Who did you tell him?"

Evan locked his gaze on her. "I picked a name randomly from the book. I was so surprised to see you when you showed up. I figured you were close to catching him. I was still worried that if I told you, he'd kill my mother and O'Connor, so I didn't say anything. But I asked you how to keep him safe. Do you remember? I was trying to do my best. I didn't know where to find him. I could have given you a name, but it wouldn't have meant anything. I tried researching Ronny Pallazzo but didn't come back with anything other than this house. I couldn't verify anything else about him. Nothing about him being a private investigator. Nothing. I assumed it was a fake name. That wouldn't help you with anything. I wasn't even sure until I came up here that the house was real and belonged to him."

It was a wild tale and Kate wasn't sure how much she believed. "That night when you went back into Cardinal O'Connor's house. Did you see him?"

"I'm sure that's who stabbed me," Evan said with too much hesitancy in his voice to make Kate comfortable.

"That's not what she asked you," Declan said, his tone still simmering. "Did you see the man you knew to be Ronny Pallazzo kill Cardinal O'Connor?"

"Who else would it be?" he asked, his voice rising an octave. Kate and Declan didn't need to press the issue. Evan clutched his stomach and leaned against the house for support. "I didn't see him."

"What did you see?" Declan asked.

"It was dark and there was a figure coming out of the bathroom. Cardinal O'Connor was bloodied and beaten. The guy was holding a mace. I confronted him and he charged me. I never saw his face. He was wearing all black and had a hood up. Before I knew what was happening, he jabbed the pointed end of the mace into me. Once and then another time. I fell to the floor."

"You never saw his face?" Kate asked again and Evan confirmed. "Was there something covering it?"

Evan raised his head and stared past Kate as if trying to summon the memory of that night. "No, his hood was up and he had some kind of ski mask on."

Kate stepped back deflated. He'd not seen the man who attacked him.

"You can't say one way or the other then that it was Ronny Pallazzo who killed Cardinal O'Connor. Am I understanding that correctly? You don't know who stabbed you."

Evan remained silent for several moments, then shook his head slightly. "I guess I don't know for sure. I never saw his face."

"Was the man you saw the same height and build as Ronny?" Declan asked, trying again. He glanced over at Kate. She knew her disappointment was evident on her face.

"It all happened so fast. I can't be sure. I thought it was him. Why wouldn't it be him? He asked for the directory. He threatened them. It had to have been him." He looked at Kate with hope that she'd confirm his suspicions, but she couldn't.

All Kate could ask was, "What are you doing here? You were in there looking for something. What were you hoping to find?"

"Evidence," Evan said as if he couldn't believe he'd been asked the question. "I knew I wasn't safe in that hospital. I figured with Ronny in Boston, I was safe to come up here. I wanted to see if he lived at the address I found online. I needed something to bring back to you."

"Did you find anything?"

Evan shook his head. "I haven't been here long enough." He clutched at his stomach again and groaned.

Without hesitating, Kate stepped toward him and lifted his shirt to reveal the two stab wounds. One had remained stitched and covered in white gauze and medical tape. The other had lost its bandage and blood oozed out through broken stitches. "We need to get you medical care. You're not going to make it back to Boston."

Evan shook his head. "The next town over. Not here. Not in Salem. I don't know when he'll be back."

Kate raised her eyes to Declan, wondering if it was possible to wait. He didn't think so either. "We'll be with you the whole time. We will keep you safe." She didn't trust him not to run and he was the only person who could identify that Ronny was in Boston asking about the local Catholic priests. She didn't know if it would be enough for a search warrant. She also didn't know how Evan's break-in would impact the case. She would need to call the local police right after she took him to the hospital. "We need to go."

Evan relented, not that Kate or Declan were giving him a choice. "Let's make this quick and get me out of here." After he made the demand it must have occurred to him that he could be in serious trouble for what he said and he turned to Declan. "Am I under arrest?"

Declan gripped his arm again as they headed for the car. "That's yet to be determined."

That was all Kate needed to hear to know that Declan might not be buying Evan's story either.

CHAPTER 25

Two hours later, Evan was lying in bed hooked up to IV antibiotics and sleeping off the sedation after a minor surgical procedure to stitch up his insides. He had torn himself more than the initial stab wound and had lost a considerable amount of blood. The doctor scolded them for taking the time to interview Evan in the driveway rather than rushing him to the hospital. Kate would have felt guilty for that if she wasn't still suspicious of Evan. There was something in his story that still wasn't adding up.

After the procedure, the doctor insisted Evan remain in the hospital and be given antibiotics to prevent any infection from the open wound. Not to mention he needed healing time before being moved again. The doctor insisted on it no matter how much Kate protested. She wanted Evan back in Boston where the Boston Police Department could stand guard and ensure he didn't escape again. She had to settle for the Salem Police Department, not that they weren't competent. She trusted Briggs and his team above all.

While waiting for Evan to undergo the surgical procedure, she sent Declan to explain the situation to the Salem cops while she called Spade. What they needed more than anything was a search warrant to go into Ronny's house. Given the information Evan had provided coupled with the information Ned at the library had given, Spade thought with the egregious nature of the crimes, the judge might be accommodating. He said he'd make a few calls and file the paperwork for them.

Kate waited at the hospital for the go-ahead to search Ronny's house. While she waited, she flipped through three of the books she had brought in from the car. It looked to her like Ronny was researching all things metaphysical from black magic spells to the history and usage of the tarot to how to harness the power of the universe. He was also reading about astrology. None of the pages were dogeared and he had not written in any of the books, so there was no way to tell what had sparked his interest. There were, however, more books on the power of the tarot than anything else. His reading fell in line with that of the killer. She hoped that would be more than enough for the search warrant.

Kate closed the book and rested her head back against the wall. It was a long day and if the search was approved there was no telling how much longer they'd be there. As Kate closed her eyes, her cellphone buzzed against her hip. She sighed and sat forward, opening her eyes as she reached for her phone.

"Briggs," Kate said as she answered. She had been checking in with him on and off all evening.

"Kate, I hate to bother you. I'll get right to the point." He paused only briefly before delivering the blow. "We've had another homicide. A man and a woman in room 501 at the Fairmont Copley Plaza. Do you know when you're coming back? I've called Sharon's team and the medical examiner. I can handle it. I just didn't want to hold them off too long if you weren't going to be back for a while. I know you like to see the scene as it's found."

Kate cursed softly. They couldn't hold the scene for that long. They'd have to see this one from video and photographs. "We are waiting to see if we can get a warrant to search Ronny Pallazzo's house. I'm having Spade pull a few strings for us. Did anyone at the hotel see or hear anything?"

"It's fresh, Kate," Briggs explained as noise from the hotel echoed in the background. "I'm here now. There was a scream, which is what prompted a call to the front desk. They sent someone up to the room and found them dead with stab wounds to the chest. The Lovers tarot card was in the woman's hands. There was also a cupid doll sitting on the nightstand. I assume that's from the killer since there is a cupid with a bow and arrow in the imagery on the card."

Kate cursed a long streak under her breath. She was surprised the killer hadn't used a bow and arrow. However, Kate assumed that probably wasn't practical to get in and out of a hotel. "Do you know anything about the victims yet?"

"The man is Vince Macek. He's the one who rented the room. We found his wallet and he has an address out of Framingham. We also found the woman's wallet and her name is Meg Stiles and she's local to Boston. We don't have much other information on the couple right now." Briggs paused again and Kate knew he had something else to say. "We found a wedding ring in the man's pocket. Given they live in separate cities and he wasn't wearing the ring, I think it's safe to assume he was having an affair."

Kate rolled her eyes to the ceiling in frustration. That death notification would be harder than most. She swallowed hard having to think about telling a woman that not only was her husband murdered but he was murdered with his mistress. It was a double punch to the gut that no one needed. "Do you need us to come back?" Kate asked, hoping he said no. As much as she was needed at that scene, she still had hope that she'd hear from Spade soon.

Briggs started to say something then stopped and asked her to hold on. There was shouting in the background then Briggs groaned in frustration before barking orders. He got back on the phone. "There's been a shooting, Kate. One of the Boston MBTA drivers was shot."

"What?" Kate asked, not sure she was understanding him correctly. "While he was driving the train?"

"I don't know. I don't have all the details yet."

Kate grabbed the book about the tarot on the chair next to her. "Hold on, Briggs. This might be connected."

"Connected to this tarot murder case? How is that possible?" He continued to bark orders to his team while Kate looked up the information she needed.

When she got to the page, Kate jammed her index finger down on the image, knowing she was right. "If he just killed The Lovers, the next card in the tarot is The Chariot. We don't have horse-drawn carriages all over Boston. The T is the main method of transportation people use. It makes sense. I'm telling you when you go to the scene, there will be a card."

"Two in one night, Kate? This guy is imploding."

That was the perfect word for it. Kate knew she needed to get back to Boston soon. "If I don't hear back from Spade soon, we will be on our way. If we get the search warrant, we will work with the Salem Police Department to search the house and then get back to Boston as soon as we can. I can call agents from the Boston Field Office to assist if you need it until we are back."

"I appreciate it, but I have it. Another homicide detective is heading over to take a look at the shooting. I'll tell him if he finds a tarot card, to back off and wait until I can arrive."

Kate did not doubt that Briggs could handle it. "We'll be back as soon as we can." She thanked him for all of his hard work before hanging up. Kate had barely rested the phone in her lap when her phone rang again. She fumbled to grab it, catching it as it started to fall to the floor. She was tired, hungry, and her dexterity was slipping. It was Spade calling. She brought the phone to her ear.

Spade didn't waste any time, not even waiting for her to say hello

"You got the search warrant, Kate. Go tear that place apart."

The relief washed over her. "There's been two more murders, Spade. Three more dead." She should have said the subway driver was a possibility, but Kate knew it was connected. She detailed the other murders to him including the plan Briggs had. "We are going to search the house and then head over there as soon as possible. Can you send an agent up here to Salem to watch Evan and then bring him back to Boston when he's stable enough to be moved? I don't know his involvement, but there's more he's not telling us."

Spade agreed he'd do that. "Is there anything else you need, Kate?"

"Have you checked on Leo? We bailed on him when we came up here to Salem. With his head injury, I wanted him to rest." It was hard having to think about someone else on her team. She had gotten so used to it just being her and Declan for so long.

"Spoke to him about an hour ago and he's doing as well as can be expected. Hard start out of the gate for him. He'll be okay. He asked if there was anything he could be doing and I told him to rest."

They spoke for a few more minutes before Kate texted Declan that she'd need a cop from Salem Police Department to head over to the hospital so she could leave. She informed him they got the search warrant. She could sense his elation in his text.

An hour later, they were standing in Ronny's house with three detectives from the Salem Police Department and one of their crime scene techs to search the house, catalog evidence, and process the scene. Kate wanted anything that held the man's DNA as well as anything that might relate to the murders.

The house had five bedrooms, three baths, a family room, living room, formal dining room, and a kitchen. There was a lot of ground to cover. When they arrived, the neighbor next door – an older man Kate had spoken to earlier when they were asking around about Ronny – stepped out onto his porch and reminded them to check the hidden cubbies of the house. When Kate inquired what that meant, he told her that the homes had several secret areas behind the walls and under the floorboards. It had been built that way. Knowing that reaffirmed Kate's suspicion that the Langmores had left behind information about the Order of the Magicians. They thanked him for the information and got down to work.

The tip proved to be useful when a search of the home turned up nothing. There wasn't even much DNA left behind for the crime scene tech to sample. There were no dirty clothes or dishes. The fridge and freezer were bare as if he had emptied it never to return. Some shirts and pants were hanging in the closet and clothes were in the dresser drawers. They would fit a man about the same height and weight as Ronny had been described.

The home was sterile – it lacked family photographs, knick-knacks, and other personal items found in most well-lived homes. The walls had generic art of seascapes and colonial homes found around New England. The family room couch was the only piece of furniture that looked like it had much use. There was a desk in the far corner of the family room too that held a stack of books – a mix of history, fiction, and metaphysical. There was a faint outline in the dust where a laptop had once been and a surge protector plugged into the wall that didn't have anything running to it.

All five of the bedrooms had beds and furniture but only the master suite's comforter had the softness as though it had been laundered a few times.

What was lacking was any evidence that Ronny Pallazzo had committed the crimes. There was also nothing about his past. The crime scene tech had already lifted prints and was heading out when Kate decided to take the neighbor's advice and start feeling along the walls for any levers or springs to access a hidden space. It was the only thing they hadn't tried.

Declan focused on stomping on the floorboards and listening carefully for a sound differential to indicate an open space underneath. He was downstairs stomping away while Kate slipped into one of the upstairs spare bedrooms. She had already searched the master and two of the spare rooms.

She felt along the wall, knocking and feeling with her hands. Kate continued until she reached the antique white wooden armoire. It stood about six feet tall and three feet wide. It was massive in size. She opened the doors but found that it was empty. Kate tried to move it aside but it wouldn't budge. She had no idea how much it weighed but it was more than she could manage alone.

Kate stepped back from it, noticing a thin gouge in the hardwood floors. She traced the track of it with her finger…it led right to the armoire. Someone had been dragging it out and pushing it back so frequently that it left a groove in the flooring.

Kate called out and asked for help from one of the Salem detectives. She took one side and he took the other as they slid it out from the wall. As soon as the heavy piece of furniture was moved, Kate saw the break in the wainscoting. The detective felt along the break for a way to open it. Kate asked him to step back so she could try. She didn't think it would be as simple as to just pull it open. She ran her hand down the wall moving over the whole area until she felt something small and round at the palm of her hand, a button of sorts on the inside of the wall. She pressed her palm hard against that section and the doorway built right into the wall sprung open. As she reached for it to pull it open wider, she was knocked back by the smell.

It assaulted her nose and stung her eyes, making them water.

It was the putrid stench of death – remarkably, decidedly human death.

"Is it an animal?" the detective asked, putting a hand over his mouth and nose.

Kate shook her head. "It's human and fresh." She knew the smell of death. Had smelled it more times than she cared to recall. "I'm going in."

Kate clicked the flashlight app on her phone and aimed it into the darkened space.

She suppressed a gag as she stepped inside, shining the light in front of her. She took three steps to the right, trying to limit herself to short shallow breaths. The light shined on the floor and caught the bare feet of a man. Kate hesitated as her hand shook slightly and raised it to the man's unclothed legs, to his naked torso, finally resting on his face – his mouth hung open, eyes slightly parted. His skin was a discolored gray.

Kate steadied herself as she backed out of the space and screamed Declan's name.

CHAPTER 26

Kate stood next to Declan in the county morgue, trying not to lean on him for support. All she wanted was a scalding shower, her favorite pair of pajamas, and to crawl into bed to forget the entire day had happened.

It started with a trip to Salem and ended with four murders.

As soon as the medical examiner came to access and retrieve the body, it was determined that it was a homicide. Out in the open, under the lights of the room, the harsh reddish purple line across the victim's throat indicated he had not died by natural means. Why he was naked or how he had ended up in the room had yet to be determined.

Before the medical examiner could give any official statement, she had to perform the autopsy. Her initial findings were off the record and something she had shared only with law enforcement, but it was in no way intended to be an official statement. Dr. Mary Gibbs had stated that at least three times. She did not give them an official manner and method of death. It was merely an observation of the body.

Kate didn't need the official statement. What she needed was a positive identification of the corpse. She spun up countless theories after finding the body and her mind continued to reel. Declan had to talk her down and remind her that nothing was a fact until it was proven.

"I'm here," Ned said from behind them as he was ushered into the autopsy bay by one of the staff. "I still don't understand what's going on." He approached Kate on her left and looked over at her. "You found a body in Ronny's house? Is that what you said on the phone?" His face had paled from earlier and his whole body was rigid and tense.

Kate couldn't blame him. Having to come to the morgue to identify a body wasn't something she wished for anyone. She explained to Ned again about the search warrant and how she had found the man in the hidden room. "We have yet to see a photo of Ronny. There were none around the house and no one in town had his photo. Did you know he didn't even have a driver's license in the system?"

Ned pulled back in surprise. "I've seen his driver's license. How can that be?"

"Forged," Declan said on the other side of Kate. "You were right when you said Ronny Pallazzo probably wasn't his real name. We don't know where he came by the identification card, but it wasn't registered in the official Massachusetts Registry of Motor Vehicles. It means he didn't come by the license by legal means. A good forger created it for him."

"I don't understand why." Ned's confusion was evident on his face. "He was a strange man but to essentially be a ghost. It's so odd. He bought that house, surely to get a loan he'd need legal identification."

It was all questions Kate and Declan had earlier. There were still no answers.

Declan gestured toward the body with the sheet over it. "Because we have not seen any photos of Ronny, we have no idea if this is him. Whoever this man is doesn't have fingerprints in our database, which only means that whoever this is has never left fingerprints at a crime scene or been fingerprinted for any official reason."

Kate felt bad for Ned. She put her hand on his arm. "I know this isn't easy. You have had more contact with Ronny than anyone we have come across." She wasn't going to ask Lily or Christa to be here at the morgue with them. As difficult as it was, she felt like Ned could handle it, which is why it had been an easy decision to call him in.

Ned looked over at the body. "Let's get this over with. I don't like being in here. I don't know how anyone works in here all day." Realizing what he said, he apologized to Dr. Gibbs who told him she understood.

She approached the stretcher, tugged the white sheet down off the deceased man's face, and held it there for Ned to take a look. "Do you know this man?" she asked.

He leaned forward and studied the man's face for several beats. He breathed three heavy sighs and nodded his head. "That's Ronny all right. See the freckles on his cheeks and that scar on the side of his face, the one that runs along his jaw line. He told me he got that ice fishing in Alaska. What happened to him?"

"I won't know until I do the autopsy," Dr. Gibbs said as she covered him back up.

"Let's go outside and talk." Kate put her hand on his back and guided him out of the bay. Once they were in the hallway and the door was shut, she explained, "We were able to get a search warrant to search his house. We believed until we found his body that Ronny was our killer. With the information you provided and other sources, I was positive we had him. Then we found his body."

"I don't understand. Does that mean he can't be the killer?" Ned asked, as confused as Kate.

"There were two separate homicides connected to these cases in Boston this evening. They could not have been committed by Ronny. Yet, we know that someone using the name Ronny Pallazzo with this address threatened someone connected to the case. We haven't shown him a photo of the deceased yet, so we are uncertain if it was the same person or someone using Ronny's name." Kate paused for a moment, realizing she wasn't explaining things well. "To be honest with you, Ned, it's all rather confusing. Agent James and I are working to sort out the details."

Ned pointed to the double doors of the bay. "That's Ronny in there. I'm sure of that. There's no question in my mind it's him. I don't care about the license or the fingerprints. The man who has been living in Salem the past few years and calling himself Ronny Pallazzo is that man in there."

"We believe you," Kate assured him. She stared at the doors, frustrated by the turn the case had taken. "We appreciate you coming here and identifying him for us. Do you know if he had any family or anyone close to him we can notify?"

"He never mentioned any family specifically. I have no idea."

Kate turned back to him. "What about other people you've seen Ronny with? Did he ever introduce you to anyone he called a friend? Out of town guests, maybe?"

"No," Ned said with a shake of his head. "The only people I ever saw him talking to were other people I know in Salem. Do you think he was working with someone else?"

That had been Kate's initial thought. She was also wondering if Ronny confided in someone about the Order of the Magicians and they exploited him for the information. Then killed him before going on his killing spree. "When was the last time you saw Ronny?"

"About two weeks ago. As I said, it didn't seem strange to me that I hadn't seen him. He didn't come into the library on any kind of regular schedule."

Kate knew the body they found hadn't been deceased for two weeks. She'd be surprised if it was more than forty-eight hours. "You haven't seen him since that time? Not at the diner or grocery store?"

"Not at all. I wasn't by his house for any reason either. Did you find his truck?"

They hadn't found any vehicle in the garage and there was nothing found registered to that address since using his name was pointless. She explained that to Ned. "What did he drive?"

"He has a brand new black Ford truck." Ned provided her with a license plate number. "Could the plate be a forgery too?"

"It might be or it might be stolen." At this point, Kate had no idea what they were dealing with. They had a deceased man who was practically a ghost. He had no records coming back to the name he was using. His truck was gone as was any identification in his home. Kate admitted to him that there was still a lot left to explore. "We are in the early stages here of sorting things out. But we know for sure that if Ronny was involved in the murders, he wasn't doing it alone. He was working with a partner, who is still killing." What she didn't tell him was that they would be photographing the deceased and visiting Evan in the hospital to see if this was the man he had met.

"Is that common? Serial killers working with each other?"

"It's not common but it's not unheard of either. We don't know what we don't know," Kate said with a sigh. She thanked him again for coming down to the morgue. "If you think of anything else, let me know."

Ned promised her that he'd call her if he thought of anything. "Let me know if there should be any warnings going out to the community. I can help you connect with the mayor." He thanked Kate for all she was doing to help solve the case before he turned and left.

When Ned was gone, Kate slumped against the wall trying to make sense of the situation. She had been so sure that Ronny was the killer. Now they were even deeper in deaths and still didn't have a lead. Kate flinched at the hand on her back. "Sorry," she said, "you startled me."

"Were you hoping that wasn't Ronny in there?" Declan asked.

Kate wished he had pulled her into him and held her for a moment.

The way he might have in another case. He was cold and distant but she wasn't going to press the issue. "It would have made more sense to me."

"It doesn't make any sense, you're right about that. If Ronny isn't the killer, then why all the intrigue? Why the obsessions with mysticism? Why the fake name or forged license?"

They had far more questions than answers. Something occurred to Kate. She pulled out her phone, scrolling through the sketch of the man who had given River the letter to deliver to her house. She stared down at it, surprised by what she saw. "This man doesn't look anything like Ronny." Kate turned the phone to Declan. "I forgot we had the initial sketch of this man."

He took the phone from her and studied it. "Even if this guy was wearing a fake beard, it still doesn't look like Ronny. Neither did the man in the video, what we could see of him. They don't have the same facial shape, eyes, nose, body structure, or height. River said the guy he spoke to was over six foot and Ronny wasn't that tall."

Kate gestured toward the autopsy suite. "Are we done in there?"

"Dr. Gibbs said we can go and she will call us with her findings. Do you want to go to the hospital?" Declan seemed as tired as she felt.

"We need a place to stay tonight," Kate said. When he asked why, she explained, "I need some sleep and I want to go through Ronny's house one more time tomorrow before we take off in the morning."

Declan didn't like the idea of staying in Salem but he agreed. "Will Briggs be okay without us?"

"He's doing fine. Sharon is with him and they have been going through the evidence, not that there is much. The hotel is full of fingerprints and fibers. They aren't going to get much there. Briggs was able to figure out the location of the shooter from the angle and location of where the driver was shot. He found a note up on the rooftop congratulating him on finding the location."

Declan shook his head. "It was addressed to Briggs?"

Kate had forgotten to tell him the latest from Briggs. Briggs had called her on the way to the autopsy and she hadn't had a chance to share the information yet. "I wanted us to focus on one thing at a time. During the last call from Briggs, he told me the driver wasn't killed up close as originally thought. He told me about the note too."

"How did the tarot card end up with the driver?"

"Briggs thinks it must have been stashed there before the shooting. It was found on the floor of the driver's train compartment. He thought initially it had been on the body. It was on the floor though, so there's no telling how long it was in there."

Declan blew out a frustrated breath. "This guy…"

"I know," Kate said, reaching for his hand. "He was watching us and probably saw us leave town or he suspected we were out of town when we didn't show up to the hotel homicide."

"Either way I don't like that he knew it would be Briggs who found his shooting location. He's watching us too closely."

"He saw Briggs on the news with you. He knew his name. If he didn't see us at the hotel, then maybe he suspected we were chasing down a lead. It didn't surprise me," Kate said matter-of-factly. She wasn't sure if that was wholly the truth. When she heard the news from Briggs, it had been like another shot to the gut. After thinking about it, nothing was really surprising in the case. "Let's get to the hospital. That's the only way we are going to know if Ronny was involved directly in this case or not."

As Kate started to head down the hall, Declan reached for her. "Is there any part of you that wonders if Evan could have killed Ronny?"

Kate stopped in the middle of the hall. "I don't know, Declan. I've thought about it. If he did it was more than a week ago. Why would he come back?"

"What if he was looking for something that ties the cases to him?"

Declan moved around in front of her. "I didn't want to say this earlier because I have no proof, but hear me out."

"Say whatever you need to say."

"The killer sent the first communication to the FBI office in D.C. It was only after you visited Cardinal O'Connor and met Evan that the next one came to your house. What if he followed you home, Kate? He could be working with someone and following you. Then gave your address to the other guy who approached River and who committed the murders tonight. We know Evan didn't commit those. We have no proof that he didn't kill Ronny. The guy is involved somehow – I know he is, injured or not."

The timing was so fast that Kate hadn't stopped to consider that. "I wasn't home from the Archdiocese more than an hour when the second communication came."

"We have to consider it a possibility." Declan stared down at her, his gaze fixed on hers. "I don't trust him. If he was so scared of this killer, why come here to the man's home to confront him when he's injured? I didn't buy the story when he said it. I'm even more suspicious of him now that Ronny is dead."

"Okay," she said agreeing with him. It's not that Kate hadn't considered what he was saying. She hadn't drawn any conclusions.

"There's one more thing," Declan continued. "If Ronny visited Evan ahead of time and threatened him, then why not finish him off when he had the chance? If Ronny was the killer then why not end it there? He left Evan alive to identify him later. That doesn't seem like something this killer would do."

Kate bit the inside of her cheek and breathed through her nose, considering that. Declan was right – it was counterintuitive to everything the killer was doing.

Everyone who could identify him was dead.

CHAPTER 27

"Are you sure?" Kate asked Evan after showing him the autopsy photo of Ronny. "This man is deceased. His coloring is off. You're going to have to look past all of that. I know you said the man you spoke to had a beard and this man has no facial hair. Look again for me and take your time."

Evan lowered his head to the phone again. He took probably thirty seconds of staring at the photo and raised his eyes to Kate. "I'm telling you this isn't Ronny Pallazzo or at least the man who came to see me who called himself by that name." He handed the phone back to Kate. "It's not him. The man who came to me had a bigger head. He was broad and big and scary. His arms were tattooed. That guy doesn't look like he could scare a five-year-old. He might be creepy but he isn't scary."

Kate had no idea the distinction but she accepted Evan's answer. She scrolled to the sketch and showed that to him. "What about this guy?"

Evan took the phone back and barely even glanced at that photo. "That's him! That's the man who came to see me. That's who called himself Ronny." He raised his chin. "Are you telling me that the real Ronny Pallazzo is dead? There was a dead guy in that house when I was in there?" His pale skin turned a ghostly white.

Declan moved from the side of the room to Kate's side. "Help me understand why after this man attacked you and killed Cardinal O'Connor you'd feel safe enough to come up here? You said you left Boston because you didn't feel safe. Yet, we found you standing in his living room. That doesn't make a whole lot of sense to me. It didn't the first time you told us and now that I'm repeating it, it's frankly unbelievable."

Evan lowered his eyes to his hands. He handed Kate's phone back without looking at her. He was stalling for time. He raised his shoulders in a shrug. "I can't explain it any better than I explained it before. I assumed the killer was staying in Boston. He's been killing there so I figured he'd remain there. I thought this was my chance to come to Salem and find some evidence to stop him."

"Why did he let you live?" Declan pressed.

"I can't answer that. Maybe he thought I'd bleed out before help arrived."

"No," Kate said. "This killer is highly skilled at murder. He knew that you wouldn't die based on how he stabbed you. If he wanted you dead, you'd be dead."

"That's why I wanted more information," Evan admitted. He sat back on the bed and stared at them. "I don't know what else to tell you. I've told you everything I know. As soon as I got that communication that night, Cardinal O'Connor sent me to find you. I couldn't have been killing him while I was coming to get you. I can't be in two places at once."

"That's convenient," Declan said with a sneer. "Something you're telling us isn't adding up for me."

Evan closed his eyes and sniffed. "I don't know what to say." He opened his eyes and looked right at Declan, not shying away from eye contact. "Do you believe that I'd kill Cardinal O'Connor? I worked for him for years. He was a mentor to me." A tear formed in Evan's eye. He wiped it with the back of his hand. "I was closer to him than my father. He meant everything to me. I wish I could turn back time and not have left Cardinal O'Connor alone. If I had known, I wouldn't have done it. I'd have fought the guy if I could have. I had nothing to do with his murder or any murder for that matter. Yes, I handed over the directory of priests in the diocese. If that is a crime, then arrest me. Take me in. If not, leave me alone. I'm tired and in pain and I don't know anything else."

Kate was worried Evan might call the doctor and they'd be asked to leave. "Get some sleep, Evan. There's an FBI agent outside your door, making sure you're safe." *And making sure you don't take off again.*

It wasn't until they were out of the hospital that Declan said with anger searing his voice, "I don't believe him."

Kate wasn't sure if she believed Evan or not. More debating wasn't going to solve it. "We need some rest and food." Her body was shutting down and she needed to refuel.

An hour later, they were camped out at a hotel outside of the city. It was the only one in a twenty-mile radius that had any rooms available. Given the popularity of Salem in October and the many ongoing events happening, everything from cheap motels to nicer hotels and bed & breakfasts was at full capacity. Even if they weren't going to search Ronny's house again tomorrow, neither of them was in any shape to drive back to Boston.

Kate had taken a hot shower and was curled up on the bed scrolling through social media on her phone. She had a few dummy accounts so she could look.

"Burgers and fries are our only option this late," Declan said as he entered the room. He was holding the handle of a large brown bag that looked big enough to hold dinner for several people.

"I don't care what it is. I'm starving. It looks like you have enough to feed several people," Kate said as she slid off the bed and walked over to him. She took the bag from him and set it down on the desk.

There were two food containers and then two milkshakes wedged between them. She leaned up on her tiptoes and kissed him. "How did you know I wanted a chocolate milkshake?"

"You always do when you're stressed." Declan pulled her into an embrace. "I'm so sorry I've been such a jerk. I know I've been cold to you. I don't know what's wrong with me today."

Kate didn't know what was wrong with him either, but it felt too good to be held to argue. She stood there with him until he released her. He pulled his shirt over his head and tossed it to the floor, heading to the bathroom. "Your food will get cold," she called after him.

Declan gestured to the microwave. "I can reheat it. I need to shower. You start eating without me."

Kate knew better than to try to convince him otherwise. As much as she wanted the milkshake, Declan wanted the shower. She pulled her food out and sat down on the small sofa in the corner of the room. She grabbed the remote and flipped through the channels looking for the news. Finally, she settled on a national news channel as a panel of "experts" discussed the cases in Boston. There were all kinds of wild speculation about what was happening and the failings of the FBI. Not one of them had any real insider information. Briggs told Kate he had refused the interview request and so had Spade for them. The last thing the case needed was more national attention.

Kate dug into her food while processing the events of the day. Even after seeing him again tonight, Kate didn't know how Evan factored into it all. She was more on the fence about him than Declan. She had never quite seen him take a dislike to someone so quickly and forcefully, and she knew he wasn't going to let it go.

What Kate focused on was Ronny. He was either involved initially and the killer bumped him off or he had become friendly with someone who had used him and then killed him.

Used him for what was Kate's question.

There was no telling what Ronny found in the house about the Order of the Magicians. Kate couldn't help but feel that it was a factor in the case. Whatever Ronny had found, and Kate believed it was something, led him to research more. He had a knowledge base that fit the killer. He had access to Christa and learned about her uncle in Boston. All of it added up to Ronny being the killer – and yet he wasn't the man who had threatened Evan and he wasn't the one who had killed the couple in the hotel and the subway driver.

They still didn't know Ronny's real identity.

Kate continued eating while she focused on that factor. It was going to be a challenge to figure out who he was and why he was living in Salem under a false identity. As Kate sat there processing, she got an idea and reached for her phone. It was late but Spade would be up.

"Everything okay, Kate?" Spade asked as he answered.

"I want to send you the prints for Ronny Pallazzo. He's not coming up in the database and his license is a forgery – a good forgery based on those who have seen it. He even got a mortgage with it. I don't know too many people that pull that off. I know that you have access to resources that we don't. Could you ask around and see if he's in the system someplace?"

"What do you think?"

"I don't know exactly. CIA? NSA? Witness protection? He's living here and doesn't have a job. He's told people he comes from money and has investments. He was able to get a mortgage for a rather large historic home and renovated it completely. He's a bit of an enigma and now he's dead, murdered in his home. He can't be our killer or at least not the lone killer."

"I can explore it," Spade said with some hesitation. "You know I might not be able to tell you much, provided what I find."

Kate knew her security clearances only went so far. "Spade, the man is dead. If he has family out there or friends, someone should know he's dead. If he's involved in this case, then learning his real identity might help us. I know there are rules to this kind of thing. I'm not asking anyone to destroy their career to get me information, but he's deceased now and we have a serial killer terrorizing Boston, there's got to be some wiggle room."

"Let me see what I can find." Spade paused before he hung up. "You sound tired, Kate. I know these murders are coming at you fast and there are a lot of unanswered questions. There's not much you can do tonight. Get some rest."

Kate assured him that she would.

"Who are you talking to so late?" Declan asked as he came out of the bathroom wearing a loose pair of sleeping shorts. He was towel-drying his hair and eyeing her.

Kate explained she had called Spade to ask about running his prints. "You know he has access to every agency. Spade should have access to the U.S. Marshals Service to see if they have someone in the program. I would assume it would have an FBI case."

Declan grabbed his food from the desk, leaving his towel on the back of the chair to dry, and joined Kate on the couch. "That's a good idea," he said as he opened his food, plucked a handful of fries, and put it in his mouth. "Still hot enough." He looked over at her. "Everything okay?"

"Okay enough. Spade didn't ask about you tonight. He told me to get some sleep. I think he might know about us."

Declan didn't seem bothered by that. He continued to eat. "Why do you think that?"

"I think he assumes we are always together."

"We were always together before we were *together*, Kate. I'm sure Spade questioned it long ago. I know everyone around me did."

"Even your mom?" Kate wasn't sure how she felt about that.

"Especially my mom." He leaned back and saw the worried look on her face. "Relax, Katie. My mother always liked you more than my ex anyway."

"I'm worried because Spade could separate us."

"We'll deny it till the end. Besides, I don't think anyone wants to work with me."

"You've been better," Kate said, leaning her head on him. Since being with him, she'd allowed herself to explore a softer more vulnerable side to herself. Kate wasn't sure she liked it, but she was trying to lean into it. "Tell me why you think Evan is involved." She knew she shouldn't open this can of worms this late.

"Granted his story made more sense than it did earlier." Declan finished off his food and sat back on the couch with his milkshake. He took a sip. "There's something squirrely about him. That's all I have, Kate. I have no evidence of anything. I probably shouldn't be pushing so hard. It just makes no sense to me that he'd come up here looking for the man who stabbed him."

"He said he was looking for evidence. He thought his family was still at risk." The more Kate focused on Evan, repeating his words, the less it made sense to her. Not that Declan was convincing her. "I don't think he had anything to do with Cardinal O'Connor's murder. I truly believe he didn't know that was going to happen."

"That I agree with. It might have been exactly what he said. He was helping someone who was threatening his family. Then when he could get out of Boston to try to find evidence, that's what he did. He seemed eager to help you protect Cardinal O'Connor."

Kate thought back on that conversation. Evan knew then what the killer was doing. He had direct contact with him and hadn't told her. He had a real opportunity to help and didn't.

Declan set his milkshake down on the table. "Can we stop talking about work now?"

"Sure, we should go to sleep. It's an early morning." Kate yawned for good measure. She watched his face fall. Normally, she would have known what the look meant. After today though, she wasn't sure. She raised an eyebrow in a question.

"I know I've been off today and I apologize. I thought I'd make it up to you. We'll sleep after some stress relief." As if reinforcing his words, he leaned into her and kissed her. When she didn't resist, he scooped her up and she allowed herself to be carried to bed, grateful for a moment to escape the horror to come.

CHAPTER 28

The next morning Kate and Declan rose earlier than the sun and went for breakfast at the diner where Christa worked. The young woman wasn't working, but the food was good and the service excellent. Kate thought they'd grab a quick bite to eat and some coffee before searching Ronny's house one last time.

When an older man slid into the booth next to Kate, it took them both by surprise. "I think I know something you need to know," he said quietly.

Kate caught Declan's gaze as his hand lowered to his gun. She didn't think that was necessary. She slid over in the booth against the window and introduced herself and Declan.

"I know who you are," he said with his eyes wide. He gestured toward the other patrons in the diner. "The whole town knows who you are and why you are here."

"What's your name?" Declan asked, relaxing his posture.

"Martin Stevens. I live three houses away from Ronny. We didn't get a chance to speak yesterday when you came by. You spoke to my wife and she didn't know anything."

Kate recalled meeting a Mrs. Stevens. She couldn't recall the woman's first name, but she had an image of a petite woman with short gray hair and a pleasant smile. "You said you know something we need to know."

"I heard that you've been asking around about him, wondering if he could be the serial killer in Boston. Then you found him dead inside his house."

"That's correct." Kate knew the community was small and people talked. "What is it you think we should know?"

Martin looked around to see if anyone was paying attention to them. When he realized everyone was focused on themselves, he leaned in and lowered his voice. "There's been a guy coming and going from Ronny's house late at night. He looks like one of the fishermen from the docks, a rough-looking guy. I was out walking my dog one night and Ronny looked like he was up to something, so I followed him down to the docks."

"That was brave of you," Kate said, looking at the older man. He had a tuft of white hair and a face weathered by the sun. Now that she was looking at him, she noticed the muscle in his forearms and biceps. He might have been well into his seventies but he was strong and had kept himself in good shape. "What did you see down on the dock?"

"Ronny went to the man's boat. They were standing on the back of it talking for quite a while. I couldn't hear what they were saying. I thought maybe he was buying drugs or something like that. I didn't see them exchange anything. Then all of a sudden the man shouts at Ronny and tells him he's the one in control of *this thing* and that Ronny would do what he was told to do. That Ronny better bring him the information or he was going to pin the whole thing on him. He threatened to kill Ronny if he didn't do what he was told." Martin shivered. "The whole thing was quite unsettling. A couple of days after that, another man showed up at the house wearing nice dress pants and a shirt tucked in. He had a beard and looked pulled together. There was something familiar about him – something about the way he walked, a bit of a swagger. That's when I realized it was the same man. He had cleaned himself up."

"Why do you think this relates to the murders?" Kate asked.

"I'm getting to that," Martin said with an air of frustration for being rushed. "Ronny let him into the house and they were arguing. I could hear it down the block. Then the man came out with what looked like a metal pole with spikes on the top of it."

"A mace?" Kate said, letting the word slip out of her mouth. She reached for her phone and pulled up a photo of a mace and showed it to Martin. "Is that similar to what you saw?"

He lowered his head to look at the image. "That's nearly identical to what I saw. The one I saw had kind of a crown shape at the top that flared out on the sides and the pointed end was at the very top above that."

Kate gave Declan a knowing look. Martin was explaining the weapon that had been used to kill Cardinal O'Connor. There were pattern marks like a crown on his skin. "You saw this other man leave with the mace?"

"If that's what you call it, yes. That's what I saw."

"Have you ever seen this man at Ronny's house again?"

Martin rested his palms flat on the table. "That's why I'm here. So the day after Ronny gave that man the weapon, they left together in Ronny's truck. I don't know where he was going but he took off out of here going pretty fast. Then they returned. But here's the catch. The two of them went into the house together and only that man came out. Ronny wasn't with him and I haven't seen him since."

Kate had to slow him down because he was talking so fast and she wasn't sure she fully understood. "Ronny and this man showed up to the house together?"

Martin nodded. "Ronny was driving and the other guy was in the passenger seat. They went into the house together. Then the other guy came out a few hours later and left in Ronny's truck, which I thought was weird. I told my wife and she told me to mind my own business."

He made a shooing gesture with his hand. "She's always telling me to mind my own business. Sometimes you have to pay attention to what's going on around you."

Declan asked, "You said you hadn't seen *him* again? The man or Ronny?"

"Well, either of them. I had a kind of weird feeling about it, so after the man I didn't know left, I went to check on Ronny. He didn't answer the door. I figured he wasn't up for talking to people, so I thought I'd give him a couple of days. It's not like he's a friendly neighbor. We don't chat over coffee or anything. Still, something seemed weird. The most neighborly thing I could do was make sure he was okay. No answer though."

"You didn't check again?" Kate asked.

Martin shook his head. "I didn't have time. I had to go watch my grandkids out of town. I got back late last night. That's when my wife told me you were by. You were hard to track down this morning. I finally heard from someone that you were having breakfast at the diner." Martin sighed deeply and heavily. "I think that man killed Ronny."

It was as promising a lead as they had had. Kate asked, "Do you know anything about him?"

He pulled a slip of paper from his pocket, surprising them both. "His name is August Wynn. Most of the guys down at the dock call him Auggie. They said he's pretending to be a lobsterman, got a commercial license and everything. But he's a rich kid from the Wynn family fortune. He's not out there much. He lives in a big house up in Rockport on the shore."

Kate knew Rockport was about thirty minutes or so north of Salem. "Does he have a place where he lives locally or does he commute in?"

"I don't know," Martin said, explaining that the other fishermen he spoke to at the docks didn't know August well. "He's a guy who keeps to himself. A few of them said he had a wicked temper and most stayed clear of him. They only found out about the house in Rockport in passing. I don't know where exactly it is. I'm sure the guys at the dock would talk to you. They didn't hold back with me and I'm a nobody. If the FBI heads over there, surely you'll get more information."

"We appreciate you tracking us down with this information," Declan said, catching Kate's eye. This was the most promising information they had to date. She saw the relief on his face that they had stuck around.

Declan pulled out his phone and showed Martin a photo of Evan. "Did you ever see this guy with Ronny or the other man?"

Martin leaned on the table to get a better look. "No, I don't know who that guy is. Never saw him around Salem or with Ronny. He doesn't spend much time with too many people. I see him talking to the women here at the diner. I think he eats dinner here most nights. A lot of people do. I've seen him with Ned at the library and then that new guy. As I said, he's not the most friendly neighbor. I'd never expect something like this to happen."

Most people didn't. Kate turned to him. "Is there anything else you think we should know?"

"I don't have anything else. My wife didn't even want me to be here. Mind your own business, Marty, she said to me this morning," he mimicked her tone. "Always mind your own business. You can't do that in a community, especially not when you care about what's going on."

Kate tried to hold back a smile. She could see Martin's wife giving him that lecture. While she was friendly with Kate and Declan, she didn't talk to them any longer than she had to. "You tell your wife we appreciate your help."

Martin gave a curt nod of his head. "I'm glad to help. We need more people in the community willing to help. I know I probably shouldn't ask, but do you think Ronny was involved in the murders?"

"We don't know," Kate answered honestly. "Do you think he'd be capable of something like that?"

"I don't know. He was a weird guy. I don't know that I could see him being a crazed killer. From what I saw on the news, the person who is doing this has to be truly diabolical. I'm not sure Ronny fits that description. He might have gotten himself caught up in something that he couldn't escape from." Martin sat back against the booth. "I kind of feel bad for the guy. He never talked about family and didn't seem to have any real friends. He was isolated. His personality didn't help with that either. It's too bad. We are a good community here and he could have made new friends easily." Martin slid out of the booth and wished them luck. Kate got his phone number before he left.

When he was gone, Declan asked, "What did you think about that?"

"I think we need to head to the docks before we search Ronny's house again." Kate knew they might even need to drive up to Rockport too if they could find an address for August Wynn.

Declan pointed to her half-eaten food. "Eat up before we go. Who knows when you'll get the chance again today."

While Kate ate, she did a quick background search for August Wynn and found a photo of a clean-shaven man who had donated a large sum of money to the Boston Children's Hospital. He had the same height and build as the killer. His facial features were not too dissimilar to the sketch either. "Look at this, Declan." Kate handed him her phone. "That's August Wynn. The article says his family is involved in the shipping industry and has business here and abroad. His family has donated millions to charities, including this million-dollar donation to Boston Children's Hospital. He went to Yale." The man fit the profile of the killer in many ways. Kate knew she couldn't get ahead of herself. All they had was a statement from Martin. It was enough to explore it.

Located on the North Shore, Salem Harbor was home to both commercial and recreation vessels. It didn't take Kate and Declan long to find their way over to the commercial fishermen, most of whom had already left for a hard day of work.

They spoke to the few who were around and learned that the information Martin had provided was accurate. Two of the men remembered Ronny coming down to the docks twice to speak to August. No one overheard the conversations. One of them said it seemed tense but no blows were exchanged.

When the matter turned to August Wynn, no one had a nice word to say. Pompous. Arrogant. Entitled. Violent. Those were the words that came up more than once. The biggest consensus was that the men didn't know why August Wynn even had a commercial fishing license. He was rarely on his boat, hardly ever caught a lobster, and wasn't running a commercial fishing business.

They knew the Wynn family was involved in global shipping and assumed Auggie had been able to get the license because his family pulled some strings. One of the men at the dock had called Auggie, an *overgrown entitled kid with too much money, not enough sense, and red-hot rage running through his blood.*

Kate had never heard a more apt description of the killer. When asked if the men thought Auggie could be the one terrorizing Boston, no one said no. They all thought not only was he capable but it was probable.

The biggest challenge they had now was that no one had seen Auggie in weeks. He had taken his boat and left the harbor for Rockport. He didn't tell anyone why he was leaving or when he'd be back.

The timing matched up.

No one at the docks had seen Auggie since the murders in Boston had started.

CHAPTER 29

Declan drove them north to Rockport. Kate had found an address for an August Wynn Sr. in the database. She assumed correctly he was Auggie's father. Auggie, who had turned forty-seven over the summer, was his only son and the youngest of his four children. The father was seventy-five.

From what Kate could find, Auggie was a screw-up in every way. While he had attended Yale, he failed out his junior year and then went to work for the family company. That employment stopped a few years in and that's when records for him ran cold. Kate had no idea what Auggie was doing for work, other than living off his family's money. She had found an article about the "Wayward Wynn" as he'd been called in the press. He'd shown up on gossip websites as a party boy in Boston, running the circuit of bars and parties, flirting with the right women, building connections with powerful and wealthy men.

The photos of him had run the gamut of clean-shaven and professional to fully bearded and menacing. He had a tattoo sleeve on his right arm and several additional tattoos on his legs. There had been rumors about drug and alcohol addiction. The latest article indicated that the senior Wynn had chosen his eldest daughter and her husband to take over the company when he retired.

That was nearly seven months ago now.

That could be the trigger that had set Auggie off on the rampage.

She looked over at Declan while he drove. "He's been like a pot ready to boil over for a while. I haven't found the reason for all of the rage and bad behavior. I don't know if it's a childhood issue or if he's just a bad seed. He's been in trouble from day one. His father didn't choose him to run the company. There's a quote here from Auggie saying his father was a terrible person when a reporter asked him how he felt about his sister taking over the company."

Declan whipped his head around to look at Kate. "He told a reporter his father is a terrible person?"

"Yep," Kate said barely believing it herself. "Auggie has never held back when it comes to the news. He outed the youngest of his sisters as a lesbian and told the world his other sister was pregnant before she got married. I'm not sure if these were things the family was trying to keep out of the press, but there was no comment on either from August Sr. Their mother passed away when Auggie was a kid. That might have been the cause of some of this, but it sounds to me like he's always had issues with Auggie."

"Where are you getting this information?"

"A mix of traditional news sites and gossip sites. I'm taking the latter with a grain of salt but it seems like solid information. The photos are of Auggie around Boston playing it up for the camera. August, the father, has given several interviews given he's the CEO of a global shipping empire."

Through the articles and interviews August had given, Kate came to learn the Wynn family corporation was more than a shipping business. They were an empire that had their reach across the globe. They were the name behind many of the more common shipping companies. It all tied back to Wynn Global, Inc. It was a business that August's great-great-grandfather had started that had been passed down through the generations. Auggie would be the only son who'd not inherit the company from his father.

Kate's research was interrupted by a phone call. An unknown number flashed across her screen. She hesitated to answer it but it was a Boston number.

"Agent Kate Walsh," she said as she answered.

"Kate, it's Carmen. I want an update on the case."

Kate switched the call to Bluetooth so Declan could participate. She explained to Carmen how things had gone in Salem. "We have a promising lead. I don't know what we are going to find in Rockport, but it's the most promising we've had."

"Good," Carmen said with an edge in her voice. "I have the media breathing down my neck here, wanting to know what's going on. Det. Briggs has been doing a good job running the two newest investigations. I'm not saying people didn't care when it was the Davenports or Kirk Eagen. The city is boiling over. And you know who's next, right?"

Kate had been trying not to think about it. The Justice card. She and her colleagues were at risk. She wondered if there was some subconscious desire to remain out of the area for her self-preservation. Kate pushed the thought aside. She had never been that cowardly and didn't think she was starting to be now. "Do you have added security? I can send an FBI agent over if you'd like."

Carmen rejected the offer. "I have security. I'm more concerned about Judge Keaton Thomas and his colleagues. I've told them that they need more security at the court and their homes. I don't know if they are taking me seriously or not." She sighed into the phone and cursed. "Listen, Kate, I had hoped you would have caught this guy by now. I didn't want to get to this place. I certainly never thought it would happen this quickly."

Kate had been surprised at the fast pace of the case too. She didn't have an answer for Carmen. At least, not one that would appease her. "I assure you we are doing the best we can. It was worth the trip to

Salem. I think we are getting closer."

"When will you be back?"

"As soon as we can," Kate assured her. "Briggs has the case under control. He's running down leads and Sharon from the FBI lab is heading up all the crime scene evidence. Even though we are out of the city, I assure you, it's under control."

"I assume Declan is with you?"

Kate's back tightened at his name coming out of her mouth so casually. "Yes, he's right here on speakerphone. We are together working the case."

"I see. I was hoping he might swing by my office for a moment. I'd like to speak to him."

Declan raised his eyebrows and stared over at Kate. He looked afraid to speak. "Ah…" he started and stopped.

"Right," Carmen said frustrated. "This isn't the time or place for the conversation. When you're back, Declan, please come to my office." She paused and added forcefully, "Alone." Then the phone clicked and the line went dead.

"What?" Declan turned to Kate with his mouth open. He gripped the steering wheel tighter. "What was all that about? I don't want to go see her alone. She scares me."

Kate felt like Carmen was playing chicken with them, forcing her to admit that she and Declan were more than work partners. "I don't think we should worry about that now."

"I'm worried about it. I feel like she's going to get me alone and wrap me up in her spider web."

Even though Kate's mind was fully focused on the case, she couldn't help but smile. "You're acting like a child. She expressed interest in you and you simply turned her down." Kate side-eyed him. "If that's what you want."

"Of course, that's what I want. I wouldn't date her even if you and I weren't together." He could see that Kate still wasn't convinced. "Katie, she's a gorgeous woman. There's no denying that and she's rich and powerful."

"I'm not hearing a downside."

"She's terrifying!" Declan looked over at her and swerved the SUV at the same time. He focused back on the road. There was a hint of a smile on his lips when he explained, "You at least pretend to give me some control in the relationship. I'd be like her lapdog if we ever were to be together. She'll have my balls in her purse in five seconds flat. You're good at pretending I have a say in things."

Kate turned her head to look at him. "You have a say in things. I'm not pretending." She had to admit that being a strong woman who worked with men most of her career, she could run over most men if she wasn't careful. She assumed that had been the problem for most of her dating life. It was hard not to take the reins in her private life when she had to do that so often at work. She wasn't going to submit in a relationship the way some women might. Kate aimed for partnership and thought she had been doing it well…until now. "You know I'm not really in control, Declan. Right? You have a say."

Declan slowed to get off at an exit. "Don't overthink this. I like us exactly as we are."

It didn't answer the question, but it would have to suffice for now. Kate read him directions to the address that she had found in the database. She didn't know what they'd encounter when they arrived. The Wynn family had many homes. The family was originally from Boston and that's where the headquarters of the business were located. The Wynn siblings had scattered across New England. Kate wasn't sure where the senior August Wynn resided now. She didn't know if anyone would be in the home in Rockport or if they'd encounter Auggie there.

If he was the killer, Kate assumed he'd be back in Boston plotting his next murder.

They drove down one narrow lane after another, taking a left and then two rights. The final turn took them by a yellow sign that told them there was no exit. The next sign was marked private property and to turn around. Declan kept driving until he reached a tall wrought-iron gate and gatehouse.

A man with a thick neck and menacing scowl stepped out as they approached. Before they even came to a stop, the man gestured for them to turn around. "You should have seen the sign. You don't belong down here. It's private property."

Declan applied the brake and stopped the car next to the man. He put down the window and flashed his badge as he introduced them. "We are here to see August Wynn, Jr. This is a police matter."

The man bent down to the window. "You have an appointment or a warrant?"

"No," Declan said, his tone gearing up for a fight. "It's urgent that we speak to him. We can come back with a warrant if needed. Given the family's reputation, we were trying to keep this out of the court record, if you catch my meaning."

The man righted himself. "Let me make a call." He went back inside his gatehouse and picked up a black phone attached to the wall. He turned his back to them so Declan and Kate couldn't hear what he was saying. When he hung up, he opened the gate and waved them forward. "You can park in the circular drive at the top of the hill. August Wynn Sr. will meet you at the front door."

"That was an effective lie," Kate said, grateful that he had thought quickly on his feet. "I assume since we are meeting with the senior Wynn that Auggie isn't here."

Declan drove the car up the winding hill where heavy tree cover paved the way to the largest Victorian home Kate had ever seen. There was an expansive green lawn and sea views. Declan followed the road to the driveway and parked just past the door of the home.

"Are you ready for anything?" Declan asked as he unclasped his gun holster. "As we were driving up, I had a moment of concern that we shouldn't have come alone. If Auggie is in there and he is the killer, we might have a fight on our hands."

Kate looked up at the house. "I don't think he's here. If I had to guess, his father has no idea what he's done, if he is involved." She unclasped her gun holster for good measure but opened the SUV door with confidence that they would be fine. As her feet crunched the stone drive, the front door of the home opened.

A man with a full head of white hair, round glasses, and a thick gray cardigan walked out into the fall sunlight. He took a few steps toward the car and waited until Declan was fully out and standing next to Kate. She started to introduce herself but the man stopped her.

He told them he was August Wynn Sr. Then pointed to Declan. "I know who he is. Agent Declan James. I've seen the news. You're here about Auggie." The man pulled his cardigan around him tighter even though there wasn't much of a chill in the air. "What has he done?" His face registered resignation as if he knew his son had done something truly terrible this time – something he could never come back from and that might take down the whole family.

Kate had a moment of empathy for him. She extended her hand. "I'm Agent Kate Walsh. To be perfectly honest with you, sir, we don't know what Auggie has done. We got a lead on some information in Salem that we are following up on and we were hoping to speak to him. Is he home?"

"No. Please come in and we can talk." August didn't wait for them to respond. He turned around and walked back into the home and called out for a woman named Betty to bring some refreshments into his study. "It's this way, follow me," he said as Kate and Declan entered.

They followed him through the foyer across the front of the home and down a short hall to his study. The room had a masculine feel with leather furniture and dark accessories. There were tall windows that offered a perfect view of the ocean.

August stood in the middle of the room. "I work in here. Lately, I've been sitting staring out the window wondering where exactly I went wrong with Auggie. He's been so troubled for so long and nothing I do seems to work. I'm sure you've read in the news that I didn't leave the company to him. What could I do? He'd destroy something that took generations to build. Financially, he'll be taken care of for the rest of his life. I had to break tradition and give the company to his sister. Not only is she vastly more qualified, but she's also more responsible." He gestured for them to sit on the couch and he took a chair across from them.

Kate wasn't sure how much of her hand she wanted to show. "You said Auggie isn't here. When was the last time you saw him?"

"A few weeks ago, he brought that stupid junker of a boat back. The one he uses to pretend he's a fisherman. That was one of the things I bought to support him. I thought then he'd get his life together if he found a passion." August tsked and shook his head in disgust. "It was a hobby, something to have."

Kate started to ask another question but August stopped her. He leaned forward. "Let's skip all of this. When I asked you what Auggie has done, I think I know. You think Auggie is the killer terrorizing Boston, and I think you're right."

Kate and Declan sat too stunned to speak.

CHAPTER 30

"Excuse me," Kate said not sure she had heard him correctly. The look of confusion on Declan's face told her he was feeling the same. "I'm not sure I heard that right. You believe Auggie is the killer terrorizing Boston."

"That's correct," August said evenly as he crossed his legs. He seemed far too calm for the information he shared.

Kate wanted to keep him talking. "Take all the time you need to explain."

August took a deep breath, his chest rising then falling. "There are things I know that once you hear, you'll believe he's guilty too. I've not been able to reach him. He's been 'off the grid' as they say since a week before the first murder."

Declan appreciated his directness. "We believe Auggie might be involved in this case. Agent Walsh was serious when she said we don't know the details or how exactly he's involved. Just that it's probable he is. Our understanding is that he was seen with a man named Ronny Pallazzo in Salem. We have a witness who saw Auggie arrive with Ronny at his house and then leave with Ronny's truck. Ronny was found murdered."

Kate pulled out her phone and brought up the autopsy photo of the man's face. "Have you ever seen this man with Auggie?"

August stood and met Kate in the middle of the room. He winced when he looked at the photo and handed it quickly back to her. "I've never seen him before. That doesn't necessarily mean anything. He doesn't bring people back here. While he does technically live here, he's gone more than he's home." August closed his eyes and turned away from them. "I have failed my family in many ways."

"What about relationships with women?" Declan asked, urging the man to stay with them.

August turned to face them again. "He's never shared that part of his life with me." He sat back down in the chair and Kate returned to the couch with Declan following her.

August gestured toward the phone. "You believe Auggie killed that man?"

Kate gave him the most honest answer she had. "We don't know. Auggie's behavior with him is certainly suspect. From what we know from the witness, Auggie was the last person seen with Ronny when he was alive. Do you believe your son is capable of killing someone?"

August didn't even need to consider the question. "Yes, unfortunately. I believe Auggie is capable of horrible things." The man took three shallow breaths and then looked right at Kate. "I tried to get Auggie help when he was young. As you probably know, his mother passed away when he was fourteen. My wife had been sick with cancer for a while." Kate offered him sympathy for the loss when he held up his hand to stop her. "I don't believe that's how she passed."

"What does that mean?" Declan asked, his whole body shifting.

"I believe Auggie smothered her with a pillow," August said with heavy sorrow in his voice. "She would have passed regardless. Auggie was terrible when she was sick because it took all the attention away from him. He couldn't stand it. He asked me several times how long it was going to take until she died. He showed no compassion or empathy for her. He didn't offer her a kind word, help take care of her the way his sisters did. He did nothing to help me or the family during that time. He was almost angry that the family was focused on her."

The grief was still evident on August's face. Kate wasn't sure how he could bear the thought of his son killing his wife, the child's own mother. It was too sick to contemplate. "Do you have proof that this happened?"

August shook his head. "It's why I was never able to do anything with it. She was seriously ill and had already stopped treatment. The doctor said she had a couple of weeks at the most. A nurse caught Auggie in the room with her, telling her she should be dead already and that if she didn't hurry up and die, he'd rush her along. The nurse came to me immediately but he denied saying it. My wife was in and out of consciousness. I don't know if she heard him. I pray that she never had to hear such a thing."

August looked away as a heaviness settled in the air around all of them. "I've tried to be honest with myself over the years, my wife was always afraid of Auggie. He was destructive as a child. Had a short violent temper. He'd be fine one minute and strike out at someone the next. He'd punch or shove his sisters and then lie to us with a straight face that it never happened. He stole things and lied about it. He was so good at lying a psychologist once told us that he wasn't sure if Auggie even knew he was lying. It was pathological. We tried all kinds of talk and behavior therapy as well as medication and nothing seemed to work."

Kate had seen this before and she felt for the parents. With some children, there was nothing that could be done. "I assume you believed what the nurse told you?"

August met her gaze. "I did. I knew how well Auggie lied."

"When you confronted him, did you tell him you knew he was lying?" Kate wasn't sure if it would have done any good.

"I didn't confront him so much as just asked what he said," he admitted. "I had three other children to look after, a dying wife, and a business I was trying to keep running. A fight with Auggie at the time wouldn't have done anything for anyone. In the past, any confrontation made Auggie angrier. I suppose I was trying to prevent more chaos."

Declan didn't seem to understand. "Weren't you concerned about the threat he made?"

"Absolutely. After that point, we never allowed Auggie in the room with her alone. It wasn't that hard because he didn't want to spent any time with her."

Declan started to say something, but Kate put her hand on his leg to stop him. August was deep into a painful memory and she didn't want anything to break the spell of it. The more detail, even as painful as it was for him, that he could share, the more Kate would come to learn about Auggie.

August collected himself. "The evening it happened, I was in my office working. My daughters were in their bedrooms doing their homework and I thought Auggie was off with friends. I didn't even know he was in the house. He had stayed late after school. As I said, we didn't allow Auggie in the room with her alone. A nurse or one of us was always present. That evening with Auggie out of the house, we were all a bit relaxed with the rules. The nurse had walked to the kitchen to refill the water pitcher without calling one of us to be with her. She returned to find Auggie standing over her. My wife was deceased. No one witnessed it. She screamed for me and I came running. Auggie said that she was dead when he entered the room. He said he went in thinking the nurse was in there. He said she took her last breath and he was about to call us when the nurse walked in."

In any other situation, Kate would have believed the story. The poor woman was dying. It could have happened at any time. "Did you question him?"

August shook his head. "Not immediately. There's no proof of anything different and I didn't want an autopsy. The nurse said she couldn't have been gone for more than fifteen minutes. I don't even know how long Auggie had been there. He could have just been walking by. As I said, he never cared enough to go in and check on her. It seemed too much to accuse him of with no proof."

Kate understood all of that. "Yet, here you are now, thinking that he might have killed his mother. Something must have changed."

"I think I suspected all along. It was too much for me to process." August grew quiet for a few beats in the way Kate had grown accustomed. He was a thoughtful, contemplative man. "It was my daughter, Ellen, who suggested it a couple of years later. She and her sisters were talking and she said she found it strange that Auggie had just appeared home that night, earlier than planned, and was the one with their mother when she took her last breath. Her sisters agreed with her and expressed their own suspicions. They brought it to me and I couldn't deny the possibility. I implored them not to confront Auggie about it. No good would come of it. Auggie was seventeen then and had grown bigger and stronger than all of us. We were all a bit afraid of him."

Kate found herself sitting on the edge of the couch in anticipation. "I assume Ellen didn't listen to you."

"She tried for a while, a couple of years. Ellen is a lot like my wife. She's a bit of a spitfire. She's a personal injury lawyer and made for litigation." August rose from the chair, leaving Kate to wonder what he was doing. He turned his back to them, walking to the window. He stared out of it as he spoke. "Ellen confronted Auggie on one of her college breaks. She wasn't living in the home anymore, none of the girls were. They were all away at college. I was the only one home with Auggie. Ellen didn't sugarcoat it. She came right out and asked if he had killed their mother. He exploded in rage, screaming at her and calling her all kinds of names. Ellen didn't flinch. She remained calm and watched him rage. When Auggie realized he couldn't bait her, he broke into hysterical laughter and told her that even if he did kill their mother it put her out of her misery."

"Did he admit it?" Declan asked.

August turned to them. "About as close to an admission as we were going to get. He said if he were the one to have done it, he would have smothered her with the pillow. After he left, Ellen implored me to call the police. I knew he'd never admit anything to them and I had zero proof."

Kate knew he was also concerned about the scandal and his family business. "What other violent acts has Auggie committed over the years?"

"Too many to name," August admitted, shaking his head. "He has a violent temper that comes on as quickly as it dissipates. None of his sisters want anything to do with him. They won't come here if they know he's here. I've lost staff because of him. I'm at my wits end. I finally stopped trying to manage him and just stay clear of him. It's the only way I've been able to survive. Well, up until a few months ago."

"When you left your business to your daughter," Kate said, filling in where he had stopped. "How did Auggie respond?"

"I honestly didn't think he'd care. He's never shown an interest in the family business other than the money that's earned from it. Auggie has never worked an honest day in his life." August blamed himself for that. He explained that he hadn't made any of his children work while they were in school. He told Kate and Declan that their only job was to get good grades and excel in their education. "I expected them to go to college and find stable employment in something they loved. All three of my daughters did that successfully. They were raised the same as Auggie. It never stuck with him, so I was caught off guard when he came back here and flew into a rage when he found out I was turning the business over to his sister. He has no business degree and no experience. It would be insane of me to leave him the business. His monthly stipend will continue, so it's not like he was losing his income. I didn't understand it."

Kate figured it was about control. "Is that the last you saw of him?"

"No," August admitted. "He's been in and out of here over the last few months. We hardly speak when I'm here, which isn't often. You're catching me between work travel. My daughter isn't running the business fully on her own yet. It will be another couple of years until I'm fully retired."

Kate needed to come back to something August said at the start. "You told us that when you first heard about this case in Boston, you thought Auggie might be responsible. I understand your concerns about him and his temper and even potentially killing his mother. That's a big leap to serial killer. What am I missing?"

August held his hand up. "Right. I forgot. Auggie is obsessed with the metaphysical. Ever since he was young, Auggie was obsessed with tarot – studying it, using the cards, trying to garner power from it. I'm not really sure what got him into it. His mother and I thought it was a weird hobby but didn't see the harm. I figured he'd grow out of it, like a kid who was obsessed with magic or something similar."

Kate saw the reasoning behind it. "I assume he never grew out of it."

August gestured for them to come with him. "Let me show you. You'll want to search his room."

Kate and Declan shared a look. They were getting to the heart of things now.

CHAPTER 31

ugust stood at the door at the end of a long hallway. "Auggie has had this wing of the house for years. He's been—" He didn't get to finish because Kate's phone buzzed in her pocket at the same time Declan's rang.

She reached for hers. "Leo is calling me," she said as Declan showed her the screen. It was Briggs calling him. Kate looked up at August. "I'm sorry, we need to handle this first."

August left them alone in the hallway, going back the way they had come.

Kate answered as Declan took a few steps away to take his call. His back was to her as she spoke. "Leo, is everything okay?" she asked even though she was sure it wasn't.

Kate braced herself for the news.

Leo didn't waste any time. "Carmen Langston is missing. She never showed up at the office this morning. She had two early meetings that she missed with no explanation. Two of her assistant district attorneys went to her home looking for her after she didn't answer any of their calls. They thought she might be sick or something. They found her security guard dead in the backyard and glass shards due to a plant being thrown through the back door. She's gone, Kate. There are signs of a struggle in her bedroom but no sign of her."

Kate sucked in a sharp breath as if she'd been punched in the gut.

"Any tarot card left at the scene?"

"No. It looks like a kidnapping not a murder."

Kate knew there'd be murder. If not at Carmen's house, she assumed the woman was probably already dead and it was only a matter of time before someone found her body. "Was the whole house searched, top to bottom?"

"Everywhere, Kate. The Boston Police Department has been over there all morning." Leo grew quiet for a moment as she stared down the hall at Declan. The tight jaw, furrowed brow. "There's more, Kate. Are you there?"

She realized Leo was still talking. "I'm sorry. Did you say there was something else?"

"Carmen isn't the only one who's missing. Judge Thomas is gone too."

Kate stumbled back against the wall, her hand moving behind to brace herself. She couldn't have heard that correctly. "Judge Keaton Thomas?"

"He's gone, Kate. There was a similar scene at his house. His security is dead and his wife was attacked, hit in the head. She's alive at Mass General, holding on. But she's not conscious yet. Things happened so fast. I know Briggs was trying to get a handle on the scenes before calling you in. He's called Sharon already."

"He's on the phone with Declan now." Kate's voice sounded hollow to herself. It was like a fog had come over her. She couldn't make sense of any of it. "How long ago did all of this happen?"

"Not even an hour ago. Briggs called me directly to make sure that I was okay at home. He's called a few other people too to check on them. He was trying to make sure that no one else was missing."

"Anyone else?"

"No, just the two."

That was enough. Kate had no idea what to do. "Is the media aware of what's going on?"

"No one has called them yet. Briggs brought in a team of detectives. It's too much for one person to handle. Are you close to finding the killer?"

Kate turned around and looked at the door they had been about to go through. She had no idea what was on the other side. "I think we're close. There's no definitive proof yet but the circumstantial evidence is there." Kate went on to explain about Ronny and Auggie. "They are connected. I don't know if Ronny was involved, but even Auggie's father believes he might be the killer. He was about to allow us to search part of the home when you called."

"Search, Kate. Find whatever you need to on this guy so you can stop him. I feel useless on this case but I'll help in any way that I can."

There was nothing he could do. "We'll be back as soon as we can." She hung up without even asking him if he was okay. She turned back to Declan and slammed right into his chest.

He steadied her. "I assume Leo told you about Judge Thomas and Carmen."

Kate nodded. "They are both missing." She found it hard to even say the words. "What did Briggs say?"

"The scenes are nearly identical. The back doors of the homes had been breached. Security is dead, shot. Signs of a struggle in the bedrooms. Mrs. Thomas was struck once in the head and is at the hospital. The prognosis is good and Briggs has someone there with her making sure she's safe." Declan hitched his chin toward the door. "Briggs needs us back. Let's catch this guy, Kate. If Auggie is the killer, then let's hope something in there tells us that definitively."

Kate's mind started to clear from the shock of the news. "If he's kidnapped them instead of immediately killing them like the others, he must be holding them someplace. We need to know what properties he has access to." She moved quickly past Declan down the hall, calling

August's name as she went.

He turned the corner from the living room and met her halfway. "I'm here, Agent Walsh. Is everything okay?"

"No, it's most definitely not okay," Kate said, anger tinging her tone. She had no more time for drawn out stories. "Two prominent people are missing in Boston. Carmen Langston, the district attorney, and Massachusetts Supreme Court Judge Keaton Thomas. I believe both of them were taken by Auggie. The Justice card was next and that's all about law. This killer has never kidnapped anyone before. He's always killed them in their home. This is new. I need to know where Auggie might have taken them. While you're showing us Auggie's room, I need someone who works for you to get me all the addresses for your properties. Anywhere Auggie might have gone."

"Of course," August said with a nod of his head. "Let me phone my daughter and she will send you everything by email."

"What about banking and credit cards?" Declan asked. "Do you have access to any credit card statements or his banking? If so, we might be able to track him."

"Banking, no. Auggie has an account that I deposit money into but otherwise have no access. One of his credit cards is mine and he's an authorized user. I can check it. Let me give you access to his wing of the house and then I'll call my daughter to save time. You can be searching while I do that."

August took a step around Kate and she reached for him, putting her hand on his arm. "Many fathers wouldn't be so helpful. I know this must be difficult for you."

August offered her a warm smile. "This is something I should have done years ago. Had I gotten law enforcement involved instead of protecting him, we might not be here now. Do not wait for a warrant, I'm giving you full access. You want to go through anything, let me know and it's yours." He raised his head to Declan. "Let me unlock that door, call my daughter, and then we can go through the credit card information together."

"We appreciate that." Declan stepped out of the way to let him pass.

August pulled a key from his pocket and unlocked it. "Auggie has his own entrance and I keep my side of the door locked as I don't want him coming into my office while I'm not home. He has no reason to be on my side of the house when I'm not here. He has a small kitchen and all the amenities he needs. When I built the house, I kept this as an in-law apartment for my parents. They never needed it, but Auggie moved in when he was kicked out of Yale. He's been here ever since. The housekeeper cleans it once a week but otherwise, he's the only one over here."

"Was there something specific you wanted to show us?" Kate asked, remembering their earlier conversation.

"Follow me." August led them down a short hall to an open concept living room and kitchen. The space wasn't huge but it was bright and clean with newer furnishings. He went through the living room to a door on the other side. "This has two bedrooms," he explained, opening the door. "Auggie uses this space for an office." He reached inside and flicked on the light as Kate and Declan walked through the door.

Kate's eyes shifted around the room, not quite sure where to land. There were symbols drawn all over the walls and images of tarot cards blown up and fixed along another wall. There were notes on each of the cards in a black scrawl that Kate couldn't read from her position. She'd need to get closer. "What is all of this?" she asked pointing to the symbols.

"Astrology," Declan said, surprising her. "They are astrological symbols for the zodiac. See there's Pisces, Taurus, and Cancer. The other with the circles look like birth charts."

Kate wanted to ask how he knew all of that. "Can you understand the meaning of all of it?"

Declan glanced over at her and nodded once. "Believe it or not but I took a history class in college that included information about astrology. I can do my best." He turned to August. "When is his birthday?"

"July 30, 1977."

"He's forty-seven," Kate said almost to herself. That would put him right in the middle of her profile. She hadn't been off about that or much else. "Does his birthday relate to all of that, Declan?"

He crossed the room to the circular chart on the wall. He traced his finger down each line. "Yes, it's his birthday chart from the date and time he was born." Declan explained to Kate how things were positioned and what they meant. Then he moved onto another chart. "This details positioning of things for this year. He was looking for the most favorable time. It doesn't say for what but my guess would be to pull off these murders and get away with it."

Kate sighed loudly. This was such nonsense. "Does it give any indication about where he is now?"

Declan looked over his shoulder at her. "Astrology doesn't provide that kind of information, Kate."

She threw her hands up in the air. It was useless to her. Turning to August, she asked, "Is there anything specific you wanted to show us in here?"

August crossed the room to a bookshelf. He started pulling books and small boxes from the shelf and tossing them down on a nearby table. "This is all his tarot information. When the murders started, I thought of all of this. He has boxes and boxes of tarot cards. He's been collecting them for a while. I had no idea tarot cards came in this many designs and styles. He told me he'd paid some significant money for some hard-to-find cards. It seems like a total waste to me."

Kate thought back to the card that she was sent that looked unlike the others. The ones that Baird told her were originals to the Order of the Magicians. "Are there any that look particularly old or that Auggie maybe said were rare?"

August grabbed a box a little larger than the rest and pulled it from the shelf. "Auggie came home about two months ago and said these were the rarest of them all. I didn't pay attention to him."

Kate pulled gloves from her back pocket and tugged them over her hands. She took the gold box from him. There was an intricate design of a sun and moon on the front of the box as well as small symbols Kate had come to learn represented the wand, sword, cup and coin, in each of the corners. Kate carefully pulled the cover off the box and stared down at the first card – The Magician. It was in the same design as the card she had been sent. It was the same golden color, faded by time. She was sure these cards in her hand had been done by the same artist as the Justice card she had been sent.

Kate went to the table and put the box down. She bent at the waist and carefully pulled out each card, laying them in a pile next to the box. They seemed to be in order from what she had remembered. It didn't take her long to realize the Justice card was missing or at the very least not in its rightful order. There was nothing between The Chariot and The Hermit where Justice would have been. She kept going through all of the cards to see if Justice had been ordered incorrectly or tucked away among the others. The only one missing was Justice. Kate was sure her card had come from this box – it was physical evidence tying Auggie to the case.

Kate's head snapped up. "August, what did your son tell you about these cards? Did he say where he got them?"

August pointed to them. "No. He never said. He said they were from 1694. You'll see it written on the back of the box."

"The Salem Witch Trials were in 1692." Kate wasn't sure why she had remembered the date so well. "Did Auggie ever mention the Order of the Magicians?"

"No. As I said we rarely spoke. I was surprised he even told me about this tarot deck. He seemed excited by it. Said it would be powerful for him."

"I'm going to need to take this with me," Kate said, gesturing to the box of tarot cards. "August, call your daughter and search the credit card expenditures and we can connect after that." Kate wanted privacy so they could tear the place apart.

Kate was sure now they had their killer. Catching him would still be a challenge all its own.

CHAPTER 32

After a thorough search of Auggie's suite, Kate and Declan came away with a trove of information about the Order of the Magicians and Auggie's interest in the subject. There was solid evidence that Auggie had been in contact with Ronny. Emails went back and forth between them discussing the Order of the Magicians.

Kate and Declan confiscated all the evidence about the Order of the Magicians, a laptop, the tarot card set, and guns. There were even directions and the makings for the silicone fingertips that they had suspected him of wearing. They also found fake beards and wigs in a bin shoved in the closet. It was more than enough evidence to connect him.

The most incriminating evidence Kate found on the lowest bookshelf stashed behind a stack of books. Auggie had a notebook with notes on each of the tarot cards and detailed ideas for each of the murders. Each card had a page with a highlight of what the card meant and the power that could be gained. Kate wasn't sure if he had taken that information from somewhere else or if it was his interpretation.

Under that there were names of people Kate believed were potential victims. None of the victims that had been chosen were listed except for the Davenports. That was the most direct tie from Auggie to one of the murders.

Even though they had found all the evidence needed to tie him to the murder, there was still the question of how Ronny was involved. It was one of the reasons why they were headed back to search Ronny's house. They had just enough time to do that and get back to Boston for a press conference scheduled for later that night, which Declan would lead.

Sharon and Briggs were hard at work processing each of the scenes. Briggs had called in every detective and officer that could be spared to search. He had also alerted the Massachusetts State Police and Declan had sent over FBI agents from the Boston office. Everything that could be done to find the two was being done.

Declan had pored through the credit card statements but found nothing helpful. August was working to see if there was any way he could access his son's bank information but it was unlikely. Kate and Declan would need a warrant for that. To get that, they'd have to make their case to a judge. Even then it might be a slow process and they didn't have time for slow.

Kate and Declan had reviewed the list of properties where Auggie might be hiding. They had dispatched FBI agents across the United States to those locations. Spade had been a tremendous help in working to coordinate all of it.

On the trip back from Rockport to Ronny's house, Declan had remained quiet for most of the trip. He had focused on the road as Kate processed in the passenger seat.

"You're unusually quiet," she said as he turned off at the exit.

"A bit of a headache and I'm worried about coming back here to Salem. I didn't like how I felt when I was here. All the heaviness seemed to dissipate while we were up in Rockport. I can feel it coming back again."

Kate had noticed his shift in mood. She hadn't wanted to call attention to it. She reasoned that if she didn't point it out, he might not notice or connect it to Salem. Kate thought maybe the power of suggestion about what a haunted town Salem was might have influenced him. She saw now that she was wrong and it was real.

"I promise I'll try not to be too long here," Kate said, staring over as he navigated the city streets. A pang of guilt bubbled up for not believing him about how he was feeling. "Is there anything I can do to make you feel better?"

As if some unknown force was answering for her, the sky lit up with lightning followed a few seconds later by the roar of thunder. All at once the sky opened up and the rain fell in torrents.

Declan turned his head to see her eyes wide. "You just jumped in your seat. Okay?"

Kate relaxed her shoulders. "I wasn't expecting a storm."

"I was. That's why I was hoping we'd be back in Boston before it started." Declan turned back to the road, going down one street and then another. The rain cut the visibility down to about twenty feet in front of them. The wipers sloshed back and forth at the highest speed and it still wasn't keeping up.

Kate's phone rang jolting them both. "I don't know the number," she said as she glanced down at the screen. She engaged the call. "Agent Kate Walsh."

"It's Ned from the library," he said with a tension in his voice he hadn't had when they were speaking earlier. "Are you still in Salem?"

"We are just pulling back into Salem. Is everything okay?"

"I thought of something earlier and thought I should tell you," he said, pausing to clear his throat. "I remembered something about Ronny. There was a man with him one afternoon in the library. I didn't realize at first that they were together. They came in at different times. I heard them arguing in the stacks on the second floor. Someone else grabbed my attention and I had to help them find a book. By the time I went back, they were gone."

"Do you remember what they were arguing about?"

"The man was telling Ronny that he had to help him. That he wasn't going to be able to do it alone. Ronny said he wanted no part of it and that he wasn't going to help him. He told the man to leave him alone or he was going to call the police. I never had any context as to what the *it* was. Whatever it was sounded serious and something Ronny wanted no part of. The whole exchange concerned me, but it was right at the time the other person wanted my attention. I was alone here at the library and had to help. When I went back to check on Ronny, they were both gone. I never did follow up with Ronny to see what it was about."

The information might exonerate Ronny as far as committing the murders. "Do you know if Ronny ever went to the police?"

"He didn't," Ned said with resignation in his voice. "I just called a friend at the police department to see if Ronny ever made a report. They didn't have anything from him. I'm not sure if any of that helps your case. It happened a couple of months back and kind of slipped my mind. Sorry I didn't think of it sooner."

One of the things Kate and Declan were able to get while in Rockport were recent photographs of Auggie. Declan was able to pull them off the man's laptop. "Before we leave Salem, I'm going to come by and I want you to look at some photos to see if you recognize the man."

"Are you close to solving the case?"

"I believe we know who is committing the crimes. Catching him is something else entirely. You might have seen the news that Carmen Langston, the district attorney in Boston, and Massachusetts Supreme Court Justice Judge Keaton Thomas have been kidnapped. We are trying to sort out all the details before a press conference tonight. Their disappearances are connected to this case."

"Oh," Ned said not hiding the surprise in his voice. "That's truly terrible. I won't take any more of your time. I'll be here until six and then back home. If you're later than six, you can call me and I'll meet up with you wherever you want. I'm confident I'd recognize the other man if I saw him. He was big and muscular, mean looking."

It sounded like Auggie. Kate promised that she'd try to get to the library before it closed. When she hung up, Declan was watching her. She explained the call from Ned. "It looks like Ned can corroborate that Ronny and Auggie were seen together."

Declan drove directly to Ronny's home, parked in the driveway, and they entered through the back, moving the crime scene tape that covered the doorway. They decided to each take a floor. Kate had no idea what she was looking for or why she felt such a need to search the home again. The local police had gone over every inch of the home with Kate and Declan the first time.

Kate thought back to what Lily had told her – *just follow your instincts and you'll do well*. Kate was honoring that now, even if it made little sense to her and frustrated Declan. She ascended the stairs and started with the closest rooms. She searched everywhere – every nook and cranny of the home, pressing on floorboards and walls as she had the first time. She moved meticulously from one room to the next and even searched the hallway. Every space was devoid of any evidence of Ronny's involvement or anything pointing to Auggie.

Kate saved the bedroom for last – the one where she had found the secret room that had been hiding the man's body. She left it for last because she didn't want to go back in there if she didn't have to. She stood in the doorway and scanned the room. It looked relatively undisturbed except for the mess of white dust from the crime scene techs looking for fingerprints and other evidence.

Kate searched the whole room before moving to stand in front of the hidden room. The wall had been left slightly ajar. As she reached out to open it wider, her phone rang. Kate tugged off a glove and reached for her phone.

"Spade," Kate said as she scrambled to answer. She was hoping he had good news about finding Carmen and Judge Thomas. "Any news yet?"

"Nothing yet," he said much to her dismay. "I'm calling about Ronny Pallazzo. He's been in witness protection for the past seven years. Well," he paused and said that wasn't quite right. "Let me be clear, he went into witness protection seven years ago. He took off three years ago and no one has seen or heard from him since. He's been living off the grid, which is why his driver's license didn't come back to anything. His real name is Ronald Pauly. He didn't change his name that much when he dropped the new name the Marshals had given him. They have been searching for him. He was supposed to be in Madison, Wisconsin."

"Do you know the case that landed him in witness protection?"

"It was an international arms and money laundering case a decade ago. Ronny was living in Miami and laundering money for an international arms dealer. He got in over his head and was about to be taken out. He went to the FBI instead. He made a deal and was put into witness protection. He testified at the trial and the Marshals moved him again. This time to Wisconsin. Seems he got bored of his suburban life and ditched the program. The guy I spoke to said they suspected all along that Ronny had kept a stash of cash in the millions. He didn't have much family when he went into witness protection. A sister and her children and the FBI informed her back a decade ago that Ronny was killed. She already thinks he's dead. I'm sending out an agent to talk to the sister to gently see if she still believes he died a decade ago or if Ronny stupidly contacted her recently. He'll deliver the death notification."

Kate couldn't imagine having to be on the run like that. Not that she had much family of her own, but that life wasn't one she'd do well with. She understood Ronny's need to take back control of his life. "Did the Marshal tell you anything else about him? I'm sure you mentioned we were looking into him as a potential suspect."

Spade confirmed he had. "They didn't think Ronny fit the killer type. They said he was a money guy. The man in the shadow pulling strings. He wasn't violent or a killer. They said he was mild-mannered if not a bit odd. He was obsessed with the occult and was good at keeping secrets. When they searched the house in Wisconsin, they found all sorts of secret compartments in furniture and the walls. He was a master at that. That was the biggest takeaway."

"That's why we are here searching the house again," Kate explained. "I feel like we missed something." Kate gave him the overview of everything they had learned about Auggie. "We need a decision by tonight if we publicly state he's a person of interest and put his photo on the news."

"We don't have a choice, Kate. If this is the guy, he's kidnapped two prominent government figures and who knows who else he's going after. Get his name and photo on the news and run him underground if we have to. Let the public help us."

Kate agreed with him. They chatted for a few minutes more about the press conference later that evening. Kate promised to call as soon as she had any news.

She took a deep breath, wanting to be anywhere other than where she had found Ronny's body. The flashback of him lying there discolored and dead flashed in her mind. She shook off the feeling of dread and advanced into the small space. She had to use the flashlight app on her phone to scan around the small enclosure. Kate felt along the floorboards and the walls.

Just as she was about to give up and exit, a board creaked under her foot. She stepped back and toed the board, pushing harder and then releasing.

Kate got down on her hands and knees and pried the board up with her hands.

There, lying under it, was a small red thumb drive. Kate knew it would be significant.

245

CHAPTER 33

The drive back to Boston had taken too long for Kate. Declan had to fight heavy traffic and the downpours. She wanted to know what was on the thumb drive and every mile they drove felt like ten. Declan was surprised Kate had found anything but hadn't been nearly as surprised by the information Spade had given her about Ronny's background. He had remembered hearing about the case in the news and the witness who had been in protective custody that had testified on camera from an undisclosed location.

After finding the drive and accepting that nothing else would be found in the home, they left for the library, catching Ned at the end of his day. Kate showed him the photos of Auggie and he confirmed that's who had been in the library with Ronny.

They were closer and closer to finding the truth. Kate was sure of that.

Declan pulled the car into the driveway and sat staring at the back of the house. "I don't think I've ever been so happy to be home."

Kate had no time for him to pontificate some greater meaning of life. She saw the look on his face and he was heading down a contemplative path. "As much as I love you and want to hear what you have to say, we need to know what's on this drive."

Declan turned his head to look at her. "You're relentless." He wasn't letting her move on from it that quickly. He leaned over, took her face in his hands, and kissed her thoroughly. When he pulled back, she was sure he saw desire in her eyes. He leaned his forehead against hers. "When we catch this guy, I want about a week of rest with you not talking about work at all."

Kate wanted to lean back over and kiss him again, forgetting the missing and the dead and the killer who still needed to be stopped. The drive burned in her hand, bringing her back to the present. "You have a deal."

The rain had not let up on their drive back and it still came down in torrents. They ran from the car to the house only bringing the bare essentials with them. The rest could be brought in later when the rain stopped. Kate had checked the forecast, hoping for a reprieve, but the rain would continue for the next few days.

Once inside, Kate punched in the alarm code and Declan did a quick sweep of the house. She went directly to her office and fired up her laptop. Kate wanted to look at whatever was on the drive first and foremost. She didn't even care that she was dripping puddles on the hardwood floor.

Declan finished the sweep, yelled out that all was clear, and came into the office with two towels. He handed her one and dried off with the other as he stood behind her.

Kate thanked him for the towel and took a few seconds while her laptop was queuing up the drive to wring out her wet hair. She got herself as dry as she could and sat down in her chair while Declan pulled up another seat. Kate navigated the mouse to the drive and clicked.

There was one lone video file saved. Without thinking about what virus could be imbedded in the video if she clicked it, Kate pressed on. She brought up the file, which in the small video screen showed a dark-haired man sitting in a chair awash in light. She clicked play and the video sprang to life.

This was the first time Kate and Declan were seeing an animated Ronny. He remained seated during the video, leaning slightly forward and back as he spoke.

"If you're seeing this video, I'm probably dead," he started with his voice clear and calm. "I wanted to go to the police but my life is too complicated for that. I've been on the run for a long time. There are people who'd kill me if they had the chance, and because I ran from witness protection, I'd be in trouble with the government. I have to take my chances on my own. I'll be honest it doesn't look good. As I said, if you're seeing this then my chances weren't good. I'm dead and you're probably wondering about my involvement in murders connected to the tarot in Boston. It was my fault after all for sharing what I found in my house with the wrong person."

Ronny took a breath and gnawed at his lip. "To be fair, how was I supposed to know he was a homicidal maniac? I found antique tarot cards in my wall and a whole book filled with rituals from the Order of the Magicians, which I later came to learn was a secret order operating in Salem since the witch trials in the 1600s. No one was able to tell me about them in the community – that's how secret they were. I tried to look up information online and at the library. I even talked to people in the community who denied their existence. I had the information though. I made a mistake in talking about it so broadly, but in my defense, I was curious about its historical relevance. I've always had an interest in the occult, which is what brought me to Salem. It seemed like a good place to escape to and the community was eclectic and nice. I figured I'd blend in easily enough and I did for a while, until I met him."

Ronny looked away from the camera as if he'd heard a noise. He paused and then focused back without explaining. "I met him in a rare book shop in Boston. I was looking for more on the order and he was looking for rare tarot cards. You could say fate brought us together. I had a rare set of tarot cards that I bragged about. He wanted to see them and I didn't see the harm. He said he was from Rockport, not far from Salem. We ended up becoming friends, I guess you could say, for a while. Then the conversation turned darker based on some of the rituals in the book. He told me he knew about the order. He never said how. He told me that I didn't know what I had and that taking a life would bring him great power. Honestly, I don't believe any of that was true – he was just looking for an excuse to kill. He seemed enthralled by the idea – excited."

Kate paused the video and turned to Declan. "Ronny has to be talking about Auggie."

Declan gestured toward the video. "Let's keep watching."

Kate pushed play again.

Ronny continued. "I didn't think he was serious at first. Who'd be serious about something that insane? I honestly laughed it off until he told me that I had to help him kill people. I couldn't do that. I've done a lot of horrible things in my life but never murder. He took the tarot cards from me and the book. I tried to get them back but there was no reasoning with him. That's when I should have called the police. I was afraid for myself though and what would become of me. I didn't know what the government would do if they found me. Worse, I didn't know what my enemies would do if they found out where I was living. There were no good options, so sadly, I did nothing."

Kate could see the strain on his face. There was no time and date stamp on the video but she could see that he was struggling with the decisions he'd made.

Ronny lowered his eyes. "Actually, that isn't completely honest. I tried to talk him out of it several times. But then he found out about my secret – that I had been in government witness protection. I had been involved in money laundering in a case out of Miami more than a decade ago. I was a witness for the prosecution in exchange for witness protection. I don't know how he found that out but he did. Maybe I wasn't careful when he was in my home or he could have seen my license and realized it was a fake or maybe he found no information about me online. Whatever it was he knew. He told me that he'd expose me if I didn't help him."

Ronny paused, got up from the chair, and walked away.

Kate took the time to process the information. The threats made against Ronny were similar to the ones Evan claimed Auggie had made to him.

Ronny returned with an explanation for the pause in the video. "I'm paranoid with every sound I hear that he's back for me. I asked him what he'd do with me since I know his identity. He promised me that as long as I didn't get in his way, he wouldn't kill me. I don't believe him."

Kate wanted to know when this video had been made – if it was before the murders had started or if they had begun. The medical examiner put Ronny's death about a week back, right before the first murder. She'd have to get tech support to see if there was a date on the video.

"You might ask why I'm recording this now. I can't go on the run again. I did that for years. I'm settled here in Salem and happy with my home and community. I won't run again. If it takes my life, then that is my fate. But I want to leave a warning as I should have done all along. He wants me to go to Boston with him to help him scout locations for The Tower card in the deck. He sees The Tower as his grandest plan of all. If he gets away with that, then he said he could easily finish the mission."

Kate's heart quickened at the thought of it. She'd seen the card – with its tall brick tower in flames and people falling out of the windows. The card meant disaster, endings, and destruction or collapse of what was once known. The card shows a building struck by lightning and set aflame – an act of nature that can't be prevented. She supposed in life there were many tower moments, a tearing down of the old to get ready for the new. Auggie had taken these things literally and it had been on Kate's mind since she saw the card.

She focused on Ronny.

"I didn't want to go to Boston with him. I wanted no part in his destruction. I think he was engaging me to go with him to make me as guilty as he was – buying my silence in a way. He can't replicate the storms that caused The Tower to burn, so he's going to do the next best thing."

Ronny shifted in his chair and leaned into the camera as if speaking to Kate and Declan directly. "He's going to blow up the Prudential Center with a truck bomb like the Oklahoma City bombing. He's truly mad. I feel like this is my one last chance to talk him out of what he's doing. I don't know how to stop him. He's a chameleon. I know he's befriended a few people he intends to kill in Boston. He's not told me their names so I cannot warn them. One is an older couple, very rich. He's gone to the husband as a potential business associate. This man's family comes from great wealth so he knows how to blend in, to walk that walk, so to speak."

Ronny sat back and sighed deeply. "This is like a runaway freight train that I don't know how to stop. Yes, I could go to the police. I know I should. I know if you're seeing this, you'll blame me for not doing more to stop him. But it's also my word against this man and his family is very powerful. I don't even know that I'd be believed. I'm looking out for my interest. There's a part of me that doesn't think he'll go through with it. He hasn't killed anyone yet. At least, I haven't seen it on the news. I'm hoping it's all a big ruse, a game he's playing. If not and I'm dead and he's gone on to kill people or worse, actually blow up the Prudential Center – then give this to the FBI. The man they are seeking is August Wynn Jr. He's a madman. I don't know how you'll stop him, but you must."

Ronny wasn't quite done. He glanced away from the camera and a moment later back at it. "Forgive me for having failed to stop him. Forgive me for not going to the police when I should. If I am dead and you're seeing this, know it's August who has killed me. Please, you must help."

The video ended, leaving Kate and Declan too stunned to speak.

Auggie was going to blow up the Prudential Center, killing countless people.

CHAPTER 34

Kate stared at the screen too stunned to speak. She slowly turned to Declan who was already on his feet. "What are we going to do?" she asked with the words catching in her throat.

"I'm calling the ATF," he responded with his phone in his hand. "You call Spade then we can call the rest of the team." Declan glanced back at her. "I want to tell you that everything is going to be okay, but we both know I can't say that. He's a madman, Kate, who has been several steps ahead of us this whole time."

Hearing Declan's words, Kate's mood shifted. Anger replaced the fear.

She called Spade and the phone rang longer than it usually did. She was to the point of impatience when he finally answered. "He's going to blow up the Prudential Center or another similar building," Kate said as he answered. She didn't even wait for him to say hello. "Ronny hid a video recording of himself talking about Auggie. He found out about Ronny's past and was blackmailing him. He told Ronny he already knew about the Order of the Magicians. I'm not so sure. There was a ritual book Ronny found and the tarot cards. Auggie took them. Ronny didn't necessarily believe in the rituals found in the book. He was more interested in the historical information. Auggie thought he could gain real power from the tarot cards left behind and the murders. In the end, Ronny admitted that he went with Auggie to Boston to scope out locations for The Tower card. Do you know what that is, Spade?"

"I saw the card, Kate. I've been worried about it since I saw it. I had been hoping that it wouldn't get that far."

Kate had been hoping the same thing. They had failed to stop the man. "Declan is on the phone with the ATF and we have that press conference scheduled for tonight. I think we need to release Auggie's photo. If it runs him underground, then so be it. At least it will give us more time."

Spade didn't argue with her about that. "What about mentioning the Prudential Center? Do you want to go public with that?"

Kate had been hoping that Spade would have the answer because she wasn't sure. "I will contact security at the Prudential Center today and alert them. We only know about it from Ronny. For all we know Auggie changed his mind. I think we need to keep the name of the building out of the news and send a general alert. This way all building security will remain on high alert. I have no idea what he's planning. The Prudential Center is the perfect target. But if he sees security being tightened there and can't get near the building with the truck bomb, he'll turn to secondary targets. I don't want anyone to let their guard down."

Spade agreed with the reasoning. They talked about the plan for a while longer, including using the FBI's tipline for sightings of Auggie. They'd need a way to expedite the information to get it to them quickly. Spade said he'd handle all of it, working with the FBI and the Massachusetts State Police.

Spade had one final focus. "We need to discuss Evan Crandall, Kate. I was waiting until you got to Boston to tell you. He's confessed a few things to the FBI agent who has been watching him."

Kate lurched forward. *Confessed.* "What did he do?"

Spade didn't waste any time. "He admitted to following you from the Archdiocese that first day when you went to warn Cardinal O'Connor. Evan said that he followed you home and gave your address to the man he thought was Ronny. As you figured out, Auggie was posing as Ronny."

Kate felt as if she'd been punched in the gut. "Is there anything else?" She sensed Spade had more to say.

"There is," Spade said through a frustrated breath. "He admitted that he ran ahead of Leo and that he was the one that hit him on the head. He knew, Kate, that Auggie was going to kill Cardinal O'Connor. Auggie wanted to lure the FBI to the scene to kill them. Evan didn't follow the plan. He hit Leo over the head outside to stop him from going into the house. Then he went upstairs alone and that's when Auggie stabbed him. It was retribution for not bringing the FBI to the scene."

"There was the same pattern on Leo's head as on Cardinal O'Connor though."

"There was another mace. There were several stored in the basement of the Archdiocese. Evan is the one who gave Auggie the weapon as long as he promised Cardinal O'Connor would be dead by the time he used it. That's when the suicide, sacrificing himself scheme came into play. He was back at Ronny's house looking for the mace – the one connected to the Archdiocese. He was surprised no one found it's match outside in the grass where he threw it before running into the house."

Kate knew with the focus inside Cardinal O'Connor's house no one was looking out in the grass for anything. She thought back to how easily Evan had lied to them, played up how distraught he'd been by the cardinal's death. "How'd the FBI agent get him to confess?"

"It didn't take much. After Evan realized he wasn't going to be able to run, he told the FBI agent everything. He said he was sorry and that he was still terrified. He figured if he exchanged information, he'd be let go. That's not going to happen. He's in custody but the agent there wants to know our plan."

The same would have been true if Ronny had lived. "We need to use him for information while we can," Kate said evenly. "Since Evan is so comfortable with the agent, try to see if he knows anything about the bombing plan in Boston. Auggie might have wanted to use Evan again. That's why he kept him alive."

Spade agreed with the plan. "Do you need anything else?"

Kate considered the question. Outside of resources on the ground to hunt for Auggie there wasn't much else she needed. "Those addresses we provided. Can we check them again?"

"We'll keep watch on them."

"Auggie has to be staying someplace in the city or close by in the suburbs." Kate didn't know how she knew but there was a part of her that sensed he was close. She wondered if he knew they had gone to Salem. Evidently, he had never found the video that Ronny made. Kate wasn't even sure if Auggie knew that Ronny was willing to give him up to the police.

"I'll let you know when I know more," Kate said before hanging up. She pushed back from her desk and walked to the hallway to find Declan. She caught a glimpse of herself in her standing mirror and grimaced at the sight. Her hair had untwisted from the top of her head and hung to the side in a twisted heap of wet mangled hair. Her skin paled a lighter shade than usual and her makeup had long been gone from her face. She rarely appeared on television during a press conference but she'd have to fix herself to even stand among the crowd. She'd take care of that later.

"Declan," she called as she stepped into the hallway.

"Here," he called from the bedroom that had once been his before he started sleeping in her room. He still kept his clothes in that closet.

"What did the ATF say?" she asked as she walked into the room and found him standing in just blue boxer briefs in front of the mirror. There were pressed pants on the bed along with a fresh shirt and tie.

He turned to look at her. "The ATF wants to be at the press conference as a show of force."

"We're fine with that." She stepped into the room closer to him.

"I figured it was fine," Declan said, explaining he'd already green-lit it. "They are going to start calling all the truck rental places and hunting down where Auggie might be getting the supplies."

Declan reached for his pants and put in one leg and then the other leaving them resting on his narrow hips without buttoning them. "The Oklahoma bomb was agricultural fertilizer, diesel fuel, and other chemicals. The ATF agent said that he must be storing this somewhere. Auggie has to have enough room to put it together. Did any of the addresses August provided have space for that sort of thing – a warehouse, maybe, far away from everything else? Auggie would have to be getting all of the supplies in and then the barrels or whatever he's putting it in to place in the truck. There has to be space, probably not right here in the middle of the city. It would arouse suspicion. He's also holding Carmen and Judge Keaton if they are still alive."

Kate didn't know all the details of all the properties on the list. "I told Spade to send people back out. Do you think they should hold off on any properties like you described and wait for the ATF?"

Declan buttoned and zipped his pants and fixed his belt in place. "Call August and ask if he knows of any places he might not have mentioned where Auggie would have that kind of room." He turned back to the mirror and finished dressing. "I'd like to be on the scene and so would the ATF."

Kate sat on the edge of the bed while Declan finished dressing. "We are going to need to get Briggs up to speed before the press conference. I want to attend the press conference in the crowd, Declan. Now that we know what Auggie looks like, we can look for him. I suspect he might be attending."

Declan buttoned his shirt. "He didn't look anything like the sketch we put out, Kate. He is probably wearing a disguise. Do you think he'll come? He's holding Carmen and Judge Keaton. Do you think he'd just leave them wherever he's holding them?"

Kate hadn't forgotten about the hostages. "He has no idea what we are about to announce. Once we put his name out there, he's going to be forced underground. He'll have to be more careful than he's been. Up until now, he's had free access to the city and anything else. He's been walking among all of us free to carry out his insidious plan. Auggie has no idea, but this next hour is the last that he has to walk freely."

Declan finished dressing and appraised himself in the mirror. He turned around to her with his arms wide. "Okay enough for national news?"

Kate rose from the corner of the bed and walked to him. She straightened his tie and kissed him sweetly. "This is going to be a real show of force tonight. I'll be in the crowd looking for him."

"If you spot him, don't go after him alone, Kate. He's dangerous." Declan stepped back and looked her up and down. "You're not going like that are you?" He cracked a smile to show he was teasing her.

Kate touched her limp ponytail. "I need to get myself ready. Should I meet you over there?" The press conference was being held at the Boston Police Department in the lobby. It was raining too hard to hold it outside as the previous ones had been.

"You can. I'll go ahead and catch Briggs up to speed," Declan said, leaning down to kiss her again. "I don't think Auggie is going to show up, Kate. I don't think even he has the balls to go to the police department."

Kate wasn't so sure about that. He got off on the risk. "Let me worry about the crowd."

"Be safe," Declan said as he headed out leaving Kate alone in her house for the first time since the case started.

She stayed in the bedroom for a few minutes longer, just accepting the feelings that were rushing over her. For the first time, maybe ever, Kate didn't feel safe alone in her home. She'd been targeted before but not like this. This killer was something she'd never witnessed before and she hoped never again. Kate pushed the feelings aside long enough to get herself ready for the press conference.

Twenty minutes later when Kate stepped out onto her front stoop, she felt ready to face whatever lay ahead. The rain had tapered off from torrential to a steady cold rain that at least gave her some visibility. She glanced down the street toward Leo's and noticed that the light on the second floor glowed a hot orange. She had not checked in on him recently.

Kate checked her watch and frowned. She wouldn't have time to go see him now and make it to the press conference. She started to pull out her phone to tell him to watch the news when she noticed a man jet out from between Leo's house and the one next door. He stared up at the house and then disappeared down the alleyway.

Kate didn't get a good look at him. She'd only caught the back of his head. She texted Leo that someone was lurking around his house then she bounded down the front steps and jogged toward his house to investigate.

She didn't have much time, but she wasn't going to leave Leo to handle it himself.

CHAPTER 35

Kate slowed her pace as she approached the narrow passage barely wide enough for a single person to navigate. Most of the neighboring houses stood shoulder to shoulder, but Leo's residence was a looming figure with its own space, flanked by a slender alleyway.

Unlike the conventional layout of nearby houses, Leo's boasted an array of unique features. Its basement floor was concealed, guarded by a fenced-off enclave of foliage. Turrets punctuated each level, a stark departure from the turrets found on only the upper floors of neighboring homes. The detailed carvings on the front of the home hinted at the artistry that lay inside.

Before venturing deeper into the alley, Kate glanced at her phone, hoping for a response from Leo. Silence echoed back. She sent another urgent message, stowing her phone away just as the sharp shatter of glass pierced through the air.

With a swift motion, Kate unholstered her gun, her senses heightened. She cast a wary glance over her shoulder, then plunged into the alley, hugging the shadows of Leo's imposing home. The cacophony of breaking glass mingled with the grating of metal on metal.

"FBI!" Kate yelled, cutting through the patter of rain. "Come out slowly, hands where I can see them."

A sudden hush descended.

Heart pounding, Kate inched closer to the rear of the house, tightening her grip on the gun. She recalled the layout from a previous visit when the house was still under construction. A back porch, modest compared to the grandeur of the front, offered access to the kitchen and the back three windows.

With gun raised, Kate rounded the corner, eyes scanning the dimly lit backyard. A figure leapt from the porch, crashing into Kate before she could react.

Fists lashed out, a relentless barrage aimed at her face. Kate's instincts kicked in, but not swiftly enough to evade the punishing blows that knocked her to the ground. The sickening crunch of bone echoed in her ears, drowned out by the rush of adrenaline and the sting of water in her eyes. Another strike forced her head to collide with concrete.

Summoning every ounce of strength, Kate fought back with ferocity. She knew what to do. She had trained for this, spent years in the gym and sparring for this very scenario. But with the punches to the face and the thumping of her brain, her resolve diminished.

Still, she fought.

As he took another swing, Kate raised her knee to his groin as hard as she could muster. As he let out a guttural groan and lurched forward, Kate grabbed him by the jacket and pushed as hard as she could to the side, rolling him off and freeing herself from his grasp. Aching everywhere, she scrambled to her knees just as he began to rise.

Frantically, she scanned and slapped at the ground searching for her gun, but it had vanished amidst the chaos. Time was slipping away as her assailant regained his footing. Ignoring the relentless waves of dizziness and nausea washing over her, Kate fought to stand, her muscles protesting with each attempt.

As she got one foot under her, she buckled. Collapsing back to her knees, she cursed softly, her hands sinking into the cold puddles beneath her. Summoning a final reserve of determination, she attempted to get to her feet again, groping with her fingertips for the stability of the porch wall.

As she righted herself fully, a sharp intake of breath heralded the onset of another wave of sickness, and with a gut-wrenching heave, Kate emptied the contents of her stomach onto the sidewalk.

As she doubled over against the house, Kate's assailant halted mid-escape, turning back to her with a chillingly calm demeanor. "Kate," he said softly, a hint of mockery in his tone, "you're never going to catch me. You're never going to win."

Struggling to lift her head, Kate peered through blurry vision, locking eyes with Auggie and his smug, self-assured smile. "August Wynn," she began, her voice faltering, "you're under arrest for…" Her words trailed off into silence as she slumped to the ground, unable to hold herself upright any longer. A punishing defeat.

"You'll have to catch me first." Auggie's taunt lingered in the air.

She felt his presence over her, his hand touching hers before darkness enveloped her.

Hours later

Kate's eyelids fluttered as she tried to pull herself to consciousness. She expected to feel rain pelt her face as she reached for her gun but found nothing but softness. The rain had stopped too.

"We have to…" her cotton-filled mouth couldn't get out her words. She had no sense of time or space. All she felt was the heaviness of her body – as if she'd been weighed down.

"I'm here, Kate," a man said off in the distance. It sounded to Kate like he was miles away beckoning her. She felt an unfamiliar hand slide over hers. "Kate, I'm here with you."

Kate knew by the voice and the feel of his hand that it wasn't Declan. She breathed heavily as she forced her eyes open. They closed again.

It was as if they too were tugged down by weights. "Where am I?" She turned her head to the voice and tried to push herself upright.

A hand on her shoulder gently pushed her back down. "Kate, don't try to sit up. You've been injured. You're at the hospital. You're safe now."

She remembered then – Auggie's violent attack, her inability to chase him, and the taunt. The fear and agitation rose in her at once. "We have to stop him," she tried to say again, hoping her voice was stronger. Kate brushed off the hands on her and opened her eyes. Through blurred vision, she took in her surroundings. The light blue walls of the hospital. The hum of a television on low. The faint overhead light. "How'd I get here?" She tipped her head back to see Leo's face. She was glad that it was him. If it couldn't be Declan, she was glad Leo was there with her.

Leo reached for her hand again, holding it tightly and slipping his fingers through hers. "I saw your texts, Kate. I heard the commotion behind the house and went to see what was going on. I found you there on the ground, unconscious and bleeding. I spoke to Declan briefly. He's running down a few leads with Briggs and Agent Terry Chaplin from the ATF. He said he'd be here as soon as he can."

Kate couldn't get a sense of time. "How long have I been here?"

"At the hospital about two hours. Here in the room less than thirty minutes. I should go tell the doctor you're awake."

Kate reached for him, asking him to stay. "Did you catch him?"

Leo shook his head. "You were alone out there when I found you. I called 911 and was able to get the Boston Police Department over to the house. They found your gun." Leo held her hand tightly and locked his gaze on hers. "They found something else, too."

By the look on his face, it was something that scared him. "What is it?"

"Three tarot cards – The Hermit, Wheel of Fortune and Strength.

You had two of the cards clutched in your fist. I found The Hermit card lying on the ground not far from you."

Kate didn't remember grabbing anything when she was struggling with him. She remembered his taunt and how he had walked back over to her. She had been too weak to fight. Kate wondered why he hadn't killed her. "I don't understand any of this."

"I think maybe he was there to kill me and you stopped him," Leo said uncertainly. "That's all I can assume. I don't know why he'd try to break into my home."

"August Wynn Jr. Does that name ring a bell?" Kate didn't know why he'd target Leo or how he even knew anything about him. She reached for his other hand in the hopes he'd help her to a sitting position. She couldn't lay back and have this conversation. "Please help me sit up and I could use some water."

Leo smiled down at her. "You're demanding things. This is a good sign." He helped her sit up and adjusted the bed and her blankets.

Her brain still felt fuzzy. "Did they give me pain medication?"

"They did, Kate. Your face…" Leo didn't finish his thought as he crossed the room to the water pitcher and cup. He poured some into the cup and walked it back over to her, holding it for her as she sipped.

When her mouth no longer felt bone dry, she raised a hand to her face and felt the bandages. She recalled how many times Auggie had hit her and the ferocity of the punches. "How bad is it?"

Leo grimaced. "You'll recover but it looks like you went a few rounds in the boxing ring with a stronger, tougher fighter." When she closed her eyes trying not to remember, he tugged on her blanket to get her attention. "You have a broken nose that the doctor fixed, a fractured cheek bone, and a nasty cut above your left eye that required a few stitches. You still have your teeth and the rest will heal. In the long run, it's more cosmetic than serious. The CT scan didn't show any damage. You're still beautiful, Kate. I don't think much could change that. The doctor said you have a tough head."

Kate had heard that before from doctors. This wasn't the first punch she had taken and it probably wouldn't be the last. She raised her hand to the back of her head. "There's something back there."

"I forgot," Leo said evenly. "You needed a few stitches to the back of your head too."

Kate reached for the cup of water. Leo handed it to her this time and she sipped it slowly. "Why am I here in a room? If it's not that serious, why'd they keep me?"

"You were unconscious when you were brought in, Kate. Don't you remember throwing up?" Leo pulled up a chair and sat beside her. "They want to keep you overnight for observation. This is the first you've been conscious since bringing you in. That's why they did a CT scan. They thought something more serious might have been going on. You must have hit your head against the concrete pretty hard."

"He got the better of me," Kate said with regret. "I wasn't ready for him to leap over the side of your porch like that and land on me. He's agile, Leo. Moreso than I anticipated. I didn't stand a chance against him. He knocked the gun out of my hand. I don't understand why he didn't kill me when he had the chance."

"I don't understand why he wanted to kill me at all," Leo said, bringing them back to the initial question Kate asked.

"You never answered me. Do you know him?"

"After I saw the photos Declan sent me after we brought you in, I realized I had met him briefly two days ago." He looked up at her and caught her surprised gaze. "I didn't know it was him. I was out in front of the house tending to that small flower garden and he was walking by. He commented about the house and noted that he was taking on some new clients. He told me he's a house painter and that if I was ever in the market for any inside work I should give him a call."

"Did you let him into the house?"

"No," Leo said with a shake of his head. "I think he wanted me to invite him in. I didn't offer and he didn't ask, but he looked disappointed. He asked me what the interior was like and he kept hinting around about seeing it. He never asked directly. If he was trying to kill me, that might have been what he was going to do once I let him in. Maybe he just wanted to get the lay of the house for when he broke in later. He did a number on the back door when he couldn't breach it."

"Did he give you a business card or phone number?"

"Business card. It's back at the house. I saved the number though." Leo pulled out his phone and read her out the phone number. "It's a local Boston number. I've not called it."

"Was he wearing a disguise or anything?"

"No. He looks just like the photos that Declan gave to the media and he went by the name Auggie Wynn. He wasn't trying to hide his identity. Maybe he was trying to test me to see if I knew him. Spade said Evan Crandall confessed to hitting me in the head. Is there any chance that he told Auggie my name or where I live?"

"Anything is possible," Kate conceded. "Evan said he told Auggie my address. He's not someone we can trust. He's disclosed some information to the agent with him, but I assume he might know more. I'm hoping the agent keeps building rapport and Evan tells him more." Kate gestured toward his head. "How is the injury?"

"It's fine. I've been fine and wish I could help you more with this case. I'm out of my element. I know art theft." Leo shook his head in disgust. "I had a conversation with the killer and didn't even know I was talking to him. He lied well and I don't trust anyone. Usually, I can sniff out that sort of thing. I believed he was a housepainter looking for work."

Kate couldn't fault him for that. Before knowing his identity,

Kate could have easily had the same conversation. "He's a master manipulator. This is what he does. He meets and connects with people. He was staying at the Davenport house and no one was the wiser. I think he gets off on fooling people. He told Ronny, the guy in Salem, that he was a lobsterman and met him at the docks. With the other fishermen, he was rough and violent. He wouldn't have been able to be that way with the Davenports. He's changing up his appearance and how he speaks to connect with his audience. His family is from great wealth. He went to an Ivy League school. He knows how to blend in."

"What do you think about the tarot cards he left?"

Kate wasn't sure about those. "He didn't kill me but Wheel of Fortune makes sense for the situation. He one-upped me after I found out his identity. That card is all about a twist of fate, a change. Circumstances in the case have changed. We have more information now. I don't understand why he left the Strength card."

"You're strong, Kate. Maybe he found you a worthy adversary." Kate couldn't argue with that. When Leo looked over at her, he added, "I have been a bit of a Hermit since getting to Boston. It's been a rough transition. That card fits me. He's never left them when people were still alive though."

"No, he hasn't. Then again he kidnapped Carmen Langston and Judge Keaton." Kate couldn't help but wonder if all of this was just a race to The Tower and the bombing he planned. She didn't go into those details with Leo. She was having trouble forming thoughts and keeping her eyes open. The pain medication made her feel heavy and tired.

Leo noticed it too. "You need to sleep, Kate. I'll watch over you."

"Wake me as soon as Declan arrives," Kate said.

"The moment he arrives." Leo stood and pulled the covers up around her. He stood there by the side of her bed until Kate was asleep.

She trusted him – this man who had once held her hostage – to protect her.

CHAPTER 36

Kate had a rough night of sleep. The nurse came in frequently to check on her and give her more pain medication as she needed it. She tossed and turned, not quite able to get comfortable, the sheets twisting around her legs. With each waking moment, Kate worried about what Auggie was doing on the streets of Boston and the fate of those in his hands.

Through it all, no matter the hour when Kate opened her eyes, Leo remained in the chair at the side of her bed. Each time she opened her eyes, he remained awake, watching her and making sure she was okay. She'd fall back to sleep only to wake an hour or two later to Leo remaining steadfast at her side.

Declan had never shown up. He texted Leo at close to midnight to let him know that he was running down a potential lead with the ATF and he'd be at the hospital as soon as he was back in Boston. He hadn't provided any other details. Leo hadn't pressed him for information, much to Kate's annoyance.

It wasn't until eight that morning that Declan arrived with three coffees and a bag full of bagels and donuts. He got one look at her and froze, his gaze roaming over her battered face. He struggled to find the words. Finally, he released an audible groan. "I had no idea, Kate. I'm so sorry I didn't get here sooner." He dropped the coffees and the bag on the tray and rushed to her side, smoothing down her hair and kissing her on the forehead.

She was so glad he was finally there, even though she understood the case had to take priority. Even with Declan, it was hard to be taken care of in this way. In the middle of the night, she had thought back to a time when she was eight and she had to have her tonsils out. Her mother had doted on her and even then Kate was antsy to get out of bed and do for herself. It was an ingrained part of her personality. Having that taken away from her, leaving her with no option but to remain in a hospital bed, she struggled.

"I feel better this morning. I understand why you didn't get here sooner." Kate had told the nurse earlier that morning she didn't want any more pain medication. She wanted to remain clear headed, even if she experienced pain. Her body still ached in places she didn't even remember hurting. Her left shoulder was stiff and her right knee pulsed in sporadic pain when she moved it a certain way. "Leo was here with me all night. He's the one who found me."

Declan turned his attention across Kate's bed. "I know. He told me, Kate." He turned back to Leo. "I can't thank you enough for helping us. If it's not too terrible to say, you look like you didn't sleep all night."

"He didn't," Kate said, beating Leo to it. "Every time I woke, he was right there watching me sleep." Kate reached out a hand to Leo and he tentatively took it, leaning forward in the chair. Kate noticed as he was holding her hand, he didn't look directly at Declan. "Go home and get some sleep. We can get a Boston police officer to meet you at the house if you'd like."

Declan added, "We can get you security. It might not be a bad idea to have someone on the street watching both houses."

Leo let go of Kate's hand, their fingers caressing as he retracted. "I'll be fine. Now that I know how much I need to be on guard, I'll be ready next time. I hadn't realized I was a target. You should have someone watching Kate when she gets home. I can come over and stay with her when you're out, Declan."

"I appreciate that."

"You're both talking about me like I'm not even here," Kate barked, losing her temper in a way she hadn't intended. She wasn't going to let them baby her into submission. "This isn't going to stop me from working this case. It's just my face. My head is already feeling better and I'm not dizzy or nauseated any longer. My face will heal, but it won't prevent me from working."

They both started to argue with her.

"Enough!" Kate yelled, startling Leo but not Declan. "I'm going to see this case through to the end." Kate wasn't going to take any coddling by either of them. She let go of Declan's hand. "Tell me about the lead you were following."

Declan knew better than to press the issue. "Agent Chaplin with the ATF got to work as soon as we provided him the information yesterday. After we released the photo of Auggie, Chaplin got a call from a truck rental place in Springfield that they rented a truck to someone who matched the photo of Auggie. He said his name was Ronny Pallazzo. The guy didn't even look at a license. I think ultimately he was trying to frame Ronny for these crimes. He rented the truck for three days and claimed he was using it for a local move. He hadn't returned the truck."

"That required you going all the way to Springfield?" Kate asked.

"There was some surveillance video that the owner wanted to show us. He would only provide so much information over the phone. I think he was worried about never asking for a license. There was a place in Springfield where Agent Chaplin thought Auggie might get some bombing supplies. Chaplin wanted me to go with him there. Turns out he was right. Auggie was there and picked up the fertilizer and some of the chemicals. We have him on surveillance video in both places."

"There was no one questioning him about the purchase?" Leo asked.

Declan raised his head. "Everything Auggie bought could be used for agriculture. They didn't have any concerns, just said Auggie seemed a bit aloof. The guy said it wasn't his job to judge his customers and we couldn't argue with him about that. He was willing to share the information. He could have made us jump through hoops to get it."

Kate wasn't done. "What about a phone number? Did he leave one?"

"At both locations." Declan rattled off the phone number that Leo had provided the previous evening.

"He's using the same number," Leo said, explaining about his brief interaction with the man. "It was on the business card he gave me. Is it normal for a killer like this to be so public about his interactions with people? I'd have assumed he'd be trying to fly under the radar."

"Most serial killers blend very well into their communities." Kate gave Leo a rundown of a few infamous killers and how well they interacted with others. "Most of their victims would have never guessed their true identity until it was too late. That said, Auggie is toying with us. I remember the sick smile on his face last night. I think he left me alive to have to live with the fact that I nearly had him and he bested me and got away. I don't believe he has any intention of ever being caught."

Leo's forehead wrinkled. "What does that mean?"

"He's not going to be taken alive," Kate explained, wishing that it weren't true. That she didn't feel in her gut how the ending would come. "It's either going to be him or us. I'm not going to let it be us. If by some miracle we are able to stop him, he's going to make us kill him."

Even Declan seemed surprised by her admission. "Do you really think that's the case?"

If there was one thing in the case Kate was sure of, this was it. "He won't sit in a prison cell. He has wanted ultimate control this entire time. He made friends with the Davenports to toy with them. All the while knowing he was going to kill them. He used Ronny Pallazzo, someone who didn't have many friends, and then used him for the information he had before killing him and trying to frame him for murder."

Kate hadn't told anyone but Spade the information about Auggie's mother. She had kept it out of the conversation with Leo, mostly because she didn't know how he'd react to it. Even with his life of crime, he spoke highly of his mother. There was a softness in his features and his voice when he spoke of her. "Leo, I know this might be difficult to believe, but Auggie is suspected of killing his mother who was dying of cancer. She was defenseless and he had already threatened that he wanted to rush the process along. It wasn't a mercy killing – it was cold and calculated."

Leo reached for the back of the chair. "How could someone be so cruel?"

"That's what we are dealing with." Kate had told him now to drive home the point that if Auggie lacked the ability to even care for his dying mother, the man would show no mercy to anyone else. "We all have to be prepared for the end. We cannot under any circumstance allow him to blow up a building in Boston. It would be the ultimate failure on our part and might very well end our careers." She looked up at Declan. "Do we have any leads about where he might be? He still has Carmen and Judge Keaton. Can we track the cellphone?"

"Already tried and it's been disconnected." Declan looked down at her, frustration on his face. "We are doing everything we can, Kate. We have his photo all over the news. All major national news outlets were there. Spade has a team searching the other properties for him that Auggie's father provided."

"I asked Spade to send the team back out again," Kate said, interrupting. "I need to call Auggie's father to see if there are any properties like you mentioned – something remote enough and with a structure where he could stash a truck and build a truck bomb. I never got to do that. He has to be somewhere in the suburbs."

Declan agreed with him not being in the city. He had other thoughts about where Auggie might be. "I'd say even further out than the suburbs, Kate. The areas around Boston are still pretty tight for a big moving truck to be sitting at the curb for that long with no one moving anything in or out of it. Not to mention the amount of fertilizer he'd need and diesel fuel."

That reminded Kate of the other supplies he'd need. "Do we have any idea where he'd get the fuel from?" She wasn't even sure how much he'd need.

Declan moved closer to her, pulling the covers slightly up around her. "Kate," he said softly, "the ATF is handling all of that. I know you don't want me to argue with you about this, but you need rest. Can you rest for at least today? You can get back to it tomorrow."

Before Kate could snap a response back at him, the doctor came in, shooing Declan and Leo out of the room. He asked Kate how she was doing and she explained that while she was feeling some slight pain, it didn't warrant pain medication. He checked the stitches above her eye and the back of her head before assessing her fractured cheek and broken nose.

When the doctor was done, he lowered his head and met her eyes. "I'm allowing you to leave, but I want you to take it easy over the next few weeks. Your cheek and nose are going to take some time to heal. If you damage your cheek bone further, it will require surgery."

It was as if Kate hadn't heard a word he said. "I can go back to work though as long as I take it easy. Is that what I hear you saying?"

The doctor shook his head. "You are at a significant risk of further injury." He put his hand under her chin and tipped it back, shining a light in each of her eyes. "How is your vision?"

"It's fine," Kate said with an edge of annoyance. The truth was it was *mostly* fine. There was still some slight blurriness. She assumed it was from the swelling in her face that caused her eyes to narrow. "I'm ready to go home and I have the two of them who will take care of me."

"See to it that they do." When the doctor left, Kate sat up straighter in bed and swung her feet to the floor. She put one foot down and then the other, cursing softly because she needed to steady herself with her hand. Kate stood up straighter and took a few slow deep breaths, bracing herself for how difficult the next few days, possibly weeks would be.

The door creaked open and suddenly Declan was at her side. "You should have waited for me. Let me help you."

Kate opened her eyes and leaned on him. "Is Leo still here?"

"He's headed home." Declan had her lean against the bed while he went to the closet and pulled out her clothes. There were dark streaks of mud across her pants and her blouse looked like it had seen better days. He apologized as he handed it to her. "I should have brought you clean clothes."

"It's okay. I'm going to shower when I get home." Kate expelled a breath and locked her gaze on his. "I hate admitting this. I might not be as strong as I think I am. I'm going to need your help today."

"You're going to need my help for longer than today, Katie." He saw the tension on her face return. "Let's just start with getting you dressed and we can take care of the rest later."

Later that afternoon, after Declan helped Kate shower and got her dressed in her favorite silk pajamas and had her settled in front of the television in the living room, he left to continue working on the case with Briggs and Agent Chaplin. She had asked if there were any leads she could follow up on while at home and he shut that down quickly. He promised her that tomorrow if she woke feeling well enough he'd make sure she had something to do.

About thirty minutes after he left, the doorbell rang. Kate threw off her covers and walked slowly to the door, not sure that she would open it. Surely if it was a threat, Auggie wouldn't ring her bell. There was supposed to be a police unit watching the house, but if he slipped past them nothing would surprise her.

"Hello," she called out from behind the door. She got up on tiptoes and looked through the small security hole in the door. "Leo! What are you doing here?" She tugged the door open and took in the sheepish smile on his face and the brown bag in his hand.

"I figured since you were over here alone, you'd want a snack and a little company." He held up the bag. "I brought you a warm ham and cheese croissant." Leo raised his eyes to her. "I made the croissants myself. I also grabbed you a milkshake from the ice cream shop you like around the corner."

If Kate was going to be relegated to staying home, this was at least the way to do it. "Come on in," she said as she opened the door wider. Kate was feeling a little better already.

CHAPTER 37

The next several days went by at a snail's pace, especially for Kate. Declan worked with Briggs and Agent Chaplin until the leads ran dry. Kate did what she could at home. She had followed up with August Wynn Sr. to figure out any potential properties that might be remote and large enough for Auggie to carry out his diabolical plan.

After discussing it with Declan and Spade, Kate had confided in August what his son had planned. To say he was horrified was an understatement. He told her that if she needed anything of him, including getting on television and making a plea to his son directly, he would do it willingly. August didn't care about his reputation or that of his business if it meant he might be able to prevent his son from killing anyone else.

While Kate appreciated the offer, she didn't think Auggie would listen to anyone – let alone a father he had never respected and never listened to. She felt August might do more harm than good, if that was even possible.

Declan had wondered if Auggie had felt them closing in and disappeared underground for a while, taking a chance that temperatures would cool and the residents of Boston would become complacent and lax in their security again. Kate didn't believe that's what was happening. Auggie still had Carmen Langston and Judge Keaton.

Their bodies hadn't been found and there were no ransom requests made. Kate could only assume they were still alive and being held someplace.

Kate had no idea why he had changed course and not killed one of them immediately and left the Justice card. Then again, he went after Leo and had attacked her but left her alive. While they knew he had placed the Wheel of Fortune and Strength cards in her hand, Declan, Spade, and Leo assumed he had dropped The Hermit card in the scuffle. Kate didn't know what any of it meant.

She had been expecting more bodies.

She had expected Auggie to carry on with his plan. Maybe even go back and target someone who represented The Hermit more than Leo did. She wasn't even sure how Leo would have fit that card – unless of course Auggie knew about Leo's past. But that couldn't possibly be. Kate had to set that aside because it was too disastrous to contemplate.

Kate focused on the four more cards to come before The Tower – The Hanged Man, Death, Temperence and The Devil. They had remained on high alert waiting for those bodies to be found, but the days dragged on with no sign of Auggie's destruction.

In that time, Kate had long discussions with August Sr. as well as the sisters to see if they had heard from Auggie and explore where he might be hiding out. Briggs and his team, along with the Massachusetts State Police, were scouring the city and state looking for any sign of Carmen and Judge Keaton. There were just no signs of life or death. It was like the two vanished into the night never to be seen again. It cast a glaring spotlight on Boston and the FBI.

Why weren't they finding them and holding the person responsible?

Briggs and his team were even exploring the possibility that their disappearances might not be connected to the case and someone else, some unknown criminal, had a vendetta against them both. They all knew that it wasn't the case. Briggs felt his due diligence required him to explore all potential avenues. Kate couldn't fault him for that. He was doing his job and doing it well.

Every day Kate got a little bit stronger and the throbbing pain in her cheek and nose subsided. She had a follow up appointment with a specialist who checked on the progress of her cheek fracture and he noted that her healing was coming along nicely. Each day after work, Leo and Declan doted on her. Being home for the week, she had grown closer to Leo who'd come over each day, helped her with research, and filled her with stories about his time as the world's most infamous international art thief.

Kate supposed she probably shouldn't enjoy his previous adventures, which was how she had grown to think of them rather than crimes. She couldn't help but smile and be thoroughly enthralled with his capers. In the end, she figured Leo was doing good, returning Nazi-looted art to its rightful owners. His ingenuity for pulling off the heists would be put to good use later on in other cases. Kate was sure of that. She even found herself learning a thing or two along the way.

She got herself into such a routine, forgetting temporarily the ongoing horrors of the case, that when Declan had arrived home in the middle of the day and found her and Leo having lunch in the kitchen that it didn't even occur to her that something might be wrong.

The look on his face told her otherwise.

"What's happened?" she asked, getting up from the chair and walking over to him. "Has someone else been killed?"

"No, thankfully," he responded with a sigh. "Evan Crandall is back at his house under the watchful eye of another agent. The FBI agent Evan had connected with needs to be recalled to do other things. He called me and said that Evan didn't disclose anything else to him, but has been overly anxious about finding out the progress in the case. He also said something curious. There wasn't one phone call to Evan checking in on him while he was in FBI custody and not one going out. This family he was so concerned about protecting – there's been no contact between them."

"I never found any family for him, Kate," Leo echoed from the table.

During their days of research, Leo had tried his best to find more information about Evan. Kate hadn't put too much stock in Leo not being able to find much. It wasn't unusual that Evan didn't have social media pages, given his work at the Archdiocese. They had found information on Evan's mother and sisters with addresses. Two of the sisters had social media but the pages were private. There really wasn't much else available.

Evan had no prior criminal convictions and had never been arrested. He was in good standing with his creditors and wasn't in debt that they could find. There was nothing in his background that would have caused any alarm.

It's why when Declan provided her with this new information it was hard to justify. "He said the whole reason he did what he did was to protect his family. Is it possible he was still trying to protect them but not be close to them?" Kate was trying to square that in her mind and it wasn't adding up even as she said it aloud. The reality was Evan was a wildcard in the whole situation. He'd be charged and prosecuted for his crimes. There was no doubt about that. His overall involvement with Auggie was something that had yet to be determined.

"I don't know," Declan started, giving her a look that told her he hadn't trusted Evan all along. "If you're feeling up to it, I need you to come with me to speak to him. He needs to be interrogated this time without the kid gloves. I need you to do your thing with him. He knows more, Kate. Please trust me on that."

"I trust you, Declan." Guilt washed over Kate that she had been downplaying Evan's role even when Declan had been so persistent. "Let's go now. I'm feeling up to it."

"How can I help you both?" Leo asked. When both Kate and Declan hesitated, he persisted. "There must be something. I've been trying to keep you occupied over the last week, Kate, so your downtime didn't feel so bad. There must be something more I can be doing."

"Do you know how to do property searches?" Declan asked.

Leo offered a faint smile. "It comes with the territory of stealing art."

Declan had assumed as much. "Pretend you're going to steal from Evan Crandall. Do all the background research you would do in that situation. He has a painting you want and all you need to do is find it."

Kate thought that was an ingenious way to position it. She wished she had thought of it herself. She must be a little off her game. "You have the access to the database and everything we do. Text or call us if you find anything of interest."

Kate thanked Declan as they headed out the front door. "I've not been much of a partner to you on this case. I should have listened more about Evan."

"You listened, Kate, and you reasoned with logic. I had no logical reason to suspect him. I just couldn't shake the feeling. For a while I thought I was imagining it. Things keep not adding up." He stopped her at the door and reached for her hand. "Are you sure you're up for this?" Declan lightly traced her injuries with his finger. He'd been so tender with her while she was healing. Kate didn't realize he could be so gentle with her.

"I'm fine. I had more than enough time to heal." The bruises hadn't faded much and she still looked like she'd gone a few rounds in a boxing ring and lost. Kate wasn't vain about her looks. The bruises and cuts would fade and she'd be back to normal in no time. Declan believed her or must have truly needed her because they left without another word spoken about her injuries.

They arrived at Evan Crandall's house and rang the bell at the front door. The FBI agent with him answered. Evan was right behind him.

He didn't appear surprised to see them at all. His surprise came when seeing Kate's face. "My God, what happened to you?"

Kate stepped into the house from the porch. "I was attacked by Auggie Wynn, similar to you. For some reason, he left both of us alive. I need to speak with you."

"Certainly. Come into the kitchen and sit down," Evan said stepping out of the way.

Kate looked back through the front door to the porch and raised an eyebrow in a question to Declan.

"I'm going to be right here. I think the two of you should talk alone," Declan said, leaning casually against the porch railing. He gestured for the other agent to follow him out. Declan locked his gaze on Evan. "I'll be right here," he reiterated, punctuating each word. If Evan caught the meaning, he didn't show it.

Kate knew what Declan was doing. He was allowing Kate to bargain with Evan, if need be, while leaving Declan as the threat. Once she was seated at the square, four-person dining table, Evan asked again if she was okay.

"If you're talking about my injury, yes, I'm fine. If you're talking about the case, not so much." Kate folded her hands on the table and stared him down, causing him to flinch. "I think we both know that there is a lot you're not telling us about this case. You know Auggie Wynn Jr. a lot better than you've let on." When he started to argue, Kate kept going, not giving him a chance to speak. "I didn't catch on as quickly as Declan and that's unusual for me. I truly felt bad for you, even when you were giving a serial killer my address, hitting Leo in the head, and helping Auggie kill Cardinal O'Connor."

"No," Evan said, raising his voice. "I had to help him. My family—"

"Who you haven't heard from once since you were stabbed," Kate said, interrupting him. "Nor have you reached out to them. Your story isn't adding up, Evan. It doesn't make any sense to us." She pointed toward the front door. "Declan wants to arrest you today. Bring you in and charge you with the murders. He believes you're an accomplice to all of them."

Kate expected Evan to protest. He stared at her for several moments then sat back against the chair, folding his arms across his chest. "If I were an accomplice, would I have allowed myself to be stabbed? Would I have gone to try to find evidence in Salem?"

"You went to Salem to find the murder weapon that you gave the killer. You were trying to clear your own name, Evan." Kate didn't falter. She also took in his defensive body language, challenging her almost to catch him. She was seeing now what Declan had been sensing all along. There was a shift in him, subtle but palpable. "We have enough reason to arrest you. The evidence of your complicity in these crimes is piling up. Only you know the *why* of what you have done."

Kate leaned into the table and smiled as best she could, pinching the fracture in her cheek. "The why doesn't even matter anymore and it's not going to matter when you spend the rest of your life in prison. Is that what you want? Prison for the rest of your life? Auggie has done a good job of trying to frame Ronny Pallazzo. What he doesn't know is that we found his body and a taped confession. We have all the evidence we need. But when Auggie is brought in, he's going to need another scapegoat. How long do you think before he points the finger at you for orchestrating all of this?"

Evan's breath caught in his throat and he shifted his eyes away from Kate.

"You know what I'm saying is true. You have time to make a deal." Kate waited until he turned back to look at her. "Tell me where to find Auggie and his plans of bombing the Prudential Center." There was a flicker of recognition in his eyes. "That's right, Evan. We know all about his plan."

"I—" Evan never got out another word.

Declan rushed into the home, banging the front door and calling for her. "We have an address. Leo found it." He pointed directly at Evan. "It's owned by a company where you are the primary investor."

"Leo," Kate said his name in a breath. She didn't know how he did it so fast and she probably didn't want to know. She turned to look at Evan. "Is there anything you want to say?"

Evan's tongue shot out between his lips like a snake, licking his lips nervously. "I want an attorney."

"You're going to need one," Declan sneered, offering his hand to Kate. "The Boston Police Department are on their way."

CHAPTER 38

They waited on the outskirts of the home until nightfall before the planned raid. They wanted the cover of darkness to use as their advantage. Kate had insisted on going in with them even though Declan and Briggs tried to talk her out of it. She could see clearly, her vision long since returned. Even though bruised and battered, Kate was strong, competent and ready to go. No one was going to stop her – even as well intentioned as they were.

They had a full force of people with them from the Boston Police Department, the Massachusetts State Police and the ATF. There were two SWAT teams, the bomb squad, and a host of well-trained officers ready to do whatever was asked. Sharon was there with two of her crime scene techs ready to access the scene when they were done. A raid like this took precision and skill.

There'd been little movement on the property as far as they could see from the road. The ten acres of land was in Sudbury, roughly twenty-five miles from Boston. There was an old farmhouse that looked like it should be torn down rather than rebuilt and a barn that had also seen better days. SWAT had done a perimeter search and found that the property line backed up to a thick wooded area that separated it from its neighbor. SWAT had quickly cleared the property behind and had the residents driven to safety. There was no one else around.

The area was remote and yet close enough for Auggie to come into the city and wreak havoc but far enough away to have some refuge. Evan Crandall had bought the property five years prior. Kate guessed this wasn't his intention for the property but along the way had gotten mixed up with Auggie. Evan was in FBI custody and had been given no chance to reach out to Auggie to communicate anything about the raid.

Judge Keaton and Carmen Langston were still missing and it was likely they were being held here if they were still alive. They couldn't go in with guns blazing and cause collateral damage in the process. Declan had been instrumental in slowing everyone down and creating a strategy for the process. He and Briggs worked together with the SWAT commander to come up with a plan. So far, all was going as agreed.

As the clock ticked relentlessly toward eleven, Declan's signal sent a jolt of adrenaline through the team. Despite his earlier argument with Kate about her involvement, he positioned her cautiously behind him. The tension crackled in the air as they moved in.

Under the cover of darkness, they advanced swiftly across the expansive lawn. Kate's heart pounded in her chest, her breath shallow as she fought to maintain composure. The weight of their mission pressed down on them, the stakes unbearably high.

Their approach to the house was stealthy, the darkness cloaking their movements. With guns drawn, they pressed forward, each footfall echoing ominously.

As they reached the porch, Declan's rapid ascent led the countdown to confrontation. Kate followed closely, her senses on high alert as they prepared to breach. The ancient wood of the porch groaned beneath them. Kate hoped it would hold their weight.

Once everyone was in position, Declan banged once on the front door. "August Wynn, this is the FBI. Come out slowly with your hands up." Declan informed him that SWAT was in position and the enforcement agencies were present.

They all held their collective breath while they waited for a response. The seconds stretched into eternity as they awaited a sign, any sign of their elusive target. They were met with silence.

With a signal from Declan, they surged forward. The door splintered under the force of SWAT's battering ram. Declan, Briggs and then Kate filed into the home. The floorboards creaked under their footfalls. A musty smell hung heavy in the air. Kate followed as they cleared room after room on the first floor. Other officers had ascended the stairs and took the second floor.

The home was sparsely furnished. An old couch in the living room the only furniture. No tables or television. What would have been the dining room was a large rectangle of open space. Dirty blinds hung closed on all the windows. There were no curtains or other coverings. No keepsakes or family photos on the walls.

It was only in the kitchen that they found signs of life. Three plates were stacked unwashed in the sink with forks tossed on top. A new toaster had been left plugged in on the far counter and the microwave door had been left open, letting a sliver of light shine in the otherwise darkened space.

Kate pulled the refrigerator door open to reveal a recent grocery haul. There was milk and juice, some sandwich meat and vegetables. Someone was eating well in the home.

"There's food in this cabinet," Briggs called from the other side of the kitchen. "Someone is definitely living here."

Someone above them yelled an all clear much to Kate's dismay. She had been hoping that since no one was on the first floor Carmen or Judge Keaton would have been found on the second.

The house had no basement in the architectural plans and no attic to speak of other than a crawl space. "Maybe they are in the barn,"

Kate said hopefully.

Declan radioed to the other team and the SWAT commander's voice cracked through the speaker. "Truck isn't here. No suspect or hostages. A lot of bomb making material."

Declan and Kate cursed at the same time. "Where is he?" Declan growled what everyone was thinking. Kate didn't have any words of encouragement to offer him. It was clear Auggie had been staying there, but with no truck and no hostages, the raid had been a bust.

Just as Kate considered all hope lost, someone off in the distance called her name. Declan's followed. "Is that Sharon?" Kate asked him, not sure she was hearing correctly. Sharon had been waiting at the perimeter of the property until she was given the sign to enter. She wasn't supposed to be anywhere near the house.

Sharon called their names again.

Declan took off through the house toward the front door in a run with Kate and Briggs right behind. He took the porch steps two at a time and stopped when he got to Sharon on the front lawn. She was out of breath and her eyes wild.

Declan grabbed her by the arms. "What's going on? You're supposed to be back by the cars."

"There's a woman yelling. I heard it as soon as you guys got into the house. I can't figure out where it's coming from. Can't you hear it?"

The only thing Kate could hear was her breath and the beating of her heart. She turned around and told the officers behind her to remain still. Silence fell over them and they followed Sharon to where she thought she'd heard it.

"It can't be that far from the road," Sharon explained, marching the group of them back toward the cars. "I haven't been able to pinpoint it. I think it's coming from underground."

Kate had studied the land plans and the only buildings on the property were the house and the barn. This wasn't the south where tornado shelters were common. Still, if Sharon heard a woman yell, they were going to explore it. Declan barked orders to the rest of the officers and then with Kate and Briggs stepped off the concrete pathway and started combing through the shin-high grass in the area where Sharon had heard the woman.

"Where exactly did you hear this?" Kate asked, looking up at her.

"I don't know. It was hard to tell. It was faint at first then got louder, so I ran to get you. It's quiet now." Sharon pointed to an area on the left side of the home that was shaded by a tree. "I think it was more in this vicinity." She bent forward as if to try to hear it again.

Kate walked slowly through the grass, taking careful steps. A faint cry stopped her cold. "I heard something," she said hardly above a whisper. She tiptoed closer to the sound and heard it again, this time louder. Kate forced herself upright and yelled for the team. "I'm close!"

Declan rushed to her side. "I haven't heard anything."

"It's faint." Kate pointed in the direction of the sound. The cry started and stopped as they surveyed the area. All at once, the faint cry turned into a scream for help.

Declan lurched forward. "I heard that." He dropped to his hands and knees combing through the grass and fallen leaves. He along with Kate took it slowly, inch by inch, until they got to an area that was more dirt and leaves than grass.

Declan put his ear right to the dirt. "There's someone under here," he said with surprise as if he couldn't believe it himself.

Kate sat back on her heels and shifted furiously through the fallen leaves until the back of her hand struck something hard and metal. She plucked at the leaves, brushing away the dirt to reveal a small metal handle. "Declan, over here!"

He moved quickly to her side and reached for the handle, helping her tug it open. They both had to get to their feet for more leverage. As they stood and pulled, the earth opened up revealing a small wooden staircase.

"Help me!" the woman shouted, louder now and easily heard. Her voice was recognizable.

Kate rushed to go down the steps but Declan stopped her. "I'll go. We don't know what else is here."

Kate stepped back as he climbed into the hole and disappeared down the steep staircase. She bent over watching him go, surprised by its depth. "Carmen, Declan is coming down! Is Judge Keaton with you?" There was a moment of relief that Carmen had been found alive. At least that was one thing going in their favor. She turned back to Sharon who was right behind her. "Thank you so much for being so attentive. We might not have found her."

Sharon glanced back at the house and then to the ground. "It must be a root cellar from when the house was first built. That's probably why you didn't see it on the plans. It was added later."

"Kate," Declan called a moment later. "I need your help."

Sharon offered Kate a hand as she stepped onto the first step. By then, Briggs and the other officers had noticed what they had found and were rushing to aid them. Kate looked up from the steps. "Get some lights in the area and call for an ambulance. Carmen is going to need some assistance." Briggs assured her he'd get everything she had requested.

Kate went down a few steps and felt Declan's hands grasp around her waist, steadying her as she climbed down the rest of the steps into the cold, dark root cellar. The temperature was significantly colder. She could see her breath when she spoke. "Is she okay?"

"Don't ask him. Ask me," Carmen shouted from the corner of the cellar. Declan shined his flashlight over so Kate could see her. The once formidable prosecutor was slumped in a rocking chair with a thin blanket twisted around her legs. There were streaks of dirt down the sides of her face and most of her nails were broken and chipped. "I'm most certainly not okay. He's starved us. I'm freezing and dehydrated. I'm not even sure that I'm going to be steady enough on my feet to get out of here."

Kate flicked on her cellphone's flashlight and walked over to Carmen. She crouched down next to her. There were several questions she could and should ask, but one seemed more important than the others. "Where is Judge Keaton?"

Carmen pulled back when she got a good look at Kate. "What happened to your face?"

"It's too much to explain, but Auggie attacked me. Judge Keaton?"

Carmen looked up at Declan and toward the stairs. "He's gone. I don't know the man's name. He never told us. A few hours ago…" She paused and shook her head. "Actually, I can't get sense of time down here in the dark. It could have been hours or maybe a day ago. But he came down here and took Judge Keaton with him. We tried for days to get that door open but he did something to it and you can't open it from the inside. We were down here together. He never said anything to us. Judge Keaton was down here when I arrived. He took him first. We tried to find a way out. We both tried talking to him, reasoning, finding out his plans. Anything to be helpful and humanize us. Nothing. He's a monster set on destruction."

"Do you know where he was taking Judge Keaton?"

Carmen closed her eyes and shook her head. "To his death, I'm sure. We both knew that we'd die." Her head snapped up then. "You haven't found his body?"

"No," Kate said, pleading. "Anything you can remember. He must have said something."

Carmen took a beat to remember, rubbing the side of her head. Her eyes flicked up. "The one thing he did say was that he was going to put the judge on display. A symbol for all the judge's bad decisions. He'd get the same treatment that judges over the years had shown prisoners."

"The Hanged Man," Kate said in a rush of breath. "He's going to hang the judge somewhere public."

"Boston Common," Carmen said in a rush. "It was where all the hangings took place. Near the old oak that's no longer there." She explained in detail where the oak once stood. "You'll be too late. I'm surprised he hasn't been found."

"It's only a little after eleven," Declan explained. "There are still people out in Boston Common tonight."

Kate asked Declan to shine his light on her phone as she showed a photo to Carmen. "Is that him? Is this the man who kidnapped you and held you down here?"

Carmen leaned forward to look at the photo. "That's him. There's no question in my mind. That's him. You have the right man. The side of his face in the sketch, it was a fake beard. But see there, he has a small birthmark. That's what I think River saw."

Kate had noticed that in the photos she had from August. Hearing that from someone who had been up close with Auggie confirmed it.

"Did he say anything about a bomb?" Declan pressed, his hand reaching for Kate. They'd need to go quickly if they were going to prevent the judge's death.

"No." Carmen's hand flew to her mouth. "Is he going to bomb something? Maybe that's why he was saving me."

Kate had no idea. She didn't have time to get into it all now.

Judge Keaton's life literally hung in the balance.

"We have a whole team who can help you out of here," Kate explained as they backed up toward the stairs. "They will get you out of here and get you medical attention."

"Go!" Carmen shouted at them when they hesitated to leave her. "Stop this madman!"

CHAPTER 39

Kate abandoned her SUV, the engine still ticking as she bolted through the intersection of West and Tremont Streets, the nearest entrance to Boston Common where the ancient oak once loomed. Her mind raced with the urgency of finding the marker.

Ahead, Declan disappeared into the shroud of night, his pace leaving Kate struggling to keep up. Every step was agony, her body protesting from the recent attack. The Freedom Trail's starting point passed in a blur as darkness enveloped Boston Common, far quieter than she anticipated. The drizzle of rain and gusts of wind conspired against her, amplifying her sense of isolation.

Despite her cramping calves and aching thighs, Kate pushed forward, each stride a battle against pain and fear. The wind howled, a chilling reminder of her vulnerability, mocking her determination.

"Declan!" Her voice echoed through the empty expanse as panic seized her. She scanned her surroundings, an instinct warning her they were not alone. The city lights dimmed as they neared the heart of the Common, and with each turn, Kate's heart pounded louder. The path ahead lay empty and foreboding.

Pop. Pop.

Kate froze, adrenaline coursing through her veins.

"Declan!" Her cry held desperation now, etching lines of worry on her forehead as she pushed her weary legs harder, tears mixing with the stinging rain.

Arriving at the center of Boston Common, Kate's worst fears materialized. Declan's silhouette loomed against the pale moonlight, frantically cutting down a figure dangling from a tree. The rope, thick and cruel, still coiled around Judge Keaton's neck as he slumped to the ground. She raced toward them, slumping to the muddy Earth beside him. Declan's urgent CPR instructions merged into a blur of noise, overwhelming Kate.

When Declan abandoned the post, Kate had no choice but to take over. Each compression a desperate plea to revive him, counting in rhythm with the rain that now fell heavier. "Please, please," she whispered, willing life back into the judge's motionless body.

Moments stretched until, finally, a gasp shattered the tension. Judge Keaton convulsed, his sudden movement knocking Kate back. "Judge Keaton, you're okay," she reassured him, her voice a mix of relief and exhaustion. As she removed the rope from his neck, she could feel his weak pulse beneath her fingertips. Kate identified herself so he'd know she was there to help.

"You're going to be okay," she repeated.

His hand went to his throat and he rubbed the raw rope-burned spot. He struggled to get his words out. "That man was impossibly strong. I tried to fight him but he hoisted me up there from a standing position."

Kate had wondered how Judge Keaton had been hung. There was no ledge on the tree from which he could have been pushed. He was not a small man and the strength needed for Auggie to pull the rope over a tree limb and keep pulling to get Keaton off the ground was nearly incomprehensible to imagine. He must have done it though and looped it around the tree to hold it because that's what she had seen Declan cutting.

"Carmen," Keaton said, fear flashing in his eyes as he struggled to sit up. "She's being held underground on…"

"We have her. She's safe." Kate put her hand on Keaton's shoulder.

Keaton gripped Kate's arm. "He has a truck bomb and he's going to park in the Prudential Center garage and blow up the building first thing in the morning as people are coming to work. The hotels. The businesses. Do you understand the devastation?"

Kate absorbed the information, wondering if Auggie would change course now that he knew there might be a chance Keaton would live. "Did he mention any other targets?"

"No. He might blow it early now that you rescued me. All those people in the hotels. You'll never have time to evacuate them all. I can't imagine he'd think I'd still be alive." Keaton reached into his pants pockets and pulled out The Hanged Man tarot card. He handed it to Kate. "He was sure I'd be dead. He was going to blow up the building and go back and stab Carmen. He didn't even consider the possibility that the FBI would stop him. He said he could have killed you when he got the chance. He let you live because he didn't see you or your partner as a threat."

Kate struggled to find the words. "He's right. I couldn't stop him when I had the chance." There was so much to be done but she couldn't leave Keaton lying in a heap in the middle of Boston Common. "I need to call you an ambulance. You need to get medical help. You weren't breathing for a period of time. It took CPR to bring you back."

Keaton held his hand up to stop her from talking. "Call the bomb squad. Call everyone you know who can get to the Prudential Center and evacuate it. Now! I don't care if I live or die. You have to focus on saving the others."

Kate started to protest but Keaton wouldn't hear of it. "You must stop him. He's done enough damage. The Prudential Center is the center of commerce and business. Think of the hundreds, if not thousands, he could kill."

Kate knew he was right. She left Keaton there on the ground and called Briggs, shouting the information at him. Her head was swimming with information and details. The sheer size of the evacuation would take the entire police force. Briggs assured her he was on it and would act immediately, getting the plans and everything underway.

"Take care of Judge Keaton, Kate. Let me handle the Prudential Center."

Kate thanked him for the information and hung up, feeling relieved. She called an ambulance next. When Keaton insisted, she helped him get to his feet.

"I will not be found like this. Walk me to the edge of Boston Common."

Kate tried to protest but he left no room for argument. He leaned on her as they walked. He was slow and required a good deal of assistance. Kate managed to get him to a bench just outside the Common back on Tremont Street. Kate wanted to run toward the Prudential Center and help, but Declan was still gone.

Time moved too slowly and Keaton urged her to go.

"I'm waiting for my partner." Kate realized then Keaton had never asked her about the man who had done this to him. "Do you know the name of the man who kidnapped you and tried to kill you?"

"Never saw him before. He didn't tell me his name."

"August Wynn Jr, the son of August Wynn."

A flicker of recognition took hold. Keaton knew the name. Most people in Boston did. Kate asked Keaton a few questions about what Auggie was driving when he brought him to the Common. Keaton didn't know, he was blindfolded in the root cellar and the blindfold didn't come off until they were near the tree.

"He didn't tell me anything when we left the root cellar. Only that he was going to hang me where the guilty had once been hung. How'd you find me?"

"Carmen," Kate explained. "As I said, she's safe. We found her right before we came to rescue you."

A moment later, Declan jogged toward them cursing a blue streak. His face red and his temper flared. When Declan reached them, she explained what Keaton had told her about the Prudential Center. "We need to get there as quickly as possible. The whole team is headed there now. Which way did Auggie go?"

"Out the other side and headed toward Newbury Street. I lost him in the alleyways. The rain and the wind, I lost my footing and slipped." Declan cursed again. "I wasn't even close. He had distance on me and I wasn't able to catch him."

Kate knew it was because he was saving the judge. He had made a split second decision – save the judge or kill the suspect.

Sirens wailed off in the distance. Kate noticed that Keaton's shoulders relaxed back. He knew he was going to get the care he needed. He caught Kate's eyes. "Did you catch his accomplice?"

Kate thought of Evan Crandall. "We have someone in mind, but we aren't sure how he's connected. He took orders from Auggie and did as he was told. We don't know much else."

"No," he said, insistent. "This isn't someone Auggie was giving orders to. He was taking orders from someone. Auggie didn't come up with all of this on his own. He called the man master. He was doing what he was told and said he would honor the order in his sacrifice. I think he's willing to die for the cause or maybe that was the plan all along."

Kate peered down at him. "How do you know this?"

Keaton didn't waste any time in responding. "The person called him while I was tied up in the truck. He didn't seem to mind speaking in front of me. I was a dead man anyway. He never thought I'd live to tell anyone the information. I can say with absolute certainty someone else is calling the shots."

Kate groaned inside. The case couldn't possibly get more compli-cated. "Any idea who it is?"

"I wish I did. I wish I could be more helpful. I have no idea. The phone rang and he picked it up, listened, said yes a few times and then ended the call. I tried to remain still. I was hoping that once I got out of the truck, I could run or fight him." Keaton swallowed hard and sighed. "He's just too strong. I was no match against him."

There really was no time to interview Keaton in depth. Kate asked one more question. "Did he give you any indication why he's doing all of this?"

"No," Keaton said slowly and Kate knew that wasn't all he was going to say. "I think someone found an easy target to corrupt and mold the way they wanted. Someone powerful found a psychopath and is exploiting the rage and violence that lives inside that man. He mentioned a payday after this. He might have been speaking literally – the person behind this might be paying him or maybe it's power. He spoke of that a few times – the power of the tarot. My sense is he's been given a set of instructions and he's following them out to the letter."

That certainly put a new spin on the case. "We'll stop him," Kate said as she helped Keaton to his feet as the ambulance arrived. Keaton didn't want to greet the paramedic sitting down. Kate thought it ridiculous but the man's pride bubbled to the surface.

Keaton refused the stretcher but allowed himself to be helped into the back of the ambulance. Declan shouted after them that he needed protection at the hospital. The paramedic said he understood then they were gone.

Declan reached for Kate's hand. "You ready to stop this finally?"

Kate was as ready as she was ever going to get. They raced together toward the Prudential Center and only stopped running a block away. Briggs had already closed off the block and had a line of cops stationed at each entrance. Kate knew they weren't far enough back if the parking garage did have a truck bomb. There were streams of people in nightclothes being ushered into the street.

The Prudential Center was part of the Hynes Convention Center complex, which also included several chain hotels and Copley Place malls, which were attached via indoor walkway and skybridge. All the shops were closed this time of night. By the number of disoriented people filing into the street looking scared and blurry-eyed, the hotels were probably near capacity. Kate was only seeing one side of the crowd. The complex was massive and there was more than one hotel. At least the evacuations had started before an explosion.

Briggs waved to Kate and they were let through. The chatter of cops, crackling radio transmissions, and vehicle noise made it hard to hear. "Briggs, how would he get in the parking garage? Isn't there a guard at the gate? I would have assumed they'd be more cautious as to let this kind of truck through."

Briggs leaned into her to respond. "As I'm sure you can imagine, the complex gets a number of deliveries and supplies brought in. Some come through the Prudential Center garage. The guard didn't let any moving trucks in, the kind that we told them to be watching for. We have to consider that Auggie is using something else."

Kate had considered that. "Where are the deliveries made?"

Briggs pointed to the entrance to the parking garage. "There is a special area under the building that takes in the supplies. We've got SWAT and the bomb squad with their dogs down there now going through everything. If there's a bomb in there, they are going to find it. The team is ready to disarm it too." Briggs was much more confident than Kate was at the moment or he was good at faking it.

Declan raked a hand through his hair and cursed. "There's no way to do this with a robot or something? They shouldn't be in the structure." He realized his mistake as soon as it was out of his mouth. Someone had to go through the trucks to find the right one. "There's got to be a better way."

Briggs agreed with their reasoning. "They are trained for this, Declan. This is what they signed up for. Don't get any ideas about going into that parking garage. I was under strict instructions not to let anyone in."

That was going to be easy for Kate.

Declan seemed itching to get into the thick of it.

"Did the Oklahoma City bombing have a remote detonator?" she asked.

"No," Declan said, trying to remember the details. "He set the fuse and walked away. Unless there was C-4 or something similar, there isn't a detonator. He might have a fuse on a timer."

The reality was they had no idea what kind of bomb they were dealing with. They knew Auggie had purchased some fertilizer but they never confirmed any diesel fuel. They were working with very little information. There was something that struck Kate as odd. "The bomber in Oklahoma parked the truck in front of the building in the road. He set the fuse with room to walk away. There is no way Auggie could light a fuse in a truck in that parking garage and get out alive. If he's talking about a payday at the end of this, getting out alive is his endgame."

Declan agreed with her. "Then he's not doing that. That doesn't negate the use of a timer."

"If he's set a timer and he's long gone from the building, then it's only a matter of time and we are all in danger." Kate stared over at the building. A truck bomb on the lower level might take down the whole thing and surrounding buildings depending on the strength. It would certainly take out all the law enforcement inside looking for the bomb and the ones outside manning the perimeter. She grabbed Briggs by the arm. "We need to get everyone back further. Much further."

Declan wasn't paying attention to her. He was scanning the area around them. "He's here, Kate, watching us. I can feel it. He's not going to take down this whole building and not stick around to watch his handiwork. Timer or remote detonator, he's here."

Kate had the same looming suspicion. She barked a few more suggestions to Briggs and then turned back to Declan. "You and me right now. Let's go find him. I am so sick of this guy and his games and him being one step ahead." She pointed to the building, a surge of determination swelling inside of her. This case had all but broken her but her fighting spirit was surging back. "I'm not going to let this guy win. Not today. Not tomorrow. Not ever. The bomb squad is doing what they do. We need to do what we do best."

"I'm with you, Kate. Till the end."

CHAPTER 40

K ate and Declan scoured the surrounding area, trying desperately to figure out where Auggie could be lurking. They looked in parked cars, in traffic flowing by, in the buildings that could be accessed. All the while they shouted at people to clear out of the area. Nearly an hour into the search, they heard the swirl of helicopters overhead.

Kate tipped her head back as a local news station flew by. Their searchlights illuminated the street below. Kate shielded her eyes from the light and screamed at them to get out of the area. There was no chance they heard her over the turn of the blades. "They are going to get themselves killed," she muttered to herself.

Declan didn't hear her.

"Where is this guy hiding?" she shouted, through sheer exhaustion. The rain had started and stopped, making their task even harder. "He's got to be somewhere."

"The bomb must be on a timer," Declan reasoned and Kate agreed. "Otherwise, I think it would have blown by now. If he's around, he's got to know there has been enough time for most of the hotels to be evacuated. Maybe his intention wasn't to kill thousands of people."

Kate couldn't venture a guess at the man's intention. A psychopath for sure but whose motives were still hidden from her. He was bent on destruction but when he seemed to have the opportunity to bring the city to its knees and kill thousands of people, he wasn't taking it. There was nothing she could say to Declan, she was out of her depth on this and that was saying something.

Each minute that passed, they were closer to detonation. They had no word from Briggs that the bomb squad had found anything. There were a lot of trucks to go through not to mention all of the cars and other vehicles in the parking structure. There was no telling what Auggie did with the bomb, if he was even telling Keaton the truth of his plans. Kate hated to think all of this was for nothing.

"This sicko is probably hiding someplace watching all of us scramble," Kate said, stopping in the middle of an alleyway. She fought back tears of frustration and physical pain. Everything hurt including her pride. Declan stopped his search and walked back a few feet to her. Worry was written all over his face. He put his hands on her arms as she held back tears of frustration.

She spat, "What if he's somewhere else with the truck? He could be stashed away watching all of us. The people in the street from the hotels. The cops, SWAT, and the bomb squad. Even us running around the street like we have lost our minds, which I'm fairly certain we have. What if we do all of this and then in the morning when all is calm again, he simply drives the truck right into the Prudential Center garage and walks away, detonating on the street? What then, Declan? Thousands of lives are at stake."

Declan reached for her and pulled her close to him as she rested her head against his chest. He cradled the back of her head and allowed her to cry out the tears of frustration she was desperately trying to hold back. He gave her a moment to let it out and another for her to collect herself. Then he straightened her and wiped the tears off her face. "Kate, look at me."

She locked her gaze on him.

"You can get into his mind. I know you can. Think of all of his crimes. What would he be doing right now? If you were him, what would your plan be?" Declan stared at her and wouldn't break eye contact. As she turned her head away from him, he gently nudged her chin back. "Think, Kate. You've got this."

Kate resisted at first. She didn't know what Auggie was thinking. They'd been so behind in the case from the start. Declan urged her to take a few deep breaths and clear her mind. He told her to relax more than once. It was the last thing she could do standing in an alleyway with the rain beating down on them. Kate turned her head up to the sky and let the rain wash over her. She closed her eyes and tried to do what he asked.

All at once, it was a little akin to being struck by lightning. She could see Auggie's plan and it was exactly what she had shouted moments ago. She lowered her chin and locked eyes with Declan. "The truck isn't at the Prudential Center. If it was, he would have detonated it already. He's waiting until he's exhausted us all. He's lulling us into a sense of safety just like he did with the Davenports and probably Kirk Eagen."

"Where is he?"

"Hotel, probably close by. Someplace with a parking garage to keep the truck out of sight. Someplace with self-parking where there isn't a gate guard who'd stop and ask to see inside the truck." The details were coming to her now. It was as if someone was whispering them in her ear. She knew without knowing through her senses. "He's watching and waiting for the right time."

Declan stepped back from her and took a moment to himself. "I know, Kate. I know exactly the place you're describing." He reached for her hand and pulled her with him as he ran out of the alleyway and went a block to the west. Kate didn't have trouble keeping up. He was jogging slowly enough for her to keep in step with him. Declan stopped once he got to a name-brand chain hotel with a parking structure as Kate described. The hotel had twelve floors and Kate guessed if they were on the top floor, they'd have a good view of the happenings down the street at the Prudential Center.

They slipped into the open garage and didn't have to go far. On the second level in the back near the elevators was a moving truck parked right next to Ronny Pallazzo's stolen truck. The plate of the moving truck didn't match the one that had been rented. There was no denying it given the proximity to Ronny's. Declan went around to the front and checked the VIN.

"It's a match, Kate," he said through steely resolution. "We need to get the bomb squad over here now."

Kate instinctively backed away from the truck. "If he's watching out the windows and sees the bomb squad headed here, he'll blow the truck up, Declan. He won't wait and it will take out this garage and the hotel and everyone inside. We have to be careful."

Declan stopped pushing the buttons on his phone. "What do you want to do?"

"I know what to do," she said softly and turned and walked out of the garage without waiting for him to follow.

Nearly ninety minutes later, after Kate approached the man at the front desk, pulled him aside to explain the situation and confirm that Auggie was staying at the hotel, having checked in not long ago with no luggage, the hotel had been cleared of people. The staff worked diligently knocking on doors and ushering people out the back stairwell to the staff doors opposite the hotel from Auggie's room. While this was happening, the bomb squad was snuck into the hotel and ushered through a connecting door to the parking garage.

It was only after the entire hotel was cleared and the bomb squad was still hard at work trying to dismantle the bomb, a task that was proving to be nearly impossible, that Kate and Declan stood in the lobby together knowing the whole case was ending – one way or another.

They were risking their lives to do it.

They rode the elevator to the twelfth floor. Stepping out of the elevator, both calmly unholstered their weapons and shared one last loving look between them. Declan gave a curt nod of his head and they moved quietly down the hallway to Auggie's door.

Kate slipped the master key into the lock and held her breath. They were counting on Auggie not having any of the other safety features engaged. The door clicked, she turned the knob, and Declan put his shoulder and all his weight into the door. It sprang open before Auggie had a chance to react. His back was to them as he stared down at the chaos he caused on the streets below.

Declan aimed his gun at the man and took several steps into the room, charging him. Kate was right behind him but moved to the center of the room instead of following.

Declan shouted, "Put your hands up now, Auggie! Turn around slowly." Declan had closed half the distance between them when Auggie turned around and aimed a gun back at Declan. He had a detonator in the other hand, which he held up proudly.

Declan stopped near the end of the bed, the men only a few feet from each other.

Auggie offered him the same smirk as he had Kate after he had beaten her. "I don't think so, Agent James. I think you and your partner are going to leave here and let me continue my work. Otherwise, I'm going to blow this building with all of us in it. Think of all of those innocent lives that will be lost."

Kate knew then he had no idea they had cleared the building. She believed he'd detonate the whole thing. She also knew that this wasn't the kind of criminal who could be reasoned with. Kate stared the man down as if daring him to either pull the trigger or detonate the bomb or maybe both.

"That's never going to happen, Auggie. This isn't like the alleyway. You're not going to win this time," Kate said, drawing his attention to her.

As Auggie took his eyes off Declan and turned to her, he opened his mouth to speak but the words never crossed his lips.

Kate expertly raised her gun and took two shots in rapid succession – one bullet entering through his forehead and the other into his cheek.

She couldn't say the second wasn't payback for what he'd done to her face.

The detonator flew from his hands as his body jerked back, slamming into the glass.

Declan dove headfirst after it, catching it right before it collided with the carpet. With it firmly in his grasp, fingers nowhere near the switch, his body slammed hard into the floor. Kate lowered her gun, realizing then that her hand was shaking. She holstered her weapon, ignoring the adrenaline coursing through her veins, and rushed to Declan's side.

Bending down over him, she saw the detonator firmly in his hands. It was only then that relief rushed through her. "I can't believe we pulled that off," she said in a rush of breath.

Declan turned his body and pushed himself upright. "I can't believe we pulled it off either. Where's his phone? We have one more thing to do."

Kate wasn't going to look for the phone yet. She didn't trust that Auggie was dead. The man was missing half his head and the blood coagulated under him. Still, she reached for his bloodied wrist and checked his pulse. Nothing. She pried the gun out of his dead fingers and set it on the desk next to his phone. She picked it up, realizing then it needed a thumbprint to engage. She walked back over to Auggie's body and lifted his hand once more, applying his thumb to the security screen.

Kate went to his most recent contacts and scrolled to his call log. There she saw a familiar number but couldn't quite believe what she was seeing. She raised her head to Declan. "I know who he was working for."

Kate looked at a few of the other apps on Auggie's phone including a banking app. More than two million dollars had been deposited into his account throughout the murders. There was a pending transaction of a million more.

Keaton had been right – for Auggie at least, it was partially about the money.

Two hours later, after working with Briggs and Sharon to secure the crime scene and checking in with the bomb squad to ensure that the bomb had been defused, Kate and Declan found themselves in her SUV headed back north following the same path they had days before.

They went down the same streets and crossed familiar intersections. The person they were headed to see had no idea why they were coming. She was sure it would take him by surprise. She didn't think there'd be much of a fight.

Declan parked on the side street in front of the well-manicured home and cut the engine.

"I just want to know why," Kate said, feeling only a little relief after Auggie's death. The whole case made little sense to her – all of this tied up in the tarot. She couldn't unravel it.

"We might not get that answer."

Kate would have to live with that but she was still willing to try. They got out of the SUV and followed the concrete walkway up to the front porch. Declan stepped up to the door and knocked loudly. When that didn't elicit a response, he rang the bell.

A moment later, a man grumbled inside that he was coming and to stop all the racket. He pulled open the door, his eyes wide at the sight of them.

"Agents," Baird Howe said, his voice stiff. "Is everything okay? What's happened to have you call on me so late?"

Kate stepped forward and pulled the screen door open. They were standing inches apart. "Baird Howe, you're under arrest for the murders of…" She listed each one of the victims' names. Then she pulled him out of the home in his pajamas and twisted the old man's arms behind his back. He didn't protest or argue with her. He didn't deny it either.

Baird only asked one question. "The bomb?"

"Defused before it did any destruction," Kate told him, not hiding the smugness in her tone. "Judge Keaton was rescued by Declan and Carmen Langston was found alive. Your protégé is dead. I was the one who put two bullets in his head. You're going to wish you had the same fate."

Baird dared to smile at her. "You'll never convict me of this and you know it."

Kate was afraid he might be right. The evidence other than the money transfers was weak. The judge barely wanted to issue the arrest warrant. Kate didn't care, she was going to savor this moment for a long time. The rest would come later.

Kate marched him to the car with Declan right behind them, watching her back as he always did. "I want to know why, Baird. Why would you do something like this? I can't believe this had anything to do with the Order of the Magicians. It's a silly old tale. The theatrics of all of it. Why?"

Baird stopped walking and turned to look at her. "I'm not admitting to anything. All I'll say is this – if I was involved, I have just cause."

"What could that be?"

He gave her a knowing look. "Revenge for the sins of your forefathers."

"The Salem Witch Trials?" Kate asked incredulously. "You can't possibly…" She didn't even finish her thought. It was such a ridiculous notion that someone had held a more than three-hundred-year-old grudge. It couldn't possibly be true. She also knew that serial killers rarely had a real motive. They often made up one to justify their actions. It hardly ever made sense to the average person. "Why Ronny?"

Baird couldn't resist that question. "I've been looking for that ritual book for decades. The rumor was the Langmores had it hidden away, afraid of its power. My family was never afraid."

"The Order of Magicians was all about revenge?" Kate asked, not sure she understood. "Why now?"

"I have no heirs. It was now or never. I had a chance at immortality. No one would forget me after this."

"How could you seek revenge for something that happened three hundred years ago?"

All at once his body roiled with laughter, shaking himself against Kate. "You know what they say about revenge. A dish best served cold."

There was nothing she could say. She shoved him toward the car as Declan opened the door. She unceremoniously dropped him in the back seat.

"You can't reason with a psychopath, Kate," was all Declan said as he moved around to the driver's side.

Kate took one last look over the streets of Salem. If it was truly revenge, it was the most insane diabolical plot she had even encountered. Kate wasn't even sure that's what it was all about. Maybe they did believe the rituals in the book that said taking a life could bring them ultimate power. Maybe this was the Order of the Magicians' plans all along – revenge through destruction.

All Kate knew for sure was that justice didn't prevail back then but she was going to make sure it did now.

CHAPTER 41

After a day filled with administrative paperwork and interviews with Baird and Evan Crandall, Kate figured she'd be ready for sleep. Instead, she was still running on adrenaline from the events of the night before and Baird's and Evan's arrests.

Evan was being charged as an accessory to Cardinal O'Connor's murder and a slew of other charges. He finally admitted that he'd been helping Auggie. During the interview, he had expressed some hatred for O'Connor but no solid evidence as to why he'd been helping Auggie. He told Kate that after he hit Leo on the head, he rushed up to the bedroom. He tried to explain to Auggie that he couldn't get the FBI to come with him. Evan said he wasn't going to be responsible for any FBI deaths – even he had his limits. Auggie stabbed him twice for his failure. He rinsed the mace off in the tub and left, narrowly missing Kate and Declan's arrival.

Baird was being held on first-degree murder charges for all of the cases as well as a conspiracy charge and kidnapping that Carmen Langston assured her would stick. Kate received a call late in the afternoon, long after other FBI agents combed through Baird's residence, that he was tied directly to the account that wire-transferred money into Auggie's bank account. A search of his home had turned up notebooks like the one found at Auggie's house with details of the murders. Kate assumed that Baird had taken the lead on the plan and strategized with Auggie on pulling it off.

Kate had insisted on being the one to call August Wynn Sr. to explain that his son was dead by her hands. August had been kind to her, assuring Kate that he held no ill will and that she did what she had to do to stop him. Kate started to explain about the bomb and other details, but August stopped her, explaining that it was too much for him to bear. Kate knew he felt a tremendous guilt for not stopping his son sooner.

Kate didn't know if anything would have helped Auggie. He had one of the strongest psychopathic minds of anyone she'd ever met, possibly rivaled by Baird.

"Do you honestly think this was all about the Salem Witch Trials?" Leo asked, sitting on one of Kate's porch steps. The three of them had gathered outside early in the evening to pass out candy to the kids trick-or-treating in the neighborhood.

While Kate realized that morning she hadn't bought candy or even that it was Halloween already, Declan informed her that he had already gone shopping and had been stashing bags of it away in an upstairs closet.

After Kate finished a few things at the Boston Field Office, she returned home to chowder simmering on the stove and freshly baked bread in the oven. He uncapped her favorite fall beer and handed it to her before pointing out the large buckets of candy on the table for the kids.

Kate couldn't argue because he looked too happy with his plan. Declan was so earnest and excited about sitting on the porch after dinner and seeing all the kids that she readily agreed. They had invited Leo over and tabled any discussion about the case until after dinner. They all needed a break.

The rain had subsided and it was a nice night for the end of October.

Kate had been sitting there thinking about Leo's question – could it all have been about the Salem Witch Trials? The only answer she had for him was the one Declan had given her.

Kate smiled up at Declan and then turned to Leo. "As a great man once told me, you can't reason with a psychopath. Baird had his reasons. Now whether he truly believed he'd garner some power from the murders or if it was all an act of revenge for what had happened to his ancestors, who knows. What matters is he orchestrated it all and found the perfect man to do the job for him. Auggie wanted to kill. It was bubbling up inside of him for a long time. Auggie then used the people he needed – Ronny and Evan. Both I think were struggling and susceptible."

Kate assumed Baird had orchestrated the relationship between Auggie and Ronny from behind the scenes, playing off both of their interests in tarot and the metaphysical.

"Have you ever had a case this complex?" Leo asked.

Kate shook her head. "Not a serial murder case. This was complex. I still don't know if they truly believed the tarot would bring them power or if it was more performative. It's left a lot of unanswered questions but then again, the topic of tarot and psychics and all that leaves a lot unanswered too."

Leo raised an eyebrow. "Did you become a believer?"

Kate couldn't say that. She gestured toward Declan. "Earlier in the case, Declan said that he couldn't explain everything in life, so he left room for the unknowns. I'm a little more willing to admit there are unknowns. I'm slightly more comfortable with it now than I was before this case."

What Kate was still struggling with was Ronny's hesitancy in going to the police. He was the least involved but wasn't blameless in the whole situation. He could have stopped it before it ever got started. If he had, there was a chance no one would ever have known about

Baird's involvement.

After Baird's arrest, Kate contacted Lily in Salem and explained before she saw it on television. It didn't seem to surprise her as much as Kate would have assumed. It was then that Lily reminded her she had told them it was a layered, complex case and that the person was close. At the time, Kate believed she was talking about Ronny. It turned out, Lily led them right to the door of the master of the conspiracy.

Kate didn't think it was particularly prophetic. Still, she couldn't help but smile at Lily's prediction and help during the case.

Carmen recovered quickly and was already a star of the national news circuit, describing her harrowing ordeal and how her office was handling the prosecution. Carmen mentioned Declan a few too many times for Kate's comfort. Her name was mentioned only once as the partner of Agent Declan James. Declan hid his smile from Kate when he saw it on the news.

Carmen was making a play for him and they both knew it.

What no one knew and hadn't made national news was how instrumental Leo was to the case. She reminded him then that had he not found the address, they wouldn't have been able to save Carmen or Judge Keaton. "I'd say for your first case, Leo, you did exceptionally well."

"You did," Declan echoed from the porch step next to her. "We didn't ask how you came by the information so quickly, and I don't think we will. Probably better off not knowing, huh?" There was a teasing tone in Declan's voice.

Leo smiled in return and nodded. "You wanted me to bring my skills to your team. You have them. Sometimes you're better off not asking questions."

The kids started to come faster than the trickle they had before. They handed out handfuls of candy to the kids, the parents remarking on Kate's decorations and the lit pumpkins that lined the stairway of the porch. Kate felt good, happy even. There with Declan and Leo. It felt right, enjoying her time, smiling, and laughing with her neighbors for the first time in a long time. The house, which had once remained quiet and dark, was coming to life much like her spirits.

At close to ten, long after the kids and parents had gone home and they chatted happily on the porch finishing their beers and getting to know Leo better, Kate's cellphone rang.

"Spade," she said, holding it up and showing them her screen. She engaged the call, wondering why he was calling so late. It couldn't be good news. She braced for the inevitable, hearing they hadn't made a good enough case against Evan or Baird. "Hello, Spade. Declan and Leo are with me too."

"Good. I'm glad the three of you are together." He paused too dramatically for her liking. "I have your next case."

"Already?"

"Five incredibly wealthy women, two Americans, three European, are dead. We believe it's the work of a conman. He seduces them, steals their money, and murders them when he's done. We know of the five. There could be countless more he hasn't killed."

Kate took a moment to digest the information. "The FBI is wanted on this case?"

"You've been requested by Sam Harris, your counterpart in London. You worked with him on the Close Killer case."

Kate knew him well. She looked down the steps at Leo. "Will we be going to London?"

"Three of the women were killed there."

"What about the victims in the United States?"

"Los Angeles. You'll start there and work your way over to London. Wheels up tomorrow afternoon. Can you be ready?" Spade asked the question but knew the answer. It was a question of choice – of course, they'd be ready. "Kate, I know you won't be happy. I might need you undercover on this one. If so, we'll need Leo's chateau in France."

Kate closed her eyes, dreading it already. "Yes, I understand." She ended the call with Spade, knocked back the rest of her beer, and looked over at Declan and then down at Leo. She explained what he said. "No rest for the weary. Wheels up tomorrow for Los Angeles."

Once back in the house after Leo left, Kate put the rest of the candy in the kitchen and the three beer bottles in the recycling bin. She flicked off the lights and double-checked that the back door was locked.

She met Declan on the stairs. He pulled her into his arms and left a loving sweet kiss on her lips. He tucked the errant strands of her hair behind her ear and whispered, "I know we should be tired. I'm not ready to go to sleep yet."

Kate searched his face, so happy he was hers and she was his. "We have a long day ahead of us tomorrow and who knows where this case will take us." He frowned as if she'd ever turn him down. She rested her hand on his chest. "Sleep can wait. I need you tonight."

"Good," he said, taking her by the hand and leading her up to the bedroom.

There were only certain times Kate allowed herself to be led.

She knew she'd follow Declan anywhere, to the ends of the earth if that's what he asked.

About the Author

Stacy M. Jones was born and raised in Troy, New York, and currently lives in Little Rock, Arkansas. She is a full-time writer and holds masters' degrees in journalism and in forensic psychology. She currently has three series available for readers: the completed cozy paranormal Harper & Hattie Magical Mystery Series, the hard-boiled PI Riley Sullivan Mystery Series and the FBI Agent Kate Walsh Thriller Series. To access Stacy's Mystery Readers Club with three free novellas, one for each series, visit StacyMJones.com.

You can connect with me on:

- http://www.stacymjones.com
- https://www.facebook.com/StacyMJonesWriter
- https://www.bookbub.com/profile/stacy-m-jones
- https://www.goodreads.com/StacyMJonesWriter

Subscribe to my newsletter:

✉ http://www.stacymjones.com

Also by Stacy M. Jones

Watch for the next FBI Agent Kate Walsh Thriller in Feb 2025

Access the Free Mystery Readers' Club Starter Library
PI Riley Sullivan Mystery Series novella "The 1922 Club Murder"
FBI Agent Kate Walsh Thriller Series novella "The Curators"
Harper & Hattie Mystery Series novella "Harper's Folly"

Sign up for the starter library along with launch-day pricing and special behind-the-scenes access. Hit subscribe at http://www.stacy mjones.com/

Please leave a review for The Magician. Reviews help more readers find my books. Thank you!

Other books by Stacy M. Jones by series and order to date

FBI Agent Kate Walsh Thriller Series
The Curators
The Founders
Miami Ripper
Mad Jack
The Fuse
Dead Senate
Close Killer
Diamond King

PI Riley Sullivan Mystery Series
The 1922 Club Murder

Deadly Sins
The Bone Harvest
Missing Time Murders
We Last Saw Jane
Boston Underground
The Night Game
Harbor Cove Murders
The Drowned Boys
What He Saw
Fear City
What Stays Buried

Harper & Hattie Magical Mystery Series
Harper's Folly
Saints & Sinners Ball
Secrets to Tell
Rule of Three
The Forever Curse
The Witches Code
The Sinister Sisters
Scandal Knocks Twice
A Treasure Most Deadly